Copyright 2024:
All rights appertaining to the contents of this book remain
the intellectual property of the author.

Cover design by Skip Evans

Me & My Shadow

Skip Evans

Disclaimer: **Me & My Shadow** is purely a work of fiction. Any similarity that may seem to arise to any actual person living or dead is entirely unintentional and is purely coincidental.

Other books available from Amazon by Skip Evans:

A Bear Named Canadian Joey

Timbe

Clive's Drive
Just an Ordinary Joe
Not an Ordinary Joe
Eve of Annihilation

Dedicated to all who work for
…help-out in any way
…donate to or just buy from
The charity:

SHELTER

Me and My Shadow 1927

Officially the credits show this song as written by Al Jolson, Billy Rose, and Dave Dreyer, with Jolson and Dreyer being shown on the sheet music as being responsible for the music and Rose the lyrics. Al Jolson was often given credits on sheet music so he could earn more money by popularizing them, but it is said that he played no actual part in writing this song.

Me and My Shadow 1927

Shades of night are falling and I'm lonely
Standing on the corner feeling blue
Sweethearts out for fun
Pass me one by one
Guess I'll wind up like I always do
With only
Me and my shadow
Strolling down the avenue
Me and my shadow
Not a soul to tell our troubles to
And when it's twelve o'clock
We climb the stair
We never knock
For nobody's there
Just me and my shadow
All alone and feeling blue
When the sun sets on the far horizon
And the parlour lamps begin to glow
Jim and Jack and John
Put their slippers on
They're all set but we're still on the go
So lonely
Me and my shadow
Strolling down the avenue
Me and my shadow
Not a soul to tell our troubles to
And when it's twelve o'clock
We climb the stair
We never knock
For nobody's there
Just me and my shadow
All alone and feeling blue.
When I go out at night
With my old pal
We never fight
About any gal
It's just me and my shadow

BEFORE THE BEGINNING

Darkness reigned over the formless firmament
All was empty & tranquil
Then came light
And the first shadow fell
I am shadow
I am timeless
I am traveller
Journey awhile with me if you will
Cross the vastness of my realm… The Eternal Emptiness
I am as one with the velvet blackness of the void
Come, we shall visit one of the multitudes of spiralling wheels of
light & colour
Yes… this one in particular…
Dive with me through clouds of stars scattered as dust.
Here we are, this is your miniscule neighbourhood
Look, a small yellow star illuminates it
Its dim light, lost amongst billions of far brighter stars
To you though it is…
The Sun!
Orbiting here, there lies a carefully hidden-away,
a sparkling blue jewel
Held fast in orbit by the iron grip of gravitational embrace.
Descend with me down through the celestial blue vault
to your home
A Planet you have named The Earth

Sit with me a while above this tranquil green valley
Watch empty millennia spinning by…
Until we see scurrying creatures swarming all over the land
Now they work like ants to create a channel,
they fill it with water
They sail proudly up and down on the water in boats
More scurry around alongside the water, they work
with brick and stone
A mighty edifice grows up from out of the ground
Encased are we now by many an iron beam
and sheets of glass.

They bring into life a giant hissing monster
It breathes out fire and steam
Smoke blackens the valley for a while
Until the beast falls silent to quietly rust
Then it is gone

Now more creatures scurry into this newly empty
and vast space
Tables and chairs appear as the creatures come and go
I will slow down the passage of Time now
so we may observe these creatures more closely
Sink down to join them
Here we are with two of your kin
They shine brightly
Radiant beings of light
Let me place scales over your eyes
Dim your vision to perceive their world
To see them
In the way they see themselves…

One is seated, another approaches
One is thin youthful, brightly dressed
The other one old, bearded, bedraggled
They force air out from their mouths to create pressure waves in
the air, they call this *sound*
The sound passes between them entering their ears
They are communicating
They are *speaking* to each other
Will we listen to what they are saying?
Shall we eavesdrop?

Come…

For Jude,
None of that Sci-Fi or fantasy nonsense this time! Thanks for checking it over too...

CHAPTER ONE

"Hi there, my name's Andy... Andy Robinson. Would you mind if I joined you?"

"Eh?... What you say?"

"I... err... I said... my name's... err- Andy! Would you mind if I joined you?"

"Join me in what? The fight to save our planet? Or on a little crusade to rescue humanity all of your own?"

"Sorry? Oh I see, *ha-ha*... well no, although, in a way yes! Of course, I do mean... Yes! But for now at least, I only meant, may I sit down here at your table with you. Maybe have a chat with you?"

"Well for starters it's not *my* table sonny, it belongs to this 'ere place don'it? So as far as you sittin' down there goes... hell man! Feel free! I ain't gonna complain! You've as much right as anyone else 'as... though lookin' at yer... from what I see's of ya... y'don' look that destitute to me, wi y'nice new and very clean blue anorak on!"

"*Ha-ha-ha*... no of course not! Thank you. So... I'll sit here and join you. Mmm... oh...dear..."

"Pah! Just one sip o'that coffee 'as gone an' wiped that self-satisfied smirk off y'shiny young face an't it? Not quite up to y'Costa or Starbucks as y'd normally sup eh? That overpriced stuff as y'ave in them fancy cups as y'walks down't street wi'... tryin' to, what?... '*look the part?*' When all as y's'doin is bein' a part o'their unpaid advertising machine! Joinin' in wi' all t'other sheep as they're 'erded along, an' all't'time y's thinkin... '*Oh look at me...*' Mind you I 'ave to say, them cups does come in 'andy for beggin' for change wi! Y'know after you lot's done wi'em an'dropped-em on't'floor wherever y'appen t'be when yer finished wi'it! *He-he-he...*"

The old man paused and smiled at the young man, revealing teeth that were dull and brown round the edges. He went on,

"No but really son, that shit y've got there's terrible for sure! Terrible's t'only way to describe it, eh? All'as stick wi't'tea in 'ere lad! It's mebee stewed to buggery, but it's 'ot and if y' puts some sugar in it's sweet an'all... bit o'free energy t'put ya on... and at least y'can just about tell what y's'drinkin'!"

"Thank you! I'll do that if I ever have the pleasure again! May I ask your name Sir?"
"Sir! *Sir* is it! *Ha-ha-ha-ha!*... Been a long time since I were addressed by anyone as *Sir!* (*he coughs... a rattling phlegmy cough*) Now see wha' y'gone an' done... set me off coughin'..."
"That sounds really nasty... err... Shouldn't you have that looked at, don't you think, err...?"
"Bill! Me name's Bill, okay ... '*Err-Andy*'... so, pleased to meet ya! Nay lad, doctorin's for folk as they let's into their surgeries innit?"
"But surely there's someone who you can see? That really is a nasty cough."
"What's the point? If it kills me off, so be it! I don't 'ave an 'ell of a lot to live for!"

"Bill, I feel I must say to you... I'd hate you to have a bad impression of me... You see, I *never* discard my empty coffee cups onto the street, in fact I never litter at all! I think it's disgraceful behaviour... littering, that is! Also I always buy my coffee, well... when I can afford one that is, from an independent coffee shop, *Big Business* is destroying everything worthwhile on our planet!"
"Well good f'you lad an' shame on an old cunt like me for mekin' snap judgements on ya, an' f'slaggin' ya off an'all! My apologies to ya... Andy."

"Oh that's okay Bill, from where you're sitting, I guess I must look like some, wet-behind-the-ears, middle class twerp of a kid who's revelling in slumming-it? Yeah? Having a day off from college and my usual lifestyle of getting drunk or high on drugs? Nothing in fact could be further from the truth though, I'm appalled by the way our country is being run into the ground... by people with no morals or any sense of responsibility or accountability to the people who elected them! They are people without honour or any sense of decency!

"I want to be part of a fight for change, to force a return to decency, a return to a better, kinder and more inclusive society!"
"Aye well lad, y's preachin' t'converted 'ere! And sorry for judging you! I were a tad 'arsh! Us folk's as come 'ere, ain't under any illusions 'bout 'ow well t'system's workin right now!
"So yer's a Socialist then? Up the workers! An all that eh?"

"Well naturally I am, I find it impossible to imagine that anyone who isn't a totally selfish bastard, just out for themselves could be anything else!"
"Well good for you lad! Y'gonna make the world a better place for us all are ye?"
"Yes I truly hope to do so! I'd dearly love to go into politics one day, make the whole democratic process relevant to the people again, so many have simply given up on it, allowed themselves to be put off, discouraged, distracted and entertained elsewhere with the tsunami of trivia and nonsense that can so easily overwhelm us nowadays!"

"Well, I wish y'every success in getting t'y'Brave New World, doubt as 'ow I'll live to see it 'appen though...
"Any'ow what ar y' doin' 'ere today, to further the cause Comrade Student? Y'know, to fight for t'revolution, armed as y'are wi' only a clipboard?"
"Yes well... so... me and my girlfriend Nat, are doing a joint project on homelessness for our post grad, we're particularly focussing on the work of this place here, The Folks Factory in our own town, it's an amazing, inspirational concept and the fact that it's all privately funded too is bloody amazing! The guy who's putting up the money is like some rich dude I believe, a true philanthropist, like there were back in the days of The Victorians, when they ploughed back some of the money they made from their factories and yeah, from the ruthless exploitation of the people they gave jobs to, I do get that... and yeah too, that they were self-righteous and condescending at the same time, but you can never take away from them that they actually *did* put something back! That they had a conscience! Not like so many of the rich bastards of today, who just get rich off us then salt-away their ill-gotten gains in off-shore Tax Havens, all so they can dodge their dues, not pay their taxes! I mean we still have the legacy of The Victorian philanthropists with us today don't we? You only have to look around our town, or any town... if it hasn't been gutted by private equity business bastards, ripping everything down to make even more money from unnecessary *rebuilding*... despite all that, we still have fine buildings, libraries, schools, museums and hospitals! I mean even the infrastructure they built... the bloody water supply and sewers! Many still working today and well over a hundred years

old now! Today they think in planning terms of a decade max! There's no foresight, no vision, no passion for doing anything well... for doing it properly..."

"*Whoa there* Sonny! Save it f'ya soap box! Aye, you'll mek a fine politician one day I'd say... wi' all o'that passion an' bluster! Well y'will if ya carries on like that anyhow!"

"But no lad, seriously, I love it that you 'ave that burnin' passion, I 'ope you can carry it wi you all through y'life, that y'never lets that fire die! You keep it stoked-up son, an if y'ever feels like givin' up... an' trust me there'll be times in y'life, when things ain't so rosy and shiny... times that y'll'want to give up on it all... Y'know y'remind me of a man, a politician I means, one as I do 'ave a lot of time for... Jeremy Corbyn."

"Oh my God yes! He is one of the few for sure! Pardon me for pinching his favourite slogan and turning it on its head! But in the context of him being one of the few decent men in politics! But look what that bastard Murdoch and the media gang of criminals did to him, even the BBC were in on it too, all the lies they made up about him, it was bloody disgraceful...."

"Precisely! But that were where it all went wrong in't first place wannit? Jeremy! I mean... fa-fuck'sake! E's a lovely man but 'es no leader, never was, never would be... never could be!"
"I think that's unfair! Look at the following he had, especially with the young! We loved the man!"
"Aye well, fat loada good it did for ya'all? Eh? Man were doomed from day one! Y'know 'as 'ow Tories registered an voted for 'im, t'be leader, cos they knew 'ed be a disaster?"
"What? How..."
"Oh aye, they was besides 'emsels wi glea over 'im being elected! T'were meant t'be a joke, y'know? 'Im standin' f't'leader in't first place? 'Alf o't'PLP were agin 'im from moment 'e were elected, plottin' an schemin! Nah... y'see where they went wrong in't first place, were puttin' wrong brother in charge even before Corbyn. If they'd med right choice back then, Corbyn'd never of 'appened! 'E'd a stayed where 'e belonged as an activist on't'back benches."

By now Andy was looking quite perplexed, "You mean they should have elected David Milliband rather than Ed?"
"In a nutshell lad! Just think 'bout what y'jus said eh?"
"What, that they should have elected David Milliband rather than Ed?"
"Aye… What'd'ya call 'em, eh? Eh? David & Ed! Not David and Edward, David not Dave! See the difference? Look what the bastards did… straight off, it were… *'Ed the Red'* eh? I mean yeah Ed's a great bloke in'e? But they fell straight inta th'ands o't'bastards wi'im! Custom made t'be ridiculed!"
"So in your opinion, they should have chosen the straight guy! The one who would have fitted the bill? The one who looked the part, whether or not he was the best man for the job?"
"Fuckin' right they should've! 'Ow many politicians 'as been brought down f'ow 'e was seen eatin' a bacon butty? Lookin't'part fer t'camera is ninety percent o't'battle today!"

Harry Protherow who was leaning on a table some twelve feet away from this odd couple, had observed them over the tin rim of his coffee mug as they sat there talking so intently, now as he observed old Bill tentatively reaching out his hand across the table towards the young student sitting opposite him, he froze. Bill was as ever, wearing his fingerless gloves, his *filthy* fingerless gloves! Even from where Harry was, he could see that the fingers that protruded from the dirty knitwear, with their blackened fingernails were equally filthy…

So it was with interest that he watched as the young lad despite this, gamely took the old man's hand and shook it anyway… Harry smiled to himself as he watched the lad immediately afterwards trying to discreetly wipe the palm of his hand on his jeans out of Bill's sight, below the table top.

Bill was a large man, he had broad shoulders and stood-up straight was about as tall as Harry, at near enough six feet, but he had quite a stoop to his back now, maybe owing to his age? It was hard to determine with much accuracy how old he actually was, he had a mass of long hair, a mixture of white, grey and black which fell out from under his dirty baseball cap and down onto his shoulders, his face was nearly completely covered up to his eyes by a thick and wild beard of similar colouring. Given the right outfit to wear he could easily have passed as a wizard or as his mother would have said as, *The Wild Man of Borneo!* Whoever the hell he might have been!

Harry unobtrusively carried on listening in on their conversation as it progressed from the handshake. Bill was quite a character, he'd been frequenting the shelter for a few years now, but had steadfastly resisted every attempt Harry or anyone else on his staff, had made to get him to… *'come inside,'* to accept the help that The Folks Factory Project could offer to homeless people such as him.

Harry was the manager of the place, it was a fully registered and paid-up charity. He'd come to the project after it had been up and running for just over a year, his expertise in project management had seemed a good fit and he'd been given the job. He was thankful for the opportunity as his career path's upward trajectory at that moment in time had ground to a halt! He'd left his last post after his boss had totally cocked things up but had then very neatly landed the blame onto him! He'd been lucky with the interview as the guy who he met was very philosophical and understanding…

A few weeks into the job he'd come to the conclusion that the main reason he'd got the job was more likely to have been because there had been very few, remotely suitable applicants, rather than because of his suitability or qualifications! Apparently running a *doss-house for tramps,* as he'd since heard the place unkindly described as, hadn't seemed such a rosy prospect for too many people! Harry on the other hand had become inspired when he toured the old building and saw the work that was being done there. There was such attention to detail being put into the whole scheme, whilst all the time there was a devotion to preserving and utilising the giant hulk of the old industrial building by returning it to a new purposefulness.

The original Project Manager had left suddenly, hence the vacancy arising and it seemed there was something of a mystery as to why he'd left and where he'd got to! It was clear that the project had been beset with many practical difficulties and additionally there had been significant opposition from some of the local residents and assorted *nimby's!* The sheer scale of the task of converting the old building alone must have been challenging enough even without any of that extra hassle.

His predecessor had been the only person who'd had direct contact with the millionaire backer and initiator of the whole idea, since his departure all contact with them was now made through a board of trustees.

Harry had been in the job for nine years now and despite his early reservations he had come to love it. Managing any business situation or commodity had its similarities and running a project whose customers were unfortunate folk was little different in many ways to dealing with any other group of the public. Surprisingly he'd found that helping people in need and being in constant contact with others who shared the same aspirations was quite uplifting, the willingness of the majority of his clients to be readily appreciative probably had a lot to do with it.

Harry had somehow let himself drift into looking like an ageing academic bachelor, favouring tweedy looking sports jackets, worn over a t-shirt and jeans, his bespectacled face topped by thick curly grey hair, which kept itself naturally tidy with little maintenance from him, all adding to the impression.

'Come Inside' was the name of the plan he had initiated on the instructions and with the watchful oversight of the trustees. It was an open invitation to anyone who was homeless, to literally *come inside* and see what the project was able to offer them. It was deliberately non-coercive and everything was always offered without any pressure, it was simply an invitation to do literally nothing more than… *come inside* …to just have a meal initially. If they were interested in more once their bellies were full, this could then be followed-on with an introduction to '*the stepping stones*' as they were presented in the plan. They would tell the *guest* that they were now standing on the first stepping stone, that it was the one where they'd accepted a meal and they were now being shown how the steps could progress one-by-one towards a better life, each one taking them further away from the streets where they presently found themselves, to show them that these stepping stones were there for them, if they chose to walk along them.

The second step was to accept one of the beds they offered to anyone who was sleeping rough, it was just a single bed, in a dormitory setting, in one of the ground floor rooms, one of the many rooms that had once been machine shops in the days when the factory had been working. This second step was on a turn-up-on-the-night basis, with no commitment other than signing-in, using the name they had given when they registered.

There were many more stepping stones available to those who were willing to be led along them, the final step being that of re-integrating back into society once again, either out there on their own or in one of the affordable flats that they had for rental onsite.

Many of the clients were instantly defensive and to say the least, less than enamoured by the entire idea of course! They had rejected Society and all of its entangling embellishments, or as was often the case, they felt that they had been rejected by their fellow citizens and evicted from 'their' Society!

The idea of accepting the helping hand that was being held out to them, of walking along *'their bloody stepping stones'* could seem to them like an attempt to merely haul them back into it all… back to all the things that they'd left behind? All the things of their so-called and ever-so-precious to them, *'normality'*… that place where the enfranchised dwell, or seen obliquely… the prison within which they live… without even being aware they are incarcerated, unable to see the invisible bars that hold them!

So of course *they* would think that you'd want to jump at the chance to re-join them! Well they would wouldn't they? Deluded idiots that they are, living in their Fool's Paradise! Join them? With all their boxes to tick, their endless forms to fill-in, their charity to beg for, their hoops to jump through, all that shit they insist on, to become accountable for all of that, all over again… To be mugged into taking on the responsibility for all their bills, to put themselves back into the chains that bind them! To have to pay the rent, the Council Tax, the gas bill, the electric bill… help them to put back in place one-by-one all the bars to make their very own cage that would imprison them once more, enslave them? …all of this, of course, to be accomplished while you then had to go out and slave away for long hours, for next to no pay, simply so that you could go home to your gilded cage at the end of the day, exhausted and with no energy left to do anything but slump in front of your telly to watch how wonderful life is for other people, to see how the rich live a life of leisure, in idle luxury and splendour laid out there before you on your TV screen!

Of course there were some of their *clients* who did accept the offered hand and in due course, if they chose to, who would ultimately re-join mainstream life, although equally they could progress only as far as the stepping stone that suited them and go no further… That was the approach of The Folks Factory, to offer help and give as much as they were asked to give. If that meant that the client did no more than get off the streets it was a win, whether they just slept there or if they moved to the stepping stone that gave them a pod or a room, providing them with the vital address they needed to gain access to benefits.

Old Bill here though was a total refusenik! He'd staunchly rejected pretty much every attempt they'd ever made to reach out to him. He was grateful for the free food of course and glad of a mug of sweet tea and occasionally he would turn up to get a bed for the night, usually when the weather turned bad, cold was a killer when you lived on the streets, it eats into your bones… But he had always shrugged-off any invitation Harry had offered to him and equally any offers made by the most persuasive of his staff… to *come inside*!

Harry'd had many a long conversation with Bill… although what his real name was, nobody knew! He was one of the many who refused point blank to give their name when they were asked to register. The staff had been told when this happened to politely suggest a name for them, one for them to use whenever they wanted to use the facilities at The Factory, solely for registration and for record keeping purposes of course, also for Fire and Safety Regulations. They had a list of names to use, to give out to them, to provide them with… ticking off the name from the list as they gave it out. *Bill* had clearly been registered early on in the scheme and he had adopted the name himself and used it ever since.

It had been quickly apparent to Harry that Bill was despite appearances, a highly intelligent man. Despite his slovenly speech pattern and lazy enunciation, with aitches, letters and missing syllables clattering to the floor with every sentence he uttered! It was what he said that mattered though, his words as they poured out at you, truncated as so many may have been, were still strangely articulate and comprehensible enough... in the most part at least! They were clearly the product of a lifetime of detailed observation and a meticulous, in-depth interpretation of all that he'd experienced. In fact Harry had deduced that Bill made a study of observing life, of people, of everything he experienced, that he lived completely 'in the moment,' he would often allude himself to that and to other Buddhist concepts if you could get him talking.

He was also extremely well-educated and extensively knowledgeable, across a wide range of subjects too. It was clear to Harry that this was a man who had once *been someone*, had held a place in society, that he'd most likely had a good job, a home of his own and probably a family too, along with all the other trappings and paraphernalia most of us accept as normality.

He wondered what it was that had befallen him, had brought him to where he was today, to be living as he was on the fringes of society. How had he fallen, what event or series of events and setbacks had he been through, had he suffered? The list of potential causes was endless, let's face it staying afloat in today's society is like walking a bloody tight-rope, there's precious little margin for error too and often there's no safety net either! Yeah it's fine and dandy if you're up there with a good income... a nice fat monthly salary to rely upon, but then again along with that big salary come big and expensive aspirations to fund! The big house, the big car... big bills... none of that comes cheap, so it's the same tight-rope but with an even bigger fall? They say most people are only a month or two pay-cheques from the street don't they?

If he had known the real truth about Bill, Harry would have had enormous difficulty in believing it, of accepting it! Most folk would have done.

He reproached himself for thinking earlier that Bill had once '*been someone*!' Come on! Bloody hell, he *still was* someone! That type of lazy thinking grew out of the very attitude that he was constantly fighting against, the view that a large part of Society now held with regards to his clients the homeless, that they were no more than the dregs of society, druggies and criminals, that they were merely the remnants of people, what was left of someone who although they had maybe *been someone* once, had failed, hadn't measured-up, weren't good enough and that now they were less than nothing! That they deserved to be where they were because of their own ineptitude! It was a view actively fostered by recent governments of the day and the evil people they employed to assist them in their aims of seeping their foul poison into the minds of the populace with their despicable vitriol.

Bill *still was* someone, he reproached himself for feeling the need to affirm this fact! He was a living breathing human being, he was a person... he was a man. It was said that the true measure of a society was to check-out how it treated its weakest members, the old, the sick, the mentally challenged... and surely that *had to* include the homeless didn't it? Well if that was the yardstick to measure a society, then this one was a total fucking failure! The very existence of homelessness, the acceptance of it as a fact of life was utterly abhorrent, it was a stain on the soul of their nation, in his opinion and yet he harboured a belief that for the powers that be, it was considered more as a tool, a weapon to be wielded to keep people in their cage, working away and paying their taxes and producing. Producing in one way or another, wealth and profit for England plc, which of course is owned exclusively by the rich. When it had suited Society, during the Covid19 farrago, they had taken people off the streets, proving that it *could* be done and that the only difference between then and now was the will to do it!

Lost in his musings Harry was taken by surprise when Bill, abruptly spun his head round to face him directly...
"If ya's that interested 'Arry, why don't ya come'n join us, 'stead o' eavesdroppin' on us conversation like Key'ole Kate!?"

Despite his abruptness, there was no animosity in Bill's tone, the flash of a smile confirmed this, it was intended as a smile but it was more of a fleeting and revealing glimpse of a few discoloured teeth inbetween the small occasional gaps in the overgrown luxuriance that was his moustache, he was gesturing to the empty chair next to Andy as he spoke…

Harry was a bit taken aback, it had been happenstance alone that had brought him to be *eavesdropping* on Bill and the student's conversation, there had been no intention whatsoever in it! He had simply paused on his way across the dining room to finish drinking his coffee… it wasn't that bad, was it? Hmm… actually it was pretty dire! Perhaps he should check out what was actually inside the catering size Nescafé tins they spooned it out of? If there was another fiddle going on for him to discover he would be ruthless this time, stealing to survive was one matter, but substituting cheap coffee and flogging the tins of Nescafé they'd ordered in was something that he found unacceptable!

He hadn't even noticed the pair sat in conversation until he had temporarily parked himself up, he'd been lost in his own thoughts as ever… running the Factory was an all-consuming job!

On his way over to the proffered empty seat, he was still pondering on the coffee problem as he sat down alongside the red haired lad with the clipboard. A chance to listen to Bill in full flow, was not to be missed!

The student seemed to be an earnest sort of lad, full of idealism and enthusiasm… for now at least… Harry smirked to himself, he was all too aware of how life had a habit of knocking all that sort of admirable stuff out of you! He turned and offered his hand to the lad,
"Hi I'm Harry, The Manager here, we've not met but it was me who you spoke to on the phone last week, when you asked for permission to work with our clients."
"Oh yes… Of course. I'm Andy, but you already know that, please do join us."

Harry mused to himself that Andy was just about as close to the personification of a student you could arrive at! Well as you imagined a student to be if you were an ageing, over-the-hill, last-chancer type such as himself! Andy peered at him through the lenses of his black, heavy framed… *retro?* (well, he guessed that would be what they were termed!) …glasses, they were similar to the ones his Dad had worn back in the nineteen-sixties, but these were more rounded. He had the wispiest of red whiskers on his top lip and about his chin… *bum-fluff* he would call it if he were being cruel! When it was probably in reality there more out of a desire to put off the day when he had to decide if he was going to scratch away at his stubble for the rest of his life or not!

Harry realised he was rubbing his fingers across the stubble on his own chin, a sensation something akin to exposing them to contact with the heaviest grade of sandpaper! Why he bothered shaving at all when he could only manage to bother with it a couple of times a week was something he often asked himself, thank God that *designer-stubble*… or as he described it… *looking like a scruffy-sod*… was once again fashionable, at least for the time being! A glance at the tangled mass of Bill's massive grey, black and white beard was the only reminder he needed as to why he needed to shave his own whiskers off, albeit infrequently!

Andy had the typical complexion of a red-head, pale skin and even the freckles too, the kid was lucky to be living now and not when Harry had been a lad, it had been anything but trendy and *a bit cool* to be a carrot-top as it was today, back in his own youth!

Andy must have caught Harry's gaze as their eyes met momentarily, he had green eyes, big magnified green eyes as seen through the lenses of his spectacles… there was something about green eyes that had always fascinated Harry, maybe it was their rarity, at least as far as he was concerned? He looked away, a little embarrassed to have been caught studying the lad and spoke to Bill,

"So Bill, you'll tell your tale to this young whippersnapper, but remain clam-like most of the time when I ask you anything, that's how it is, is it?"
"Aye, well 'es not jus' some nosey bastard who's sole purpose in life is to rid the streets of us sorts 'cos 'is masters as told 'im to! Sorta like a Pied Piper for 'em, y'know… like a vermin control exercise! This lad 'ere… *'E's* actually interested 'e is! Andy 'ere's gonna change the world for the better, aren't you lad?"
Harry held his hands up in surrender,

"Okay! Please continue then and I shall sit here in silence, as an unwilling stooge of the masters and await enlightenment!"

Bill shuffled uneasily on his chair, he shook his head slowly a few times and then shoved the chair back, pushing it with his legs to make the feet scrape noisily across the stone flagged floor! He put his hands on the top of the table and used them to help push himself up onto his feet, all the while glowering at Harry then looking over at the startled student, he said,
"I've changed me mind son, sorry an' all that, you go over and 'ave yersel' a nice chat with ol'Louie o'er there, he loves to ramble on!" He nodded in the direction of the wreckage of a man, who was sat staring blankly into space, a mug, long empty on the table in front of him. Having said that, Bill leant down, grabbed hold of one of his backpack's straps and slung it up onto one shoulder, turned and shuffled his way out of the dining hall.

"That went well!" Andy scoffed sarcastically, giving Harry an accusingly reproachful look.
"I'm sorry if I threw a spanner in the works there Andy!" Harry apologised, "You'll probably not have found out yet that some of the staff here call him 'Gruffalo Bill' will you?"
He laughed, "No worries, I'll catch-up with him later."

An hour later Bill caught sight of Andy as he came out of the door to the refectory, he was now with a girl, the two of them were headed onto the large open and paved ground that ran alongside the south side of the old industrial building where he was sitting. He was sat at one of the picnic tables enjoying the spring sunshine. He took a last drag of his rollie, pinching the minute, burning stub between his thumb and forefinger, before flicking it away onto the stone flags. He beckoned to the students who had seen him and they ambled across to him holding hands as they strolled, he smiled to himself thinking how young they were, how exciting it all still was for them… being alive! All that freedom along with the joy of discovering sex thrown in too! How much life had yet to throw at them, all the chances there would be for so many an unexpected disaster to swoop down upon them from out of the blue at any moment or to spring at them from out of the shadows…

"Hi Harry, this is Nat" Andy announced proudly, she smiled... it was a thin little smile and slightly forced! Bill deciding in that moment that the whole idea of *getting down with the homeless and the tramps* was very much Andy's plan and much less Nat's! She was a pretty enough little thing he thought, tiny he'd say, what was it they called a girl her size nowadays? *Petite?* or was it *Size Zero?* Yeah that was it, well she were *just that* in fact... reet petite! She was a good foot shorter than Andy, she had purple hair and was wearing heavy make-up, particularly around her eyes he noted as he took in the youthful, yet to him weird and clown-like apparition that he beheld before his eyes... and her piercings! God how Bill cringed at that! One through the side of her nose, another through the skin by her eyebrow, one through the skin below her lower lip and an assortment of all manner of things dangling through and from her ears!

Andy was saying something which turned Bill's bemused and somewhat horrified attention away from his girlfriend,
"I was sorry you didn't feel able to chat earlier, maybe we could try again tomorrow?"
"Sit down 'ere and we can do it right now! It weren't you in there that were't'problem lad, I'm not for talkin' infront o' that vulture as come and swooped down aside o' you though! So lad, what do ya wanna know? You get your pen out an' go down the list on y'clipboard there an' I'll do me best to answer ya!"

Andy looked a little pained now that they were stood alongside Bill, he glanced down at Nat as she looked up at him, as she... *gave him a look*... There was something sulky about the girl, was it just the make-up? Nah... it was there in the way she held herself, in her body language. She leaned her weight onto her right leg so that she was standing a little awkwardly. She had both of her arms wrapped tightly around her waist, looking as if she was almost in need of holding herself together? All it did was make her bust seem larger! She had those wonderfully firm and pert breasts that many young women still possessed at her age, before time, gravity and having kids themselves inflicted their weighty woes upon them! There was no need to provide support for those tits he thought and as she was wearing a thin, white cotton T-shirt it was very clear that she *was not* wearing a bra! Her T-shirt was low cut with a curved sweeping line to it and her cleavage was very much on-show!

Her nipples were very evident too… it was as if there was two eyes staring at him! He snatched his eyes away, he'd not been perving over her, he was just *seeing her*, taking in everything about her appearance and her essence as he did with everything else that he observed, took note of, but he'd suddenly realised that it could easily have been misinterpreted as perving! He felt his cheeks glow a little, thankfully concealed beneath his wild beard, as Andy replied to his earlier remark,

"Oh, err… look I'm so sorry Bill but we have a lecture to get to… right now… err maybe…" Bill interrupted him with a dismissive wave of his hand,
"No worries lad, I'll be sat 'ere tomorrow mornin' same time same place, we can do it then if you'd like maybe? You kids run along…" With that he turned away from them, to gaze into empty space… to look at nothing. Once they had turned and were walking away he glanced at their backs, Andy had his arm around her and she was leaning into his shoulder as they sauntered across the stone flagstones, all their lives ahead of them… she had a very shapely, if *petite* bum too, he noticed! It wasn't a lecherous thought though, that kind of thing was long behind him now! But it explained why young Andy was so happy… at least for the time being!

The sun went behind a cloud, prompting him to move on. He pulled up his backpack, threaded his shoulders into the straps, groaning a little as he took on its weight, before he wandered off in the direction of town. As he was passing through the thickly constructed iron gates that stood in the opening of the tall stone wall, he turned and surveyed the massive long, old mill building standing five storeys tall, once a proud, thriving centre of industrial enterprise and manufacturing, owned by a forward looking man of vision, a man of his day, of his times! A Victorian entrepreneur… it was now operated by a charity to house the cast-off's of today's somewhat less industrious descendants.

Once upon a time, exactly where he was standing now, hundreds of workers would have streamed by, pouring in and out through these self-same gates to go and work their long, arduous shifts, then to wearily head for home at the end of the day. He accepted that it had been gainful employment for them back then, hard and demanding work no doubt, but from their perspective, they'd been grateful to have a job and at the end of the week they had a pay-packet to take home to provide for their family! It was difficult he thought, for us not to look at things like this through a modern day prism, a time when so much has improved since the heyday of the mill so long ago and however much it may have slipped back in recent years, the expectation of those masses employed there were vastly lower than those we have today.

Nowadays all that type of work was done overseas, it was better apparently to have people unemployed here rather than pay them a decent wage to work, preferable to give the jobs to workers in overseas countries! It was simple economics, the people in poorer countries would work for much lower wages, under worse conditions and with fewer provisions for their safety, all of which cost money to provide for and consequently resulted in less profit...

Today it was quiet standing in that gateway, there were only a few people drifting in and out, there were no hordes of people at the gates of The Folks Factory. It was still a truly magnificent structure regardless of its fall from its intended purpose, a full five storeys high with windows the full length of it on every floor. Built with millions upon millions of red bricks, incredibly skilfully laid, with yellow ones built-in to form intricate patterns.

If you took the trouble to go around and view the edifice from the canalside, what had originally been the business side of the factory, proudly emblazoned out across the central clock tower, you would behold the lettering, ARMSTRONG MILL the shapes of each letter having been formed out of intricate brickwork!

It was a good thing that it had been saved, so many similar and now disused mill buildings lay derelict all over the north of England, or had been demolished to create warren-like estates with housed crammed in on top of each other as tightly packed as possible... the destruction of such fine buildings as these was yet another testament to the crass stupidity, ignorance and indifference of the people who ran the country or more like their desire to profit from such vandalism and increase the wealth of their compatriots in crime.

He turned back and strolled off in the direction of the town centre, stooping to pick up a newly discarded and hence clean(ish), Costa coffee cup that had rolled into the gutter. He flicked off the plastic lid, sending it flying like a mini-Frisbee to land back onto the floor, sniffed at the remnants of the coffee, tipped it up to drain them out, squeezed the rim flat and shoved it down into his pocket.

Town was quite busy today with people scurrying around everywhere like ants, all very purposeful... busy, busy, busy, rushing around, bustling their way through their day, every minute accounted for and allocated to a pre-determined schedule, all with meaning and purpose... He sat down on the floor outside one of the doorways to the M&S store, not the best place to get money despite the fact that a great many of the people who went in and out of their doors clearly had plenty of it, most of that type liked to cling onto it for themselves though he found!

He sat there today not only because it was nice and warm in the sunshine, but also because he liked to be a prick in the conscience of *that sort*, to present himself before them as a sort of opposite of them, to be a horrible reminder to them, providing a *through-the-looking-glass* reflection of *their* society to them, a mirror of conscience? To challenge them! To show them that the lovely shiny, affluent life that they lived... with so little appreciation, all of it taken for granted as being their entitlement... accepting as some sort of God given right the position they occupied in the echelons of society and yet knowing all the while that it was underpinned by a sub-culture with equally as many other, lower positions... levels descending down below their own station in life, down through many layers of misery... down through the levels of the low-paid workers doing all the menial jobs, often having to do more than one job to make ends meet, then down through the unemployed who were forced to perform their pointless tricks, jump through the cruel hoops at the commands of the merciless ringmasters of The DWP ...like sullen, reluctant performing seals in a Water Park of Misery... so often having completed their ritual humiliation to be denied their fish from the charity bucket anyway, because they had failed to complete the trick *precisely* as they had been instructed to! Then you could descend right down to the dregs of society... all the way down to the very bottom level, where folk like he himself lived... or rather strove daily just to exist, to survive, to get through another day.

A few of them put one or two coins into his Costa cup during the hour or two he sat there, before a *Special Constable* or whatever they called this sub-division of The Police nowadays... had *moved-him-on.* He went and sat on a bench across the square until the cop had gone out of sight and then went over to the Wilko, people who shopped there were far more generous in the main. He guessed they had more of a sense of how much closer their own precious lives were to being in the same predicament as he was himself?

He was thinking of moving on when he saw the shuffling form of Mad Malky heading in his direction, he'd evidently spotted Bill sat there and had unleashed his mighty grin in recognition, showing off all three of his teeth! Given the choice and if he'd been on the move, already up on his feet, Bill would have avoided Malky, he was harmless enough but he was hard work, something Bill tried to avoid. It didn't help that the old guy really stank too!

His pungent odour settled down along with him as he shuffled onto the ground to sit alongside Bill, prompting him to rapidly commence work on a rollie...
"Ah sure, would you be sparin' one o'those littel rascals for an ol'unfortunate such as yourself my fine fellow William?"
"Good morning to you too Malky!"
"Top o'the morning to yourself!" Bill finished the cigarette and handed it over, immediately starting work on another for himself. As his fingers deftly formed the thin tube of tobacco, having had Malky's company forced upon him, he made an effort to have a conversation with him.
"I 'eard ya afore... over by t'monument, in full flood y'was today! Liked the bit about all them folks in y'audience bein' now't but plastic people an'them not even realisin'it! Y'certainly knows 'ow to win a crowd over eh?"
"Ah away wi'ya man. I do the work of the Lord as and when he commands me to, it's not my own words that issue forth from outta these old lips! Them's as been damned don'wanna hear the word!"
"But you tell 'em any'ow!"

Bill made short work of his rollie in order to take his leave of Malky at the first opportunity possible! A solitary old guy sat begging outside of the Wilko was one thing to be tolerated, but add in a decidedly unsavoury vagabond, with his shopping trolley full of placards and plastic bags, parked-up next to him and you were asking for trouble!

Malachi McGranahan was another regular at The Factry and not someone you could miss with his wild white hair and whiskers and his almost toothless grin. Some claimed he'd been in the clergy in Northern Ireland, it was evident from his dulcet tones that he hailed from there, others claimed that he was a priest who'd had to flee from The IRA for preaching for peace! Minds lacking the over stimulation of modern everyday life that the majority of us have inflicted upon us, were free to create their own imaginary stories!

Once he was away from Malky and as he'd scraped together enough change by lunchtime, he bought a sandwich at the Pound Bakery, the girl behind the counter sneaked a paper cup of tea onto the counter as she passed his sandwich across to him, looking furtively back over her shoulder to see if her boss was watching her as she did. She smiled at him as he nodded to her and mouthed '*thank you*,' quickly turning and leaving the shop. Little acts of kindness like that was what kept you going, the realisation that for all the nastiness and meanness that was everywhere, there still remained a little spark of decency, of compassion and humanity that was alive and burning in the hearts of many a person.

Drifting across town, all the while heading westwards... following the sun, he mused... he begged here and there. Lidl's carpark was en-route and he got a few coins there. He'd long ago noted that it was people who got in and out of the older cars, the more battered, dirty, unpolished ones that gave him something, the bigger, the flashier, newer and shinier the cars were the more it seemed that those who drove them pretended not to see him, or looked down disdainfully at him or even now and then would say something, sneeringly derogatory to him. Yeah, he thought sadly to himself, the ones with the most are the meanest. When you need help, always ask for it from the poor.

The daily rush and bustle of activity as the schools disgorged their open-prison inmates out onto the streets came and went, as it did every weekday in term-time around this time of day. It was all a part of the ebb and flow of life that was the time-keeper of Bill's days. He bought a pouch of baccy and some papers from a scruffy corner shop, that was happy enough of his business, along with a quarter of whisky, then made his way up to the canal where he sat on one of the few benches there still were, well ones that were intact and not vandalised or even burnt out!

For a few hours he watched the day slip gently away. He smoked a couple of ciggies watching as life went by… a few dog walkers passed, a jogger or two, a few kids on their way home from school, one or two folk with carrier bags of shopping… Most passed him by without paying him any attention, or consciously ignoring him, one or two smiled, said hello or *afternoon* at least acknowledging his existence… A few of the kids giggled or made rude remarks about him, he didn't care in the least about any of them… As the sun dipped behind the trees of the wooded copse across the murky water, to cast the towpath into shade, he carried on wandering westwards along the towpath, heading away from town.

He had a nice little spot to bed down, at least for now he did! The downside of it was that it was at least a mile and half out of town, just off the towpath. The canal was a favourite haunt of his but for exactly the same reasons it was also frequented by many other homeless guys as well, more unfortunately it was also used by the little gangs of youngsters who were most often up to no good, with their bloody drugs or larking about like dickheads once they'd consumed them!

He wasn't that bothered about the distance he had to walk, walking was the activity he was most involved with… or call it by another name… tramping! He'd always enjoyed walking anyway, the only snag for him now was that it burned calories, precious and scarce calories he had to acquire from somewhere!
He chuckled to himself as he twisted the metal top of the whisky bottle, breaking the seal and taking a swig, '*ahhh!*'… he exclaimed as the neat spirit ran across his palate, down his throat and into his stomach. He screwed the top back on, then slipped the bottle back into his pocket as he looked up and gazed around

him at the glorious wonder of the tall trees on the bank of the far side of the canal, with glimpses of blue sky through the greenery of their ever shifting leaves, the celestial blue vault of the heavens overhead, scattered with a puff of white cloud here and there and through the fence along his side of the canal, next to the towpath the sweeping expanse of green and yellow fields that surrounded him now, all so near to town too! Town, with all of its hustle and bustle, traffic and fumes, noise, dust and people… the small flask-bottle was made to fit in your pocket with its neat curve in the glass, clever that was…

Half an hour later he was wandering along a stretch of the canal that was heavily wooded on both sides, away to the south he could just about make out the motorway flyover higher up the valley, it seemed as if it were high up, running through the tree tops! Occasionally visible were the brightly lit shapes of some of the larger vehicles as they flashed past, still catching the low sun up there, on the parapet. The land rose steeply to the south where the motorway ran, a stream had painstakingly carved a small valley out of the hillside over the last million years or so as it had splashed its way downhill. A little further along it fed the canal with one of the many vital sources of water upon which it depended.

He too, once upon a time had driven across that very motorway bridge, high up there spanning the valley, a great many times in fact he had done so… It was a fine, elegant structure with a drop measured in hundreds of feet to the valley floor far below… now it was others who roared along the tarmac artery and never he, others who still lived in the world that he had left behind…

He came to a long stretch of the canal that had tall palisade fencing running along the edge of the towpath, it was old fencing but it was still doing its job despite that, the galvanising was now dull and matt, with the reddish-brown powder of rust showing through all over the place. Someone had once wanted to keep people out of the land that it bordered, land that behind it fell away steeply down through the woods. There were no structures visible to show what the fence had been put there to protect, maybe whatever it was, was some way down the hill, or maybe whatever it had once been was long gone now?

There was a small, single gate in the fence squeezed inbetween two heavy-duty posts, once there had been an access point here. Bill looked up and down the towpath to be certain no-one could see him and then reaching through the square opening, he carefully tugged at the rusty old padlock that was holding fast the bolt from being drawn. Once it was released he slid the bolt over and pushed hard against the gate so that it budged, with a tortured squeal just enough for him to squeeze himself and the his backpack through the gap, as soon as he was through he pushed the gate shut again, slid the bolt back across and threaded the hasp of the padlock through the eye on the bolt, squeezing it tight, so that it looked as if it was actually locked.

Ever so carefully he stepped away from the fence, placing his feet only on rocks and hard ground to ensure that he left no footprints, no trace of his passage! That was what gave your hideout away, *a path,* an indication of somewhere someone had passed, leaving a tell-tale message that whoever it was had been going somewhere... so why? What was there for them to go to? That was why so many places you could find to bed down weren't safe, or at least would already be occupied... they were just too obvious.

He made his way down the slope of the woods, careful not to leave footprints or crush the undergrowth too much and form a clear path. He took a leak up against a massive oak tree before making similarly careful progress as he entered the dense undergrowth of a mass of rhododendrons. Easing a branch back here and there he passed carefully through, until finally he had descended to a particularly dense patch that grew up against a vertical rock face some fifteen feet high. He eased a branch back and stepped over another one that was a couple of feet off the ground enabling him to duck into a small clearing about six feet in diameter, a clearing he had made by cutting back the branches with a little saw he'd got from a car boot sale. It had been rusty and blunt when he'd bought it for ten pence, but sitting for a few hours with a suitably sized stone he had worked at it tooth by tooth putting an edge on each of the teeth and then twisting them alternately to create the *cut*. Something his grandpa had shown him how to do, long-long ago in a life that no longer seemed to have ever belonged to him, a life that was more of a remembered dream than a reality... *"Look after your tools son and your tools will look after you!"* The old man had often told his six year old self.

He unslung his backpack and hunkered down to sit alongside it, leaning his back against the rock with his legs stretched out infront of him. The familiar smell of the damp rock, with its coating of moss filling his nostrils. He rolled a cigarette and sat there luxuriating in the smoke and feeling the effects of the nicotine... Sucking the last life out of it he stubbed it out and undid his backpack, there was a cereal bar in there somewhere... he rummaged until he found the box, his fingers finding only emptiness in the box, annoyed he snatched the box out, but once he tipped it up, a single bar fell into his palm! He smiled gratefully as he shoved the empty box back into the backpack and carefully split the plastic wrapper open.

He took his time eating the cereal bar, making the most of each bite, chewing it carefully before swallowing, always resisting the urge to gobble it down in response to the gnawing command of hunger that his stomach constantly growled up at him in its anger ...

Now it was time to settle down for the night. Kneeling on the ground he reached over to the far side of his clearing to retrieve a rolled-up piece of dark green canvas tarpaulin, frayed at the edges where it had once been torn away from a much bigger sheet. It was amazing what you could salvage, if you kept your eyes open that is, from the things people discarded. It was probably part of a cover for the back of a wagon, he'd found it in a corner of a yard where lorries parked so it seemed likely! Firstly he tied it to the branches where it was lying, about three feet from the ground with bits of string and rope. Then when he unrolled it, he was able to tie two of the other sides up similarly. The fourth side was now tight to the rock and fitted beautifully just beneath where there was a slight overhang, so that when he pulled it tight it made a half-decent seal. By tying one side at about four feet from the ground he gave a quite effective pitch to his makeshift canopy, enough to get any rain to run off, at least keeping the worst of it off him.

Although it was a dark colour, he always untied it and rolled it up whenever he left his shelter, the less there was to see the better.

Above the canopy he had used a piece of old galvanised stock fencing he'd found discarded where it had been replaced with a new section. He had taken it back to his den and painstakingly untangled it to form an arch over his clearing and then tied branches of the rhododendrons to it so that in time it created a green vaulted ceiling of sorts! It also provided extra cover to keep him safely hidden.

The canopy tied in place he settled back down leaning-up against the rock. He pulled the backpack up to his side underneath his arm, having removed and unfolded his waterproof blanket. He carefully spread it out over his legs, putting a rock on either side of it next to his feet and then he retrieved his whisky from the side pocket of his jacket and pulled the cover up to his chest.

He pulled his hood up and over his baseball cap. The cap seldom left his head, it was a navy blue souvenir hat from the 2012 London Olympics, it had their logo printed on it, that strange amalgamated jumble of orange shapes that someone had come up with! It was made up from the five rings and the union jack all mixed in together! His cap was the type with an elongated peak, so that once it was pulled down low and if you kept your head well down, wherever *they* had *their* CCTV with their 'facial recognition' spyware... you were practically invisible to the bastards! It was also handy to pull down to sleep. Most of his clothing and his possessions had come from one or another charity shop, the Salvation Army maybe or one of the ones at The Factory, they had stacks of items that others discarded as being no longer of any use to them but they were essential to folk like Bill. The hat however had been his son's, he'd taken it off the mirror in the lad's bedroom as he'd grabbed the rest of his gear on the day he walked out of his old life.

As dusk crept up slowly, the deepening shadows stalked-up on him relentlessly through the trees. He slowly drank the whisky, to the accompaniment of the last few songs of the day that the birds still felt like singing, *giving thanks for the day that they had just lived through?* Maybe... The backing track to the songs was the dull monotonous droning of the traffic on the motorway as it hurtled along, hundreds of feet in the air above him higher up the valley apiece, as it went across the bridge... it would die down as night followed on after dusk...

Draining the last of the whisky he tipped the bottle high and licked at the glass opening of the neck to get out the last drips, he screwed the top on and laid the empty bottle down at his side, he would take it away from his hideout, leaving as few traces as he could that he had been there. It wasn't that he gave a shit about littering! Nah... that wasn't his motivation! As soon as he was away and along the towpath it would be unceremoniously dumped! Maybe sent with a plop into the water! Why should he care? So many of them didn't! Once he would have been full of scorn for that type of behaviour... when he'd been *one of them*... Still worried about littering, like that lad Andy had said he was!

It was more or less dark now, so he pulled the zipper of his jacket right up tight to his chin, took one last look around his outdoor bedroom and closed his eyes, allowing his ever present companion of weariness to well-up and then to wash up over him like an incoming tide, his mind beginning to wander... he hoped that he didn't snore... silly that was... I mean who'd be out in the depths of the woods, late at night to hear him? For some reason he thought of a day... a day from way back that floated up to him from the sleepy depths of his memory, a scene from a lifetime ago, when he was a still a small boy... 'what on earth has made me think of that? He sleepily wondered, maybe meeting that student boy? He was so young...' *Anyone* could be out in the woods, what was there to stop them being there?... Other homeless guys... It was the day of his sixth birthday he was remembering, wasn't it?... or... He was fast asleep before he gave it another conscious thought...

CHAPTER TWO

Picture a 1950's living room, sat on the floor surrounded by torn and crumpled-up brown paper, a massive smile on his young face is a happy boy. A long cardboard box was next to him, its lid resting in front of him, partly across his outstretched legs. The lid was a shiny blue colour and had the word 'VOSPER' emblazoned across its top in bold red, capital letters that were outlined in black, it also had 'RAF ELECTRICAL CRASH' in smaller letters and also the word *Tender* in a wonderfully swirly script!

On his lap he was cradling in his arms a beautiful model boat, the shining black plastic of its hull gleamed and underneath it, at the stern (that was what you called the back of a boat!) there were two highly polished brass propeller shafts each ending with a wonderful little shiny, brass propeller! In addition to this, each one had a tiny rudder behind them, fully adjustable ones too! There were little brass thingy air-vents sprouting up on the top of the cabins too, even tiny hand rails as well as a white lifebelt! The lifebelt was also a switch that you rotated to start the electric motor that made the propellers turn! It was wonderful! With a beaming face he looked up to say,

"Thank you daddy, it's *magnificent*! I love it! Can we go to the boating lake today, please, please… please…" His father smiled as he looked down at his happy six year old son, watching patiently as his lad enthusiastically showed and demonstrated to him all the features of his new boat. He was pleased that his present was well received and that the memory of the tantrum in the toyshop was now forgotten, at least in the little lad's mind! The tantrum he'd thrown when he was told that he had to choose *between* having the crash tender *or* the ocean going liner for his birthday present and that *no*, he most definitely could not have both!
"I can steer her, look daddy with the rudders, so she won't get stuck out in the middle of the pond like my yacht did!"
"Yes it is *magnificent*, you're correct son!" He had to say he was impressed with the his son's habit of *collecting* words, but especially that he made sure that he understood their meanings and more importantly, how to use them in the correct context, *magnificent* was one of his latest acquisitions!

A little while later the lad was crouched down on the paving stones as he launched his boat out onto the water of the boating pond, the pond was about thirty feet in diameter and was in one of the bigger parks in their town. He set the boats electric motor running and put it gently onto the water, giggling as the propellers sprayed water up at him as they contacted the surface of the pond. The boat surged forward and headed out across the lake, scattering a duck that flapped and quacked angrily before it was left behind bobbing in its wake. He was on his feet, jumping up and down ecstatically watching it go with his hands raised for a few moments... until his face fell and turned into one of shocked horror as he realised the boat was heading at *full-speed-ahead* directly for the stone surround of the pond on the far side! The terror of realising that *she would be smashed into smithereens* when she hit it and would be sunk on her maiden voyage was an unbearable agony for him! He yelled out, *"NO!!..."*

Then he saw his Dad, who was, as ever ahead of the game, he was already strolling around, on his great long legs to where the boat would arrive on the other side... His face changed in a moment from horror to joy, akin to the sun coming out again from behind a thundercloud...

Back home and listening to the babbled tales of his boat's 'maiden voyage', his mother tried hard to smile encouragingly before gently interrupted him to say,

"This came for you, the postman brought it while you were out. A late birthday present!" As she spoke, she was handing him an envelope. He turned it over in his hands, admiring the stamp which he would cut-out later to save. He recognised the small, neatly written and meticulous script of his grandma's handwriting.

The envelope was already opened! He looked up accusingly at his mother, the look on her face told him to say nothing on the subject of the *shocking invasion of his privacy* that had quite clearly and outrageously taken place! He reached inside the thick envelope, took out and unfolded the single sheet of crisp blue Basildon Bond writing paper and there inside the fold of the thick paper there was something else, a slither of much thinner paper!

He let the letter fall onto the table top at which he was now sat and held the small piece of thin paper outstretched inbetween the fingers of his two hands. It was about five inches by three, white, with black printing on it, some of it was intricate too! It had a feint blue pattern beneath the lettering too! (Intricate... good word!) Beneath a picture of The Queen's crown the words PREMIUM SAVINGS BOND were printed, then in smaller letters, which he was reading out loud of course... it said, "Issued by the Lords Commis... si-on..?"
"Commissioners." His Mum read over his shoulder,
"...Lords Commissioners of H.M.Treasury... Look Mum it's a pound note! See here, look there it says £1!"
"No love it's a Premium Bond! You can't spend it!"
"Ah... so what use is it then?"
"Well love, you see that number there..." She points,
"This one? *4AW 277941?*"
"Yes dear, well they have a special computer in Lytham St. Annes called Ernie and..."
"Why is it called Ernie if it's only a computer, that's a type of a machine isn't it, not a person?"
"So why do you call your bloody boat *she*?" She snapped back impatiently before adding more soothingly...
"It's an acronym...!" She knew that would distract him! Giving the little sod a *new word* to memorise and then repeat all the bloody time for a week! Here it comes...
"What's a..."
"It means a word that is made up out of the first letters of the words that describe it!" Like *'ALS'* she sniggered to herself as mentally she invented a new *acronym* for him, *Annoying Little Sod!* She managed to stop herself from providing her son with this demonstration of how to make up an acronym... But only just!
"Oh... I see?" He looked up at her clearly still wrestling with this new concept. She elaborated,
"It stands for 'Electronic Random Number Indicator Equipment'.
"Oh righto. What does that mean?"
"Ask your father! I've got tea to make!" With that she swirled away out of the living room into the kitchen, he listened with *pricked-ears* as he heard the click-click of her cigarette lighter, to

be followed shortly by the smell of her ciggy smoke as it wafted through...

'It's him... he makes me smoke!' He replayed in his mind the outburst his mother had unleashed on his Dad recently when he had dared to reproach her yet again for *smoking too much!*

'He's just a lad! Have some patience will you?'
'It's alright for you! You just bugger-off out to work every morning, leaving me here on my own with him! I have to put up with the little sod all day long!'
'Oh right, so when did he stop going to school, eh? Forgot to mention that did you, didn't think to mention to me... his father! That he'd been expelled?' ...hmm he noted, *'expelled'*, another new word, he'd thought! Another one to write down, then look up in his Nelson's School Dictionary, one of his *special* books, one his Dad had given him, a really old book, one that he'd had himself, when *he* was a boy! The replay of his parent's conversation was still running in his head...

'Ha-bloody-ha! Such a bloody comedian you are, aren't you! Should have been on the stage in Blackpool, you should... Might have earned us a bit more money too! Well the little devil may as well be here all the time, by the time he's gone to school it's only five minutes later, or it may as well be, before he turns up back here again, bouncing-in, full of his bloody endless chattering and mithering!"

'You really are a miserable bitch aren't you? You should be grateful for all you have instead of whining-on all the time! You're an ungrateful wretch! I have to go off to work! ...WORK! It's not a day of fun and laughs you know. I have to work damn hard to keep a roof over our heads, clothes on our backs and food in our bellies, while you just swan around here at home pretending that having seven hours... all to yourself... is just five minutes! Maybe if you did a bit more housework, kept the place a bit tidier... The lad even takes himself off to school now and comes home on his own, how many kids of his age do that? He's six for God's sake! What do you expect from him? You've got the maternal instinct of a rattle-snake! You make me sick, you selfish, ungrateful bitch!' SLAM! ...and that's Dad gone out to his garage...

'Bitch! & Wretch!'...They both went on the list on the page headed 'naughty words!' to sit in the company of others such others as *shit, fart & bugger*.

His mum and Dad'd always make-up later on, now *that* really did make him sick, hearing her purring to his Dad and getting all over him, all slimy, smarmy and sneaky! He hated her! Dad was right, she *was* a bitch! Why did he have to have such a horrible, nasty old bitch as a mother? His friend Nigel's mum was lovely, she was kind *and* she was pretty too, why did he have to live here with *her*? He liked going around to Nigel's house, he wished he lived there with their family... except he'd miss his Dad, he loved his Dad... He worshipped his big, tall, strong but ever so kind Dad...

He looked down at the little circles that were appearing on the thin paper of his Premium Bond, he put it down on the table and tried to brush off the tears that had fallen onto it... but they had already soaked into it! It was ruined! He had ruined his brand new Premium Bond, even though he didn't really know what it was, apart from knowing that a man called Ernie had sent it to his Gran, who'd then gone to all that trouble of posting it on to him... but now it was ruined! He angrily screwed it up and threw it across the room as he emitted a pained and wailing cry, to be followed by endless sobbing as he buried his head in his arms on the table top.

His mother came through from the kitchen,
"What the hell!.." She stood for a moment, her arms akimbo, ready to bawl at him, but seeing his distress her heart softened... she did love the little bugger really despite everything... before she had time to think she heard herself saying, "Oh dear, what's the matter love?" She had her arm around his shoulders a moment later, she ran her fingers through his thick brown hair, gently lifting his tear streamed and tragic face up to hers,
"What is it? What's the matter love?"
"I've...*sob*...I've ruined my Premium Bond... *sob*... my Premium Bond that Grandma...*sob*... sent me... *it's ruined*!"
"What? Why? Where is it?" He pointed a trembling finger in the direction he had thrown the screwed up bit of paper...

His mum went over and picked it up, un-crumpling it on the top of the table,
"Why on earth did you screw it up?" A hint of annoyance was now returning to her previously soothing tone…
"I cried all over it… my tears got it wet and ruined forever!"
"Come here you daft apeth!" She reached out to her distressed little lad and he sprang up into her arms where she hugged him tightly to her body, lifting him right off the ground as she spun around with him..
"Shall we dance baggy-pants…"
"Yes of course droopy-draws…" He joined, as the clouds of despair were being swept away by the force of his naturally sunny disposition and the rare glow of his mother's love for him… She leant back, from him as she held him in her arms and looked into his eyes,
"Why were you crying over that in the first place love?" She let the question hang for only a moment before brushing it aside with,
"Oh it doesn't matter… many a tear has to fall… it's not ruined anyway, just a bit crumpled! I'll iron it, that will restore it to its former glory!"
"Now? Can you iron it now? Please mum, please, oh please…?"
"What, you expect me to stop everything I'm doing and get the flipping iron out right now, just because…" The transition from joy as it was rapidly returning to abject misery that was sweeping across her son's face melted the chill of her rising ire,
"Oh, alright then! The things I do for you! You my lad, should go on the stage, the way you can pull that fizzog of yours around, turning all that emotion on and off like a tap and with such conviction too! You could be the next Sir Laurence Olivier, you could…"

Bill stirred in his sleep, he blinked his eyes open for a moment, it was still early but it was already becoming light, he gave thanks… *that he was still here*… even though he sometimes wondered about how much *'still being here'* was a blessing and how much it was a curse! He guessed that if he ever thought that the balance had tipped too far into the camp of the latter then…

Dismissing those thoughts, he shuffled himself into a more upright sitting position, he had woken-up to the beautiful, shrill sound of a blackbird's song as he greeted the new day, his song was wonderfully loud in the stillness of the clear and crisp early morning air, the woods still relatively quiet as the traffic had not begun to properly wind up overhead for the morning rush-about. The blackbird had some backing singers today, provided by two or three pigeons with their rhythmic but un-syncopated coo-cooing... Of course they were scattered around on branches in different trees, unlike how they were in Bill's imagination... sat on a branch in a line, side by side alongside the blackbird...

For a moment or two the dream was still with him in that vague, transient and ethereal space between sleeping and waking... hanging around for a few moments like evaporating mist in the sun... Ah yes... That Premium Bond he remembered and all that it had meant to him, when so very long ago he was incarnated as his six year old self!

CHAPTER THREE

Harry Protherow walked out through the front door of The Folks Factory into the Spring sunshine, he tipped his head back to feel the warmth of the sun on his face, catching a glimpse of the two students sitting at one of the picnic benches off to his right, they were drinking coffee, looking at their phones, chatting intermittently and now and then showing each other what they were looking at on their screens.

He pondered for a moment whether he should go over and have a chat with them, make out he was interested in what they were doing even! He supposed he should, also that actually he *really should* be interested in any way that he could use to promote the mission of the project he headed-up, it was a case at that particular moment though of... could he actually be arsed to bother right now?

He was not in the best of moods having just sacked the catering manager Viktor! At that moment the very man himself came storming out of the doorway, he deliberately caught the large bundle of work-clothes he was carrying against Harry's arm, jostling him a little as he did! He took a pace or two more past Harry, then paused as if in a moment of indecision perhaps? If it had been, once he'd decided, he turned and his face was full of rage and thunder as he spoke out very loudly... just short of yelling... in his heavily accented Romanian manner,
"You haf not heard de last of thees! I sue you for unfair dismissals, you will be seeing! You call me thief! Is defăimare! Is no right!"
"Your workwear belongs to The Factory Viktor, can you leave it please?" With that the furious and now even more outraged man threw the bundle at Harry's feet, this time truly shouting he yelled out,
"Le duceam la spălat! I only take to wash them, bastard! Du-te naibii!" With that final outburst, he stormed off!

Harry bent down and picked up the bundle of clothes, he needed a sit down now as he was trembling all over in reaction to the confrontation with the angry man, so he decided he would after all go over to the two students who had been watching it all go down... Oh no! He thought to himself as he realised that the bloody girl had been videoing everything that had just transpired on her phone! For fucks sake!

He placed the bundle down on the table and squeezed himself in to sit next to Andy,
"You okay man?" Andy asked,
"Yeah, all in a day's work for The Project's manager!"
"Sure but that guy was like, proper aggressive y'know? Real angry! I thought he might've even smacked you one!"
Nat spoke up now,
"What was it all about, he was making out like you'd accused him of stealing? Was that it?" She was so sweet and innocent he thought as well as... well no need to think like that... but although obviously intelligent enough to be at uni... she nevertheless did seem a bit *thick!* Maybe it was his own prejudice on account of all the piercings or perhaps the purple hair? *Purple* for fucks sake he thought to himself!

"Well you know how our coffee's been tasting like ditch-water of late? Well I have invoices for several one kilo tins of Nescafé from the catering suppliers and the tin on the shelf in the café *is* one of them, however in the storeroom there is no sign of the six tins we had delivered according to the invoice! When I rummaged about I found three tins of some cheap and nasty stuff from some cash and carry, damaged tins that he'll have got on the cheap somewhere. So I had a look in the tin they were using to make brews with and compared it with the tin I'd had delivered direct to me, by arrangement with the rep. Guess what?"
"It wasn't the same stuff!" Andy volunteered...
"Give Poirot a cigar!"
"You're like devious dude, you should be a detective!" Nat remarked then she added,
"Bit harsh sacking him though? I mean how much would the guy have been making out of his little scam?"
"Not the point love," Andy volunteered, "If he was doing that what other little fiddles did he also have on the go? There's all sorts they can do, like signing for stuff they don't get and getting a deal off the driver, or just ordering too much and simply whizzing it!" Harry asked,
"So how do you know all that Andy?"

"I worked in a supermarket last summer, you wouldn't believe what goes on!"
"Right… Thing is it's not the first time I've caught him out, I gave him the benefit of the doubt that time, but this time, well I caught him red-handed, I mean stealing from a charity, how low can you get?"
Andy volunteered an answer,
"Y'know if you're on a low income today, life can be really tough… trying to get by, pay all your bills, keep y'head above water? He's probably working another job as well as this one here. Maybe he really needed to do it, just to stay afloat, even to feed his kids perhaps?"
Nat piped up at that point,
"Stealing's still wrong, and *it is* from a charity too! So Harry The Factory is a charity is it? Like it's registered and all that sort of thing?"
"Very much so Nat and definitely with *every sort of thing* it entails to be a fully Registered and Official Charity!"

There was a little pause in the conversation before Harry asked Nat,
"Would you do me a great big favour love and delete that footage you just shot of my little contretemps with Viktor?" She looked affronted so he carried on,
"Please, don't take offence, you see anything that reflects badly on Folks Factory is not only bad for me personally as manager but it's also bad for our reputation in a wider sense too. You know when it was first being set-up there was a massive outcry against it? Protests even, folks with placards, if you can believe that? The Press were on it like vultures back then and they're still there, always circling over our heads waiting to swoop on anything they can to *get a story*, to dish out more dirt. I know you didn't mean any harm by filming it, it's second nature for folks nowadays to film everything, but if you post it anywhere, you'll instantly lose control of it and it could be on the front page of the local rag tomorrow!"
Andy intervened,
"Go on Nat be fair, Harry's been bonzer with us, giving us free access here for our thesis."
"Okay…" She held her phone up and demonstratively deleted the clip.

"Thanks Nat, I really appreciate that. Now then, what brings you here, I mean sat outside and not interviewing our illustrious guests?"
Andy replied,
"We arranged to meet up with Bill today, but he's a no-show by the look of it. We can go in and see if anyone else will chat maybe? Nat?" She nodded, Harry commented,
"They're notoriously unreliable you know, most of our guests, Bill more so than most, in fact I would say he's the most difficult one of all of them, quite an enigmatic character though is old Bill. You do know that Bill isn't his proper name, just one that we gave him? We give names to folks who won't provide us with one?"
Andy: "So you know next to nothing about him, not even his real name?"
"Yeah, maybe you picked the wrong one if you wanted to hear his tale of woe!"
Nat: "You're not that sympathetic towards them are you Harry? To your... *clients?* That's what you refer to them as isn't it?"
"Off the record?"
"Off the record yeah, if you like…"
"Phones switched off and on the table face-up?" Harry nodded at Nat, she stopped recording the conversation and switched her phone off, Andy did likewise as he asked,
"Like why Harry, what's the beef with being upfront… *being on the record?*"
"I have no *beef* with it lad, but I have a job to do here and that's what it is to me, a job…nothing more… nothing less. If I could get a better paid job I'd be gone in an instant! They don't come that easy though for a guy my age and this one does pay pretty well. But I'm no missionary, I work here for the same reason ninety-nine percent of people do any job… for the money! It's like I said before, bad publicity is the last thing I need if I'm to keep this place open and myself in a job!

"So far as dealing with this lot of vagabonds… Well, I'm basically a business man, trained in systems management and the organisation of people, the basic nuts and bolts of running this place, the maintenance of the property, the accounting are all relatively simple tasks, I answer to a board of trustees, they hold the purse strings and have the final say on any financial decisions, apparently they're in touch with the guy who

originally funded the whole project some Millionaire…" Andy interrupted him,
"Who is this guy, the one who's money and vision this whole project grew out of?"
"That Andy is a question no one knows the answer to, or at least anyone who may know, is willing to divulge! The board deal with a go-between, an agent who acts on behalf of the benefactor, he was the one who did all the negotiating right from the start, from fighting to get planning permission, right through to contracting the builders and services that created it all. It was no mean task to renovate that there colossal old building you know!" Andy asked,
"So who's this go-between?"
"His name's Jos, Jos Armstrong, I've heard a whisper that no-one has seen him for quite some time though, but that he left everything so well set up that funds are readily available to sustain the operation under the supervision of The Board pretty much indefinitely, especially now as we generate a lot of our own funding. I've been told by someone close to the board that they think he's been reassigned to the philanthropist's next project, now this one is up and running and has become self-sustainable. But if that's true nobody's aware of where that new project may be."

"Right, he *so* is a *mysterious* benefactor then eh?… that's really cool eh? Nat?" She shrugged disinterestedly,
"Didn't you find it a tad funny that this Josh character had the same name as the Mill? Like… *Armstrong*? Come-on!"
Harry smiled,
"It's simply Jos, not Josh, and yeah it didn't miss my attention! When I asked him he said it wasn't entirely coincidental, his great-great grandfather, (I think that's the right number of *greats*!) was a cousin of the Victorian industrialist who built the mill. He said he couldn't fathom out what relation it actually made him to Ephraim, Phineas Armstrong other than *pretty distant*!"
Andy laughed,
"Ephraim Phineas! They loved to have a gob-full of names didn't they back then!"
"E.P.A. Nat chipped-in! I've seen that carved into the stone around the building! Now we know why!" Andy nodded,

"Yeah! Like AS was for Arnie Saknussemm in journey to the centre of the earth!"
Harry and Nat looked at him blankly... He shrugged and went on,
"Well for all that's real fascinating like, I'm not particularly interested in it, my angle is on the people using it today, these guys who depend on the hand-outs they get here and one thing I have noticed is that they're all guys too, well from what I've seen, aren't they Harry?"

"It's true that they are mostly men for sure, but we do have a few women coming through now and then, but they seem to be more willing to take the steps... you know about the idea of *the stepping stones*?" They both nodded. Andy asked,
"So they move on, get off the streets and don't need to come here again, by and large, unlike many of the guys?"
"Yeah, the stepping stones idea came from the founder apparently, we can provide a bed for the night, no strings attached with just a name for registration. The next step is to be offered a cabin, that's what we call the pods, they're a mini-room on the first floor, they were all once factory machine floors in there you know? The cabin gives them an address, they have a key for their door and they can come and go as they please."
Andy jumped in again,
"So that means they're able to access benefits, as they have an address, they are in fact technically no longer homeless?"
"No *technicality* about it Andy, they *aren't* homeless anymore! That's the beauty of it. We have advisers that come in regularly, they help folk to navigate the minefield of claiming benefits, they know how to fill-out the forms online correctly, we help with that of course and they also know how to succeed with any appeals that often arise if they try and turn down the claim.

"The Benefit System's set up to deter claimants you do understand that? They set the hurdles as high as they can get away with, yet all the while seemingly offering help... so it can appear that way for the public press releases and then they try to trip people up at every opportunity! Their task it to hold the purse strings as tightly as possible, to minimise spending rather than to provide the services that people are legally entitled to. Whenever you hear the government quoting figures about the cost of benefits, bigging-up the huge amounts that are being spent, what they never tell us is the amount that they would actually have to spend if they gave everyone what they needed and were entitled to. You understand what I mean, it's like however much it is if it's not enough the scale of the amount is meaningless without proper context."

Nat: "So basically what you're saying is that you and your whole operation is a bit of a thorn in the flesh of The Establishment?"

Andy: "Not scared they'll like… take you out?" He laughed at what he at least considered to be his witticism!
Harrry just shook his head and answered Nat's more sensible question,
"Yes indeed, we are a thorn in their flesh Nat, very much so! I think the Government would love to find a way to shut us down, our Council is run by Labour thank God, so they do try to be as supportive as they can with the ever more restricted funding they're given by Central Government… but of course even Labour is moving to the right now…"

Andy: "So do you think that they see homelessness as a… I dunno, err… a deterrent maybe? A sort of way to instil fear into people… like sort of, work hard keep your nose to the grindstone or you'll end up on the streets?"

"Absolutely Andy! You've hit the nail right on the head there lad! Our project, what we're doing here is anathema to the Tories, even though we're more or less self-financing now and we don't get a penny directly from The State, they still hate us as we get more benefits for our clients out of The System than they would otherwise have got. They see us as subversive, think we're commies at worst, Socialists at best!"

Nat: "Are you then Harry? A Socialist?"
"Me?" He laughed… "Nah, I'm a *Harryist*! Sorry if that disillusions you love, but like I said, to me this is a job, nothing more. Our clients… I mean… *clients*? Mostly to me they're just the commodity I trade in today, in this particular job, something to be dealt with! Herded-in, fed and watered, washed and cleaned-up if they want to be… housed overnight if they'll let us and then herded-out again in the morning!

We do offer the opportunity for them to be moved-on and move back towards society as well, if they want to… too many of them simply don't though! Does that surprise you?"

Nat: "Yeah! I've found that myself in talking to them, like why would you choose to live like this?" She pulled a face, Andy disagreed though,

"Actually I can see it Harry, the way they feel is like, well… societies damn well rejected them y'know, so now they feel sort of defiant, so they reject society right back? Why would you want to take a step that will just lead you back into the same shitty trap you were in before you fell through the safety net? What would make you want to go back to the same shit that drove you out onto the streets in the first place?"

Nat: "I've not seen any showers or suchlike, do you provide that, you said something about them getting *washed and cleaned-up*?"

"Well you'd probably not want to see that, they're bad enough with their clothes on!" He chuckled, "I'm sorry, haven't you had the full tour? We do indeed provide showers, even baths! We have a laundry for the clients, they hand in their clothes, we bag & tag them and return them washed and as clean as we can get them. We also have a clothes store too, we work very closely with many charities to source second hand clothing, shoes and stuff like that, you've been in our *shopping mall* area and seen that?"

Andy: "Yeah where all them types of shops are, the food store that's like a foodbank with donated stuff, The Shelter advice shop and all of them, yeah 'have to say that was impressive."

"Yes, that's the place. Look…" Harry looks at his watch, "I don't know if you've noticed the media types coming and going today with all their gubbins and what-nots, but I'm giving a press conference in The Media Reception Room, it's through the main door over there, then left along the corridor to the bottom, we're in a constant battle with The Press like I said, even nine years into the project! The latest Kerfuffle is over our housing project next door, you'd think someone building low cost housing would be cheered-on wouldn't you? But no, the Nimby's are all out jumping up and down shouting and waving their placards and banners all over again, they'll be along too when the Press

Conference starts, you can count on that, should be great material for your work!"

Andy: "What do people have against the housing project you're funding? Why would anyone object to someone building affordable homes?"
"Why indeed? I mean the site was derelict, it was a mess, an eyesore with fly-tipping and health hazards galore! We come along buy the site, have it cleared, cleaned-up and fenced-off then apply to build a modest development of houses and flats, to provide a final stepping-stone back to being part of the community for our clients! And lo... the objections come flooding in thick and fast! Stuff like: 'It will destroy the amenity of the area, create friction in the community! Giving houses to people who don't deserve them!' That's the sort of bull they come out with!"

Nat: "Really? Is that what they say? But surely you don't just give the houses away?"
"Of course not, but neither do we seek to make a big profit from them as any other Housing Developer would. They'll become a part of the charity naturally, but in practice they will actually create a small income over time to help maintain our work."

Nat: "Will you win in the end? I mean will you get the go ahead and eventually build it?"
"Oh yeah, we will for sure! Their arguments are spurious and argumentative at best, they have no real grounds or substance other than pathetic, mindless prejudice and some sort of nasty objection to anyone getting more easily what they've had to fight tooth and nail for themselves! Instead of blaming the shitty, corrupt housing market that we have here today, they turn on us! You'd think they'd be glad to see someone pioneering a better way forward, trying to buck the system? But no, they won't even try to see it our way, they just see someone getting an easy ride that they never had the opportunity of taking for themselves!"

Andy: "That really sucks man! Like they're in the system, they're a part of it, know it's shit but still they won't try and fight it or support someone who is willing to!"
"Yep! That's about it, that's the thing with the housing ladder, anyhow the way I think that they see it is that once they've got

themselves up onto it, even if it's only as far as getting one rung up from the bottom… many of them seem to want to pull the ladder up behind them! They look at how much their own house goes up in value and they're fooled into the thinking that they have their very own pot of gold under their very own rainbow, they imagine that they are rich! Even though the vast majority of them are in hock to a building society or a bank!

"But of course it's all an illusion! A fool's paradise? More like a croc-of-shit because unless you sell-up and move to the back of beyond, the value of your house is irrelevant, the worst thing about it though in this false market is that it forces rents to go up accordingly."

Andy shrugged, "But what do you do? How can it be fixed? Why has it gone so badly wrong?"
"Because it's propped-up Andy, it's a fake market. If they really let *Market Forces* work, allowed the market to get on and do its job properly then there would be property price slumps too, the market would get ahead of itself and then it would fall back, drop like a stone as it used to do periodically. Not anymore though, there's too much money invested in property today, it's seen as a commodity nowadays and not as housing, providing homes for people to live in has little to do with anything, it's simply a massive business!"

Andy: "Yeah that's why in London they buy houses and just leave them empty, the value goes up and up, it's like gold but makes a higher return so they make a killing for doing nothing!"
"Precisely so my young friend. Look I've only got half an hour now, so I need to go and get ready. Come in and listen, it should be fun when they get to ask questions at the end!"
He took a couple of passes from his pocket and handed them to Andy,
"Here, you'll need these to get into the VIP area at the front with the Press and invited dignitaries." Andy beamed as he took the passes, clearly delighted to receive special treatment. Harry left the kids and headed to the main doors, *fun* was one thing he was sure it *would not be*, at least not for him, having to do battle with the ignorant prejudice of a mob of ovine, selfish people! Even the Media would focus their questions on the concerns and prejudices of *their public*!

Already there was a small crowd of people gathering outside the building, thronging around at the main doors with security guys already getting set up with crowd control barriers to allow press and media people past and keep the rest out until later, when a limited number of the public would be allowed in along with ticket holders! The dignitaries had their own entrance of course! He squeezed through the throng and into the building.

CHAPTER FOUR

Earlier on in the woods just outside of town, Bill realised that he must have dozed off again because this time it was the swishing, hissing noise of rushing traffic on the wet road up on the bridge that woke him. The air was damp now, it seemed darker than it had been when he'd stirred earlier to listen to the blackbird's solo part in the dawn chorus. He once more shuffled himself up against the rock to be sat more upright, in an attempt to relieve the backache that plagued him every night. What he'd give right now for a couple of those Co-codamol 30/500 tablets he'd once used! Just another thing he'd taken so much for granted in the life he'd left behind…

As his eyes got nearer to some sort of focus… he'd lost his prescription specs years ago… he could see clouds of misty drizzle drifting around in the rhodies, the rich smell of damp earth permeated his nostrils as he rummaged into his backpack to retrieve his water bottle.

He unscrewed the top of the military surplus canteen, letting it dangle on the little chain that secured it and took a deep swig of the cold liquid. He wiped the back of his gloved hand over the unruly whiskers that mostly covered his mouth and let his head rest back against the rock. His bottle was nearly empty, a vital daily task to complete, but it looked like it needed to be completed sooner rather than later this day. Leaning forward a little, he pulled his hood back from over his hat, it was like flicking a switch, immersing him into the full range and volume of all the sounds that surrounded him…

His mind was drawn back to the disconcerting dream he'd had earlier… what had it been about? It had been disturbing, that much he could still remember, he could still feel the emotions it had stirred-up, deep within him. He felt as if he could almost grab onto it, hold it back from burrowing back down into the inaccessible depths of darkness deep in his subconscious mind … Then he had it! There it was! It was that bloody Premium Bond he'd had as a kid that he latched onto, that had been a part of it! He mentally grabbed on tightly to it and as he held onto it the whole dream came flooding back to him!

He shook his head slowly, what the fuck was that all about? Revisiting his childhood? It had an unpleasant hint, a nasty whiff of all those therapy sessions he'd forced himself to endure when things had got really bad for him, when he was still desperately trying to cling onto the life he'd once had, when he still had the remnants of a futile hope that it all could still be alright for him… that it would come right again, that life would get better… in the end… But of course it hadn't.

Had it been a conscious decision to finally accept that as an incontrovertible fact? To stop desperately trying to cling onto his life, to accept that it required more than he had left in him to hold onto it? Had he accepted that, admitted defeat and simply released his grip on it… just let go? Now he lived trying to keep it all locked away, to see it as gone and forgotten, as if all of it had happened to someone else, that it had nothing to do with him, why the fuck wouldn't it stay that way?

As if to rub his nose in the fact that it wasn't going to be denied, he found himself remembering the time when he found himself waking-up on the floor in a street he didn't recognise. The first time he was mugged. He was cold and wet, it was still dark, he was bruised and bleeding with the leaden tick-over of a soon to develop hangover from hell about to rev-up… he had no wallet, no watch, no phone… and no memory…

So in that first instance he hadn't 'let go' at all, consciously left behind all that his life had been up until that moment in time? Had it been the mugging, or had it been a case of the load on his mind, the pressure of the mounting strain of all his problems bearing down on his tortured psyche that had caused it to hide itself away as it finally broke, snapping like an ancient tree as it finally surrendered to the last gale? He'd stood tall and resisted all the trials and tribulations that had come his way throughout his long life up until then, it was what we all did, wasn't it? He'd been like that tree then, when it was young and supple and in his youth he'd bent with the wind too, was it the hardening of his attitudes akin to the thickening of branch and trunk in the stricken tree of his imagination that had led to his demise under the onslaught of that final storm? To cause him to break asunder, shattering completely as his resistance was finally insufficient to resist any longer? They say it is the addition of a single straw that finally breaks the camel's back do they not?

A poem he'd once written came to mind...

It was called, Fallen Giant:

Oh fallen giant now laid low
No longer do your branches go
Thrusting upwards towards the sky
Now broken down with you they lie

The wicked wind with banshee song
Cared not that you had stood so long
The more your branches vainly flailed
The more screeching became its wail

With shattering crack your life it took
The woodlands trembled as they shook
To thunderous blow, splintering of wood
Empty the space where you had stood

No longer may I upwards gaze
At your majestic branches raised
As your giant arm's gnarled fingers held
Me, enchanted under your spell

So now you rest dear old friend
No dignity in this your end
To sentinel stand of centuries
Ended by the reapers breeze

In gentle decay now will you slumber
An insect home of mossy lumber
As into your cleared ancestral space
Reach up young trees to take your place

He chuckled to himself, back when he'd written that he'd clearly been able to see hope, feel that there was some continuity at least in the overall life of the trees as a community, if not of the individual. That even after it fell, what was left of the stricken tree was of value still, in a different way for sure, but continuing to play a part nevertheless. He'd been such a dreamer back then, a delusional romantic... an *idiot!* He snapped to himself!

Why the fuck was he doing this to himself? He lived *in the moment* now... The past was gone and good riddance to it! He'd left it all behind so why should he ever want to revisit it? He wasn't *broken* now, there was no *fixing* needing to be done anymore as none was needed! He was released... he was free now, liberated from all the shit that had caused him all that grief!

But it wouldn't let him go... the unformed thoughts from deep down in his subconscious mind it seemed, were turning on him like a swarm of angry wasps... The poem *was* an accurate reflection on life they buzzed, a simile, yes we may fail, be broken but even then we leave behind a legacy, as the new trees grew up into the ancestral space left by the fallen one... *bzzz...*

"SHUT-UP!" He realised to his horror that he had actually shouted out loud! '*Fuck'sake* yer loosin it man! Pull yourself together!' The wasps of his persistent thoughts were not done with him though, they likened the new trees growing up to his own kids... He simply *could not* allow himself to think about *them*! They belonged in the past, where he had left them when he walked away from that life, they were gone... forever.
All of it was gone...
He had no family...
He had no friends.
The person they had known, the man he once was, the person he was back then, the citizen, the pensioner, the husband, the father... that person was gone.
Dead if not buried!
He was someone else now!
He was Bill, the tramp!

He remembered that he'd said he would meet up with those students again this morning, what were their names? *Alan* was it? *Adam*? He wouldn't be going all that way this morning that was for sure! He could tell from the aches and pains that constantly wracked his body that his legs weren't going to take him as far as that. Although he often surmised that upon waking and later found that he could drag himself much further than he had anticipated.

Nosey little fuckers they were anyway! All of this was *their* fault he decided, with their questions, they'd stirred-up his memories they had… okay they hadn't even asked many questions… *yet*! But it was the process that they had set going in his mind, that was the problem, the cogs they had nudged into starting turning again, rusted-up and deliberately seized cogs that he had no desire to see spinning once again as he had to think about what he could say in response to their damnable queries!

All that spinning was what had led him here in the first place, to be homeless…

But he was better off here… he'd just determined that, reaffirmed it once again to himself! Why was he feeling a need to convince himself all over again? Was there a need to be convinced? Had he got it all wrong?

Andy! Yes, that was the little twerp's name. No, that wasn't fair the lad wasn't a twerp! He was well-meaning enough, young and naïve for sure but his heart seemed to be in the right place. What was the girl's name, the one he had with him? Nat? Yeah that was her name, funny kid she was though, Andy was clearly infatuated with her, madly in love with her Bill imagined would be how the lad would say he felt! He'd have said that himself about his first, proper girlfriend too, the first one with all the imagined bells and whistles attached to her, in what had been his first proper relationship! He doubted they would last as a couple, not many did after all. They seemed ill-matched somehow? He'd thought his marriage would last till one of them had died and he couldn't have been more wrong about that!

His mind was rebelling today he grunted to himself disconsolately as he realised that in a part of his mind he was casting his eyes again over the tightly stretched white cotton of that kid's girlfriend's T-shirt… tight it was, straining to contain her youthful tits… Grrr!!… he threw the blanket that was still covering his legs off him, sending one of the rocks that had been weighting it down skittering away! There was an unwelcome tightness in his pants as something stirred that he had no use for anymore, his mind would not give up though, it was on a roll and was now reliving one of the times when he had been looking down at a young and joyous face, as in a state of ecstatic

abandonment he merrily fucked the living daylights out of his wild and willing first girlfriend... He shook his head again, my God they'd had some hot sex back then... What disturbed him most of all though was that in this little montage that played out in his memory, when their eyes had met, as she moaned with pleasure as he thrust up hard into her... it wasn't Juliet's eyes that met his...
It wasn't Juliet's face at all...
It was that bloody lass Nat's!

Shit! This was bad... Really bad! Was his mind going ape-shit on him all over again? He had a fucking granddaughter about the same age as Nat, didn't he? How old would she be now? *Why? Why are you asking yourself that?* You have *no* family! Not anymore! You are *alone, by yourself...* for fucks sake! Pull yourself together!

The hollow growling in his belly pointed out that he needed to get something to eat, far more than that though, he needed to concentrate on the moment, be here now... *fucking do something* to stop yourself thinking, he snapped to himself! He rummaged into his pack and found a tin of baked beans, he had a small methylated spirit burner and a folding kit of pans and plates that he would leisurely use to heat things up normally but he was too agitated to bother with any of that this morning. He tore the ring-pull top off the tin and ate the beans cold off his spoon.

It distracted him a little as he munched on the beans, he had quite a kit that he carried around with him, it needed to be kept useable of course, things like the meths had to be bought, a lighter too and of course a supply of tins, he tried to get ring-pull ones but often the plain tins were cheaper... hence he had a can opener in his kit! It was ironic that he would often be turned away from foodbanks! There was a plethora of cheap, bargain basement shops to use though, it was a sign of the disgusting state that society had sunk down to.

Some of the guys who lived on the streets were almost a kind of survivalist! These were the ones who'd clearly at least initially had the remnants of some dwindling resources to set themselves up with, judging by some of the kit they had. Sad thing was if you had anything of value, it would be looked at by the envious and covetous eyes of other even more desperate guys... Guys who wouldn't hesitate to liberate it from you!

He finished his beans and shoved the empty can into the plastic carrier bag that acted as his bin, shoved it in the backpack, drained what little was left in his water bottle, shoved that in too, strapped his pack up and knelt-up. He'd just remembered that Harry was giving a Press Conference around lunchtime and it had spurred him into action, he could still make it if he got the bus instead of walking all the way along the meandering route of the towpath as it hugged the contour of the hillside... effectively doubling the distance he would have to walk. It was usually irrelevant on a normal morning of course when time had no meaning for him, he was no longer a slave to the clock... Another verse from a poem came to mind...

Wandering some ancient highway
Where will neither watch nor clock say
When to get up eat and sleep
In its clockwork slavery keep
Rise with birds and morning sun
Let whatever maybe come
Feel the kiss of gentle rain
Wash away some of the pain

Of course he'd no interest in what the jackass would be spouting on about once he was up on his hind legs like... but they always laid a decent buffet on for the VIP guests after! Not like he'd be considered *one of the guests,* but once they'd stuffed their already fat and full bellies a bit more... he'd swoop in before it was cleared away, it would be rich pickings!

Carefully moving the branches to exit his den, he glanced back to check the concealment was still good, he'd rolled up his tarpaulin as he was knelt on the ground before... it was all well-hidden he confirmed. He turned away and carefully stepped through the rhodies until he came to a bit of a track, he stepped a long stride out onto it and then headed off downwards through the woods. It was only about half a mile down to the site where some building had once stood, now it had been levelled and all that remained of it was just a large patch of rough and broken concrete, rapidly being reclaimed by nature. There was a gap in the fence that ran alongside the main road where a side-gate had once hung.

The buses ran every fifteen minutes so he knew he wouldn't have long to wait. He put his pack at the side of a small utility box at the edge of the pavement and stepped away from it, to stand next the bus stop, he tucked his beard into his jacket… some bus drivers would see you were homeless and drive past you, not stopping! Well, they wouldn't want a smelly old tramp stinking their nice clean bus up would they?

The bus rolled-up and grabbing his backpack Bill was through the door before the driver had a chance to drive off. He needn't have worried though as the driver was a friendly guy, a sheikh wearing a magnificently proud beard himself, who smiled at him as he asked simply *'town?'*

Bill dropped a two pound coin in the little bowl shape of the ticket machine, he ignored the driver's helpful comment about him being eligible for a bus-pass and his ticket whirred-out at him from the machine…

He sat near the front and as far away from the other passengers as he could. It was funny how the rareness of an experience made it seem all the more special! Riding on the bus was a feast of input for Bill, the sensation of the rolling motion, the rise and fall in the pitch of the sounds emanating from the big diesel engine, the feeling of swinging on the bends… and all the while the scenery whipping past outside the big windows…

It was only a ten minute walk to The Factory from the bus station and he arrived in plenty of time, although there were a couple of security guys on the main door vetting who went in. He turned right and went to the entrance at the far end, where you went to get fed, if you weren't one of the public but were one of the *non-public*… someone hungry, someone who was in no need of complaining about being sent around the side to get in, or about anything else so long as they were willing to put some food in your belly!

Once he'd got into the canteen it was easy enough, by nipping through a couple of doors, heading along a back corridor, through a fire door... marked THIS DOOR IS ALARMED... it wasn't! ...he came in through a small door at the back of the hall where the Press Conference was to be held.

The room was filling-up from the front, so he was fairly inconspicuous where he was at the back. He sat down on a bench that ran along the side of the hall and not facing the stage as the many rows of seats had been set out to do. The Security guys were busy keeping undesirables *out of the hall*, so if you were already in it...

He propped himself up against a pillar and put his feet up on the bench so that he was roughly facing in the direction of the stage. He knew he'd have to be fast to grab some food afterwards, before he got thrown out but it would be worth it! The fare presented to this lot would be a lot better than that which they served at the other end of the building!

All he had to do now was to keep his mouth shut and resist the urge to shout out and start heckling Harry... It was a tough call between the urge for some quality butties and finger-food *vs* the opportunity to hurl some yelled-out abuse at Harry, at 'The Man,' at society... and all of it with The Press present as his audience!

CHAPTER FIVE

Harry was sat nervously in the wings of the stage, making sure he had his notes in the correct order, he was finding it difficult to concentrate as his attention was continually being drawn unwillingly to listen to the low murmur of noise coming from the hall, an amalgam of many voices, a background of many talking quietly but with a louder one here and there heard more clearly, a laugh, a cough, the scraping of a chair on the stone floor… it was a cacophony of sound, he couldn't help thinking it was akin to the breathing of a mighty beast as it lay there, just out of sight, poised ready and waiting for him to appear before it, as he walked out to stand there exposed and alone on the stage, fearing that it might roar angrily at him, before pouncing upon him and devouring him! He felt as if he was a sacrifice about to be put out there to appease the beast.

He was so stressed that he was barely able to read the large headings he'd created on the pages, let alone the notes he had made beneath them, as he held them with trembling hands on the small table next to him! His anxiety was growing rather than diminishing, tightening its vice-like grip on his stomach, making his chest tight and causing his hands to shake as he shuffled the pages together. He kept telling himself… it was only stage fright, that even the most accomplished of speakers and renowned actors often suffered what he was going through, it was perfectly normal…

He steeled himself, 'Oh come on! You've done this hundreds of times before, you can do it again today. This is part of your job, what they pay you for!' So… *get out there and do it!*

With that he took a deep breath, sprung-up from the chair and marched out onto the stage. A deathly hush washed away the noise of awaiting beast… *as it drew breath?* The hall was packed, with many left standing in a throng down the side that led to the main doors, all the seats having been taken! Why the fuck had they been let in? He fumed to himself! Down at the front, immediately below him they had drawn a large pack of Media today, their TV cameras and microphones were bristling like the weapons of a besieging enemy hoard, or the pitchforks of a mob of angry villagers? Sat quietly behind them were the invited dignitaries and guests.

Having placed his notes carefully onto the dais, he tapped the microphone to check it was on and working, the loud thud that echoed around the tall empty volume of space created by the very high ceiling way up over the heads of the audience, confirming that it was.

Casting his eyes quickly over the throng, he spotted Bill! He was sat on a bench at the very back of the room! The old bugger was leaning against a pillar with his feet up on one of the benches that ran alongside the wall… That would be all he needed if that lunatic started off on one of his ranting monologues in front of the media! Did he catch his eye? He did! Did he smile at him? No it was more of a smirk! Fuck! What did he have the fucking Security firm for if not to keep rabble like him out of the event?

Best get to it, he decided…

"Thank you all for coming, it is my hope today that I can address the issues that are currently of concern to our neighbours and fellow townspeople and do whatever I can to alleviate them. I would like to remind everyone that the people we aim to help here, the ones we are trying to assist in returning to become part of our community once more, are also our fellow citizens. They are our fellow travellers, people who are just like us but who have stumbled, faltered and fallen. People who find that they are in need of a helping hand to get them back on their feet and as any Good Samaritan would want to, we wish to hold out that hand to them." An angry voice shouted-up from amidst the unseated throng…

"You're attracting scum from all over the county…"
A second shouted voice…
"…and beyond!"
A third voice…
"…you're a magnet for them…"

Harry raised his hands in the air trying to bring back quiet to the hall as a grumbling murmur rippled through the crowd at the side of the hall... He noticed one of the TV cameramen turning to film them... *Shit! That was all he needed!*

"Please! Please... *please,* at the side there... please be patient, I will take any questions you may have at the end!" The murmur subsided as he noticed a small group of the marshals that he'd organised to be available on standby, in case they were needed were filing into the auditorium. At least they were doing their job properly now! Two of them took up positions in front of the stage and two in the gap in the chairs between the press and dignitaries section at the front and the rest of the public who were seated further towards the back, another three forming a cordon between the stage and the crowd at the side.

"Look, I am aware of these accusations, I have investigated them *in detail* and I can state categorically that it is only a very small number indeed of people who have actually come here from elsewhere. I would like to remind everyone here of a well-known expression that applies very neatly to the clients we seek to assist... *There but for the Grace of God go I!"* He managed to get a more positive murmur in response to that!

"As we are being televised today and will be reaching a much wider audience than usual, I feel I must present a quick overview of the vision of our founder to benefit those listening and watching who are not familiar with our goal." A groan rose up from the rabble at the side...
"We know all too bloody well what yer'about!!" Harry ignored the shouted remark and carried on...

"Our founder, an anonymous but extremely wealthy man, a man who was originally born and raised here in our town and returned here later in his life, felt that he wanted to put something back into the town that he had once loved and cherished. I say *once,* because he was deeply shocked and saddened to see the amount of deprivation and homelessness here. He was also shocked to find that this has become almost accepted as *just the way it is*, as a sad fact by so many living here in his home town. An indifferent acceptance of it as something that has *just happened*, sad for sure... but nothing to do with us or our community or our society... even though we allow it to happen, allow it to continue!

It came to a head for him one day when he was asked for change by a dishevelled old man who was sat in a supermarket carpark, a wreck of a man who held out a cup begging for some coins saying… *'Buy a drink for an ex-serviceman who's fallen on hard times Sir?'* He found himself fumbling around in his pocket but soon realised he had no change on him, he apologised to the man explaining this to him… the old man just smiled and said *'ah, don't worry'*…

"But he *did* worry, he actually felt really bad about it, so he asked the man *'to hang on a minute'* as he went over to his car and rummaged-out some change from the chewing gum tub he always kept in the glovebox, for carpark machines. He walked back and tipped the coins, amounting to a couple of quid at the most, into the old guy's cup. The man beamed back at him and thanked him profusely.

"After he'd got his shopping and got back in his car, as he was sat there about to drive away, rather than feeling good about his little act of kindness, our friend was overwhelmed by a terrible sense of chagrin instead. He knew that the wallet in his back pocket had around a hundred pounds tucked away in it, so when he realised that he had no change on him, why on earth hadn't he just peeled a note or two out from it to give to the unfortunate man? He tried to justify his actions by telling himself that the guy had only asked *for change… for coins…* That if he gave him a fiver, or a tenner the guy would only use it to get a bottle of vodka or cider, that he'd just waste the money anyway! These excuses didn't wash for him though, he realised that there was something fundamentally wrong with him, with his entire attitude over the situation and his response to it, to have done what he did."

"He gave the scrounging fucker some money! What more should he have done?" A *helpful* heckler at the back suggested!

"Thank you Sir, you illustrate the very same attitude that appalled our founder! Sadly you still possess it though! Sneer at them, toss them a few crumbs if you feel like it or just walk on by, pass them by on the other side of the road… *Change* is all they ask for, so that's all they should get, it's all they deserve!

"No, *you* may think that way but what *he* asked himself was this, he told me... *'when I realised I had no change on me, why hadn't I simply reached for my wallet and given the poor chap a fiver? Or a twenty even? What would it have mattered to me? I would spend that for myself on a bottle of wine without a second thought, why not give it to someone who actually needed it? There was something so wrong in my attitude, it was appalling to me!'*

"Cos' like 'e thought... the bugger'd just drink it away in five minutes!" A shout again from the back, followed by roars of laughter from the contingent at the side of the hall......

"Thank you once more for illustrating your sneering prejudice Sir! *So what* if he did use it to get drunk? The money would be *his* once it was handed to him. It would be his to do with as *he* chose. I suspect that's exactly what you may do yourself, isn't it Sir? When it suits you, to do so, when get in after you've had a tough day, had a row with the missus, or when you go off down to the pub? Or maybe buy a bottle on your way home? Get a bit tipsy, or even get wasted? Now imagine your *tough day* is being out there, living on the streets, with no shelter, no home to go to, with no roof over your head, let alone a bed to sleep in! Wouldn't you fancy a drink then too maybe? Fancy a way of escaping the terrible reality of your God-awful existence? Yet you jump in to condemn our friend who's begging for doing precisely the same thing?"

"Our founder was so shocked in realising the significance of what he had just done, it became his epiphany on his own road to Damascus, it was his moment of revelation! The deep sense of shame that he'd felt for his action was what galvanised him, decided it for him there and then, that he would do all he could to help these unfortunates that for whatever reason it may have been had fallen into begging and homelessness. That he would devote himself and his considerable resources towards providing a solution!"

"Secretly, the thing that had upset him most of all though was that he had recognised the man, he'd pretended he hadn't of course while he was standing infront of him, he'd even tried to kid himself too, that it wasn't him, it *couldn't be* him... but sat there snug and warm on the pampering leather upholstery of his fifty-odd thousand pounds worth of luxury car, he knew in his heart that this man *was* someone he had gone to school with... he even knew his name... I won't repeat it for the sake of his family... but he'd known as soon as their eyes met that it was him. He was so ashamed that he hadn't acknowledged him, but instead had pretended not to recognize him.

"Such was the intensity of this experience for him, what he saw as his shaming, that the very next day he set about trying to find a suitable building to turn into a refuge for the homeless, to literally put a roof over their heads and then find a way to put food in their hungry bellies!

"I could write a book about the details of what he went through to find a suitable building and then to get the necessary permissions and permits, the fights he had to win in order to drive his vision forward into becoming reality! The battles he fought against angrily whipped-up, negative Public Opinion, too many battles all of which he had to win. But he never faltered, never gave up and it was less than a year before the doors opened on the first phase of his 'Folks Factory!' *Factory* because as you can see it was this magnificent yet abandoned Victorian factory that he saved from dereliction and recommissioned to offer help and succour to the homeless.

"Once it was up and running, every step he took afterwards simply followed on as a matter of course. His dormitories provided shelter and his kitchen gave food to the hungry, but he soon realised that he needed to do more, he was just treating the symptom and not providing a cure. That was the inspiration for his 'Stepping Stones Project,' a series of steps to walk along that would lead the homeless person from living out *on the streets* to living in a home *on a street!*"

"So... to follow on from the first stepping stone, one of accepting food, the second was to provide a dormitory's roof over their head, his third stepping stone was the creation of small rooms, ready-made pods, micro-appartments if you like that the person could call their own, leased free of charge to them, giving them an address and accordingly access to benefits. Then the fourth step, the chance to move into one of the ultra-low rental appartments that areas of the factory have been transformed into.

"So successful has this been that the board he established to carry on his work now wants to initiate this, the fifth step, that of providing access to affordable housing in the new development on the six acre derelict site that has been acquired on the land adjacent to The Factory. The planning application for which is what has stirred up so much hostility and objections and is the reason I am stood here today before you explaining the thinking behind it."

"I hope I have given you adequate details for most of your queries? Before I take questions, my assistants will join me onstage to direct the microphone to the questioner who they indicate. Please keep this orderly so that people can ask their questions and then be able to hear the answers!"

The Press were offered the first questions, which were mostly the usual stuff about Planning decisions, Health & Safety, infrastructure and about the facilities and amenities to be on offer to the new development. All this was conducted in a reasonable manner but increasingly he felt that the gathering was coming under the threat of trouble in the form of a growing, discontent, from the side of the room and also from the back.

One journalist asked a particularly searching and well thought out question,
"Jennifer Stainton, The Gazette: If your housing project is successful here, would there be future plans to build similar ones elsewhere in the town?" Harry smiled down at her,
"Obviously that will depend very much on the success of this scheme, once we have it up and running, but yes it has been discussed and yes again, we would hope to do so as it would be of great benefit to our community to be able to offer more affordable housing to a greater number of people and it would also help people avoid ever needing to seek help here at The Factory by them not becoming homeless in the first place!" The reported smiled as she replied,
"Putting yourselves out of business at The Folks Factory! The response was a murmur of laughter…
Harry seized upon the opportunity…

"Nothing would please our founder more, I'm sure I can say with absolute certainty, than seeing the doors to The Factory being closed because there was no longer any need for it!"

So it went for about twenty minutes, swinging from positive approval to answered questions about the plans, to outright hostility to them, accompanied by shouts of verbal abuse from hecklers! Realising that he still had to take questions from the public, he decided to quit with The Press,

"May I have one last question please?"

"From how you just answered, can we assume that you are confident that you will get planning consent?"
"Of course!" This stirred-up a massive round of jeering and shouting from around the room, the atmosphere was turning bad in the hall, shifting in a worrying direction…

The trouble really started though once questions were opened up to the public…

"You Sir… in the red anorak…"
"Why are you only building houses for the homeless? What about decent people's needs?" 'Decent people?' FFS!… Harry thought to himself!
"We won't be doing that at all, we want homes for all! But surely by definition, someone who is homeless needs a home more than most? Shouldn't they be the first to get one? However, there *will be* a surplus of housing eventually, which *will* become available to anyone." So it started…
"People renting need a chance to have a home of their own too!" Shouted…
"Will they be able to sell them on? If they're subsidised how will you prevent profiteering?"
"Clearly that will be in their contracts, they will only be able to sell them back to us."
"What do the other house builders make of it all? What do the big boys think of you muscling-in on their action, taking their profits?"
"If we offer a better, more appealing product than they do, well maybe they should too? Perhaps *they* need to think again about *their* policies?"

"It will just bring scum into our area, our house prices will plummet!

"Why don't you fuck-off somewhere else with your Commie-ideas and..." The microphone was switched off to an outburst of jeering and shouting...

"I hardly think providing affordable housing is a Communist aspiration! *Socialist* perhaps or even *Christian* or Muslim, or any other religion you may choose to mention!"
"We don't want all the scum of the entire country swarming into our town...Go somewhere else with your big ideas!" A rowdy cheer rose up from the mob at the side...

"I have already addressed those unfounded accusations!"

The mob at the side who were already on their feet were joined in standing by many of those at the back as they began chanting the refrain...

"FUCK-OFF FOLKS FACT-RY..."
"FUCK-OFF FOLKS FACT-RY..."
"FUCK-OFF FOLKS FACT-RY..."

Over and over again...

Then some of them started kicking chairs over...
As it had been predicted there could well be a disturbance, at this point the Police who had been waiting outside intervened to assist the stewards. The Inspector in charge organised them to form a line between the public seating and the area where the invited guests and the press contingent were sitting. Some of them held back the crowd as others cleared the rest of the mob out of the hall through the fire doors they had opened that led directly onto the concourse at the front of the building, there to join with the rest of the jeering mob who despite having been denied entry, had remained outside nevertheless as they chanted and waved their placards.

Order was restored in a matter of minutes in the hall and the doors were then opened to lead the guests through into the adjoining dining room. As with most of the rooms in the old factory it was an impressively large, expansive space with only a small area occupied by some trestles with the food and drinks laid out on them and twenty or so tables & chairs that had been set out for this occasion, the remaining area of the hall was still big enough to hold a Grand Ball in and would be well suited to do so, as it was one of the few rooms that had a wooden floor laid over the stone slabs.

No ballroom music today though as the dignitaries and guests filtered in, their voices quickly swallowed up by the cavernous volume of the space they were entering into. Catering staff were on standby as they entered, offering up trays full of glasses filled with Prosecco and orange juice to the arriving guests while others had dainty *petits fours salés* tit-bits on offer.

The rather sombre atmosphere of the mostly empty and echoey giant room was instantly transformed as two musicians started to play, the gentle rhythmic and soothing music of their guitars flowed into the emptiness, their melody sweeping aside the oppressively palpable silence. It was as if the room sighed gratefully as it was enabled to release its tension.

Harry was in full *mine-host* mode! His face was beginning to ache from the almost permanent smile he was forcing to hold on it as he acknowledged people, thanked them for coming and generally greeted the town's good and great! He'd achieved an excellent turnout including the town's MP, The Mayor was here too along with an accompanying gaggle of Councillors, The Police and Crime Commissioner and The Chief Constable had also turned out, they weren't at loggerheads today thankfully as they stood chatting, drinks in hands along with an assortment of people from various charities who operated foodbanks and many more from all walks of life. He noticed a group of local C of E clergymen clustered around the local Bishop like flies around.... *stop it Harry! He reproached himself!*

Oh now *that* was encouraging Harry thought, as he realised that the little group of clergy were also chatting with the town's Rabbi and Imam! Religious pluralism at work! He was so pleased that the Imam had come, he was a great fellow who had been very supportive in the past, a glorious example of how The

Factory brought diverse groups of people together... as well as more unfortunately driving a wedge between others.

Also present were representatives from the college's Student Union, Harry nodded to Andy and Nat who he noticed were chatting and laughing with them. His massive expanded management team, of two, were all there along with him, on parade doing as he was... mingling and schmoozing! There was also a large contingent of interested members of the public who had applied for a pass, responding to a general invitation they had put out.

All in, there had to be well over a two hundred and fifty people present in the room, chatting, drinking and now tucking into the buffet that had been laid on.

Never one to miss an opportunity to promote the project, once everyone had eaten and before they started to drift away Harry was back up on his hind legs again...

Chink!...chink!...chink!... he tapped his glass to quieten the throng,

"Ladies and Gentlemen, thank you again for coming today and continuing to support our project here at The Folks Factory, without your help and the wonderful work you put in we would be unable to continue. That so many of you care about the plight of the less fortunate is incredibly heart-warming, it restores some of the faith we lose daily in response to the terrible stories that seem to dominate the headlines in The Media, I guess it's a case of bad news makes it there the quickest? But what we are achieving here is *Good News* and we need to shout about it, to make The Media listen!

Clapping...

"Our new housing project is a further step towards fighting against homelessness, yes it is only a tiny step and looked at in the grand scheme of things nationally... well, at least while we're under the oppressive yolk of a government for The Few... we can never hope to eradicate homelessness from our shores. But... *we can* be a shining light of hope, we can show that *there is* a better way, a *kinder way*, a more compassionate way to treat those amongst us who have fallen, offer them a hand and help them back up onto their feet! We want our town to be peopled by Good Samaritans, with no more of this passing by on the other side, no more of the acceptance of seeing destitute people begging for change outside our shops and sleeping in doorways, sheltering from the rain under flyovers, or huddling from the cold under cardboard on the backstreets.

"I say NO! to all of that, NO to the meanness of spirit, NO to the penny-pinching, No to allowing bureaucracy to be weaponised into wilful nastiness …

"I say YES to compassion, YES to kindness and YES to decency.

"It is said that the truest measure of any civilisation is to observe the manner in which they treat their weakest citizens, their elderly, their sick, their mentally challenged… If we accept this yardstick then it has to be glaringly obvious to one and all… all apart from the totally blinkered, that as a civilisation we are failing in this apposite test!

"Our society has failed! But that failure has not been the result merely of indifference, of lack of attention, we haven't failed by casual negligence! No! That failure has been deliberate and calculatedly orchestrated by the laying down of policy after policy that has discriminated against the weakest, the poorest and the lowliest of the members of our *excuse of a society!"*

"It is time for change ladies and gentlemen.

"You and people like you are the instruments of that change.

"I feel privileged to address you here today.

"I promise to shut-up in a moment!"
Ripple of (relieved?) laughter…

"First I must extend a special thankyou to you, our esteemed dignitaries! Brilliantly there are far too many of you present with us here today for me to attempt to list you all and risk omitting anyone, you are all way too important to our cause to risk me missing even one of you! But I really do to have to say a massive thankyou to Garry Thornbury the proprietor of Thornbury Security Services who has freely donated the provision of all of the security personnel who have been keeping us safe today and also to Marvin Lawton from Top-Drawer Catering who have provided the food and staff to feed us all today, as their contribution to our project."

"Lastly but by no means at all least, I would like to thank our two musicians for transforming what can be the mausoleum like atmosphere of this massive and empty, former industrial chamber into a chamber of delightful music. John and Paul here, no *not that* John and Paul! A different John and Paul, slightly more rarefied ones at that too, as they call themselves The Pope's*!"*

A murmur of chuckles…

"These two lads are a testimony to the work we do here, to what we can achieve when we pool our resources. They first met when Paul was a homeless busker, he'd set himself up on the central concourse one morning and began to sing and play to earn some change and as he was new to the location, what he didn't know was that the pitch he'd taken up was the exact spot that John regularly used.

"So when John arrived he was more than a little miffed, as you can well imagine he would be! However, he took one look at Paul and realised that the lad needed the money a lot more than he did himself. It was clear to him that Paul was destitute, the backpack sat on the floor next to him with all his belongings in it confirmed that he had to be homeless. Despite John being a poor student himself, he did have a roof over his head and his own bedroom in a shared, rented student house.

"So instead of getting cross, instead of confronting the usurper, he sat down on one of the walls that surround the flower beds and listened to his music. He watched as passer-by's dropped a few coins into the lad's guitar case, smiled at the little girl who stood mesmerised by the music and Paul's song as she watched, standing there holding her mum's hand and then placing a 50p piece in the case and clapping as Paul finished and she was led away, Paul took a small bow and waved to her as she looked back over her shoulder beaming.

John smiled at Paul and motioned to his own guitar case, mouthing... '*may I?*' Paul nodded his approval and started to play *Tears in Heaven,* one of John's own favourites to perform on the streets. A few bars in John joined him with his own guitar, adding more depth to the music with its harmony, then the magic cast its spell as when Paul began to sing John joined him in perfect harmony! In that respect they do share the vocal magic of that other duo, their namesakes, Lennon and McCartney. Such was the beauty of their vocalising harmony that it only took a matter of minutes for a small crowd to gather, people wanting to listen to them and as always happens when people see a crowd... more folks inevitably joined it.

"As ever the crowd demanded more and they ended up doing half a dozen songs together. When they packed-up, the applause they got was amazing and the money they'd collected in Paul's case was more than he would have earned all week!

"Paul wanted to split the money with John but he refused to take any of it, on the condition that Paul promised to come and perform with him at The Student Union on Saturday night. He did and the rest *as they say* is history! It was the start of an enduring friendship, leading to a successful career for both of them and it was all down to that chance meeting, followed by John's considered and caring reaction that got Paul off the streets!

"Thank you so much boys! Please give them a round of applause..." *A good round of clapping followed...*

"Just shows what can happen when we resist the urge to react with hostility, when we decide to work together instead, when we pool our resources... That my friends, is when we can do great things."

"And finally... *I know, at last!* Please feel free to stay as long as you wish, there is no need to hurry away. Please take the time to meet with others who share your passion... mingle! Eat the food, enjoy the drinks! Please! For any of you who have not had the opportunity already, if you would like to look around, view the facilities we provide here please ask one of our staff... We're all wearing these badges!" Harry pointed to the brightly coloured TFF badge on his jacket's lapel.

With that Harry sank gratefully back into his chair to a really enthusiastic round of applause and then the murmur of chatter re-establishing itself as some settled back down in conversation with the others sat at their table and some of the dignitaries began to filter away.

Back on his feet a short while later Harry was stood chatting with Maureen O'Brien the Deputy Mayor, he introduced her to Garry Thornbury who was nearby,
"If you ever need bouncers Maureen, our Garry here's your man!" He quipped. Garry shook hands and passed on one of his business cards... he'd given out a stack of them already, always looking to promote *his own* business to!

A little while later...
"Maureen, may I introduce you to Alan, he's a fellow legal-eagle! Deputy Mayor this is our in-house solicitor Alan Jarvis." Maureen O'Brien was still a practicing QC although it was rumoured she was soon to be appointed as a judge, she shook hands with Alan,
"I understand that you represent any of your guests who may fall foul of the law as well as your duties to the project here?" She asked,
"Yes indeed, or I see to it that someone more suitable looks after them. I have to say that I was so impressed with the project when I was involved in the initial setting-up of it that I set up a practice of my own here in the town!"
"You moved your business here as a result of that?"
"Yes indeed! And my household too! I worked very closely with the chap who was the direct liaison with the benefactor." At that moment Jennifer Stainton sidled up to Harry, she intervened, her reporter's ears picking up an interesting tit-bit...
"Did I hear you say that you worked with the benefactor in the early days?"

Harry: "Oh, let me introduce you, Jennifer Stainton, isn't it?... newshound for The Gazette... this is Alan Jarvis our solicitor...

so watch what you say Alan! And of course this lady is our esteemed Deputy Mayor."

Alan: "Pleased to meet you Jennifer…"
"Oh *Jenny* please…"
"Okay… well no, actually Jenny I never met the benefactor himself, I only met the go-between, the guy who did all the work for the one with the money! He insisted that his identity was never revealed to anyone. You never met the go-between did you Harry, he was only here for the first year of the project, you joined in the second year, wasn't it?"
"Yeah, I only ever had email contact with the guy and the odd phone call, we never actually met as by then it was up and running. It was always his plan that the whole thing should be self-sustaining once it was set-up, it was designed that way with the board of trustees established to take over from him."

The Deputy Mayor was drawn away from the conversation by The Mayor as he passed-by with The Bishop, leaving Harry with Jenny and Alan. Seeing the two students passing, Harry called them over and introduced them,
"Jenny, Alan… this is Andy and Nat, they're doing a study of our project for their degrees." They all smiled, shaking hands all round.
"It's err… post-grad stuff actually like..." Andy corrected as Jenny smiled,
"I'd love to read it when you've finished it, in fact I'd be happy to collaborate with you on it… if you'd be alright with that? I could be useful to you with my contacts even?" Andy looked a little uncertain but Nat jumped at the chance…
"That would be fabulous, that's so kind of you!" Jenny pulled a card from her purse, she turned it over to look on the back and then handed it to Nat,
"My mobile number is written on the back, call me anytime."
"I will and th…" Andy abruptly interrupted her as he tapped Harry on the arm, as he pointed across the room…

"Hey Harry! Isn't that old Bill over there, loadin-up from the buffet?" Harry looked around to see that Bill had indeed dodged the security men and got through into this hall now somehow as well! He'd presumably come through the side-door adjacent to where the buffet tables were, it led to the backstage area and then on to the auditorium beyond it! The caterers who were busily packing-up everything by now were actually joking with him and putting stuff in front of the old guy!

Harry's first instinct was to *shoo-him* out! But then upon a moment's reflection he thought… *What the fuck eh?* What harm's the old fella doing? He just replied,
"Yeah it certainly looks like it Andy! Cheeky old sod he is. If you want some local colour Jenny you should have a chat with that old rascal! Daft thing is the caterers will be taking any left-over food down to their canteen anyway!"

At that moment Bill looked-up from the sandwich he was munching on, he turned towards them, maybe somehow he sensed all those eyes upon him? He looked over in their direction, squinting at the small group who he could see were looking across at him… *he found that squinting gave him a bit better focus…* He could see Harry was amongst them and the two students too… that lad Andy and his diminutive girlfriend Nat. Nat… *he didn't want to think about her!* Then there was a tall guy stood next to Harry, he was wearing a grey suit and he had a strikingly prominent shock of very white hair, it was combed straight back, he looked vaguely familiar? For a moment their eyes met... Bill felt uneasy, as he was trapped in this guy's gaze, it caused him to turn away. He quickly stuffed a couple of chicken drumsticks into his pocket and with a plateful of food in the other hand, he shuffled-off to work his way back out by the same route he'd made his way into the hall.

He mumbled to himself, *yeah… that's who the tall guy was*, it wasn't because he knew him but that he'd reminded him of someone off the TV! It was that actor who'd played Eddie Shoestring from donkey years ago, but was then in another TV show as a much older, grey haired and bearded man, *what was his name?*

As Bill was making his swift exit, Harry suggested to the students that they might be able to catch him outside, if they still wanted to interview him, they readily agreed with the suggestion and Andy set off… realising Nat hadn't followed him, he turned and gestured his query as to why she wasn't with him, using his hands and a shrug! She shouted over,

"Go! I'll catch you up…" Turning back to Jenny, she said,

"There's something I want to show you…" By now she had her smartphone out of her pocket and was flicking her finger rapidly across the screen…
"Just a minute, I know it's here… Ah! Look at this clip off YouTube…" It was a film of the back of a man who was sat playing a grand piano and singing. Harry interjected…
"Isn't that the lobby of the indoor market?" he turned his head to look a little closer, before exclaiming…
"It is! Look you can see the library through the window!"
"Yeah, yeah it is… but wait a minute…"
"He's really good isn't he?" Jenny ventured as Nat fast-forwarded through the clip…
"He's brilliant! …here wait a minute… right!" Whoever had been filming had moved around the side, and was filming his hands on the keyboard and then his face as well…

The music stopped abruptly… He lifted his hand up infront of the iPhone,
"Stop filming me! No! Stop!" As he was shouting this he pulled up his hood and his collar, grabbed the backpack that was sat on the stool next to him with one hand and with the other hand trying to hide his face, he scooted around the back of the piano and ducked under the staircase and out through the exit onto the square, more or less running! Nat asked as she grinned,
"So what'd'ya make of that then? That was Bill for sure, wasn't it?" Jenny nodded,
"Without a doubt! Who'd have thought that the old bugger could play the piano like that?" Harry volunteered… Jenny added,
"And what a voice he has! Bloody hell! His rendering of 'Smile' was fabulous, a real dash of Nat King Cole in that voice for sure, not quite as smokily raw as Nat but if you add in Sinatra's just off-the beat timing with a little of Joe Cocker's improv' and passion… "
"Wow… You're well into your music Jenny!" Nat purred!
"My Dad loved Nat King Cole, he was always singing Smile, hearing Bill then brought a tear to my eye!" Harry was nodding to himself,
"So that's why interviewing Bill is so important to you is it Nat? I just didn't get why you'd wanted to bother, he's such a miserable old sod and there's so many other's who'd actually be

glad to chat with you, they've nowt else to do all day after all!"
Jenny spoke up again,
"Nat would you send me the clip please?"
"Yeah sure!" They blue-toothed their phones to swap contact details and send the clip, moments later Jenny thanked her,
"Thanks, got it! Y'know this newshound sniffs a story here!"
She smiled as Nat said she'd best catch up with Andy. Harry suggested she go through to the kitchens, as a short-cut…
"Just go through that door in the corner and hug the back wall of the factory all the way till you get to the kitchens, from there you can get into the refectory."
She bustled off leaving just Alan and Jenny with Harry.

Harry felt that something seemed to be bothering Alan, or that he was maybe a little unwell even, he'd gone very pale and had said nothing to join in the conversation for some time, so he asked him,
"Are you okay Alan? You look like you've just seen a ghost!"
"I err… no… well actually yes… maybe? No, I'm fine! It was just that for a split second there I was sure I recognised that old guy, the one who was digging into the buffet left-overs! It was uncanny, it was really odd!" Despite his assurance that he was *'fine'* it was only moments later that he excused himself and left.
Jenny chuckled,
"That was peculiar! I do hope it wasn't anything that I said?" She laughed a little nervously, it was a girlish giggle and for a fleeting moment it seemed to Harry that he caught a momentary glimpse of the young girl she must have once been…

She carried straight on, "So… Just you and me now eh, Harry?" She tipped her head to one side and toasted him with her glass held up at face level, smirking playfully at him as she held eye contact with him, allowing her mouth to continue on to shape itself into a smile… and what a smile it was! Harry was taken aback… *was she flirting with him?*

Up until that second when he found himself dazzled in the radiance of that glorious smile, he would have laughed at the idea as ridiculously preposterous! Dismissed it as just one more in the never ending catalogue of his wishful fantasies…she was simply *so far* out of his league!

He had absolutely no delusions about himself, or his appearance in regards to where he rated on the perceived scale of attractiveness that was today's accepted benchmark! He'd say he ranged between a four and perhaps on a really good day maybe a five or a six even? Well, perhaps on a particularly good, shaved-up, dressed-up and very well-scrubbed-up day!

This lady standing next to him rated as a bloody ten... with extra stars! No, she needed to be marked on a different scale altogether! She was tall and shapely, he was Five eleven and she was his height... and not even cheating by wearing heels... her shoes were sensibly low! She was a very attractive woman, probably in her late thirties, maybe early-forties. What was most striking about her (*after that smile!*) was her hair, or rather her total lack of it! Her head was close-shaved to show only a bare millimetre of hair! She had such a wonderfully shaped head though it made no difference to how attractive she was, in fact it enhanced her attractiveness as it suited her so well, however daring and radical the concept may have seemed to *an old stick-in-the-mud* like Harry!

She was wearing large earrings, what Harry would have described as *jazzy!* (Brightly coloured and *daring... well, to him!*) They matched the large dangly necklace she wore draped around her neck that cascaded loudly down the (well-filled front) of her equally *jazzy* three-quarter length dress.

Harry found himself entranced as he watched her face, he found himself observing every micro-expression as they merrily danced across it, fascinated by the movements in the tiny lines around the edges of her mouth and at the corners of her eyes, the way her eyebrows lifted and fell, the subtle tilt and rotation of her head... He felt like he was drifting into a trance... he was utterly mesmerised by her... he felt as if he was falling under a spell...

Nina Simone had kicked-off singing *'I put a spell on you'* somewhere in the background of his mind now... was this how a mongoose felt? Its eyes fixated and glued on a snake...

He found his mind straying to the very edge of reason and then readying itself to willingly surrender, to allow itself to slip blissfully and uncaringly right over it!... *What?* He mentally snatched himself back from falling over the threshold of rationality, to descend into insanity as he consciously realised what he was thinking... is this what *it* felt like? ... could this be *love at first sight?* Well almost the first sight!

Meanwhile, back on planet Earth... Jenny, oblivious of Harry's epiphany, had carried on talking...
"You do know that you're very good at all of this, don't you?"
His confused mind desperately scrabbled to try and bring himself back into the room from the fantasyland where he seemed to have drifted off to! For Harry the expanded one or two seconds break in their conversation had been timeless for him... He stumblingly stuttered out...

"Err...what? I'm sorry? I think I had a moment then! One of my senior moments! Please forgive me!" He wanted with all of his heart to actually say that it was because he was so entranced by her beauty... that he had fallen under her spell... that he loved her with all of his being... that he wanted to spend the rest of his life loving her...that he had seen the eyes of their children in her face... that she had touched his soul... but... well... come on now! People only said things like that in the movies or penned them in stupid, mushy romantic novels! *Didn't they?* Or was *this* what it was they were attempting to describe? Unless you'd actually felt *it* for yourself then how could you possibly know what *it* was that they were on about? However elegantly, beautifully, skilfully and articulately passionately they had attempted to try and describe *it*!?

He managed, panickingly to unleash a jumble of words...
"This? What, err... you mean the catering? You think so? Well thanks, I guess? So, a compliment... Hmm?... Now then, what sneaky journo-angle are you trying to work on me now?" She play-punched him in the ribs,

"No dumbo! You know exactly what I meant! Your whole presentational package! All very slick and professional and yet done to make it seem as if it was all spontaneous and off-the-cuff, that's the genius in what you did and how you went about it! Quite a feat to pull it off as well as you managed it.
"Tell me though, I thought you said that you'd never met the philanthropist who bankrolled the whole idea in the first place?"

"No, I took over from the agent who he had as a go between."
"So how come you had that story you told about what inspired him in the first place?" Harry looked a little chagrined…
Jenny burst out laughing as she pointed a finger at him,
"You made it up didn't you? You slick, silver tongued liar!"
"Well I err… no, I wouldn't exactly say that I *made it up*! Although it is true to say that he didn't tell me himself, well not directly."
"Oh man, I'm going to have to watch you Harry Protherow, a slippery customer you are, have you ever thought of going into politics? Come on mister… spill the beans!"

"Okay, okay… They *were* his words I promise you, well a sort of dramatised and maybe slightly elaborated version of them! You see when I took over Jos's office and it was like he'd gone home one evening and then never came back, no actually it was more like he'd gone out for lunch and never come back! I think he'd intended to return, that his departure had been unscheduled somehow. In fact I was so concerned by it all that I informed the police, they made a few enquiries and found that he had still been in regular contact with the trustees for weeks after he'd left, they said they had to assume that he had just had enough of the place one day and left. They agreed that something was a bit odd about it though, as the address he had given was merely an empty flat, their enquiries revealing that no one had lived there for many years, but that someone called to collect the mail regularly! With nothing else to go on they could do nothing more."

"Fascinating stuff for sure, but no explanation about your speech yet mister!"
"Sorry, yes well you see it was all a bit like The Marie Celeste, everything just left as if he'd been beamed-up, there one second and gone the next! I had to go through it all, to set myself up and I boxed up any personal belongings, things like a couple of framed pictures off the desk and stuff like that and a briefcase with copies of plans and notes in it, but in the desk was a journal, all handwritten that was clearly the work of the benefactor. It did have some stuff about why he wanted to start the project and okay I made up some from my own experiences of a similar incident too, perhaps over-elaborated…"
"You should definitely go into politics!"

Then she unleashed that smile upon him again! There should be a law against it! That smile! It was a lethal weapon he thought as he blushed a little for thinking that as she went on...

"And you giving me all that bull about having a 'senior moment'? Gerroff with ya'self! You're as sharp as a tack, clearly a man in his prime!" Harry was flattered, he was fifty-three and to him that was over-the-hill, the reason he knew this job was as good as it was going to get for him now. For sure, a few older men did hold some great and very senior jobs, but they'd mostly got hold of them when they were much younger or were just in that rarefied echelon where age was no longer an obstacle! He knew he could have been in much better shape than he was now too, he'd let things slip, his gym membership had expired during the Covid-19 debacle and he'd never re-joined, his love of walking the hills had been pushed aside by the time pressures of this bloody job, it could get to be twenty-four-seven so easily...

He realised, quite detachedly that *he* was asking her if she'd like to join him outside for a coffee ... He listened to *his* words as they trip-trotted ever so glibly off his smooth-talking lips, almost as a spectator, as a quietly amused observer! Who was this person that had taken control of him in such an unheralded and unbidden manner? It was as if an alter-ego had seized control, taken over his mind, shoving his normal personality out of the way when it had finally had enough of the persona that his normal blundering self was whenever he came across an attractive woman, the fool who always missed the opportunities that fate threw at his feet, who was always blind to the obvious!

Well this time alter-Harry was clearly having none of it! He listened as *he* chatted on...

"It's lovely outside on the front this morning, out there on our wonderful Italianesque piazza! I don't know about you but I could use a little fresh air right now, it suddenly seems a bit stuffy in here... *(he pretends to tug at his shirt collar and gasp for air!)* ...maybe one too many of these as well? *(He held up his wine glass)* Would you let me buy you a coffee? We have an excellent coffee-truck parked-up there!"

"Are you trying to hint that I'm tipsy? In your ever-so-subtle and most gentlemanly manner of course? Well... How rude! I'll have you know that I'm a *profeshernal jurnerlista Mista*!" She said, pretending to slur her words as she wobbled on her feet and seemingly drunkenly, jabbed a finger into his chest, missing him completely on the first two attempts whilst she demanded that he... *'schstop moving!'*
They both dissolved into laughter as Harry said, "Shall we?" and They began walking back through into the auditorium,
He gestured to the still wide-open fire-doors that led out onto the stone paved *piazza!* Jenny turned with him and laced her arm through his to walk side by side out through the doorway and into the brilliant sunlight. Feeling the warmth of the sun on her face she tipped her head back and sighed... Thankfully the mob of protestors had entirely dispersed now.
"Oh, this is nice! Yes Harry, I see what you mean, we could be strolling across the stone flags of the piazza in Saint Mark's Square!"
"Yeah, if only our canal was as attractive as theirs eh?"
Harry turned to look sideways at her as she held her head back, her eyes closed as she basked in the sunshine... she was unaware of his concentrated gaze... he saw how the sun's rays danced on her skin, it was as if they felt so much more at home on it, that it was welcomed unlike the unfortunate reaction it evoked upon the pasty white skin of the inhabitants of these northern climes! No, her skin was perfectly at home basking in the wonder of the sun's glorious rays.

He understood for the first time what they were going-on-about when they used the glib expression *'Black is Beautiful'* because it truly was, she truly was! The shade of her skin, a wonderfully rich, mid-brown suddenly seemed to him to be a far more natural colour for it to be, rather than his own horrid blotchy complexion, that it was he and all his fellow white-tribes with their washed-out, sickly pale skins who were actually the oddities!

She opened her eyes and glanced over towards him, although his initial instinct would have been to turn away in a panic of guilt for being caught-out staring at her, he found instead that *he* simply smiled at her and to add even more joy to his already full heart... she smiled back at him... and simply said,

"Just look at you!"
Harry thought to himself, 'oh boy! I hope *he* hangs around! Please…Alter-Harry *do hang around!*

CHAPTER SIX

Whilst Harry had been walking arm-in-arm with Jenny across the *piazza*, bathed in the warm spring sunshine... or *floating on air* as entranced Harry was feeling... Nat was just entering the kitchen, much to the surprise of the chef and his assistants, arriving as she did through one of the service doors! He gruffly demanded of her,
"Hello... and you are who? You are wanting of something to be coming in here this way?"
"Oh no, look I'm sorry, you see I'm looking for old Bill, you know scruffy old man, big beard, baseball hat, backpack..." She was attempting to mime all of this as she spoke! The guy was clearly amused by this odd looking girl child, performing her clumsy mime in his kitchen, so he softened his voice and smiled as he replied,
"I am knowing who old Bill is! He go out through door there, out to back. Out onto canal." He pointed to a large door with a locking bar and FIRE EXIT emblazoned in red lettering across it.
"Oh thank you!" She smiled nervously as she bustled her way across the kitchen, dodging around the large Romanian chef as she was heading towards the door...
As she opened it she called back,
"Thanks again!" He waved a hand dismissively replying, with a nod of his head,
"Cu plăcere!"

The door swung back to close itself, with a loud clang as Nat found herself stood on what must have once been a dockside for the barges when the factory had still been operating. It was cool and shaded here by the massive hulk of the tall old building as she was on its north side. Further along to her right she could see the tall opening in the back wall that was now filled with the great arched window that looked out onto the canal from inside the refectory.

To her left the quayside of the dock ended abruptly about twenty metres further along and from there onwards the back wall of the tall old building plunged directly into its murky water.
Across the water the towpath ran along the other side of the canal, she caught sight of Bill, he was sat on a bench about a fifty yards away to her left. He saw her and got up, struggling into the

straps of his backpack as he got to his feet, she called to him to wait but he turned and started to walk away! *Bloody old git!* She thought to herself! As she wondered how the hell he'd managed to get across onto the other side of the canal?

Peering down to her right she saw there was a lock gate a little further along, so she trotted down to it. Arriving breathless at the lock, she was perturbed to find that there was no proper bridge to get across on, just a black metal rail fixed onto the top of the lock gates to grab onto presumably as you shimmied across? *'Fuck!'* She muttered to herself as she determined to just *go for it!*
Her platform shoes weren't ideal for acting the part of a latter day bargee, but she managed with a considerable amount of cussing and muttering *(the quality and obscenity of which any Georgian bargee would have been in awe of!)* to get over and she set-off attempting to run... as best she could in her stupidly unsuitable footwear, after the intransigent old man.

Meanwhile Andy had gone all the way around the front of the Factory seeking out the old tramp, unable to see him, he went through to the refectory to look around in there for Nat, as he wandered about a voice called out to him from the serving hatch,
"You boy! You looking for purple hair student girl?"
"Yes have you seen her?"
"She go out back, go out and round to canal. She look for old Bill."
"Thank you, thanks..." He called out as he was already dashing for the door, he spun around to his left and vaulted the low fence that separated the quayside from the carpark, so that he was a little way along from the backdoor to the refectory kitchen. He scanned down along the canal, there was a lock further along, but no sign of Nat, he turned to look westwards up the canal... There she was, in the distance on the other side stood taking to Bill! They were so far down that they were in the sunshine past the far end of the looming brick edifice that rose up from out of the canal, Nat was animated and clearly agitated, as she was waving her arms about in the air! She looked tiny stood alongside the dark hulking shape that Bill and his backpack combined to form. Suddenly Bill turned and started walking away from her heading west, she stamped her foot and punched downwards at the air in frustration before turning around herself to start walking dejectedly back towards him along the towpath.

He scrambled across the lock gate to get across the canal and set off walking along the towpath to meet her. As they approached each other, he could she was crying, he hurried up the last few strides and let her throw herself into his arms, where he hugged her tightly,
"Whatever's the matter lovely?" She was crying but he could feel the angry tension that was still broiling within her, she stamped her foot again in frustration and snarled out,
"The smelly old bastard says that he won't talk to us now! He was so fucking rude to me too! I wanted to push the miserable old fucker into the canal…"
"Only he's twice your size and you thought you'd struggle managing it, eh?" Andy said laughing as he let her go, he leant back a little and wiped away her tears,
"Fuck-him, we'll find someone else." Andy said trying to console her, but then her face brightened…
"No we bloody won't! I've just had a fabulous idea! I'm going to ring that reporter up and between us we'll find out everything there is to know about that secretive, smelly old git!" Andy could see that she was inspired by this idea, it had peeked her interest, she could smell the scent of a good story too! "To be so bloody secretive the old bastard must have something to hide!" Andy joined in,
"Yeah, he could be on the run? A criminal, or even a gangster that's fallen foul of his mob?"
"Or a murderer who the Police can't find… Maybe he killed his entire family…"
"…and even their cat!"
"With an axe!"
"Yeah… chopped them all up into tiny, bloody bits!"
"We'll see him brought to justice, won't we eh Nat?"
They dissolved into laughter as they strolled back down the towpath towards the lock gate…
Little could they know of the prophetic nature of her comment…

Despite Nat's earlier setback and frustration, the two young students laughed happily as they strolled off, hand in hand heading for The Student's Union bar, eager to lay out their plans over a few beers as to how to deal with the intransigent old tramp and enjoy a welcome little inebriation to wind down their day.

CHAPTER SEVEN

There were no other customers waiting at the coffee truck as Harry and Jenny strolled casually across to it.

Le Camionette de Café was an old Citroen H van, instantly recognisable by its corrugated bodywork, it had been brightly painted in the combination of a brown coffee colour around the lower sections and above this it was a creamy colour, graduated to go lighter as it went higher up the vehicle. The lettering was in a scripted font and shone-out in its shiny silver finish.

They were greeted at the large hatch in the side of the van by a friendly voice calling out, the French was tinted with another accent from much closer to home…
"Bonjour! Bonjour madame, monsieur! C'est une belle journée! What can I prepare for you?" Harry turned to Jenny, what's your preference? She looked up to the guy in the van and said,
"Puis-je avoir un cappuccino s'il vous plait?" The lad who was dressed in a stripy blue Breton style T-shirt and was even wearing a beret, added a big grin to complete the image before them as he resorted to his normal and rather heavy, Scouse accent to reply…

"Alright luv, no call for showin'off is there? So it's a cappucccino for yer bird and for you lah?" They both roared with laughter as he stood there arms akimbo for a while before adding…
"You's gonna make y'mind-up fella or wha?"
"A flat white please…" Was all Harry could manage to say as he and Jenny laughed!
At that moment the lookalike Frenchman's workmate, came back into the van from the rear, the van rocking slightly as she entered, she barked something incomprehensible to the lad before she appeared, smiling at the window and purred in a liltingly soft *posh-Scouse* voice…
"Take no notice of Jimmy, soft-lad as 'e'is! 'E's 'armless enough an' one thing 'e can do is make yers a brill coffee!"
"That I most certainly can do, Michelle ma belle and that I *will* do, tout de suite!" He piped up with his back to them now as he worked away at the mighty chrome and black machine!

Michelle took payment from Jenny and said she'd bring their coffees over to them, Harry had tried to pay but Jenny had insisted it was on her! Jokingly adding that she'd claim it as expenses anyway!

"It's a lovely old van," Harry commented looking back at the coffee truck as they perched themselves down on one of the picnic benches.
"Yeah I love all of that crinkly metal!" She replied.
"It was done to add strength you know? A ribbed steel panel is much stronger than a plain one, so it saves on the overall weight of the vehicle, it was used on some old aircraft too for that very reason."
"Didn't those funny little 2Cv's have a crinkly bonnet as well? They always reminded me of a hopping frog!"

Michelle came over bringing their coffees,
"There you are m'dears. Can I get yers a croissant or anything else?" They declined and as Michelle walked away, they looked at each other for a moment before laughing quietly together again.

"Do you know the story behind the coffee truck?" Harry asked.
"No... oh this coffee *is good*! Why do you all call it the coffee truck, isn't it *coffee van,* the translation of *camionette* is anyway?"
"When they first started on the renovation of the old mill, this guy turned up here in his beat-up old van and started selling brews and butties to the workmen from out the back, he said it was a great pitch for him since it was a new one and he was just starting-up, so he wouldn't be stepping on anybody's toes... Apparently you can get into a blood feud if you cross another butty-van owner, trespass onto *his patch*! He'd painted Coffee Truck on the side of the van, with a can of emulsion paint apparently and the name stuck!"
"So how did he end up with that beautiful, pristine classic van?"
"Well, the agent for the money-bags who funded the whole project... and still does... was impressed by the lad's endeavours and a few months in he rolled up with a rented butty-van and said to him, 'I'll have your old H van restored for you and fully kitted out if you'll stay on here at least until we've had the grand opening ceremony and that will be at least twelve months from

now.' So he agreed and he's never left since! He draws people in from the offices all around here and he even gets people coming specially!"

"Wow! So it's the same van he rolled-up in originally, but restored? That benefactor guy likes to spend his money doesn't he? But it was a really nice thing to do regardless. So you really never met him, Mr. Moneybags? The benefactor?"

"Nah... no one has. Like I said, I didn't even meet the original agent, the guy who was the direct go-between that did all the negotiating and setting-up, the one who supervised the contractors and the architect and organised the whole shebang. Once it was up and running and operational he left mysteriously, as I told you we're overseen by a board nowadays."

"Do they give interviews, the board I mean, or perhaps the individual members?"

"I don't know, you'd have to ask. Their names are a matter of Public Record, we're a Registered Charity so it's all kosher and by the book... to the letter and with the last 't' crossed and 'i' correctly dotted!"

Harry finished his coffee, placing the cup back down on the table he nodded as he agreed with Jenny,

"It really is good coffee! So Jenny... how come you ended up being a journalist. A snooping, hungry newshound?"

"Oh I dunno, I just love it, the whole notion of it. I've always loved writing and reading too, I'm fascinated by literature in all of its forms. My degree's in English Language. When I was a kid, at school I had a nickname... 'Jen-the-pen' they called me, because I was always scribbling or sketching in my notebook, I'd sit under the table at home either writing, sketching or just reading a book, anything to be away from everyone and all their incessant noise and jabbering... I have dozens of notebooks, no hundreds... Hey mister... Are *you* interviewing *me*? I'm the reporter! I want to do a story on your Folks Factory! I know it's had all sorts of stuff written about it already, but I want to get a more human angle on it, find out about the people whose idea it all was, the architects, the moneyman, his agent and also the guy who runs it today... about you Harry!"

"Well good luck with getting to the moneyman, that's been tried repeatedly and no one's ever got close. The Agent was the only one who had contact with him, even the original solicitor who

worked for us had to go through a second one to gain access to him!" Jenny picked up her phone which she'd placed on the table when they sat down,
"I'm intrigued by the footage that young Nat has sent me, do you want to take another look at it? I know I do. Y'know I was really struck by your solicitor's reaction to it, he looked like he'd seen a ghost! Any idea why?"
"No, none at all. Go on play it..."
"Come on Harry...You'll have to come round here and sit next to me..." he did so and she played the video of the old man playing the piano and singing, this time in full.

After the clip ended, Harry looked up at her, he was so close to her now, he could feel her presence, their eyes met and he held her gaze for a long moment... She looked down and tapped at the phone with her finger...

"That's Bill for sure, even his twin couldn't have a wild beard so exactly like his! The way he moves too, it's him for sure! I'll get what I want out of him one way or another, this newshound has a few more tricks up her sleeve yet!"
"Good luck with that Jenny! He's like a clam, if you can get anything out of him it will be remarkable!"
"Everything just keeps pointing to the fact that Bill has a story to tell, that he has a secret to hide or has run away from something!"
"You could say that for just about any one of my clients Jenny! Regardless of who we are, everyone has a story to tell."
"Yes Harry, but some are way more juicy than others and not all of them can play the piano and sing like that, that's someone who could easily have once made his living doing it!"

There was a lull in their conversation after Jenny put her phone down again. Realising that he was sat so close up next to Jenny, in her personal space, his leg almost touching hers, Harry suddenly felt awkward...
Alter-Harry stepped-in to the rescue at once...
"Would you like another coffee Jen?"
"Oh... Jen is it now? How very forward of you Mister Protherow! I don't recall inviting you to use the familiar version of my name, a name I only allow my family and very close friends to use!" She was smirking as she spoke though and Harry

was enjoying watching her face from the closest vantage point he'd so far attained, it felt almost intimate!

"Surely you already see me at the very least as a *friend-in-the-making* though Ms Stainton? That coffee?" He asked again as he rose from the bench,

"Whoa there mister! Down boy! Yeah you back-off brother!" She chuckled as he stood-up next to their table, adding…

"No really, thanks anyway but I'm good. I really do have to get back to the office."

Harry sat back down, opposite her again now, he put his best disappointed, hang-dog look on his face as he said,

"Not even for a few minutes? You can spare that surely? It's not every day I get the chance to be grilled by a top-flight reporter and I've never been grilled by such an enchanting and gorgeous newshound before… Mademoiselle Jennifer Stainton!"

"You old charmer you! *Mr. Slick* or what? You always such a smooth talker Harry? Okay, I'll really turn the heat up on my newshound griller then!"

"So Mister Protherow, tell me all about Mrs. Protherow and all the little Protherow's, what are they all up to while you're sat here sweet talking and shamelessly flirting with a single unchaperoned and frightfully modest lady"

"Which Mrs. Protherow in particular would you like to know about?"

"Oh my God! How many are there?"

"Three, that are still living!"

"Three? You've been married three times?"

"Really Madam, for someone who claims to have studied the English language you really are incredibly assumptive and imprecise in your interpretation of what you hear!" Harry beamed widely at her… "Well now, let me see, the number one Mrs Protherow is of course my mother, she is eighty-six and the other two are both married to my brothers! I, me myself personally… have never married!"

"A-ha… so that's it is it? You're gay? Knew it! You were just too damn good to be true!"

"Really? There you go off again, leaping to unsubstantiated conclusions with no solid, corroborating facts as a basis for them! No I'm not gay, there've been quite a few ladies that have come into my life, but sadly they also determine shortly afterwards to go straight back out of it! I think perhaps I'm intolerable to be with for any protracted length of time?"

"Ah… that's sad. Why? What is it that makes you so intolerable to live with? Are you terminally boring? A hopeless sloven about the house? You snore like a bulldozer? You're crap in bed?" She made the last remark with a cheeky smirk on her face!
"No… no… no… and as far as your last question goes, you'd need to make your own mind up about that, decide for yourself!" He finished with… as inwardly Harry was mentally cringing at what *Alter*-Harry had just said! But *A.H.* still hadn't finished yet as he went straight on to say…
"Look as you're a bit pushed for time just now and I wasn't able to return the favour of buying you a coffee, let me take you out to dinner, let me wine and dine you? You can carry on with interviewing me in a more amenable setting that way?"

"Why Mister Protherow! What kind of girl do you take me for?" She declared as she put on a wide-eyed and shocked expression! *A.H.* was in full flow though now, was lapping this up and was quite unstoppable…
"I take you to be a highly intelligent, well-educated and well-read, articulate and very witty lady, additionally you are the most incredibly attractive lady I've met in… well, that I've *ever* met!*"*
At this Jenny fluttered her eyelashes, dipped her head and holding her chin in her hand, looked up at him demurely… *but unable to keep a little smirk from dancing around on her lips…* as she replied…
"Why Sir… How can you speak to a lady so!" They both burst out laughing at this performance… after a while she replied,
"You know you're a pretty-darn-slick operator aren't you Harry Protherow? And something of a smooth talking, silver tongued bastard too"
"So that's a yes then? What time shall I pick you up tonight?"
"Wow! A fast bloody moving one too! Oh I do like it! It's all so very refreshing!" She pulled one of her business cards out her handbag, flipped it over, seeing it was blank she pulled a pen out and wrote her phone number and address on the back…
She presented the card to Harry with a grand flourish of the wrist,
"I shall have the butler alert me when he has sight of your carriage, shall we say at seven-thirty?"

"I'll be there!"

With that they both got up from the table, there was a moment's awkwardness, was *A.H.* finally slacking? They stood close by each other for a just little too long, hesitating... *unless A.H. wanted her to see a little more vulnerability, see that there was a less pushy side to him perhaps...* he offered his hand to shake hers, she took it, squeezed it and then pulled him in a little to her as she leant in and gave him a tiny peck on the cheek before instantly turning on her heel and striding off towards the carpark!

Harry stood there stunned, his legs were shaking! Meanwhile, he could almost feel *A.H.* next to him, leaning casually against his shoulder his legs crossed at the ankle, grinning smugly as he flipped the lid of his silver lighter to light-up a cigarette... He was a cross between Harry, Sean Connery and Humphrey Bogart as he whispered into Harry's ear...
"*She'll turn and look over her shoulder when she gets to the gateway... You'll see. That's how you'll know I made a good impression on the dame...*" What...? The *dame*?

But Humphrey's *Harry Marlowe* voice was spot on in his analysis...
Not only did she look back over her shoulder but she gave him a little wave and turned-on that smile! *That smile... Marlowe* took over again... '*and even from thirty yards away in that moment it was as if the sun had come out shining its yellow glory across the dull gray flags of the piazza on a damp gray day in that dirty gray city...*'

Harry waved back smiling! He was quite literally stunned as he imagined that he felt a little dig in his ribs and the voice in his ear saying... '*I told ya kid!*' ...Yeah but it was already sunny..?

Then another voice, one that was in the real world rang out from over to his right...
"Nice one lad!" He turned his head to see Michelle leaning on the counter of the coffee truck grinning at him, he blushed as she gave him a thumbs up adding... "You're in there lad!" He smiled weakly, then as he was setting-off back towards the factory, he heard Jimmy's voice ring out,

"You sly ol'dog 'Arry! Eh yer'defo in there!" He glanced back once more over his shoulder to briefly see a grinning Jimmy leaning out from behind Michelle, before she playfully roughed him up scolding him…
"You's get back to y'coffee machine!"

His legs still trembling as he walked, Harry continued back towards The Factory… were they actually trembling though or was it because the hard un-giving stone beneath him was not actually making contact with his floating feet?

CHAPTER EIGHT

Although Andy and Nat had gone off for a drink reasonably happy, once Nat had calmed herself down some, things were considerably less rosy in Bill's troubled mind! He'd continued to stomp angrily along the canal for another half a mile until he reached the first bridge, which carried a minor side street over the canal. He climbed the steps and leant on the parapet for a while, mumbling to himself as he tried to quell the anger that had boiled up in him earlier when he'd been confronted by the at first insistent and then angry student.

What right did she have to think that she could interrogate him about his life, why couldn't people mind their own fucking business? Worst of all was the indignation and temper she'd shown resulting from her frustration at not getting her own way! Silly little bitch! Spoilt, bloody middle-class brat she was!

Without any conscious thought of where he was going he found himself drifting back towards the town centre. He was still thoroughly pissed-off and frustrated when he got to the shops, they were busy now as the schools must have recently tipped-out their unruly rabble to scurry around the place like vermin... He found himself at the entrance to one of the big chains of bargain stores and went in, this was what the country had come down to he thought, cheap and nasty shopping with everything at the lowest possible price, often of suspect quality, sized down to a price and presented to the public with the lowest level of service... How had we become such a penny-pinching and mean spirited bunch? That was one of the few things that actually did *trickle-down* he thought... meanness and nastiness! It seemed to be a sort of contagion, something that the bean-counters had instilled in so many of us, all done of course at the will of their wealthy masters, to whom money was no object and could be thrown around as if it was confetti.

It occurred to him that the ultimate extension of their robber's culture, in response to their extravagance and blatant banditry, a kind of counter-reaction to it, was to excuse the population from feeling any guilt in doing likewise, enabling them to feel totally justified in simply helping themselves to the measly offerings that they put out on their shelves! Society called it shoplifting, the poor called it, *feeding my kids*, or *necessity* and cast themselves in the role of latter day followers of the principles nobly established by Sir Robin of Locksley, stealing from the rich to give to the poor! Accordingly he picked up the only one litre bottle of Jack Daniels that he noticed hadn't had the security tag properly attached to its neck! With a little chuckle, he flicked it off and left it on the shelf before gradually making his way towards the tills and the exit, not that anyone seemed to bother that much when the alarm at the doorway went off nowadays.

There was a group of lads larking around by the sweets, some of them had opened cans of pop that they hadn't paid for yet and they were obviously taunting each other to put things into their pockets. Bill tapped the biggest of the lads on his shoulder, he was lanky but was nearly as tall as Bill despite being very young... still a child to Bill, a kid of maybe thirteen or fourteen perhaps. He looked like he was off one of the Estates, a lot of the other kids were Asians, it was unusual to see such a mixed group, there was even a black kid amongst their numbers.
"What you want old man?" the lad said with a sneer in his voice,
"Just wanted to see if your bollocks have dropped yet or if you're just a big lanky, streak-o'piss, scared kid who's tryin' t'act tough?"
"Yer what?"
"You 'eard me! In me old regiment we'd'a soon sorted some lil'punk like you out from the real men and done it in double-quick time too!"
"You was a squaddie?" Bill was laughing to himself inside as he rattled this diatribe off... He'd heard it all from some old guy he'd come across, who really had been a squaddie, a guy who'd been sent off to some God-Damned country to fight some God-Damned war for the capitalist swine running the show at the time... Iraq was it? Who fuckin' cared, the exact location was irrelevant, it was all about money, profits, dollars! The Army had used the old guy up, fucked him up and then got shut when he was of no use to them anymore. Dumped him back into a society he was totally unable to cope with. A society he'd left as a teenager and was returned to a broken man, an old man now still wracked by PTSD. He hadn't learned to cope with his life before he signed-up, he signed-up to get away from the shitty estate he lived on, to *learn a trade*, to finally emerge from the service a trained, competent, confident man ready to take his place in

society! That was how the adverts had portrayed it, wasn't it? The only skill he'd learned was how to kill some poor unfortunate bastards who were most likely mirror images of himself, transposed in time and space into a different but equally shitty culture!

Back in the Bargain Store, Bill continued his well-run performance... Jackie wouldn't have minded him ripping it off! Jackie didn't mind anything anymore... He'd taken a dive off the multi-story one night when his demons had become too much for him. You wouldn't find his name on any of their memorials Bill grunted mentally... Not much to glorify in the sacrifice that particular lad had made *for his Queen and country*!
Now Bill growled out... Jackie's own words again... As his own testament to the man he'd got to know so briefly...

"Damn right boy! Look at me now, this is how the bastards repay you for doin' their dirty work for 'em! For doin' their killin for 'em! Y'wanna 'elp me fight back lad? You wanna show these kids 'ere what yer made of!? What kinda man y'are?"
"What, you killed people? Cool man... what d'ya have in mind?"
"Now't good in killing people lad... but we'll leave that lesson f'nother day eh? Just tell y'gang 'ere, to get their 'ands full o'loot and then go an'it that Fire Alarm button there! Then you's'll all go an' clear out't'door wi' ya stuff and there'll be me sauntering out all innocent like behind ya' wi'mine!" He opened his coat to show the neck of the bottle of Jack Daniels that was nestling in the deep inside pocket of his coat.
"Wha... man! You wily old devil you!" He went into a huddle with the group of kids and then they *sauntered* over to the doorway into the stockroom where the red Fire Alarm box was on the wall, a quick look around and wham he hit the glass with the side of his fist and they scattered as the alarm went off!

It was total mayhem for a few minutes, as the kids grabbed armfuls of sweets, time a plenty as everyone's attention was distracted, for Bill to drift out of the doors along with other folks who were already leaving and then casually head off down the street.

He rounded the corner of the street, carried on across the centre plaza and plonked himself down on the stone seating that ran all the way along one of the walls of a flower bed. He sneaked the bottle out, keeping it under his jacked, he broke the seal on the cap. He took a good swig and then hid the bottle again. *"Blearghhh..."* He muttered as he wiped a hand across the whiskers around his mouth... bloody bourbon!

It was alcohol though, neat spirit and the full forty percent proof stuff, not like some of the cheap and nasty, fiery stuff he bought in the little quarters from the corner shop... Ah well, he thought beggars can't be choosers can they? He chuckled as he recognising the appropriateness of the expression... he was a beggar... and a thief... and he too was one of that ilk who had absolutely no feelings of guilt or remorse for being either.

Part of him knew that he was making a mistake as he took another swig of the neat spirit, it wasn't all that bad actually... once you got over its initial yuckiness he thought! American shite! He knew it was a mistake because he would normally only start drinking when he was already well on his way back to his night time shelter, in addition to that he'd have already reined himself in, by only buying a quarter bottle and even then he would eke it out. This was a fuckin' litre bottle! One thousand millilitres! As opposed to one hundred and eighty! He took another swig as he thought of Bully in the old ITV show Bulls-Eye calling out... 'one hundred and eighty!'

A sharp voice interrupted his reverie...
"Excuse me Sir, if you don't put that bottle away at once and move on I will have to either issue you with a Fixed Penalty Notice or arrest you!" The ever-so-stern voice sounded out from up above where he was sat! He looked up to find that some kid in a cheap looking uniform was looking down at him. His pink little face was still all spotty, fa-fucks-sake!

"Get lost sonny, y'mummy'll be worryin,' wondering why y's not 'ome from school b'now!" Bill slurred at the lad, why the fuck couldn't they just leave him alone! He knew all too well that the last thing the cops wanted to do was to arrest people like him, homeless beggars. I mean what were they meant to do wi'em? Give 'em a night in the cells, some food and then breakfast before turning them out again the next morning? Hardly a deterrent was it? Then they'd have an additional job of having to disinfect the cell!

"You're not even a real cop lad! What y'wanna do that for eh? 'Elp them pigs out? Ya jus' doin' all the shitty jobs as they can't be arsed wi'? You can't even arrest me any'ow! 'Ave to call-up some real pig to do that won'y ya? Think they'll wanna come out f't'likes a me? They'll laugh in ya face! If ya lucky like, an' they don'give ya a slap!"
The lad blushed so red it made Bill chuckle! But still he held his ground, all credit to the lil'fucker!
"I am empowered to confiscate any alcohol you may have in your possession, upon failure to give up said alcohol I can issue you with a Fixed Penalty Notice!"
"Fixed Penalty?... Go ahead lad... gi'me summit to wipe me arse wi' won'it? Wha's worse as can 'appen t'me then eh? They puts me in a nice warm prison f'comtempt when I don't pay it? As if eh?... 'ave to give me three meals a day and a warm bed... that'ad cost'em, I mean sounds alright t'me like... but them tight-arse fuckers wantin' t'pay'out f'likes o'me? I don't think so, do you?"

"I really must insist Sir, hand over that bottle or you will force me to take action!"
"You try and take me bottle offa me kid an' you'll be sorry... well, for't'little while y's still conscious like!" Bill noticed that the group of lads he'd encouraged to riot in the Bargain Shop had surrounded them both now. He saw that the big lad was just about to start taunting the special constable too, cheered on by his gang...
"Leave him be you Fascist! You ain't even no real copper, play acting you's is! That man's a fuckin' 'ero! He fought for this country to keep us safe, not to be bullied by no Fascist pig!" His little mob cheered him on and before he knew it the cop was being jostled by the little mob, they were getting between him and Bill... he felt a hand grab at his coat...
"Come-on while we've got him off ya!" One of the lads had his face right next to Bill's, quickly getting the message he grabbed his backpack and scurried off with him... he heard a plaintiff cry of 'Oi! You! Old man! Stop!' From the pretend cop, but he was in a scuffle now and the kids were deliberately blocking his way!

The kid he was with steered him round the corner and pointed down a narrow street that went between the shops, 'this way' he urged Bill on. At the end of the street they turned a corner and headed out of town, they slowed down and walked on for a while until they went past a big petrol station with a Spar shop. A little further on they came to a derelict site, where some kind of works had once stood, the lad squeezed nimbly around an ill-fitting gate that had once been the entrance to the yard, with Bill close behind him. Once inside after negotiating piles of rubble, they came out into an open patch of wasteland where there was an assortment of old plastic chairs scattered about amidst the rubbish, around an area that had clearly had a large bonfire quite recently, the occasional little whiff of smoke was still spiralling up from the ashes. Bill put down his backpack and slumped onto one of the chairs.

The lad sat on one nearby to him, he was laughing,
"That was so cool!" Bill took another swig of the bourbon,
"Can I 'ave some?" The kid asked! Bill looked at him, he was so young, his clean-faced innocence was only tainted by his behaviour! But who could blame him or the others? What was there for them, here today in this town? So many youth clubs and similar facilities, had been shut down by their cash strapped Council.

What did their schooling do for them, what did it have to offer other than doing enough for the box-ticking on the forms for Ofsted to be managed successfully? A tick-list of all the bullshit, yet carefully selected BS in the disguise of so called *facts* that they were forced to learn and parrot, knowledge that would be of so little use to them later on as they tried to navigate their way through the maze of life, steer clear of all the pitfalls and traps so skilfully laid out in their paths? The sickening lure of gambling and alcohol so glibly flashed in their faces everywhere they looked! How could they legitimately be condemned for saying... Fuck it! Fuck you! Fuck your whole stinking society! Wasn't that exactly what Bill had done?

However, he mumbled, "you're not old enough to drink kid!" The lad pulled a face and snarled back at him,
"Thought you was cool? Yers jus' an' old cunt like the rest o'them!"

"Well yer not wrong there son!" Bill laughed as he handed the bottle to the lad.

The next thing he became aware of anything, it was morning…

He rolled onto his side in a blind panic! Then breathed an enormous sigh of relief when he felt his backpack next to him. He sat up, shrugging off a piece of plastic that had been put over him… What? His fuddled mind tried to grapple with the hazy images that confronted him as he came around, all the while battling with the ones he had of last night… Scattered, disjointed words drifted down to him…

"Where do'ya sleep bud…
"I've got to go…
"Hope you're okay mister…
"Here… this'll keep you dry…

As his head began to pound, he saw the Jack Daniels bottle lying on the floor next to him, … at least the bottle wasn't totally empty he thought as he began coughing, trying to clear his throat, which was as dry as dust… he opened his rucksack and pulled out his water bottle… it was empty! Of course he'd not filled it up had he? His routine had been wrecked by arguing with that little stupid bitch, the purple haired student, hadn't it? Then he'd gone off on one because of it. He drained the last few drops of water from the bottle and struggled up onto his feet. He needed to get water! He held his head in his hands to try and stop it exploding as the pounding worsened!

Where the fuck was he? He needed to get to The Factory, get some water, get something to eat…

He shoved the Jack Daniels into his backpack then struggled his shoulders into the straps… His mind all the while grappling to remember how he'd got here. He could see that it was a derelict site, there was rubbish and rubble piled-up everywhere, with a track here or there running through it, there were the remains of a wall around it, the place was about fifty yards square, an old works judging by the cut stone in the walls, lumps of which were lying around everywhere. He was in a clearing by the burnt out fire, its blackened embers cold now. The plastic chairs were still there, scattered about. He must have passed out and crawled off to where he'd woke up. That lad he was with, he must've put the plastic over him?

He looked all around where he was stood, with no idea which way to go to get out. He vaguely remembered a gate in the wall somewhere, that he'd come through with the lad, that went onto the main road, but he had no idea in which direction it lay. He saw that there was a well-used track worn into the rubble that headed off into a wild undergrowth of weeds, brambles and Buddleia bushes, so he followed it. As the path narrowed, he struggled on through the bushes for a while cursing the brambles until he found a stretch of palisade fencing that held back the wild undergrowth, on the other side of the fence he could see the towpath of the canal. The path went straight up to the fence and when he examined it more closely he found that the rivet that should have fixed the upright to the cross member had rusted through and the upright could be pulled off it, the top rivet still being in place he was able to swing it to one side creating an opening, he attempted to barge through it only to get stuck half-way through and then had to struggle out of his backpack to get it untangled, as he cursed and tugged at it.

Once he was through and stood on the towpath he knew exactly where he was and how to get to The Factry. He pushed the fence rail back into place as his head pounded... the incident with that dumb-fuck Special came back to mind as he set off plodding towards the Factory, silly little fucker got way more than he bargained for when he tackled me, he smirked to himself. It was still early yet but by the time he got there the doors would already be open... he hoped...

CHAPTER NINE

Jenny returned to the Folks Factory the next morning, or the *Factry* as she'd noted Harry abbreviated the name to... she was picking-up things like that from him! She was sat outside in the main car park where she'd pulled up a moment or two earlier, thinking about the previous evening and how it had gone. He'd been punctual arriving for her... and in a taxi too... and they had indeed wined and dined together in a charming little family run Italian restaurant he was familiar with, spending a couple of hours, eating, chatting and enjoying each other's company.

He'd been attentive and interested in her, asking her lots about herself and actually listening to her whilst she told him too! He'd asked her about her own situation, how it was attachments-wise of course and she'd divulged that she was divorced with twin daughters, that they were grown-up and had flown the nest. He'd been charming and had used the opportunity to flatter her saying *'that was impossible!'* Unless she'd had the twins when she was thirteen!' Her reply of *'how do you know I didn't?'* ...was in the style of how easily the rest of the conversation had flowed... She knew that she looked good for her age, *black-don't-crack*... to use her mother's well-worn saying! She knew it and she wasn't being immodest either!

Despite being off-duty... *when was she ever as a Newshound*? She'd managed to get Harry to talk a fair bit about his *'Factry'*, She now knew that although the initial funding came from the philanthropist to pay for the conversion of the old mill and to set the whole thing up practically and get it started, it was now ninety-odd percent self-financing. This had been achieved by a number of factors as well as their own continual fund-raising efforts and events, Harry liaised with a group who called themselves 'The Friends of The Folks Factory' they worked together organising the seeking out of additional donations from a wide range of sources, he even secured money now and then from larger charitable organisations too.

The expanding rental side of the Factory increasingly chipped-in funds, the latest off-site housing project being expected to not only become self-financing over time, once construction had been completed and generate a good sized long term income to pour back in to help fund the project but also to be used towards other future initiatives.

She also learnt that despite the local and very vocal opposition that there was to the Factry, there was also massive support and cooperation too, coming from a broad sweep of the town's business communities, from the big National supermarket chains, a local Cash & Carry, a couple of fresh produce wholesalers and even right down to the smallest of shops, in donating surplus stock, especially short-dated items or less than perfect produce.

After their date, he'd dropped her off again, seeing her right up to her front door… while the taxi was waiting for him… *ensuring that there was no intrigue/uncertainty/pressure over him being asked-in*! Clever man, she'd thought, figuring out that he'd deliberately planned it that way! Once she'd opened her door and she was ready to go in he, quite unexpectedly… *took her hand*!!… For a second she thought he was going to kiss the back of it! But instead he just said, whilst holding it…
"Thank you for a lovely evening, I hope we can do this again… and soon?" She nodded,
"Thank you Harry. I'd love to." This time it was he who using her hand gently drew her in, to give her a quick kiss on the lips… a little longer than a *peck*… but by no means an intimate kiss… He turned and called 'Goodnight' to her as he was walking back to the taxi, she got a final wave as climbed into the back and then he'd been gone…

There was real promise with this guy Harry, she'd felt as she pushed the door shut and leaned back on it, definitely a tad under the influence too she chuckled, they hadn't spared the wine! Yeah, she smiled as she thought, most promising, despite him being a bit slick on the surface… which she put down to most likely a bit of macho bravado… probably to hide his nerves?… As the drink had flowed he had become more relaxed and a bit less *slick*! She chuckled to herself, but underneath all that, he seemed to be an alright sort of guy, and she felt that there was definitely chemistry between them! And she was damn sure he'd felt it too! She wondered what she would have done if he'd let the taxi go… Mmm… she thought… Y'know, he might just have got lucky!

Back from recollecting the previous evening and the accompanying titillation she'd been enjoying and realising that she had been sat with the engine running whilst the car was stationary for quite some time, she reached to the key and turned off the ignition. When she'd pulled-up at the Factry she'd parked at the farthest end of the carpark well away from the entrance in a space that had the path to the canal next to it, so that no one could park right up next to her, at least on one side, protective as she ever was of her dinky little sports car! She always tried to park away from any other cars and the associated perils of less aware or uncaring drivers, swinging their damnable car doors into her *little precious!*

She leant over to pick up the thick moulded paper tray that held the two lidded coffees, but thought better of it and flicked the door lock up on the passenger door. It was something of an art form disembarking from her tiny car, without attempting to accomplish it holding a tray of two coffees, however well the cups may be locked into it! Instead she swivelled herself around to firstly get her right leg out and then she flicked her left one out so that she was still sat in the driver's seat but with both feet on the ground… this was one of the reasons she wore trousers, since she was very exposed for that moment before she pushed up from what was essentially a low squat! It wasn't that she was averse to showing off her legs, she knew that she had a damn good pair of very shapely pins! It was rather that she preferred her *showing-off* to be done at times of her choosing, when it was to her advantage and to an audience of her choosing and not offering an unwarranted viewing of her nether regions to any random voyeur lucky enough to be looking!

Once up on her feet she flicked the door shut and walked round to the passenger side to retrieve the coffees, she'd brought them because she was hoping to find Bill there. As she'd said to Harry, she was greatly intrigued by the footage of him singing and playing the piano in that You-Tube clip they'd watched. She'd been even more intrigued by his reaction of running-off as soon as he realised he'd built up quite a sizeable audience, but most especially once he saw that he was being filmed! Her newshound's nose had been set a'twitching and it had demanded that she'd come to try and meet him and facilitate some more

sniffing around to be done, she felt sure that there was an interesting story to be had there!
With the thick reclaimed papier-mâché tray held up in one hand, she flicked shut the door, there was precious little point in locking the car with its soft-top, held down only by its readily un-popped studs!

She needn't have worried about finding Bill because as she turned away from her car to head over to the *client's* doorway of the Folks Factory, she saw him leaning on the fence that ran along one side of the carpark, he was already watching her.

"Hello there! This *must* be fate, it's you that I've come here to see! You're Bill aren't you?"

She smiled as she took the couple of dozen strides that were between them to approach the dishevelled old guy, noticing that he had a little smirk on his face, in response he grunted,

"Might be, or might'nt be! One thing as I do know is you's that lass as schmoozed 'erself all over'th'igh and mighty Lord 'Arry yesterday aren't ya? I 'eard ya, asking y'questions! All the way from't' back of th'all! An'a'saw y'afta, sat out on't'front there, giggling and using y'charms on t'great big sap!"
"Well a girl has to use whatever she can in my business you know?"
"So are jus'a nosey bitch or summit worse... a reporter?"
"We're not all bad you know!"
"Yeah well don't you go an'lead 'im too far up garden path eh love? Before y'crucify 'im like, on the cross of y'need *to-tell-the-story*! He's not as tough as 'e likes to mek-out."
"I won't, I promise you! But that's so nice... Ah... you care about him, don't you? A heart of gold still beats beneath that shabby disguise you're wearing!"
"Aye well, 'Arry's not a bad sort, despite o'iself! Not like mosta'd bastards y'come across!" Bill replied, a little taken aback by her choice of words in referring to his appearance as a disguise!

"Listen Bill... look here, see, I got us both a coffee on my way here... even managed not to spill it! The weather was looking a bit off, so I thought we'd need to sit inside and Harry said the coffee in the canteen is terrible!

"Would you at least come and sit with me for a little while and have a chat with me. If you don't want to talk about yourself, at least fill me on some of the gossip about this place? You know the sort of stuff they don't put out in their press releases, background stuff and not all the shit that old Harry bangs on about once he's got an audience. What I want is an insight into the real deal, what *you* know and how you see it. It's still a hot topic in the local news… this place is."

"Okay, I'll sit wi'ya and drink yer coffee, an' I'll give y't'inside story on this 'ere place but I'll not be talking about mesel' though… We can sit outside though, not like as'ow it's raining is it?"

She handed him one of the coffees as they walked around to where the seats were,
"I put a sugar in that one, is that okay, this one hasn't got any in if you prefer?"
"S'fine…ta! Nice lil'motor y'got there luv!"
"Thanks, it's totally impractical but do I love it!"
"*It?* It's as *she*, don'cha'know owt?" She chuckled as they walked around the corner and out onto the great expanse of stone flagging that ran across the front of The Factory, there were quite a few people sat at the picnic style tables that were scattered about across the paved area, they found an empty one and sat down opposite each other.
Jimmy in the coffee van, over the other side of the paved area, shouted across playfully as they were sitting down at one of the picnic tables…
"Eh… tha's norr-on you's two! Bringin' y'Costa Coffee rubbish 'ere! Lob it in't'bin an' I'll make yers a decent brew! On the 'ouse!"
Bill laughed and replied, mimicking Jimmy's Scouse accent,
"Eh lah… aren't you's meant-to be a feckin' Froggy like… eh wha… lah?"
"Mais oui! J'ai oublié! Tu vas te faire foutre alors vieux bougre!" He said with a massive grin all over his cheeky face!
"What'd'e just say?" Bill asked Jenny.
"My French isn't all that good but I think it was along the lines of *go and fuck yourself then you old bugger!*"

"Cheeky feckin' Scouser!" Bill called back to him.

Jenny looked across the table as she sipped her coffee, at the dishevelled old fellow who was settling himself down opposite to her now, rummaging with his backpack. Turning his attention to his coffee, he tossed aside the plastic lid for his coffee and slurped away at it, the foam clinging to his unruly moustache. They'd both been amused by the guy in the coffee truck's joking outburst, so to break the ice she said,
"I can't believe I forgot! I mean about him and his coffee truck, Like I said, I thought we'd need to sit inside. He's right too, his stuff is way better than this, I didn't think and as I was passing anyway I picked these up on the spur of the moment, at the drive-through on my way here!"
Bill chuckled as he commented,"You people an'y'fuckin convenience everything's! I mean! Drive thru-fuckin-coffee!"
"Indeed! Not a place I'd normally use." She took a swig of her coffee and thought to herself, old Bill doesn't look at all well? "Are you okay Bill you look a bit peaky?"
"Nah, luv! I've gorra bangin' 'ead, I were proper pissed last night!"
"Would you like a couple of paracetamols?" Despite what he grunted being totally unintelligible, he'd also nodded, so she rummaged deep down into her handbag, finding what she was after, she popped two tablets out of the blister-pack and tipped them into the palm of his grubby fingerless, mitten covered hand, cringing inside at the sight of the two pure white tablets against the filthy wool! He nodded by way of thanks.
"Do you want some water? I can get a bottle from Jimmy?" She asked, but he had already thrown the tablets into his mouth and swilled them down with the last swig of his coffee!
"Nah, I carries me own water in me bag luv if I wants it! Don'pay for it! Pah!… No taps where I lays me 'ead y'see! 'Ave to plan ahead! So it's Jimmy is it, eh? On first names terms wi'im now are ya? Ya presumes t'call me Bill an'all, so don'cha'think it's about time y'introduced yersel?"

"No…" Pondering for a moment on his remark she hesitated… "No, I guess there wouldn't be… taps I mean! And, yes I suppose I should have done just that by now! So, please, allow me to introduce myself… I'm Jenny. I can use your surname if you'd prefer?" It *was* a long shot…

"Jenny you say? Lil' Jenny wren eh? Hmm...?"
"*Jenny Wren?*" She smiled, "No, actually I'm Jenny Stainton, pleased to meet you..." She held her hand out to shake his, but he just harrumphed and waved it away...
"... and you are Bill, so that's *William-*..." Ignoring her second hint at trying to find out what his full name was, he just set off at a tangent...

"So, what's yer 'eritage luv? Y'didn't get that lovely skin tone from no pasty-faced fucker as infests these parts, no someone, once upon a time in't'family tree ya fell outta weren't from 'round 'ere!" Before she could reply though, he carried straight...
"Yer folks'd be from't'West Indies I'd say? Y's a tiny 'int of it in ya voice, I'm right eh? Mebbe yer grandfolks, would it be was Windrush generation?" She smiled at him in response, she was pleased to see that his grumpiness had slipped, albeit only momentarily as he smiled back! She was impressed that he hadn't asked her about her heritage in the usual... *fuckingly stupid and equally irritating manner...* as was so often the case, by inanely asking *'where are you from?'* For fucks sake! She was from just down the road, the place where she'd lived all her life and if her patience had worn thin that particular day, that was exactly how she may well reply!

"Not my nanna no, it was my mum who came to answer the call, she worked here as a nurse in The NHS for thirty-five years, met my Dad here, married him and voila..." She waved her hands extravagantly as if she were revealing herself to him as she was instantly materialising at that very second before him!

"Jamaica?" He more or less grunted it as a question, seeming to have steeled himself back into his usual state of sullen grumpiness once more,
"*Nah Man!*... me were no born back den! She come all by 'ersel, an did a'tell ya? She do *terty-five* year in *de N-H-S!*" She said smirkingly in a heavily and totally over-done Jamaican accent!

He looked blankly back at her... She explained...
"Jamaica?... D'y'make-her? My mum?" Bill continued to refuse to react! He instead asked her... in what could best be described as 'Received Pronunciation' or the very best of old school 'BBC English' ...that precise and perfectly articulated, over-enunciated

manner in which their newsreaders used to speak so very long ago!

"So moving on my dear, what exactly is it that you wish me to elucidate for you?" He reverted to his normally slovenly drawl to add...
"An' don't gi'up yer day job neither! Y'll never 'ack it as a comedian!" He allowed himself a little smirk. She laughed freely, her laughter totally genuine and relaxed,

"Okay, I won't, but you... on the other hand... Oh my God... that voice! Where did *he* come from?" He smiled again, *(second time! Yay I'm winning! She thought),* then he continued, using a totally normal and contemporary voice,
"Look, you're an intelligent girl, you probably imagine that I once led a normal life, was part of it all... all the madness that people like you pretend to accept as normality? I expect it's that bloody You-Tube clip that's got you so intrigued, isn't it? You've seen that haven't you? Was it that little twerp Nat who showed you?"

"That's a little unkind, she's a lovely kid, but yes she showed it to me, but hey it's had over twenty thousand other hits you know?"
"Yeah? Look, I know that *she's alright*, it's just that... well I'm an old fart regardless of how you perceive me whether it's as a tramp or a fallen Middle Class one! I mean Nat... yeah as such... I mean she's only a stupid kid, acting stupid, but looking at all those flaming piercings of hers all over her twerpy little face... it fair makes me queasy!"

He sat up from leaning with his elbows on the wooden table and looked at her properly, for the first time.
"I have to say you're a bonny lass, bet your mum's proud of you, is she still alive? If it was your mum who came over you must be a lot older than you look?"
"Yeah man, *black don't crack!* But nah... she died a few years back, she was well into her nineties though, my Dad died decades before her though."

"What is it that you think I'm going to tell you Jenny? Don't you grasp that I'm living the way I do *precisely* because I've left all

of my old life, the way it was then... behind me! I walked away from it all. Do you think maybe that there was a reason for that? Do you think that maybe, just maybe, there are people who also wonder what happened to me, people who would like to know where I am, if I'm still alive? People who would want me to *be found*?
"Surely a smart investigative reporter such as you are, would have deduced that from that damnable footage... that I *did not want to be filmed, ergo, did not want to be found!* Wouldn't that be the glaringly obvious conclusion to come to from that one singular fact." She sat back herself now, mirroring her protagonist's body language *(those courses were worth all that money after all!)* and she laughed heartily, she had a laugh that could stir a response in even the most miserly Scrooge ...if they were still breathing! It was no surprise then that he couldn't help himself either and he laughed along with her for a while.

Composing himself he scoffed though as he said,
"Don't think you'll disarm me, get me talking with that smile of yours and your laugh, wonderfully infectious as they both may be and however clever you think you are with your *mirroring*... I'm just not going to tell you about my life before I became 'Bill' because it's gone, it's past, it's over, it's a closed book, I moved on. I found peace by living in the moment, from no longer being entangled, freeing myself from the entrapment you pretend is society."

So the points were level again! Fifteen-all... But maybe not, she'd gleaned that 'Bill' was not his real name! That was the second time he'd used the word pretend too, why was that?

"Okay, I'll try not to underestimate you again! This vision I see before me, a wreck of a man who up until a few minutes ago was a man who grunted out his words more than spoke them, suddenly transforms into an educated, deep thinking man! So yeah, I'm transitioning in my perception of you and I'm having to question the way in which I'm going to interact with you! So carry on, tell me anything else, just talk to me! You must have stories a plenty, you must be able to spin a yarn surely?" With that she sat upright and deliberately crossed her arms. She tipped her head slightly to one side as if to indicate she was ready to listen. Resorting to *Bill-speak* he replied...

"Tha' musta' etten' a feckin' dickshonery for ya breakfast wi' all them long words... fair made me ears hurt, surprised as 'ow they ain't bleeding!" She laughed but said,
"Go on tell me something, anything! Keep all your secrets if you must but talk to me...Tell me why you think 'we'... 'us' the ones who've remained behind where you left us, still living in our 'society' only *pretend* that it's normal, that it's *okay*?"

"It's all to do with the shallowness in the way people think I suppose. They've been subtly programmed to think the way they do, the propaganda machine today is so well hidden, so embedded into the very fabric of this excuse of a society, that most don't even see it anymore and yet they are told what to think, who to hate, what is acceptable and what isn't. Take the homeless, the people using this place, we're only visible when it suits their agenda, you wouldn't believe the things that people do to us! Being spat at or having abuse hurled at you is nothing, I've heard tales here from guys who've been pissed on, while they've been sleeping in shop doorways or worse still dragged-up off the floor and had the shit kicked out of them! Stuff like that's usually done by drunks on their way home after a night out, but not always, it's a fun way to round off your night out for some arseholes apparently!
"There's a lad sat in there now, Matty we call him, his real name is Graham Spencer, formerly Leading Seaman Spencer a decorated Royal Navy veteran, they call him Matty as he was a matelot. He served in The Falklands, saw his mates burnt alive, got discharged when he wasn't functional anymore and came home to his wife and kids. But it wasn't Graham who came home, he's still on that burning ship that he's unable to leave, Matty is just a ghost, a thing that looks like him, but is no more than an empty shell.

"Vinnie was a para, another Falklands victim, decorated too, he found that shooting young Argie conscripts wasn't what he'd signed up for. He let a load of them get away and decked his CO when he challenged him, didn't go down too well for him, that act of humanity didn't. I could go on, the middle management guy who got behind on his payments, lost his home and his family trying to live beyond his means, the gamblers, the drunks the addicts...

"It's all down to the lack of decency in society… Just look how many Bookies there are on any high street today, you see their adverts everywhere on every screen to, well if you look at them. That gadget of yours, you can play poker, roulette and bet on anything with any number of their gambling apps, for shit like that you'd have to have gone to a casino a few years back.
"It's all going to hell, gone to hell…"

He stopped abruptly and looked at her for a long moment, seemingly thinking. In truth he was trying to decide what to make of this cocky and persistent black woman, persistent yes but also underneath all her performing, he could sense that she was fundamentally a warm and kindly person. After a little while he shrugged, apparently having decided he'd said enough to her,

He abruptly asked her, "Do you like poetry?" She nodded, a little taken aback,
"Love it. I love all forms of writing, I do a lot myself, hence the job! Also reading, anything and everything, I was a total bookworm as a kid, devouring literature in all of its forms, fiction, fact, biographies, you name it! My degree is in English Language. When I was at school I had a nickname, they called me *'Jen-the-pen'*…she stopped, pulled-up in mid-flow, with a sense of déjà vu before realising she'd sat at a nearby table with Harry having a very similar conversation the day before. She also realised that Bill was doing precisely what she was meant to be doing… getting her to talk, *to open up!* Clever old fucker, she thought as a wry smile crept across her lips…

He nodded slightly as if he knew what she was thinking and she saw a mirror of her own smile through the tangle of whiskers on his lips… Without further ado he started to recite a poem:

The long walk in the autumn sun
Past graves all with names chiselled upon
Words of those who passed this way
But now have ended their short stay.

Our dreams I carry in my arms
In you she did not come to harm
Heavy white casket you weigh though less
Than the weight that on my heart does press.

The church that's stood for centuries
Does in her womb encompass me
I feel the peaceful calm embrace
Of this still and holy place

A blanket of love wraps me around
From all the friends who somehow found
The time to come and be with us
Through our ordeal it really does
Give us strength in our time of need
And they are truly friends indeed

We sing to God of the Son He gave
Before we stand at the tiny grave
Ashes to ashes and dust to dust
This is the way we all go must
The fullness of time though it should take
Before any of us this appointment make

Our dreams and our hopes are now shattered all
As gently rose petals onto the coffin fall
Slowly begin people to drift away
But here part of us will always stay
A piece of our heart as if carved by knife
That we will miss for the rest of our life.

Jenny wiped a tear from her eye,
"That's so beautiful and deeply moving too... I've never heard it before, it really touched my heart... no rather, I'd say that it connected me with the heart of someone's that was broken. It conveyed so intimately how they were feeling, transmitted a little shard of their pain right into my own heart. Who wrote it?"
"Me, I wrote it. You have quite a way with words yourself Jenny." She wiped her eyes, sniffling. He had used her name! Progress! Despite feeling chuffed, she kept it to herself remaining silent for a minute or so as she looked anew at this enigmatic old man sitting across from her. Her reply when it came was blunt, straight to the point.
"You lost a child?"
"I lost two, err... well that is two as babies... *stillborn* they called it. An appropriate medical term I guess, a way to aptly describe the perfectly formed little human being that you

encounter when you're taking your first look at them, knowing that it will also be the last look you'll ever have of them as you hold your dead child in your arms. She doesn't cry or move of course, she's silent and still, so yeah… she's definitely *still-born!* She'd already stopped moving before she entered the outside world and yet somehow the term doesn't quite adequately encapsulate all of that love and emotion that's been invested in her by both of you during the time you'd spent with her though somehow does it? That time when she was there with you, alive inside her mother's womb, when you could feel her moving around in there… not really adequate is it somehow? Nor does it deal with the devastation of it, the overwhelming, debilitating and tragic sadness of it all?"

"No. There could never be a name or a word anyone could think of that would give it adequate meaning, nothing could ever do that… If there was such a word, no one would ever be able to bring themselves to speak it out loud anyway, would they?
"I'm so sorry for your loss, or rather your losses. Did you have more children? That survived?" He held up a finger in response for a moment and waved his hand aside…

"Nah, that's off piste… Like another one? Another poem?" She nodded. He launched straight into it…

Lauren never saw the light of day
She never learnt to laugh and play
The only life she ever knew
Was warm and safe inside of you

And though we never felt her touch
We really loved her oh so much
For in our dreams her life was real
Her little kicks we both could feel

We will forever ask oh why, oh why
Did we not hear your new-born cry?
We only beheld your beautiful face
In death's peaceful and cold embrace

And though we must spend this life apart
We will always hold you in our hearts
So be happy and with the angels play
Until we are together again one day

Retaining her composure this time she said,
"One of yours again?" He nodded,
"But this might intrigue you... I wrote it two days *before* my second daughter was... well, when she died at birth, was *stillborn*. It was a premonition of what was to come!"
"Surely it could simply have arisen out of you knowing what had happened the first time around, when you lost your first daughter?"
He just nodded briefly as he looked upwards towards the heavens,
"Hmmm... Maybe... I'd been told all through the pregnancy that *'lightning never strikes twice'*, don't you worry, everything will be fine, you have a son who was born perfectly normally'..." Jen pretended to scribble in an imaginary notebook on the table top! Saying as if to herself...
"...and he revealed that he has at least *one* surviving son..."
"Okay yeah I did, we went on to have two more kids that survived, another boy and a girl. Happy now?"

They laughed together... after a little while she asked him,
"So you believe in premonitions, in omens, in precognition?"
"I know them to be fact."
"But how can you say that?"
"How can you not? There's endless information on the subject and from a multitude of wide ranging samples taken from a great many people's testimonies, from all sorts of people, from very different walks of life. You must know this stuff, you said that you read a lot didn't you?"
"Yeah, for sure but they're all anecdotal and are explainable in other ways." He shook his head,
"That in my opinion is just what we're expected to believe, trained to accept, what *they* want us to believe.
"When we're children we live in a world of awe and wonder of everything as we first experience it all, it's new and exciting for us then, we see things, feel things differently to the grown-ups! They tell us that what we're saying is nonsense when we tell

them the things we see and what we think about them, they dismiss them as being no more than silly childish fantasies! We are crestfallen by their response, so we begin to question what we know to be real! That's the start of them desensitising us, of cutting us off from our higher powers, from our intuition, our inner knowledge! They seek to mould us into good little citizens, ones just like them, one's with the same closed minds as them, unable to think and see for themselves! And we let it happen, well most of us do, nearly all of us do... we allow them to steer us into becoming jaded and disillusioned exactly as they have become, we just... *grow-up*! There's only a tiny number of us who refuse to do as we are told and cling onto what we know to be true, these are often the ones who become artists, the creators and all the other people we then revere as geniuses! It's no coincidence that we claim genius is next to madness!"

"Ah so... You refer to... *'Them!'* It's what *they* want us to believe! Those terrible people... <u>*them*</u>*!* So you like conspiracy theories then?"
He shook his head and replied sadly,

"You know, the closed-mind is their greatest ally, you can bleat out all of your *baa-baa'd* ovine clichés and as many rebuttals as you like, but I can tell that you're not really *that* simple! You're not a person to be so easily tricked, you're not anybody's fool so you must be just *pretending* to accept it all, going along with it so that you can fit-in! Do you see it now? You pretend it's normal, pretend that *you're* normal, so that you can make out that you're one of them, get along with them and live with them in their delusional life, in this idiotic pretence you claim to be a society!
"Can you honestly tell me, hand on heart, that when you wake up from a nightmare into darkness, in the middle of the night... that you aren't just a little bit scared that the Obeah-man might be coming for you?"
She laughed saying in her over-accented voice...
"*Wha'd you know 'bout de Obeah man boy*?" She shook her head knowingly, sighed gently, then went on...
"Okay but what evidence do you have for me?"

"With this stuff, you have to learn to listen here, to this *(he patted his chest over his heart)* not here with this *(he tapped a finger to his forehead)*."

"Look at all the prophets, and soothsayers! I know you can say, 'what about that infinite number of monkeys typing-out the works of Shakespeare'... *personally I think they did write some of his crap!* ...but there's way more to everything than that. We barely understand what time itself is, it's a mystery and it's all wrapped up in the very existence of everything there is! They now refer to it as 'Space-time'! And for very good reasons as one is completely dependent upon the other, they are interdependent... no it's truer to say that they are one and the same thing."

"It's my belief and I have to say that it's not a new thought, many people have written books on the subject, so it's not my own idea... that we are connected to more than this existence we currently reside within, that we have contact with a being or personality... one that is all of our own and no, not God as such or any other divinity, but a being who is part of each of us, in our heads if you like, part of our mind but who also dwells, exists, on a higher plane, is outside of and above this one upon which we find ourselves... they walk with feet less clay-leaden...

"In their realm they're not fixed rigidly in space and time as we are, slavishly plodding our way along a linear track from *a* to *b*, minute by next minute, year by year, from birth to death... they can 'be' in any time, back to before we were born and also ahead of us and even after we have died, they can steer us, guide us, as they already know what is coming." She is listening intently now and responds,

"So this is a rationale to explain the reasoning behind deja-vu, why people have turned back at the airport's boarding gate, deciding not to take a flight... not to get on a plane that then plunges into the ocean on its flight? Or not to get on a train, or to take a different route to work from the one they usually take on the day there is a pile-up on the motorway? But if it was true, then why didn't all the people who *did die* in the pile-up or who did board the plane that crashed, do likewise?"

He smiled as he replied, "Since they didn't hear the voice, they weren't able to hear it, so they can't heed it, or they can but chose to ignore it, they just think it's some *silly nonsense* like the things they thought as a kid that they were told by their parents to ignore? They listen to so much of the jabbering of their own *monkey-mind*, they can't hear the words of their higher-self, they're drowned out by all the drivel, nonsense and sensory overload that you are bombarded with every waking second of your lives, not least from those bloody things!" He pointed accusingly at Jenny's iPhone sat on the table.

"So you're saying we all have this *companion*? A *mental* companion, a being who is always with us, there in our heads, like a type of Guardian Angel? But most of us can no longer hear them, or that we just chose to ignore them and their ideas, or their words or are they thoughts? That they are drowned out, are just lost in amongst all the other jumble?"

"Yes, precisely so. But I wouldn't limit their presence to being 'in our heads' as such, maybe in another dimension?" She leant back, pondering on what he'd said, it had so much resonance with the type of thinking her mum told her of, that she felt it would be disrespectful to her to merely dismiss it all as mere mumbo-jumbo! She added,

"It would neatly explain how some people claim to have past-life memories too I guess?" He nodded and went on,

"How many times have you experienced deja-vu? That strangest of feelings you experience when you're suddenly certain you have been somewhere already, or have seen something or met someone before... isn't it as if a window was momentarily opened, one you weren't even aware was there but one that you can see through clearly, albeit only for that instant before it shuts again? That feeling you have as it is when you're unable to cling onto a fleeting memory of a dream, that it shuts itself down so quickly... It shuts because it's *you* looking through it... to your rational mind it's unbelievable anyway, so you are unable to even consider for a moment that it is real... because the programming from your childhood keeps telling you it can't be so!

"More often it's just that you feel something less tangible, you sense that you have had the very same experience you are feeling in that moment, in the now... before ...that it has all happened before? That's because all of that is true, you have had the experiences already, or rather is it that at that moment you are accessing your higher self's experiences, or that you are in-tune with them momentarily, connected with them and therefore able to share their vision that extends beyond that which is normally accessible... into your future!"

"Very deep..." Jenny said with a sigh. She decided to change tack while he was lost in his thoughts...
"You intimated that you had lost another child, you said something about losing two daughters to stillbirth but went on to say, *'well that is two as babies!'* He looked up at her, discarding whatever he had been lost in thought over...
"Sharp aren't you? Work as an interrogator previously?" He smiled and she chuckled,
"My job, ferret around until I find the truth!"
"Sorry, but you're back into personal details..." He paused, had he choked-up she wondered. He had! He brushed a tear from his eye, she jumped in...
"I'm so very sorry to pry, I can see how upset I've made you. You lost one of your kids as an adult?" He nodded. She let the silence grow for a while then said,

"That must be terribly hard to bear, I truly am sorry..." She reached over and rested her hand on his forearm, he made no attempt to resist accepting her offered gesture of comfort. A moment or two later he looked up and freely offered...
"My only surviving daughter was killed in an accident on the motorway. She was the middle one but somehow she was always my baby..." Jenny sighed sympathetically as she said,
"Understandable that she would seem to be so much more precious, that she'd always and forever be daddy's girl."

Something changed in Bill's demeanour, she saw it wash over him like a shadow, the light that had seemed to appear on his face was lost once more to a darkness... even his shoulders sagged...
"Are you okay Bill?" She tentatively enquired, afraid she was going to lose him.

He leant back a little and raised his eyes up to meet hers, his face seeming to lighten a little… then finding a tangent he could go of on he said,

"Nice little car that is. How long 'ave you 'ad 'er?"

Relieved that he'd re-engaged with her, albeit steering her away from talking about what she wanted to, she went along with him,

"Seems like forever, but I guess it'll be about ten years or so?"

"Been re-built I'm guessing, in way too good nick t'be original. 'M' reg'll mek it, what 1976?" She nodded, he knew about cars she noted mentally…

"So she's gorra fifteen hundred Triumph engine then, one out'a their Spitfire model instead o'th'old original Austin 'A' Series twelve-seventy-five motor, typical BMC muckin'bout. A lorra folks don'like them big black bumpers she 'as, so good on ya, good t'see y's not replaced 'em. Car should be as it were built, not mucked about wi."

"What you mean that aftermarket kits are readily available to replace them with lookalike *non-original* chrome bumpers? Surely not?" She smirked playfully at him,

"Eh? Wha'? Y'little bugger…" She laughed merrily,

"I have to say though, you know your cars too Bill! I'm impressed. I find the fifteen hundred to be a lot less revvy than the twelve-seventy-five, it's got a lot more torque too, more gutsy, she pulls like a tractor!"

"Okay, okay, I gets it! Y're a motor-ead! Y've driven both then?"

"Oh yes, one of my brothers had one back in the day, in the 80's when he was young, wild and single!" To amuse him she added,

"Of course it was the colour that made me buy her! Tahiti blue metallic!" She twiddled her near-enough-a-match, blue painted finger nails in front of him. A deliberate tactic to make herself seem a little bit more *girly?* It failed…

"Right… and you take it to a *nice man* to service it and balance the twin SU's too?"

"Why of course, I haven't a clue how you'd even open that lid thingy up at the front, you know to get at the engine! Then the thought of all that dirty oil on my lovely manicured hands!" He shook his head a little, the look of amusement was fading fast, so she changed tack,

"My Dad was a mechanic, had his own place, it was him who rebuilt the Midget for me. Why she's so precious to me. I grew up passing him spanners, I was more familiar with spanners than

dolls... ring spanners, open-ended, adjustables, grease guns, oil cans, drain plugs!!"
Realising that she was over playing this, she jumped in with a direct question,
"Were you into classic cars yourself then Bill? What did you run?"

He looked at her, giving her a long penetrating look, before huffing gently. He gave a little shake of his head before he sat back-up abruptly... 'Shit' she thought, he's for wrapping this up, right now! A little stumblingly she changed tack herself,
"Anyhow, erm... enough of cars! We've sat chatting here for ages and never got around to what I really wanted you to tell me about! I mean, don't get me wrong it's fascinating getting to know about you, but what I want, what I asked you to give me was the lowdown, the inside story about The Folks Factory.
"You made it perfectly clear that you weren't going to talk about yourself, I'm sure it would make a great story, but to be honest it's not the angle I'm looking for on this one."

The old man looked at her, she could see him weighing her up, he certainly was a wily old fox... This could go either way she thought, as she held her tongue and waited...

"Okay then, so long as we're clear 'bout that! I don't mind telling you about the human refuse that's being swept-up all over town and dumped here!"
"Oh Bill that's a terrible way to describe Harry's project!"
"Not far from the truth though is it? If you take off the rose tinted glasses for a moment and replace them with *shit-tinted* ones, nay... just open your eyes and try looking closely at the reality of it will be sufficient! What else are they doing but clearing the homeless off the streets, removing the stain?"
"But didn't you intimate that *they* wanted the homeless on view to keep the rest of us with our noses to the grindstone?"
"Oh yes, there's duality in their approach for sure, but if you can get some of the dross back to being productive? I mean there'll always be some homeless, plus at least here you can showcase them, have them here in a shop window?"

"Okay, but what type of people are they?"

"They're us. People, ordinary people like you, like you could be at any rate, like any of you could be!

"For starters, they're men in the main, they do much better at getting the women into their program and off the streets, I mean you've got to be tough to survive out there as a bloke, never mind as a woman, so they're more willing! There is a few old birds out there, but they're as hard as nails and they're usually so barking mad that no-one in their right minds would have a go at them!

"Of course there's a lot more help for women, to avoid them getting dumped out there on the streets in the first place, refuges and charities and agencies put a lot more into helping women and rightly so.

"Most of the guys are broken, they're seriously damaged goods. Let's face it this excuse for a society is well equipped with methods of breaking people!

"Some have got lost in alcohol, isn't that how it gets described, a great servant but a terrible master? Or in many cases it's drug abuse and not necessarily the illegal type, over prescribing has played its part too, doctors who only have the resources to try to cure the mental ailments of a sick and damaged society with a quick-fix prescription of a nice and cheap little pill!

"Then there's all the money issues people struggle with, not being able to pay their bills, getting into debt, losing their jobs and finding the safety net they thought they'd been paying into all their lives wasn't there for them after all!

"The breakdown of a relationship or marriage often leads to it being the man who has to leave the home, or who is shoved-out one way or another, as all of these problems that can occur, often lead to domestic violence, as the desperate fucker starts hitting out at the nearest person he can find!

"Of course all of these factors can often lead back to the earlier ones I mentioned… they can turn a guy to drink! A vicious circle isn't it? Where else is there to go, who is there to turn to for so many of us?

"Many of you folks scorn us, you'll say… *'I'm not giving one of them any money! They'd only spend it on alcohol!'* Fine, it's your money! But think for a moment what *you* might spend it on, if you found yourself out there, so lost that you were begging for a few coins, what refuge would you seek?"

"That's just for starters... on top of that you have gambling addiction as a major issue for many of them, these poor bastards have literally *lost* everything! That includes their wives, their kids, their family, their jobs and worst of all their self-respect!
"Look at the way gambling has taken hold of society today, there's gambling shops here on every high street in the land, next door to so many empty units and the charity shops you see everywhere. It's an insidious poison that has been knowingly allowed to seep into the beating heart of society. They're allowed to advertise all over the media, they're even available for you to gamble with on your stupid bloody gadgets! Your precious iPhone is now quite capable of stripping you of all of your money as well as your dignity and humanity."

"Then on top of and as well as all of these factors there's mental health problems, there's guys suffering from the usual depression, caused by any or all of what I've already said about, but also there's serious mental illness, real psychological disorders such as bipolar and schizophrenia that don't get treated properly or are fobbed off with medication and *care in the community*... that's an oxymoron if ever there was one! We used to have specialist homes, or mental hospitals where people who aren't equipped to deal with the rigours of our brutal society were shielded and given shelter. Yes, for sure their freedoms might well have been somewhat curtailed, but they were safe, they were looked after, they felt that they belonged where they were in most cases. They'd often be given jobs to do, so that they felt of value, that they were able to give something back to their community. But today? What happens to them now? So many of them are lost, bemused and unable to cope and they're drowning in a community that simply *doesn't care!*
"There was even an national organisation called Remploy that gave jobs to disabled people, somewhere that they could turn up for work and do a job, sure it might be something small and fairly inconsequential, but in doing it they were allowed to have that wonderful work ethic we're told we all should have! They loved their job, it gave them meaning and purpose and allowed them to feel of value. So what happened to this amazing idea? Scrapped! That's what happened! Scrapped because it *cost too much*, because the mean spirited bean counting bastards decided that it was too expensive to get these *retards* to make things that could be sourced for half the price from the Far East! They made

the excuse that it was demeaning for people to work for less than the National Minimum Wage, doing meaningless work, that it amounted to exploitation!

"If ever there was an illustration of Oscar Wilde's condemnation of this vileness... *'They know the price of everything and the value of nothing!'* Then that was it!
"The most idiotic thing about their twisted thinking is that it isn't even cost effective! Today it costs them vastly more than it did then, as underfunded agencies scrabble around with next to no resources, trying in vain to pick up the wreckage of the lives of the people they threw out of a job, in addition to all the people that were thrown out of the mightily built Victorian Mental Hospitals, Institutions and communities... quickly demolished for housing estates or converted into luxury appartments... Their greed is endless, it has no limit! They have no moral compass as their Victorian predecessors had.

"On top of all of this there are ex-servicemen, sucked-in, lied-to, recruited, chewed-up and spat-out by The Army. Guys with PTSD who can be turned into a gibbering wreck or triggered into *attack mode* at the drop of a hat. The worst of them end up in prison of course, they are simply too violent to be allowed to be left out on the streets, again it costs them more to lock them up than it would to treat them, to deliver what they promised... that they would always look after them, see them right..."

Bill had become quite animated during his monologue, even using his hands and arms to express his exasperation at some points! Now as he finally fell silent, he leant forward once more and resting his elbows onto the table he put his head into his hands.

Jenny's reached her hand uncertainly, out towards him ... But as she did so, he began to stir, she pulled her hand back as he sat back and slowly shook his head as if amazed that he'd talked for so long...

Their eyes met once more and in the instant that they did she knew that the interview was over, she sensed his entire demeanour had changed after that little shake of the head. It was as if as he shook his head, he'd been thinking *what the hell am I doing*? Now he had shut down, like one of his earlier described mental windows being slammed shut, her brief view of him, her glimpse of how he might have been in his former life was lost to her again as he retreated into the hard shell of protection that was 'Bill.'

It was no surprise to her that he shuffled himself up off the bench, wearily dragged his backpack onto his shoulders and left without saying another word. She called after him, to his retreating back...
"Thank you Bill, I'm sorry if I upset you, will you talk some more with me, another time... tomorrow perhaps?" He was half a dozen yards away by now, heading towards the gates... he made no acknowledgment to her.

She sighed, what a surprise that had been! Yeah, she'd been thinking that there might've been a bit of a story here, well everyone had a story of some sort to tell for sure, but what a real human interest story the telling of that old guy's life would make? She was totally hooked, this was one that she had her teeth into now and like any hound worth its salt (should that be meat?) she was not going to be letting go of it now, she would seek out that girl Nat and find out all she'd managed to glean about this enigmatic old tramp. She felt sure that the glimpse she'd just had of who he really was, the details about him that she'd wheedled out of him had just scratched the surface, what a story he had to tell.

As Bill vanished through the gateway, she looked around to see Jimmy was strolling over towards her from Le Camionette de Café with a tray in his hand... carrying it waiter-style, up in the air on the flat of his palm! He fluidly rotated his wrist to bring the tray down and place it on the table in front of her, it had two coffees and a plate with three croissants on it.

"Thought you might need a decent brew after that muck y'ad there!" He nodded his head at the empty Costa cups. She laughed,
"Why thank you... *Jimmy?* Isn't it?" He smiled and held out his hand, which she took in hers and shook as she informed him,
"Jenny Stainton... fearless reporter and investigative journalist for The Gazette.... for sure it may only be our local rag... but

today The Gazette… tomorrow… *the world!"* His hand was slender and his skin surprisingly smooth and soft although thankfully he had a moderately firm and reassuring grip she noted… *she hated the way in which some people offered her their hand so that it felt like you were holding a dead fish!*

"Now't wrong with 'avin ambition eh luv? I saw yon ol'fella storm off in an'uff jus'now, an' thought as yer may like a fresh coffee… mebee a natter? If yer's got time? Plus it's me fag break! Our 'Chelle'd skin me alive if I'ad a fag anywhere near 'er precious camionette! I mean… fuckin' *camionette?* Oops… pardon me *French*! All o'that pretendin' to be Froggies! Me, well… I were 'appy wi' me own name of *Coffee Truck!"* He placed a cigarette between his lips and went to light it, but hesitated and looked across at Jenny…
"Oh sorry luv, shoulda asked ya? D' y'mind? D' y'wan one?…"
"I'm not bothered, you light-up…" Jenny intervened before he could finish. She detested cigarette smoke, but hey! News-hounds can't be over sensitive or too picky!

He clicked the lighter and took a deep drag, exhaled the smoke slowly, clearly enthralled by the loving embrace of his nicotine habit. He glanced down at the glowing tip of the white tube of death *(as Jenny saw it!)* and commented…
"I know… I know! 'Chelle never shuts up 'bout it either! She sneaks one in though now and then 'ersel, mostly when she's 'ad a scoop or three!"
"Harry mentioned that when you first came here, took up this pitch? Is that the correct way to describe it?" He nodded. "That you were using the same old Citroen van, but that it was in a dilapidated condition back then?"
"Yeah, it were a right ol'shed! Mind you, this place were a tip an'all so she fitted in alright back then! Now't like it is today, you couldn't see all these flags for all the trash an'shite piled up everywhere, it'd been used as a dump for donkeys! Mind you it were a good thing, stone flags like these… *sheesh!*… a few lads wi'a flat-bed'd 'adve 'ad the feckin' lot of away before y'could blink! Oh, sorry pardon me language!"
She waved dismissively,
"I've heard worse believe me!"
"Any'ow, as the place started to come together, Mister Armstrong comes over to me one day an'says, look Jimmy lad,

it's great 'ow yer's been 'ere right from the very start an'all, but see, thing is… now as we're getting things up and runnin' we 'as to portray a slightly more gentrified image! *Portray a slightly more gentrified image!* 'Ay 'e were a card were our Mister Armstrong!" Jenny interrupted him,
"Armstrong? As in Armstrong Mill, so who exactly was this guy?"
"Joss? No 'e weren't related or owt like that! 'E were the co-ordinator? Summit like that, some sorta go-between wi' the rich dude who purr-up all the dosh to do it all? 'E were in charge of everyone, builders, trades the lot!" Jenny thanked him for explaining and he went on,

"So any'ow Mister A, Joss like… says to me, Jimmy I'll make you a proposition… If you'll let me 'ave yer old H-van… see 'e knew all about old cars and stuff and about the ol' Citroen y'see? 'E drove a proper old fashioned car 'iself, one wi' them great big 'eadlights!… yeah 'e says, you let me 'take your van and I'll 'ave 'er renovated, restored to 'er former glory like…and then some! If I do that, will yers stay put on'ere right through till we're up an'running? Be 'ere for the grand opening! I'll hire a suitable van for yers while this old girls 'avein her make-over like!" He paused to take a sip of coffee and the inevitable drag on his *ciggie…*
"So I'm like okay… so were's the catch like? 'An'ow much is all this gonna cost me? No, no…no! 'E says… it won't cost you a penny son, see I 'olds the purse strings to a pot o'money size of as you wouldn't believe! I can authorise anything I think… well that I think will be beneficial to the project, and I think '*a lovely old bijou Citroen coffee van… Le Camionette de Café as we'll call it would be an asset I can easily justify… not that I'll ever have to!'* Is what 'e says an 'ow 'e put it!

"So once 'es told me all that… I'm like… yeah man! I mean it were an offer as I couldn't refuse weren'it?" He finished his ciggie and stubbed it out, discarding it in the Costa coffee cup and then stacking it into the other one, commenting, as he drained his own coffee,
"All they're fit for is an ashtray!…" He picked up a croissant and started to eat it,

"You should 'ave one, these are really good! I 'as them specially baked for me, fresh every day... at the Lidl!" He laughed as he chomped on the pastry.

Jenny smiled at him and picked up a croissant as she thought, good instincts girl, there's another little story here waiting to be told! She took a bite then thinking along the lines of fleshing out this *little story*, she asked,
"So how did you originally come by the Citroen?"
"Ah, that's a whole 'nother story! Me and 'Chelle bought her over in France, hence the left hand drive. We'd both been working for a few years by then, normal run-o'the mill jobs like, she were a secretary for some posh legal firm and I were on the production line at Ford 'Alewood's, makin' posh cars! Jaguars no less! We was savin'up for a deposit for an'ouse, y'know? But we looked around at all of us mates, busy 'avin kids an' mortgagin' up their lives... seemed like they was chainin' themselves down? Y'know? Boxin' up their dreams for later, to be 'ad in maybe twenny-year or so, if they lived that long... like once the kids 'as fucked-off... Oops, sorry again luv! So we just took us savin's..."

"...and *fucked-off to France*?" Jenny intervened! Jimmy roared as he lit another cigarette,
"I could tell you was alright girl! Yeah we decided to buy the van over there, in France like, so as to get us'sel's a left 'ooker like, safer for drivin' over there see but mainly 'cos you could get vans so much cheaper over there... well you could back then, this is all donkey's ago now... must be best part o'fifteen year back now?
"We'd no idea wha' we was lookin' for, certainly not that ol'thing there! She were feckin ol'when we bought it back then! But we fell in love wi'er!"
"So how far did you get?"
"Pretty much everywhere! Down through France, Spain, Italy, then ferry to Greece, Turkey..."
"Oh my God! How long were you away?"
"Five, six years it'd be? I'm 'opeless wi' time and dates like! 'Ave to ask 'Chelle, she's gorr'an'ead like a calendar!"
"And the old van kept going all that time?"
"Yep! Never let us down once! She was the best investment we ever made! She brought us all the way back 'ome too! There

were now't for us left back in The Pool anymore, it'd all moved-on like and without us bein' a part of it an all, so we ended up 'ere, quite by chance really. We'd learn't the 'ard way not to set up us stall just anywhere! Some o'them locals… if they got the idea yers was after their trade…" He ran his finger dramatically across his throat!

"So the van always had the side serving hatch?"

"Oh yeah…" He was stopped short by a screeched shout…

"*Oi! Buggerlugs!* Get y'scrawny arse back over 'ere! Can't you see this queue of thirsty punters?" He looked behind, over his shoulder,

"Ah shit! Sorry luv, duty calls! Lovely chattin' to ya!" With that he grabbed the empty Costa cups and the tin mugs they'd been using and darted back calling out in his most charming voice…

"I'm coming my angel…."

Jenny smiled, another story recorded on her phone sat innocently there on the table! That made two stories today! Not bad and it wasn't even lunchtime, thinking of food she picked up the remaining croissant and munched on it as she walked back to her car.

CHAPTER TEN

Bill was annoyed with himself. No, more accurately he was angry, bloody furious that he had let his vanity allow him to let that bloody reporter interrogate him! She was no hack, no local paper amateur, no that woman was clever, cunning even in the way that she had put him at ease, had teased-out of him things he didn't even want to remember himself!

That's it! He declared to himself! I'm saying nowt to anyone else from now on, ever again! That life's gone, it's all behind me! Forgotten! Dredging down into all that muck, stirring the shit up, it'll only confuse me again... Pull me back down into that mire! He was unable to stop a comparison being drawn by part of his mind to this staunch mental proclamation and the tantrums he'd regularly thrown as a kid when... *never again!* ...had featured regularly in his enraged rantings! *'I'll never speak to you again! I'll never sail that stupid boat again... I hate it!'* Etcetera-etcetera...

A sharp pain stabbed at his stomach as he passed through the old factory gates, he grabbed at it and was nearly bent double by its ferocity! Leaning with one hand on the gates to hold himself up, he tried to gather himself together... *'Fuck! That hurts!'* He muttered to himself... A disembodied voice asked if he was alright, he told it to fuck-off then inadequately tried to apologise in mime using the free hand that wasn't clutching at his stomach!

The pain eased after a minute or two and he let himself slide down the wall just outside the gates, to end up sitting and leaning against it through his backpack. He felt like shit. The hangover was still going strong, the stomping feet and giant bass drum of his resident marching band were busily booming-out their steady rhythm in his splitting head.

Someone placed a pound coin into his hand which he realised had been lying open on his thigh... it made him smile, then chuckle, as he looked down at the multi-sided gold & silver-*ish* coloured coin as it lay there in his palm, he registered that it was a very new and shiny pound coin he had there siting on his filthy woollen mitt! As he stared down at it, it seemed to swim a little before his poorly focussed eyes, that in reality could do little more than make out that it was a pound coin, but in his befuddled mind he could clearly see The Queen's face that was embossed on it and that she was looking up at him! Now she was smiling at him! That made him laugh a little, then he was laughing like a lunatic, with tears streaming down his face as suddenly he felt a connection with the person who'd placed the pound coin in his hand, the person who had magically introduced him to The Queen!

For a moment it was as if he was looking down at himself through their eyes... he was looking down at the bedraggled, dirty mess of humanity that was propped-up against the tall stone wall, pitying the pathetic wreckage they saw, remnants of what had once been a man, but now more resembled a discarded sack of rubbish dumped out onto the ground. Looked-like?... Whatever he looked like, that person had seen through it and recognised the essence of a fellow human being.

Now looking down at the coin, The Queen spoke up to him... *'Arise Sir Bill of The Lost and take up your place once more within my realm.'* What the fuck?

Some little time later, he found he'd somehow got himself back up onto his feet, he stood for a moment turned around with his palms placed flat against the wall that he was now stood facing, leaning his weight onto them, just breathing and letting his head settle down some, allow the dizziness to subside a bit.

He smirked dismissively at the little dip into insanity he'd just experienced! I mean! He was a staunch Republican at heart... not that his opinion mattered a toss like... but he'd abolish the bloody monarchy in a heartbeat if it was up to him! Bloody over-privileged scroungers that they were! But it had, he found himself having to acknowledge, still been rather nice of dear old Lizzie to take time out of her busy schedule of sponging off us, to go to the trouble of appearing to him like that and to address him personally and directly, albeit through her coinage!

He'd never held any animosity towards her personally, not as an individual, all she'd ever done was simply play the role she was born into, plus things were so much different too, way back in 1952 when the old king died, he never forgot that she had her coronation the year after that, the year of one of his brother's birth, he'd had the Coronation cup they'd given to his mother back then with the new queen's picture on it ever since!

Well he'd *had* the cup! He wondered where it was now. He tried to recall the last time he could remember seeing it, badly glued together as it had been at that point in time, from the several pieces it had ended up in... he couldn't even recall how it had got broken... after all his two younger brothers and him had been clumsy kids...

He turned around letting his backpack rest against the wall as he pondered his next move. One thing was for sure, there was no way he would get very far in his current state! The mob with the big drum had marched off somewhat! It was a little further away now, but his legs felt like jelly. Was this how it would end for him he pondered glumly? It was inevitable he supposed that sooner or later his body would end up failing him, poorly nourished and abused as it was... not to mention so far past its sell-by-date too! That was three-score years and ten wasn't it? Well I must be past that by now! According to The Bible's declaration it was the 'Best Before Date' if nothing else! He was what... Was it seventy-two? Or seventy three now?

He thought for a moment of calculating back from the current year... what was it now? ...but very quickly accepted that he simply *couldn't be arsed* working it out!

The pain in his stomach had eased somewhat. What was that all about he wondered? *Maybe it has something to with swigging three-quarters of a litre of neat Bourbon perhaps*? The helpful reply came back from the voice of one of his many and ever present internal critics. They did have a point, he had to concede.

Without making a conscious decision he found himself following the tall wall using his left hand for support, in this manner he worked his way all the way along to where it ended at the carpark by the client's entrance to The Factory. It was an entirely logical decision however it had been made, as he desperately needed help and there was only one place where that help would be readily forthcoming...

CHAPTER ELEVEN

He is floating in a cloud…
No, it is a sea of the softest downy feathers…
He becomes aware of voices drifting down to him…
He recognises the voices…
They became clearer…
He hears a voice, what is it saying…
It's Harry's voice…. "How's the old fella doing?"
Now a woman's voice… "He's sleeping, but he still has a fever, it's eased a little from what it was overnight, so I think it's most probably peaked at any rate."
"Was he injured?" She laughs… it is not a joyous laugh however, it is more of a sardonic one really… as she replies,
"No I checked him all over for any visible wounds, he was still quite drunk from the previous night! He reeked of whisky! No I think this one's wounds are all on the inside! I think he probably has a stomach ulcer, from the way he was clutching at his belly. Would you look at the man though? Taking off that great big old coat of his and what are best described as his layers of rags and he's nothing but skin and bone, it's a crying shame that anybody should come to this!"

"I know that all too well nurse! He's not the only one either, as you of all people know only too well, a lot of our guests are in similar states, or worse despite all the help we try to give them.

"Aye, y'know though there's one thing I will say about old Bill, he makes some effort to do what he can towards looking after himself! Yes I know that contradicts what I just said and swilling gut-rot whisky isn't exactly looking after yourself for sure! But bodily, hygiene-wise… well take his feet, they were a big surprise to me, after seeing the horrendous state some of these old lads let them get into! You wouldn't believe how I've had to cut away their boots… Oh My God… the unholy mess you can come across!"

She shook her head, then went on,
"Aye well, no… Bill's toenails were kept short and his feet were as clean as a whistle! Decent boots too and socks that didn't run off on their own when I took them off!" She chuckled. Harry replied,

"I do know he's one of the few who makes use of our showers and washrooms, so many of them will happily come in and take the food and drink we offer, but getting them to just pass through the doors into the washrooms... it's like they were the gateway to a bloody concentration camp with *Waschen Macht Frei*! Written over the doorway!"
They laughed together...

Someone dabs a cool, damp cloth on his forehead, it is soothing, he smiles and opens his eyes, but is unable to say anything,
"Ah see he's back in the land of the living!" The woman's voice rings out. He tries to raise a hand but finds it to be way too much effort right now, it seems that it has become incredibly heavy for some reason... he lets it fall back onto the bed with a little groan. The nurse(?)'s voice drifts down to him,

"You rest up Billy my lad! You've had a fever and you need to stay still and keep lying on your back too as you've an IV in... a drip feed going into your vein... Look, follow my hand... You see? It's only a saline and glucose solution, nothing to worry about my love. We're not exterminating you... Well, not yet!"

Bill smiles again but then feels himself sinking back into the darkness, he lets it take him, swallow him down into its inky embrace...

It seemed that he had only just closed his eyes when he awoke again! There were people all around him, the air was cold and wet! He was outside. He was on the ground.

Someone took his left arm and laid it out straight from his shoulder, then he felt himself being rolled onto his side, his leg was being brought up and a hand was resting on his shoulder as a reassuring voice was speaking to him... He could make no sense of their words, but knew that they were soothing, that the person was comforting him... He recognised her voice but was unable to place it. He could see black tarmac right up next to his face, make out the individual pieces of stone embedded into its shiny black surface...

There is a commotion now, hands are upon him, faces peer at him, someone pulls his eyelid back, shines a torch into his eye.

He is lifted up…
He is lying on something as it glides away…
A hand is on his shoulder again…
The voice is saying something…
All the while his head hurts so much…
He coughs…
His mouth is wet and tastes salty…
It tastes of blood…
The gliding stops and then there is a clicking sound and he's being lifting and then bright lights, he's inside somewhere…
The whole place is moving now, he can hear the engine, feel the motion…
He figures out that he's in an ambulance…
He's been hurt…
He was in an alleyway on the floor…
How did he get there though?
Time passes away into the inky blackness of senselessness once more.

The voices again…
"Head injury, conscious but confused…
"Bleeding from the mouth, possible internal injuries…
"Broken rib or maybe two, here on the left…
"Fracture to ulna left arm…
"Extensive bruising all over…
"He's taken quite a beating he has…

Lights passing overhead…
A needle in his arm…
Blackness…

Someone is holding his wrist.
He opens his eyes and tries to speak, but merely croaks!
"Here, relax and I'll get you a drink of water…"
A nurse lifts a cup to his lips, he takes it from her and drains it,
"Can I have some more?" he manages to say hoarsely.
"Okay but just take sips will you, take sips for me? Please?"
She refills the plastic cup and hands it him, dutifully this time he takes a few sips before asking,
"Where am I? I mean I can see that I'm in a hospital but where and why? How did I get here?"

"You were found in a side street, well more of an alleyway they said, in the nightclub district of town in the early hours of Sunday morning, you'd been mugged and badly beaten and I mean really badly beaten! Someone gave you a proper going over! For a while it was touch and go whether you were going to make it. You're a very lucky man! Your Guardian Angel must have been looking out for you!"

"Pity they didn't get me away before I was mugged though!"
"Well small mercies and all that… just be glad you're still alive."
She went on,
"Now then, seeing as you're back with us, there's some medical information we really need to know, you've had a bleed on your brain, that was the most immediately life threatening injury! They had to drill a hole through your skull… NO! Don't try and feel where… oh for the love of God! They did that to relieve the pressure the blood was causing on your brain, then you lucky man, you were put into an induced coma where you lay blissfully unaware as they were busy resetting four broken ribs and your left arm. They put it in plaster and also stitched up a couple of nasty gashes by your mouth and over your eyebrow!"

"Oh my God! How long have I been here?"
"You were kept in a coma for six days until they were happy enough to risk allowing you to wake up."
"Six days? Bloody hell!"
"Oh but that's not the end of it my love! I said they'd *allow* you to wake up! But you were just so happy lying there that you didn't bother to wake up! It's been ten days since they took you off the sedative drip, left you to your own devices so to speak. That was the cause of growing concern that you may have suffered irreversible brain damage! You're actually booked in for a scan this afternoon. Listen, I know you'll have a million more questions you want to ask me, but I'm under strict orders to get the doctor to you if you wake-up. The moment you do!"
"Sure thing, no problem! I actually feel okay, you know…"

The nurse unclipped the board with his notes on, from the bottom of the bed and took a pen from her pocket,
"Just one thing before I go, as you had no I.D. at all on you, we have some rather important details that remain blank on your record! So… can you tell me your name and address, your date

of birth and who we should be letting know that you are here with us please? It'd be a wonder if nobodies been to The Police looking for you, unless you're from out of town and they're asking at the wrong Police Station maybe?"

"Sure, it's… err… I'm… err… *bloody hell*! I don't know!" He grabs his face between his hands as if squeezing his head may force the information out… it doesn't!

"Now then, stop doing that please and don't worry! It'll all come back to you soon enough I'm sure, a bit of amnesia's not at all uncommon with head injuries like the one you've had. Don't try and force yourself to remember anything for the time being, just lie back and try to relax and most of all *stay calm!* I'm going to fetch the doctor right now." She turns and leaves the room.

He is in a room on his own. A nice room with a big window and a view out over fields and trees…

Try and relax *she says*… he thinks… How the hell can I do that when I don't even know who I am? His thoughts are like raging madmen, charging around, flying about in his mind trying to access the simple basic information that he needs, things he *knows* that he knows and yet they are hitting a blank and impenetrable wall every time they go to pluck them from his memory!

The nurse is back.
But he's not in the side-room, this is a much smaller room. This isn't the hospital at all… this is the medical room at The Factory!

"So you're awake again, that's good. We've taken you off the drip now so we can get you sat up."
He is manhandled and with help from him, shuffled-up into a sitting position, the nurse carries on talking to him all the while,
"I'll get you some soup and some toast, do you think you can manage that?" He nods as his bewildered mind becomes fully awake and realises how hungry he is…
"Aye lass, I'm starving!"
"That's a good sign!" She bustles away…

He'd been dreaming! Reliving that time from years ago after he'd been mugged in the street after leaving that seedy nightclub he'd so often frequented, but was he mugged or attacked? But why? This is what came of being interrogated, of digging down

in all that muck that was lying there in the depths of his memory. The muck of his past life that he purposely left undisturbed. Why had he let that bloody woman stick her oar in and stir it all up like she had? This is what happens, this is the result!
But the dream was still vivid in his mind as it reconnected with that other moment in time when he had awakened after being totally out of it. The thought that had held his attention back then as he'd desperately delved into his mind trying to remember who he was loomed large again now... Who would want to do such a thing to him?

Of course, as he thinks back a little more with his memory intact today, he knows perfectly well who did it and precisely why. He shakes his head trying to stop himself from remembering his past life... telling himself over and over again... it's all gone now, I've left all of that behind! I'm not that person anymore! But he knows that his memories are now out of the cage he'd locked them in, not only are they loose once more but they're out to get him, he can feel them stirring down there in his subconscious mind, seething like a bed of lava that's becoming hotter and hotter, more and more volatile and sooner or later will inevitably erupt!

After a couple of bowls of soup and some bread and butter and then toast and jam, Bill was feeling a lot better. The nurse was a kindly woman in her fifties, bustlingly helpful and constantly chatting all the while that she was tidying-up the bed Bill was sat up in.
"We have the Doctor coming in to see you this morning, just to check you over, nothing to worry about! I'll bet it's some time since *you* had a check-up eh? He'll most likely give you something for your stomach too, how long have you had that pain?"
"It comes and goes."
"I'll bet it's worse when you drink spirits too?"
"Aye well... mebbee..."
"I think you probably have a stomach ulcer, you'll need to take whatever he prescribes for you and lay off the hard stuff Bill! Stick to a beer if you must have your drink. Try Guinness, they used to say that y'know, in their adverts... '*Guinness is good for you!*' well at least it has some calories in it, you really do need to put some meat on your bones!"

The Doctor came and went, confirming what the nurse had already said and suggesting that he took up the offer of a bed here at The Factory and accept any and all of the other help they could offer him
He thanked the doc and said he'd… *think about it*.
He also arranged for Bill to be collected and taken to the hospital for something he referred to as an echocardiogram.

He must have dozed off again because it was lunchtime the next time he became aware. One of the kitchen staff brought him a cheese sandwich through, he was one of the Romanians, he laughed as he gave him the tray with the food on it along with a mug of tea and a bowl of rice pudding and said,
"*Ha-ha-ha!*… today it is the royal treatment for our old Bill yes? Old man, look how he sits up in the bed to be waited on!" He made a silly bow and backed out of the room nearly colliding with the nurse as he did so, she shooed him away…

"Gerr-out-of-it yer silly beggar!" She cheerfully reproached him!
"You've another visitor on his way in to see you Bill. Now you behave yourself for once! Remember what the doctor just told you too, you don't want what's left of you to be found lying somewhere do you, a rotting corpse covered with maggots…"
"'As anyone told ya as you've gorra lovely bedside manner eh, nurse?"
"What's this about you bedside manner nurse? Not giving our esteemed guest a hard time are you?" Harry asked breezily as he wafted in through the open doorway!
"Aye well the old bugger needs someone to talk some sense into his obstinate head! He's a stubborn as an old mule!" She muttered before adding *a very stubborn*-stubborn old mule at that!" …as she left Harry alone with Bill.

Harry pulled up a chair,
"I caught the last bit of what Helen was saying, it's not far from the truth though is it Bill? Why don't you accept the help we can offer you, get yourself off the streets before it kills you? At least stay for a while? A day or two at the very least eh?"
"What's the point eh? It'll end the same any'ow, what's the difference hmm…?" He paused theatrically as if expecting an answer, but neither did he allow sufficient time for one to be offered before he went on…

"I'll tell ya what the difference is, it's me sat in t'woods in me shelter, lettin' go as I'm surrounded by nature, bein' a part of it as we're meant to be instead o'being mauled over in a bed in some rotten, stinkin' nursin' *'ome o'death*! Bein' looked after by underpaid, overworked and most often foreign folk as only do it as they can't find owt else as pays any better! Kept alive f'no fuckin reason at all! You'd not treat an animal in such a cruel way, inhuman you'd say, mekkin' 'em linger f'years an'years like t'livin' dead!" He set off coughing after this little diatribe…

Harry shook his head, he made an effort to hold down his rising irritation, after all the old bugger was talking sense in some ways, he *was* old, he *was* undernourished and he was ailing, in reality the stark truth was that he didn't have that much time left to look forward too! He tried to think of something positive to say! The best he could come up with was,

"Aye well, what you say is maybe true, it's a bleak enough perspective for sure, but eloquently put, as ever in your own inimitable style! That's the thing Bill, you still have your wits about you man! You are an exceptionally smart guy, yeah you're a depressed, down-at-heel-smart guy, but think how many people your age have dementia, are losing their mental faculties? Your mind remains razor sharp, but you focus on the negative rather than the positive too much that's all!"
Bill laughed!
"Look, you're a decent chap 'Arry, an' I get it that y'means well, I've always said as much, but you just don't get it! Y'actually think as there's 'ope, y'still believe that y'can mebbe mek a difference, but tha's jus pissin' into a feckin' 'urricane lad! Th'ole system stinks, s'rotten t'core, corrupt beyond redemption it is! When summit's that far gone y'ave to lob it out, bin-it-off, get rid o'it, destroy it once an'fer all, burn the fuckin' thing down t'ground. Time f'what yer tryin' t'do' ere's passed, it's too late, we've let'bastards get too far ahead. It'simple… right now they've won, see… an'we've lost. There's not even much fight left in most folk n'more, they're subdued, cowed, defeated. Distracted wi'all their feckin' sport, all their celebrity shite, they're all on them iPhones as they 'ave, can't pull their zombie faces away from 'em, infected they are wi' all t'internet garbage the bloody things is full off, wi' t'social media and photos flying' around there in cyberspace like snow in one o'them

fantasy globes! Yer 'ave twats an' twits twitterin' like as they're intellectuals, when all they are is morons... they twitter and tweet like fuckin' birds in a cage... no, more like fucking pigeons or chickens... mindless unthinking, useless cunts as won't do owt t'make the world they live in a better place!"

"Wow! Bill! You paint a flaming bleak picture of how things are! Maybe you're right, I mean, sometimes I think you could be and that's a fact! I often do feel like I'm banging my head against the wall, even to get simple things done. There are a lot of times when it does feel like the system is dead set against us here and what we're trying to do! And the army of nimby, whining... " He struggles for an appropriate word...
"*Feels* like it's against us? Of course it is! Bloody 'ell! 'Is Arry seein t'light! Is 'e 'avin a fuckin'epiphany on'is very own road t'Damascus!" They both laughed...

"Oh Bill... I wish you could see things from a happier perspective. However shitty things are, there are still things worth having... things like family, friendship, comradeship and yes, even charity! If you'd just take the hand that's being offered to you, that *I'm holding out to you*! So many of the clients here have severe mental health issues, that's why they can't cope, why they are unable to function in our screwed-up society, why they can't accept the helping hand when it's offered, when it's held out to them, because they have such a level of fear and paranoia that they're suspicious of everyone, including us and all we try and do for them, but you Bill... You aren't like that, you knowingly and deliberately hold yourself away, keep yourself apart, not just from us but from the other people who come here for help, guys who are all in the same boat! You must know we mean you no harm but still you refuse our help... Were you in some sort of trouble? Are you running from something Bill?"
"Just let go o'it 'Arry! Yer like a fuckin'dog wi'a bone! I am what I am, who I am, an' that's it."

Harry held his hands up in surrender!
"Okay... I tried! But please for once in your bad tempered, narky, old cunt's life will you listen to what I say next without rejecting it before you've even heard me out? Please?"
"'Arry! Mind y'language lad!" Bill laughed so hard it set him off coughing again, the rattling cough of someone who really

couldn't afford to go at it like that! Once his coughing had subsided he carried on,

" Go 'ead son... I'm all ears! I'll gi'ya a fair 'earin'!"

"Right, so I've pulled some strings and I've called in a lot of favours to make this happen... so *do not* reject it out of hand alright? *Please!* I've got you a stay at a respite centre for a fortnight, a comfy place where you'll have your own room, three meals a day, laundry services and help, help with whatever you need! As far as you're concerned it'll be like you're taking a holiday in a really good hotel!"

A look of only mild disdain ran across Bill's face, rather than the one of furious resentment that Harry'd been expecting! Hmm... that's promising he thought, what he'd actually anticipated was another diatribe of sneering contempt as a reward for his efforts! But instead the old man asked,

"An' where pray tell is this five star 'otel located?"

"Come on Bill, I never said it was a *five star hotel*, it's on the south side of town, up on the hill, just off the road that goes out over the moors."

"They'll even come down here and pick you up, so you'll have no problem getting there and they'll drop you back here after your stay."

So far no outright rejection or refusal to even contemplate the idea Harry thought... but no acceptance either yet! He began to start wondering why the hell he bothered. The guy was impossible and he had deliberately avoided telling him the name of the place because...

"So 'Arry, what's the name of this *as good a luxury 'otel*? Hmm...?"

Well I tried, Harry consoled himself, what more can I do? He'd tried to soften the blow that he knew Bill was going to feel upon hearing the name of the place, the shock it would be to him, the wound it would inflict upon his proud and stubborn ego!

"It's a respite centre, a place where people can go who need full-time care so that their carers can have a break for a week, get some relief from the pressure of caring for someone twenty-four-seven, you have to understand that however dedicated people are, it can become a pretty oppressive burden at times..."

"So 'Arry, this place is so wonderful that it don't even need to 'ave a name at all then? Couldn't be that you're talkin' 'bout that

feckin' 'Ospice could it? That big ol'ouse up on th'ill were folks get sent t'die? That why your dancin' 'round the name like Michael fuckin' Flatley is it? You're talking about St. Jude's aren't you? Written me off 'ave ya? Well I don't bloody think so!" Harry gave an exasperated sigh and got up from the chair he'd been sitting on... But Bill wasn't quite finished yet, as he added scornfully...
"You know as she's the fuckin' patron saint o'lost causes doncha? Eh? St. Jude?" Not to be outdone Harry retorted,
"So what you're saying then, is that it's a wholly appropriate place for you then aren't you?"

The old guy just huffed at him...
"I honestly don't know why I bother with you Bill, you're now't but an ungrateful and selfish old sod! You think you're entitled to do whatever the hell you like and expect others to follow you around picking up the pieces from the devastation you leave in your uncaring wake. I'll bet you left more than a few hapless victims behind when you ran away from your life? Probably a family, a wife, kids, friends... Left them to wonder what happened to you, not knowing where you went, where you are? Not even knowing if you're alive or dead? And you're still doing it today, oh yes you're ready enough to lie in one of our beds here when it suits you, eat our food whenever you want, have a warm, dry place to come when the weathers too bad, but you're not prepared to give anything back in return, not a single grain of consideration for the effort people put in..." Helen, the nurse came into the room at that moment while Harry was in full rant and cut him short!

"Oh now come on Harry, the old chap's not well, give him a break will you? A least let me get him back up on his feet before you go and lay into him and knock him down again!" The look of exasperation on Harry's already red, angry face was pained, he shrugged his shoulders to let them slump as if he could take no more and slouched out of the room without another word, merely giving a dismissive wave of his hand to Helen as he passed through the doorway.

Helen turned to face Bill and let rip,
"You really are the limit Bill, I heard some of that. That man has begged and pleaded to get you into that place, to give you a

break to get you recovered and back on your feet, so that you won't have to go back out on the streets in the sorry state that you're in! Look at you! You'll barely be able to walk to the toilet when you get out of this bed, yet you throw his offer back in his face?"
"Yeah well, it's an 'ospice innit? 'E's writing me off, sendin' me away to die!"
"Don't act so bloody stupid you ungrateful old fart! St. Jude's is a wonderful place run by the most caring people you'd ever have the pleasure to meet! My God, I wish I'd taken the job I was offered there now instead of coming to work here in this cess-pit of a place, dealing with the dregs of humanity and getting precious little thanks for it either… having to take this kind of shit from the likes of you!"
"You have an offer of two weeks…fourteen bloody days of being looked after, waited on… hand foot and flamin' finger, in a lovely warm, clean place with the most beautiful of gardens too, and you toss it aside without a moment's thought as if it were an insult to your independence! Let me update you *old man*… you are very sick, you are undernourished and the doctor thinks you have most likely suffered a mild stroke too, you are in no fit state to be out there sleeping rough! Independent my arse!"

With that she bustled around, tidying up the room…
Bill was for once shamefaced enough to remain silent…
Helen still red-faced and angry added as she swirled around in her fury, snatching up the tray of crockery as she went to leave, added…
"…and don't think you'll be staying here tonight. It's out of the door you are this afternoon, one of two ways, either with your pack on your back to go to God alone knows where… and I shudder to think what it will be like… or you get your ungrateful arse onto the bus to go up to St. Jude's for an all-in, fully paid-up, costing-you-nothing fortnight's holiday in comfort and luxury! You think-on that, old man as you're getting dressed… putting back on the clothes that we've washed for you! Well the one's that were fit to wash, all the underclothes are from our shop, yours were so full of holes and… My God words fail me!"
He called her back as she was storming out through the doorway…

"'Elen, what'd'ya mean, might've *had a stroke*?" She just carried on with her back to him, smiling to herself as she called back over her shoulder as she left the room...
"Aye that made you think didn't it? *'Elen* is it now?" And she was gone! Leaving Bill to sit there, no longer angry but increasingly experiencing an unfamiliar feeling, one he'd not felt for many years, a deep feeling of chagrin and remorse for the way he'd behaved.

He was always defensive, aggressively so, it was just how he'd learnt to be! How he felt he'd had to be, how he'd survived, living as he had these last... what was it five? Six years? No it must be at least seven now. *Was that how long it had been*? Since he had... exactly as Harry had accused him of... *walked out on everyone who cared about him?* His angry old self surged back to stand-in as his defence... *not one of them gave a shit about me! They were the reason I left!* He knew it was utter and complete bullshit to think that, but the loss of the one person who really did care about him, who despite the person he had become, had still loved him despite all his faults... The loss of her, the one person he loved more than anyone else in the world... his daughter. Her death had soured every aspect of his life.

It seemed like hours before Helen returned, the watched kettle never boils, Bill thought as the idea of being whisked away to somewhere warm and comfortable began to sound preferable to his beloved hideaway out there in the woods, besides it was the difference in the manner of getting to one or other of the two places that suddenly seemed a bigger issue, it was true what Helen had said about him finding it difficult to walk.

He could bear it no longer, so he struggled up, swung his legs over the edge of the bed and stood up. He felt wobbly, but made his way to the door which Helen had left open when she had departed, after ever so firmly putting that flea in his ear! He tottered across to the doorway and steadied himself with a hand on either side of the doorframe, he realised that he was looking out onto the short corridor that led to the medical treatment room, then on to the medical reception and then to the main concourse of the Factory. There was also a consulting room here where the visiting GP could have private consultations, that was when Harry could find one who'd actually turn-up! GP's seemed to be an endangered species of late apparently.

Now that he was on his feet he felt a little better, the blood seemed to be getting up to his brain better, albeit a little sluggishly!

He knocked on the closed door at the end of the corridor, there was no answer so he opened it and peered around it. The treatment room was empty, on the desk a half-eaten sandwich sat on a plate next to a cup of tea... He heard Helen's voice from the next room and then the door opened, she bustled in... she had that kind of movement that seemed to make her alive with energy... she smiled when she saw her recalcitrant patient,
"So you're back on your feet. Come and sit down here while I've got you in my torture chamber!" She joshed, directing him to a chair.
"Arm on here." She had him put his arm on the examination couch and deftly flipped the collar of the blood pressure monitor around his bicep and pumped it up to send it squeezing his arm.
He grimaced as she held his wrist, she shook her head as if in disbelief of how he could be such a baby!

"Well you've still got some blood pressure! We'll leave it with less scrutiny than that I think! Hold out your hands to me..."
He obeyed and she took his hands in hers, he could not fail to see that someone had made a serious attempt to get his hands clean! His nails had been clipped very short and the skin of his fingers was now something akin to pink!
"Now squeeze my fingers, harder... a little harder... Okay you can let go with your right hand. Squeeze with your left as hard as you can... Hmm..." She went across to a cupboard and rummaged in it returning with a device she placed in his right hand,
"This is a dynamometer, it measures the strength of your grip. Squeeze it as hard as you can." He did so and she read the reading and jotted it down on a pad she had on the couch.
She told him to swap hands and repeat.
She wrote down the reading then turned the pad for him to see, she'd written: $R = 45 kPa$ and $L = 12 kPa$

"What's kPa mean?" He asked deliberately avoiding the obvious!

"Very funny! Your right hand has a fine grip, your left would be poor for an old lady of eighty! So, up on your feet. Lift your left foot up off the floor…"
He did and she steadied him as he wobbled a little before finding his balance,
"Good now use the other foot." He tried but was unable to get any sort of balance and the nurse had to help him back onto the couch.
"Can you see for yourself now how weak you are on your left side? You'll not have any idea when you had your stroke I don't suppose?"
"So I 'ave 'ad a stroke then? Bloody 'ell!"
"Oh most definitely, you've probably had a mild heart attack or two as well I'd say from listening to what passes off as a heartbeat in there!" she pointed at his chest.
"I've heard some cases of arrhythmia in my time Bill, but hearing your heartbeat is more like listening to a syncopated drum solo, being played by a one-armed, drunken baboon with no sense of rhythm and who keeps forgetting to beat the drum!
"You're a very sick man Bill and the sooner you come to terms with that, the better." He just muttered something like "A*ye*-*well…"*
 "You can dismiss it as much as you like, but you'll be dead this winter if you stay out there living like this. I'm telling you, if you go back out there you *will not* see another Spring. But then again I guess that'd be one less ingrate for me to have to waste my time and efforts over!" He looked up at her, uncertain what to say…

"Oh be off with you! Go and get your clothes on! They'll be here for you in forty minutes!"
"Who will? The bus for St. Jude's? But…"
"No, it's the ambulance to take you for your echocardiogram. They'll bring you back here, heaven help us, when they're done with you!"

Much later on in the day, after he'd been… *mauled about and sat around for feckin' hours waiting…* Bill was back at The Factory.

He made his way through to Helen's office, knocked on the door and stuck his head around it.

"Oh my God, speak of the devil and in he walks!" Her voice softened a little though as she saw the old guy was clearly wrung-out and exhausted after his trip to and from the hospital. "Come on let's get you back into bed old fella!"

The following morning he woke to a cup of tea being put down by his bed, a quick taking of his pulse and then he was left alone once more.

He drank the tea and felt as if he might doze off again but was forced to get up to go and have a pee. Instead of getting back into bed he wandered out of the room to find Helen and see what was happening today.

When he got to her office it felt like Groundhog Day as she barked at him, "Oh it's you is it? Be off with you! Go and get your clothes on! The bus'll be here for you at ten o'clock!"
"What bus is that? Not the one to take me to that bloody 'ospice is it?"
"Oh begone! Of course it's the bus for St. Jude's, do you think after all the pleading he had to do with you that Harry would cancel it just because you threw it back in his face? That he didn't know that you'd eventually see sense? That even someone as stubborn and pig-headed as you would understand that it was for the best? For the love of God, will you... GO!"

Actually shamefaced again for the second time in recent days, Bill got up and shuffled his way back to the room he'd been using. He got dressed, clean underwear! He put his coat over his left arm, his cap already shoved into one of the pockets and with his backpack hanging off his right shoulder, made his way back. He gave a little knock and went back into the room where Helen was sat finishing a late lunch,
"I'm sorry for being so much trouble and thank you for looking after me..." She put her cup of tea down and then let her head fall forward to rest on the desktop with a positive bump! When she looked-up at him, her head sideways to him, he could swear there was a tear in her eye as she said...
"Look what you've gone and done! You bastard! You've finished me off! The bloody shock of it!" She continued as she sat back upright, in a voice akin to a newsreader: *"It was all too*

much for her... being thanked! Apologised to and then thanked by the miserable old sod!
He laughed with her,
"Is 'Arry 'bout? I'd like to apologise to 'im an'all and thank 'im like."
"Aw... the man's busy! He's more to do than worry about an ungrateful old tramp like you! Y'know there's folks who come here as actually want his help, grateful people that he doesn't have to force it onto! But I *will* tell him... I'll wait till he's sat down though and I'll have the smelling salts to hand first though!
"Now go and sit out there in the refectory, get yourself a cup of tea and stay there until you see the mini-bus pull up!"
"Okay, but really 'elen, I'd... She waved a hand to silence him and said in a dramatic voice...
"Begone before I open my gates and have death pour like a torrent from within!"
"Oh so now you weaponise Shakespeare to hurl at me! Okay... I'm gone!" He smiled at her as he sidled around the door, she smiled back and gave another wave to shoo him out more quickly!

He did as he'd been instructed and as he was drinking his tea, Helen came over to him, she had a piece of paper in her hand which she gave to him,
"Give this to the reception when they book you in at St. Jude's, it's a prescription, I spoke to the Doctor last evening and he's prescribed you something to calm your ulcer down and something to maybe ward off more strokes and keep you blood pumping!" He took the paper and put it in his pocket and before he could thank her, she was walking away, calling out...
"And don't you be upsetting the staff up there! BE NICE! It won't kill you!"

CHAPTER TWELVE

Bill smiled to himself as he watched the comings and goings in the massive space that was used today as a dining room, canteen or refectory, call it what you will, but whatever label you attached to it, however you regarded it the space was dramatically underused... It was an utterly huge space, more befitting a vast arboretum housing tall palms, even trees and exotic plants reaching up towards its glass and steel roof, which was way up above him, probably some fifty feet up. On one of the artist's sketches that hung on the walls that visualised how the renovated space was to be used, the room was depicted with trees along one side, to create natural shade but they never appeared to have made it out of the sketch, to materialise into reality.

The room had been built in this way as it had once housed the massive engines that powered the mill, there were still bits of out-of-place remnants of that vast machine to be seen where pipes and ducts appeared in the bulkhead wall of the factory proper next door, they now ended truncated and no longer going anywhere anymore, there were even a couple of massive pulley-wheels idle now, held there on their heavy brackets, forever motionless, never again to spin and turn the wheels of industry again...

To Bill sitting waiting, it was all a parody of Society in England today, a once mighty and great structure, inspired and built from genius, put together with infinite care, method and efficiency, designed and built to the highest possible standard, so that it would run well and in perpetuity... but the world... away from the shores of this little and then busy and industrious island (rare in terms of the rest of the world at that time)... the world had since then moved on, moved on more rapidly and purposefully than we had done, it had left us behind until all that was left here was a broken remnant of what had once been, accompanied only now by the vastly inflated opinion we cling onto of our *greatness*, even feeling the need to carry on using the word '*Great*' before *Britain*, despite living in a country where the entire system doesn't work properly anymore. This edifice was like an empty shell akin to one you might find on the seashore, empty and no longer purposeful save for it still remaining majestic even in its redundant state of being.

Those in power seemingly imagined somehow that out of the lingering spectre, from the ghost of the machine of industry that once was, that some part of it was still present albeit in a smaller form, that the driving spirit of industry and entrepreneurship remained alive and thriving in the still beating, mighty heart of England... The simple fact though was that they were delusional idiots.

Harry had told him one time that they'd wanted to put in a lowered ceiling, accepting that although the original idea was lovely drawn out and coloured-in *on paper*, it was utterly impractical in the chilly north of England in winter! He'd said it was to try and make it more cost effective to heat, it was cold in here in the winter whatever they tried to do, but there had been objections as despite nobody wanting the building before it had been bought to be used by the charity, they had managed to slap a preservation order on it the moment the renovation had started! This had made the installation of the planned acres of solar panels on the roof unacceptable as it would *change the character* of the building's appearance! Ditto the false ceiling!

He was, as he often was, lost in his thoughts when a kindly and questioning voice sounded out next to him,
"Is it Bill, may I presume? I'm sorry I don't have a surname on my list, I'm Gordie the driver for your luxury transport, here to whisk you up and away to St. Jude's!"
"Aye, s'me! But it's just Bill. That's all 'as I goes by, no need for any extendin' on that. Thank you Gordie, lead on t'where me carriage awaits!"

Sat in a comfy seat on-board the medium sized mini-bus, Bill actually enjoyed the ride as he looked out and was whisked along the same streets he would normally have plodded along. Within minutes they were driving across the bridge over the canal at the edge of town, a distance that would have taken him an age on foot and soon they were on the road that climbed up into the hills that surrounded the town, nestled in the valley as it was and then they motored on onto the moors.

It seemed like no time at all before the driver slowed down to turn off the road and slip inbetween two large stone gateposts set in the low stone wall that ran aside the highway, to drive onto a neatly tarmacked, single track drive that led away from the main road.

The drive wound its way through trees on either side until the vista opened up to reveal a lovely sweep of gradually descending, grassy hillside, mowed by a munching army of black and white sheep, innumerably dotted all across it. Away to the right there stood a fine, old building, its brightly lit, honey coloured stone appearing to glow in the brilliant sunshine.

As Bill gazed around, in awe of his new surroundings, the driver shouted-up,
"Your first time here isn't it? Spectacular view don't you think? It was a private residence when it was built way back in the eighteen-nineties, then it was used as a hospital in World War One, then it became a priory after that, until it was converted to a Respite Care Home."
Bill butted in,
"Aye and an 'ospice, an'all! But whatever t'place mebbe, it is 'as y'say *magnificent!* Y'can see why th'old gaffer o' one o'them dark satanic mills as was down yonder in't valley, would wanna live up 'ere, use a bit o't'vast wealth as they produced for 'im down there in't'all grime and dirt, them lesser folks, y'know t'workers! An' then come up 'ere in't'fresher air, an still all t'while be able to look down on 'em all!"

The driver chuckled to himself saying,
"Well that's as maybe, nothing we can do about the past, but there's certainly a lot less dirt and grime down there today for one thing and whoever it might have been who built the place and for whatever purpose it was at the time, it's a wonderful place today, a place to come when you need your spirits lifting. The gardens are wonderfully peaceful and tranquil and the trees, well... Think on this, that owner as you clearly don't approve of never lived to see the trees he had planted grown to full maturity, to behold the final vision of what he had created for him by his landscaper. They knew only too well when they laid it all out that neither of them would ever see the vision that was sketched

out on his paper, that it was a legacy for others and not for them to behold."

"Aye, well suppose there's some truth in that, easy when y'as all that money though, don't y'think?"
"I can see we have a dyed in the wool Socialist coming to stay with us! Can't say that I disagree with you personally comrade! But I'm all for live and let live myself, no point ranting and raving about things you can't do anything about is there? Just make the most of your little interlude from the darkness, enjoy your brief moments here in the light, eh old lad?"

Bill was impressed by the driver's reply, but rather than answer, for once he just let himself settle back into his seat and watch the big house grow larger in his window until it loomed up over and above them where the driver pulled-up the mini-bus at the doors, under the shade of the portico at the centre of the tall frontal façade.

Bill was directed through double doors set in the grand entrance to the old house, where he was met in the reception area by a blond haired woman in her fifties who bristled with energy, she shook his hand vigorously as she welcomed him,
"Hello I'm Patricia Melling, the Director of St. Jude's, welcome, welcome... please come with me to my office and I'll go through a few formalities to help you to settle in here, we have a lovely room prepared for you so you'll be able to have a really good rest, sounds as if you need one from what Harry has told me!"

With that she led him away down a short corridor and then into her office, a beautiful old room that had most likely been the original owner of the house's study. By the time Bill had put his rucksack down and settled into the chair facing the grand desk, there was a steaming cup of sweet coffee being placed into his hand...

Despite his reservations, Bill found spending time at the place was a real joy. His room which was on the first floor had a large window that looked out across the valley. Way down there in the valley lay his town, the place where all his life was... nay strike that and say where his *existence was*... it was the stage upon which his life as Bill the tramp was played out, the part he'd been playing only existed down there below him too, it was his choice if the curtain came down upon it now.

The room was large and comfortable, there was an en-suite with a bath and shower facilities, a comfortable bed despite it being some sort of '*hospital-type thing*' and there were two comfy chairs and even a small writing desk by the window.
He had three meals a day, served in the dining room along with the other guests... that was the least pleasant aspect of his stay he found, at least at first! Nothing to do with the food, which was excellent but having to watch the parade of human decrepitude that passed by him, old people dithering and doddering around on sticks, crutches, or with frames, or in wheelchairs of all types, some electrically powered and operated by the incumbent whilst others were great clumsy things, needing someone to push and steer them, with a plethora of attached cylinders and gadgets combining together to act as a mobile life support system for the remnant of the person who was its cargo...

Worst of all, there were a few very much younger ones...

It was one thing to have to watch the gruesome parade of clapped-out ancient folk, old codgers who were not dissimilar to himself, people who'd simply reached or gone way past their expiry date, but to see the terminally-ill, or chronically-ill youngsters who were living out the remaining days of their way-too-short lives there, or who had come there taking a break, so that their parents or whoever else may have been their carers took a break too... *from caring for them!* Some of them had no hair on their heads because of the harshness of the life extending chemotherapy they had to endure... he found it heart breaking.

This was the harsh reality of the lives we are given, he knew that, it shouldn't have been a surprise to him and yet being here in the loveliest of surroundings seemed to make it all the more stark somehow, it was right there in your face... the awful truth that death stalks us all, young or old and even the unborn. From the moment that those cells first divide and life begins... for all of it being a truly miraculous process... we are all doomed to die, one way or another, sooner or later.

He likened this aspect of the place to some sort of hellish last pit-stop on the road to hell! He thought to himself, it was like a narrow ledge hanging out over the abyss, a last ditch point to cling onto. The cynic in him wanted to scoff at that, shrug and just say, that for the worst of the cases here, what was the fucking point of any of it anyway? He pondered over the question, what quality of life did most of these pathetic remnants actually have?
As if in answer to his question, he was given an answer…
It came in the form of an ancient and shrivelled relic of a woman who was being wheeled past him as he was finishing his meal, she noticed him look up and saw that he was watching her and lifted a hand in command to the one wheeling her and her chair stopped! Her sense of command being what was presumably a long-ago learned attitude, now probably acting purely from a lifetime of habit, then she seemingly automatically reached up her bony arm to place her hand at the side of her face, where she ran her gnarled, arthritically deformed and knobbly fingers through her snow white hair as she smiled at him… Her blue eyes were bright and alive, they seemed to sparkle, to shine out of the wrinkled visage of her face, the lines in the almost transparent skin around her eyes and mouth were multiplied by the action of her radiant smile as it revealed long, pure white teeth…

Her voice despite a slight tremor when she spoke was strong,
"I see we have a new visitor to our waiting room! And a fine fellow he looks too! What brings you here? Are you a Captain come ashore from the deck of you mighty pirate ship? Have you become tired after all of your wanton plundering?" The woman wheeling her chipped-in, as Bill was for once, momentarily speechless!
"Don't mind Eleanor, she's one of our original residents, ninety-eight and still going strong! She…"
"Oh belt-up Noreen! I *can* speak for myself! Ninety-eight *not-out* is how I like to refer to it, I'm still at the crease and valiantly batting-on, my target of making a century in sight!"
"I, err… I'm Bill… I…"
"Goodness me! A timid pirate! Is it that we have here? Why that's unheard of! I know it must be hard for you Captain, dazzled by the radiant beauty you now behold before you, but I urge you Sir! Gird your loins and show some civility!" She

smiled again and in that moment it seemed to Bill that he caught a fragment broken away from time, a chimerical glimpse of the woman she had once been as it shone out through the mask of an old woman that had slipped down infront of her face…

He found himself responding… *and in-character too!*
"'Tis true m'lady, many a year it is I've sailed the seven seas, with naught for company save for the scurvy wretches of me motley crew for me eyes to rest upon and behold! Confronted by the boldest of blaggards as I may have been… for all the fearsome seas I've battled with, tossed by waves as tall as an 'ouse… None has dealt me such a knee-weakening blow as to be confronted by such a vision of loveliness as I 'as before me now!" With that he leant across and reached out for her hand which she readily held out to him, there was now a hoity smile rippling upon her thin and pursed lips as she tipped her head back a little…

Her hand was as light as a feather in his, her skin though soft and smooth was chill, as he softly kissed it saying simply…
"My lady."
She smiled and with her left hand beckoned for her carriage to move on… simply saying,
"Noreen…"
With that she was wheeled past him, Noreen gave him a smile and a shake of the head as she urged on the horses for her ladyship's carriage …

He sat back and was deeply moved by what had just happened, how a total stranger had reached out to him and without a please or thank you… in doing so she had touched his heart. He realised he was crying. He felt a little stupid by his reaction, but also utterly humbled by the old lady, it seemed to him for a moment as if it had been his own grandmother who had been speaking to him, it was the kind of thing she would have done, play act with him and he had responded as he would have done so long ago now, back then when he was a boy, by playing the part she had put him in, stepping into the role she had cast for him and he'd happily stepped back into the shoes of his childhood self today with barely a thought.

He remonstrated at himself for having had such a closed mind and for being so blinkered, being blind to the fact that though the people here may indeed appear to be remnants, mere scraps of what was left of the people they were once… *they were still people*! Most of whom had accrued a lifetime of experiences and memories over a great many years, okay perhaps some had lost access to some of their memories or maybe their mental faculties were failing them and some may well have reached questionable conclusions about what life was all about, or maybe formed suspect views about others… it nevertheless remained their right to have them. For all the ones who weren't in good shape, there was often amongst them a gem such as Eleanor, waiting patiently there to be found by anyone who was willing to spend the time to look.

Bill felt as if he was dreaming for a lot of the time he spent at St. Jude's, there was constant input here in place of the emptiness of the days he was accustomed to, days that in his life as a vagabond he filled with his endless wanderings or by simply sitting for hours watching life go by! Here he was constantly being invited to attend one appointment or another, one with the Doctor initially, another to see the visiting optician, the physiotherapist, the counsellor and even the Director of the establishment!

He thought the meeting with the boss was probably down to his connection with Harry, apparently they knew each other through their works of charity, probably hob-knobbing over cocktails whenever there was a sniff of charity money to be had in the air! She had the same attitude of relentless enthusiasm that Harry had, although his seemed to be running out of steam a bit lately, it was a sort of *we can do it, we will do it, we have to do it* mentality towards her establishment and what it was there to achieve. He liked her…

The Doctor was a kindly chap, a tall gaunt man who was well into his sixty's. He spoke to Bill, in a very matter of fact manner and completely without judgement. He confirmed the need for Bill to keep taking the tablets the nurse had given him for his stomach problem and said he would set up a repeat prescription for him to collect down at the Clinic within The Folks Factory.

He pulled up a chair next to Bill and carried out a quick examination, looking into his ears with one gadget, his eyes with another and down his throat whilst holding down his tongue with a wooden spatula. He listened to his heart with his stethoscope and took his blood pressure with the thing that squeezed his arm! He asked him to watch his finger as he moved it infront of Bill's face, asked him to stand with his eyes closed, then to lift each leg in turn. He finally took both of his hands in his and carefully examined them, turning them over as he did so and then asked him to squeeze his hands as the nurse had at The Factory.

When he was finished he huffed to himself and went across to pick-up a sheet of paper off his desk, he leant back onto his desk and looked over at Bill over the tops of his half-moon glasses,
"These are the test results I had sent up from the hospital, it doesn't make for happy reading I'm sorry to say. You have quite advanced, heart disease, you must know this already?" He queried. Bill nodded as the Doctor continued,
"You have palpations? You experience a fluttering sensation in your chest... here?" The Doctor pointed to the left hand side of his own chest. Bill nodded.
"Do you experience any chest pains?" Bill nods again,
"Show me where..." Bill pointed.
"Shortness of breath, periods of mild confusion?" Bill chuckled,
"I'm confused a lot of the time, to be honest!"

"Well the scan you had indicates that you have quite advanced atherosclerosis, that's a narrowing of the arteries, plaque builds up and reduces the diameter of the artery, making it harder for the blood to flow through it. Bits of this plaque can break away, come loose and may then become lodged in narrower veins, sometimes in the brain or the blood vessels that supply the heart. Neither is good news, obviously!"
Bill chipped-in, "Like how the water pipes in an old house get clogged up then?"
"Yes, precisely so! This can often be treated by inserting what we call stents into your arteries, close to your heart, it's pretty much a routine operation these days and could have an enormously beneficial outcome for you too. The arrhythmia or perhaps it is more a case of bradycardia, may be aided by having a pacemaker fitted, but these are all matters that you will have to

discuss with your cardiologist. They've booked you in to see one, just take this slip with you when you go."

The Doctor held out a page he'd extracted from the file towards Bill, who just sat there looking at it, held there in the Doctor's extended hand without moving...

"What is it? You don't wish to see the cardiologist? I think that would be a grave mistake Bill! And I do mean that quite literally too, if you see what I mean?"

"As in the *grave* bit? Eh Doc?"

"Indeed Bill, you really are in very poor health, you could say that you are a heart attack waiting to happen? Or perhaps waiting for another stroke, the nurse did tell you that you'd had a minor stroke didn't she? The next one could paralyse or kill you, you do understand that?" He rustled the papers and plucked one of them out,

"Yes, she's recorded it here. What is it you're afraid of Bill? Hospitals? None of us like them you know, not even us doctors! But needs must? Is it to do with your reluctance to provide a surname? Are you in some sort of trouble? On the run even?" The Doctor raised an eyebrow and smirked as if this was a joke, however when Bill didn't share his amusement he looked down, a little crestfallen,

"Oh my Lord, is that what it's all about? Oh, you poor old chap. You would still be treated, please understand that much, I could say you have amnesia, or suchlike, no one is left untreated simply because they refuse to give their name, we're not in America, thank God!"

"Aye well Doc, if that's all? I do appreciate all y've said and 'ow ya trying to 'elp like, but we'll leave it there, if y'don't mind eh?" He was up and out of his chair as he spoke,

The doctor shrugged, tapped the pages together, squaring them up and slipped them into the folder,

"Okay Bill, it's your life, it's your decision. I do respect that, of course I do, but I feel I must say one more time that taking this course of action will almost certainly be the death of you!"

"Thing is doc, the way I see it is this, when it's your time to go, maybe it's best to just go? That fella with his sickle's following all of us around isn't he? We all know we'll get that tap on our shoulder from his bony finger one day don't we, even though most folks like to pretend they don't? So yeah, maybe we can put off the day with all our clever tricks and gadgets and maybe it's a good thing, but then again maybe it's not always! You work here, you see the relics that are left once you run out of your tricks, yeah for sure you are extending life, giving folks a few years more, but a few years more of what? Pissing and shitting in their pants, wandering around like zombies, with no idea where they are, who they are or what's going on? Okay there's some who are compos mentis, old girls like Eleanor but they're the exception rather than the rule, aren't they?"

The doctor studied Bill as he pondered over a suitable response,
"Like I said Bill, it's your choice, you're drifting off into the dark arts of philosophy there though aren't you? I'm a doctor not a psychiatrist, I just tinker with the engine and the running gear, but when it comes to the CPU if you like to think of it… Well, what you're referring to is way out of my league, totally beyond my jurisdiction!"

They laughed together, then the doctor went on,
"I think you'll find that if you decide to just do nothing and allow nature to take its course, later on you may very well come to regret it. When you do, of course you will have deteriorated further by then and any treatment offered will have become far less effective, indeed it will most likely be too late by then. I have found many times that with the impending imminence upon them, of what you refer to as that *tap on the shoulder*… Well let's just say that it can exert a remarkably focusing effect upon the mind. The instinct for survival is the most primal of urges."
"Thanks doc I know you mean well and I hear what you say. As my old Dad used to say it's all about *horses for courses*, we make decisions all the time and on this subject, I've made mine,"

The doctor just nodded,
"So! Where's my pad?" He pulled a pad out from his desk drawer and scribbled onto a prescription form,
"I'll have this taken down to the pharmacy this morning with all the other ones and you'll have your pills this afternoon, we're not linked-up yet here…" A puzzled look from Bill,
"On the computer for the prescriptions? Never mind, these are two more drugs for you to take along with the ones for your stomach, they will thin your blood a bit, help lower your blood pressure a little too… they'll help, but you must accept that they

will only help to a limited extent, they are in no way a cure! Call back here about three o'clock and I'll let you have them, then all you'll have to do is call in every four weeks and pick them up at the same place, the clinic at The Folks Factory and then of course make sure that you take them as it says on the label.

He said that he'd had to give Bill a surname, so he'd find that the prescriptions were made out to William *Williams*! As Bill was leaving he added a final remark,
"I'll get an appointment for you with the dentist, you've been blessed with amazing teeth, it's probably the only reason they're still in your head with the lack of care you've been giving them! She'll clean them up for you, they not a pretty sight presently!"

Bill had run his tongue around his teeth as he headed back along the corridor, smiling to himself that it was a strange co-incidence that the doctor had given him his mother's maiden name!
The physio was a middle aged woman and yet another charming and caring type… he was beginning to think he had died and that this was heaven! Being fed properly three times a day, sleeping well and being cared for by kindly people was something he could easily get used to! What was different to *real life,* that thing he had walked away from all those years ago, was the fact that there were no demanding, personal pressures put onto his shoulders, there were no pressing deadlines, no bills to pay, no-one to be accountable to, no one depending upon him, *needing* him to do things for them or simply just *needing* him! It was freedom!

He also found the physio's massaging of his gammy leg and shoulder and the exercises she got him to perform helped his mobility and gradually he found that he was walking much more easily.

It was when the visiting optician gave him a quick once over that he found out something interesting! The optician was an old guy, retired but still wanting to do something with the lifetime's worth of skills he'd acquired that could be of benefit to others, the kind of altruism that a place like St. Jude's depended upon, was built upon even. He had a bag of ready-to-wear specs from one of the bargain stores and once he'd tested his eyes he told Bill he needed +3 for his left eye and +2.5 for his right eye for reading glasses, he then found a pair of +3 specs and after popping out the right lens, slipped in one from a +2.5 pair. 'Ready-made prescription glasses for a couple of quid!' He'd said proudly!

He repeated the procedure with a second pair explaining that Bill would need these for reading, for up-close focus. He even apologised that he couldn't run to varifocals, Bill would just have to swop over to use the readers for close up stuff!

It was when Bill had said somewhat alarmed, that he couldn't pay him, that the old guy let it slip that along with his stay here, any other expenses incurred had been taken care of! When questioned he seemed to remember that it was meant to be a secret he had to keep from Bill, but he nevertheless relented and told him that Harry had made a generous donation to The Hospice when he'd persuaded the director to let him stay for a fortnight!

When Bill had said he didn't know that, but he guessed Harry must control a lot of money running the factory as he did, the old chap had responded quite agitatedly! He'd insisted that Harry had done no such thing, that he had paid out of his own pocket and that he was a very scrupulous man with every penny of the money he handled for the charity being scrupulously accounted for!

Bill had been quite taken aback by that bit of information. That bugger Harry! The pain in the backside Harry had paid for him to stay here out of his own pocket? It must be setting him back a pretty penny he thought! He was really moved by this incredible act of kindness, it revealed a new side to Harry he had been unaware of... he was beginning to come to the conclusion that it was he himself that was the problem, that he was little more than a miserable old twat who didn't deserve any of this kindness...

That feeling of remorse, prompted him to seek refuge in the gardens. The weather was glorious again as he strolled along a well surfaced tarmac path, it was in the dappled shade of the trees as he headed out through the wooded area to the side of the old building. It had been laid out more recently to allow wheelchairs to use it, with shallow gradients and slow bends and it was truly lovely.

He sat on a bench that was situated in a leafy glade, the woods here were filled with bluebells as they made their brief and spectacular, one show a year only performance.

He closed his eyes and let everything go…
He let his thoughts float away, unattended to…
Let them drift away like clouds across an empty blue sky…
He felt the cooling air pass over his lips…
Coming into his body…
With his breath…
He felt the warmed air pass back out over his lips…
With his breath…
It was peaceful here…
Only the sound of the gentle breeze stirring the trees…
The song of a bird now and then…
The buzz of an insect or a bee…
The sweet scent of the bluebells…
He was at peace…

It was a process he had been taught at The Haven, one that had stayed with him ever since, although rarely used in practice.

"May I join you?"

A soft female voice sounded out…
He opened his eyes to behold a pale faced young woman before him, she was entirely bald even to the extent of having no eyebrows, yet she didn't look in any way odd despite that, it simply seemed to make her eyes appear even larger than they already were.

"I hope I didn't startle you?" She asked as she carefully climbed out of the wheelchair and sat on the bench next to him, in a manner that seemed to imply that she imagined herself to be as brittle and delicate as she appeared to be.

"I love it here, I try and come here every day. It's so peaceful, such a wonderful place to meditate as I see you've discovered too." She carried on,

"I'm sorry if I'm disturbing you, if you've made this a special place too, I can leave you to your meditation if you'd prefer me to. I know how important it can be."
"No… don't be silly! Of course it's okay for you to be here too! It's not my bench, they're not my trees, or my bluebells, they belong to us all, as does everything, it's only the foolishness of people that makes them think that they can own anything, have anything all to themselves! I mean how can you own somewhere like this? Where's the guy who built the big house, or the factory he owned that paid for it all? All of this we see around us… *his* landscaping? Long gone isn't he, like we all will be. We only own one thing in this life and that is this…" The girl who had been listening intently now swept her own hands infront of herself… adding for Bill…
"Our body!"

Bill looked sideways at her, she was very young, maybe not even twenty! Her face was a ghastly pale colour, like porcelain or a painted geisha's and yet in a delicate way it remained very beautiful… She caught his gaze and smiled… a natural, totally genuine smile that came from within and not merely from the manipulation of the facial muscles around her mouth…
"In my case sadly, a very defective body!"

"I'd say I'm so sorry for you… don't get me wrong… I am… but words are just so hopelessly inadequate aren't they, you'll have heard them all before already anyway and however well-meaning, all the kindness and sympathy in the world doesn't amount to anything when it comes right down to it does it? You've been dealt a damnably rotten hand kid, life's like a roulette wheel and on your spin the ball landed in the shitty-deal slot! Life can be a total fucking bitch!"
She laughed, it was small and gentle as if it was all she was capable of, like the tinkling, trickling of a crystal clear stream, so light and delicate…
"I like that! Thank you! Yes that was the best response anyone has ever had to confronting the tragedy that is me… Abigail…"
She held out a delicate, pale-skinned hand, to him… he could see prominent blue veins running across it…
He flinched physically away from her…
She was startled by his reaction, looking a little hurt, she said…

"What is it? I'm sorry... Are you afraid to touch me? What I've got isn't contagious...
I only wanted to shake your hand...
What is it?"
She could see he was trembling now, that tears were flowing from his eyes to become lost in the luxuriant thickness of his grey and white beard... He slumped forward to rest his elbows on his knees and he put his head into his hands and mumbled to her...
"I'm s-sorry... please, please forgive me... It's... it's just that my daughter's name was Abigail too..."

She ever so gently put her hand on his shoulder, squeezed lightly then gently rubbed her hand backwards and forwards on it...
"It's alright... let it all out, I've shed oceans of tears, they don't change anything but they do wash something away, don't you think? Wash away some of the pain? Oh, I dunno! I've given up trying to figure out any of it... There are no answers, unless you decide you're gonna believe in something daft... My mum tries to convince me about stuff like that, all that sort of thing, she's a Christian or at least so she says! It's a label that a lot of folk attach to themselves of course and a great many of them are just bloody hypocrites! It's all hogwash of course, least that's what I think... What about you?"

Bill lifted his face from his hands and looked across at the girl, she smiled at him and offered her hand to him once more...
"Let's start over shall we? Hi, I'm Abigail..."
"Hi, I'm Bill, so very pleased to meet you."

CHAPTER THIRTEEN

Bill returned to the same seat the next day but today he was sat there alone. He remained there anyway, sitting still and silently, letting his mind become calm, allowing himself to slip into his meditation practice.

It had been a long while since he had felt so relaxed, felt even remotely at all well in himself physically too and the calm of his meditation today was deeper and more sublime than it had been in a long time. Without conscious thought he found himself reliving the incident that had led him away from all he knew, to leave behind his life as part of society…

By that time in his life he had already sunk to the lowest ebb he had ever been down to, losing himself in a life of drink, debauchery and nightlife… or at least making a damn good stab at trying to lose himself…
That was the problem with that supposed escape route, it simply took you nowhere apart from downwards, spiralling down in ever tightening spirals downwards and onwards to seek out ever more extreme stimulation in order to obtain any effect from it at all, what would have been unthinkable at the start of the adventure quickly assumed a banality and mediocrity that in turn meant more and more extreme stimulation was required…

The saddest part of this appalling waste of time, money, life and vitality was that it had ultimately led him to a place where he had met someone who was so different to anyone else he had ever known, that they had stopped him in his tracks, made him re-evaluate his behaviour and his life. They had literally rescued him from the inevitable and miserable end that his trajectory would ultimately have taken him to and hauled him back from the brink, made him see that there could never be enough alcohol to drown his sorrow, that no amount of cocaine could ever lift his sagging spirits and that indulging in wanton, gratuitous and meaningless sexual encounters only alienated you ever further from people rather than connected you to them, that all it achieved was to further depersonalise human contact, reducing it to being purely animalistic.

But then paradoxically, she was also quite innocently, the reason he had been where he had been drunk as he was, as they had set off home in the dead of night, when he had been so viciously assaulted, when he was attacked… there in a backstreet just out of a night club at 3am… Okay she *was* saving him… but she was only managing to wean him off his more toxic habits, slowly but surely…

It was a small difference really but drunk as he might have been, he was most definitely not stoned, having laid off the drugs for some time by then.

His assailants had been upon him so quickly he'd not had time to react, to fight back or defend himself! He'd always imagined he'd do alright in a scrap, that somehow he would release his inner berserker and fight his assailants off! But in the cold, dark and damp reality of that early morning his inner Bruce Lee had been nowhere to be seen, he had been nothing more than a punch-bag! He'd just soaked up a barrage of blows that had him on the ground before he even knew what was happening… he was reeling so badly from the initial shock of the first blow, that all he knew after that was pain… before the blackness had swallowed him up…

The beating he received and the injuries resulting from it had given him an enforced break from his journey of self-destruction, for a while at least and after he had been released from hospital, he had gone on to have a protracted stay at The Haven, a rehabilitation centre for those addicted to whatever method they had chosen to use in their attempt to destroy themselves.

His memory had been slow and fragmented in nature as it had slowly returned once he'd come around in hospital, with his mind being a total blank at first. He remembered that there had been someone there with him a lot of time, someone who had sat at his bedside, no it was a she, and she was there *for* him… Slowly he realised who she was, that it was the woman who had been with him on the night of the mugging, that she was the person who had been helping him see that there was a better way…

By the time he was well enough to be discharged from the hospital she had stopped coming. Once he had been able to give them his name and he had reclaimed some of his identity, his youngest son Jake had come in to see him, it was him who had suggested the stay at The Haven and he'd eagerly organised it all for him once his Dad had agreed to go, agreed to at least give it a try…

He'd wanted to get in touch with Del, but he had no way of doing so, he thought it odd that she had stopped visiting him before he had fully regained consciousness, how was it that he didn't have her number in his phone? For some reason he'd forgotten to take it out with him that night, although it was a regular occurrence for him to forget where he'd left it! It had later turned up where he'd left it back at his flat, her number wasn't in his phonebook when he looked for it though! Had she returned to his flat at some point and deleted it? Why would she do that? She had a key for his flat although he didn't have one for hers. He'd only been there the time that he'd woken up there and had never gone back afterwards. He knew he had put her number in the phone although he'd hardly ever used it, if she'd not been at his flat for a day or two, they just met up, she'd just always *been there* at the club whenever he went.

By now he had pieced together that for sure, she'd been *with him* when he was actually attacked too! He panicked for a moment at that thought, fearing that she might have been attacked as well! But he quickly realised that she had to have been alright to have been there at his bedside, to sit with him? Then he had the stupidest of thoughts… that she had been killed in the attack and it was her ghost that he'd seen! That that was why she'd vanished once she knew he'd be alright, because she'd been able to *move on?*

He later made a trip back to the hospital at that point, to ask some of the nurses that had looked after him, and anyone else he could find that had come and gone when he was there, if there *had been* a woman sitting with him, hoping maybe they too might have seen her, even if she was a ghostly apparition?! Most couldn't remember anyone but eventually he found someone who'd worked nights, who did. She even said that his visitor was strikingly attractive and no she was no ghost, she was very much in the land of the living!… that was Del…

His mind was still hazy despite his memory having seemingly fully returned, but how could you know if it had all come back? If there was a piece missing, it would be lost, gone and therefore it would remain unknown to you… you would be unaware you ever had it, unless someone else had shared it with you and then later told you of it, perhaps facilitating you in recalling it? He almost felt like he was in a waking dream, he'd been prescribed Acamprosate to help him through his withdrawal and wondered if it was a side effect of the drug, the doctor said he doubted that it could be, saying it was far more likely to be a result of his head injury. He had remained in this slightly bemused state before and during his time at The Haven where he was to spend the next three months.

Opening his eyes again he took in the loveliness of the woodland glade that surrounded him today, he let out a deep sigh and he set off wandering back towards the house.

He approached the building from the front and could hear someone singing and playing a guitar, when they stopped there was a murmur of appreciation, calling it applause would be to exaggerate the feeble nature of the volume of noise, arthritic old hands do not for loud clapping make!

She started on a new song, one of those sung by a contemporary singer, was he the one who'd been a busker himself? James someone or other was it? No it was Ed wasn't it? It was most likely called 'What do I know?' he assumed as much from the lyrics and it was delightful to listen to. He stood at the open French windows and looked into the lounge, Abigail was sat on a stool by the piano with her guitar, she glanced up and smiled at him through the lyrics she was singing.

She finished playing and called across to him as she passed her guitar to the lady sat next to her, who simply had to be her mum, she had the same face, older of course and framed by a full head of vibrant yellow hair…
"Bill! Come over here and meet my mum. Mum this is Bill my meditation friend! Bill this is Samantha, my mum."
"Pleased to meet you Samantha, you have a beautiful daughter that much I already knew, that she sings and plays like an angel I have only just become aware of!"

"Pleased to meet you Bill, please do call me Sam! Yes she's amazingly talented, it…"

She must have thought better of carrying on with her remark as she stopped short. However Abigail carried on for her…
"…and it's so tragic that she'll never be heard by that many people, that she'll never develop her talent or go on to perform anywhere except in a hospice!" Bill chided her,
"Abi, you're not alone in your suffering love, your mum suffers with you, never forget that." Sam sniffed back a tear and forced herself to stiffen her face…
"Yes we all suffer together don't we eh mum? At the hands of the Genetic Dragon that burst into our idyllic, comfortable little lives, breathing his fire and destruction…" Her mum put her arm around her daughter's shoulders and kissed her lightly on the forehead, Abi lifted her thin arm and patted her mum's back as she leant across her. She caught Bill watching and looked up to the heavens as if to say… *look what I have to deal with!*

A voice Bill recognised sounded out from behind him,

"Enough of all this maudliness! You Sir, you big brute of a man standing there brooding, get away with yourself and pull that stool away from the piano, The Maestro is here and the recital shall commence momentarily!

A ripple of elderly laughter went around the lounge as Eleanor's chair was wheeled up to the piano. The brakes engaged, she paused for a moment her hands raised over the keys and then started playing… For all that her long thin fingers were crippled with arthritis she played beautifully, it was the music that had been pilfered for that cigar advert once upon a long time ago, it was from a work by Bach, Bill remembered.

Playing the one piece was clearly enough for Eleanor as she demanded to be wheeled away after she finished,
"I'd play more for you if my accursed hands would do my bidding, but alas they refuse!"

Bill smiled at her,
"That was wonderful Eleanor, thank you. You still play beautifully despite your hands being uncooperative!"

"Thank you Captain! Oh but they do cooperate, that isn't the problem, it is the damnable pain they cause me as I play, so much pain that I can only force myself to endure it for a short period of time before it quite literally becomes unbearable! Do you play yourself? Why, yes! I can see it in your eyes that you do and that you're itching to do so! Play Sir!" He smiled, recalling how he'd got himself into trouble the last time *he'd done so*, but nevertheless he found himself pulling up the piano stool.

He played 'Smile' in the style of Nat King Cole, followed by 'When I fall in love' which both went down very well and he was then kept playing for the best part of an hour, urged on to do so... It being a case of *'play another'* over and over coming from his captive audience!

When he finally managed to get away from the piano he sat and chatted with Sam and Abi.
"Why don't you shoot a video and put it on You-Tube Abi? You may never get to perform on stage but you could reach more people and be seen by a wider audience on there than you'd ever do performing live. I'm telling you, if I'd filmed you when I was stood watching you just now and posted it... You'd be a star love, really you would... I got caught on camera last time I played the piano and it was all over Social Media!"
"I saw that!" Abi exclaimed! "Of course, that was *you*! You played the same stuff then, how can I not have connected it, although all the time I was talking to you, I was thinking that there was something strangely familiar about you! Now I know what it was!" Sam chipped in,
"Abi showed me that clip, it was really good, you could make a living doing it! Is it true that you err, I mean..."
"Mum I told you! Don't beat about the bush! Yes he's a tramp! Or at least perhaps I should be more PC and say that he's homeless! Well, at least he *was!* How come you're *off-the-streets* and staying here with us?"
"It's a long story Abbie, but nothing's really changed, I'm still as you put it... *a tramp!"*

Sam spoke-up...
"Oh Abi don't be so gauche!" She chided her daughter as Bill laughed,

"It's okay Sam, she's only telling it how it is. It's the way I've chosen to live, I'm not ashamed of it, it was a conscious decision." Sam asked with a look of kindly concern on her face,
"But what about your family Bill, do they know how you're living?"
"Mum! Now who's being gauche and not to mention bloody nosey as well?"

Eleanor was passing as she was being wheeled out of the lounge, she held her hand up to command as before for her carriage to be halted as she drew level with them,
"That was a fine performance Captain! Do you read music as well as play from memory?"
"Oh yeah, sure… truth is my *off-the-cuff* repertoire is pretty limited without my music, that was about it… what I just played."
"You did very well indeed! I particularly liked the Beethoven, I do love the Moonlight Sonata, well the adagio at least, the Presto Agitato was always just beyond my limits to play, well to play it quite as fast as it should be played! Beethoven was a terrible show-off apparently! I think the maestro would have forgiven you for the repeated section you played, I'm not sure if he'd have been quite so forgiving about the section you omitted playing altogether though!" She laughed… "Although he *was* a master of impromptu improvisation and adaptation himself! Did you know that *Smile* was written by Charlie Chaplin?" With that she raised her hand to signal the carriage driver to spur on the horses and she was wheeled away.

Abi, Sam and Bill laughed, Abi saying to her mum,
"Eleanor is like royalty here at St. Jude's mum, she's an amazing old lady!" Sam commented,
"I never knew that Charlie Chaplin wrote that song!"

CHAPTER FOURTEEN

Bill awoke to the sound of birdsong... he opened his eyes and looked around him, for a moment he didn't know where he was, gradually he remembered as his bleary eyes took in the light pastel décor of his room at St. Jude's, the curtains were swinging a little in the gentle breeze that was coming in through the window that he had left ajar, sleeping in the totally enclosed space of an indoors room felt too strange for him, the atmosphere seeming to be dead and lifeless, the air too still. The deadening silence was disturbing in comparison to his outdoor bedroom where there was constant noise surrounding him, albeit mostly at a low level but where it felt as if the very air itself was alive.

He rolled over and eased himself to sit upright, perched on the edge of the bed then, luxury of luxury, he put his feet into the slippers that had been provided for him... *slippers!* He chuckled. He reached over to the bedside table and picked up his specs! *His specs!* He put them on and marvelled at the little miracle that occurred as everything before him in the room jumped into sharp focus!

Standing up, he took a step or two across to the window and drew back the curtains, it was still early and the sun was barely up. He fully opened the window tasting the fresh coolness of the new morning's air as it rushed into the room in greater volume, The view from his first floor window was a sweeping vista of mowed grass that was cleverly flanked by trees and woodlands, the spacing of them arranged to create a false perspective, as it was with the width of the expanse of grass as it widened into the distance, whereas natural perspective would have created a narrowing effect. Into the flat greenness of the open area of grass a few solitary trees had been dotted here and there, now over a hundred years later they were fine, fully grown specimen trees. Amongst them was a statuesque cedar of Lebanon away in the middle distance and a little to the right, much closer to the house a mighty conifer he thought was an American blue spruce of some sort, towered up well above the level of his window and the building itself.

He turned away from the view and caught sight of the image of his own reflected form in a long mirror that was fixed to the wall, he laughed at himself, at the tall, bespectacled and decidedly lean old man who was smirking back at him wearing a pair of clean blue and white stripy pyjamas!

They were the type of cotton pyjamas he'd last worn as a kid, what had they called them back then? Flannelette wasn't it? They'd probably been the kind that caught fire, more of a risk back in the days when we had open fires with their licking yellow and hungry red flames or the glowing red elements in the bars of an old style electric fire!

This morning was day thirteen of his stay at St. Jude's, he'd imagined when arrived that he'd only last a day or two at the most, after he'd so begrudgingly agreed to the stay, that he would quickly become stifled by the place, but now? Now part of him wished he could stay here for the rest of his days! Here, he still had the open wonder of nature's splendour right on his doorstep, yes the gardens close to and around the house were tamed and trimmed and yes the path into the woods was wide and smooth tarmac, but if you carried on a bit further there was that gate, set into the boundary fence with a path beyond it that turned into an earthy track, that took you deep into natural unspoilt woodlands and went on for mile after glorious mile…

He was uncertain precisely when he would be expected to '*sling 'is 'ook!* from St. Jude's, he wondered since this was day thirteen, would tonight be his last night here? He'd seek out The Director and find out later he decided.

He went through to the en-suite, hung his pyjamas on the back of the door and took a bath. It was sheer luxury to lean back in the long, deep bath and soak in the steaming hot, soapy bubble filled water!

He luxuriated in his bath until the water began to cool and he began to hear the noises associated with the general waking-up of the hospice, doors opening and closing, snippets of chatter, the occasional clatter of something now and then.

He towelled himself dry with the thick white towel and watched himself in the bathroom mirror, he was indeed, way too thin! He thought of the irony of how being leaner had been something that he had once longed for when the comfortableness of his life back then had told its sorry tale of excess in the lardy form his body always tended towards and how he had vainly fought against it. The old warning of being careful what you wish for ran through his mind!

He made use of the toothbrush that had been provided for him by the dentist and brushed away as she had described that he should, instructing him as if he was a five year old! Rinsing out his mouth he pulled his lips back to admire the shiny white teeth that now gleamed back at him in the mirror. It had been worth spending half an hour in her chair as she'd tutted and clucked while she'd worked on them!

He pulled on the pair of freshly washed underpants, the ones provided by The Factory, they were old fashioned Y-Fronts, clearly not brand new but eminently serviceable nevertheless, likewise the socks he pulled onto his feet and all of the other clothes he donned, were of similar providence… *dead man's clothes!* St. Jude's also kept a stock of such items, left behind garments they gleaned from house clearances, charity shops and of course inevitably from departed guests of their own, that they made available for anyone who was visiting and needed them.

He smiled at himself in the mirror as he imagined the former owner of the neat grey, slacks-type trousers and pale blue polo shirt he had just put on may also have done when he was wearing them! He added a loose woolly cardigan, which he had particularly liked when he saw it and had picked it out from the clothes on offer, it had long sleeves and a zipper up the front, he liked it because he'd once owned a very similar one. He left it open and slipped his feet into a pair of brown, loafer cum-deck shoes.

It didn't bother Bill in the slightest where his attire had originated, he had been walking in dead man's boots for years, the expensive walking boots that he'd originally set out in when he walked away from his old life, had eventually given out and by that time he was doing all his clothes and footwear shopping at charity shops or more often relying on hand-outs. As long as the clothes were washed and clean, what did it matter where they'd come from?

After enjoying a hearty breakfast and since he had no appointments to see anyone that day, on what would probably be his last full day, he planned to take a long walk through the wild woods, to shake down all of the food he'd just tucked away! Prior to that he sought out the Director, to clarify exactly when he would have to leave. He knocked on the door to her office which was slightly ajar, she made a point of only closing it when she was in a meeting, or really needed privacy to make the statement that… *'her door was always open'*… as near as was possible an entirely literal one!

She was sat at her desk tapping away at the keypad of her laptop when he entered, she glanced up at him over the top of her glasses and smiled,
"Be with you in a sec Bill… Please take a seat."

She only took a minute or so to stop typing then as she sat up, she took off her glasses,
"So Bill, what can I do for you on this beautiful morning? I have to say that you look a hundred percent better than you did on the day you arrived here for your stay with us!"
"I just wanted to come and thank you for all that your establishment has provided me with this last fortnight and to say that much to my surprise I've really enjoyed my stay here, and I agree, it has indeed done me the world of good!"
"It's what we do Bill! I'm so pleased that you felt you were able to embrace our offering, Harry was concerned that for all your need of accepting it, you'd nevertheless find that you were unable to! By the way I have to say I prefer this version of you, he's such a very well-spoken chap isn't he?"
Bill blushed,
"I err, well it's like me old Dad said eh?… *it's 'orses for courses!'* When in Rome and all that!"
"Yes I can see that, although I have to say that I've met more than a few men in similar predicaments as you find yourself, who remained as well-spoken as they'd ever been, yes it always seemed a little incongruous in that setting, but there we have it, let's face it, anyone can find themselves homeless with so little in the way of any reliable safety-net left in our society anymore!"
She seemed to be pondering on something for a moment or two before she went on,

"I suppose for many simply carrying on speaking the way they always have done is perfectly natural, a way of trying to cling on to at least something? Then again of course, if for some reason you wanted to hide your identity, that could be a reason for deciding to leave your voice behind, along with the rest of your identity and your problems perhaps? If you'd taken to the streets to run away from something even?"

Bill smiled as he took up her point,
"Maybe for some people it would be, but for me personally it's something that I've always found, wherever I've lived I tend to pick-up the prevailing accent, I think it's a sort of chameleon mechanism some of us use to fit in? Aren't most of us running away from something, in one way or another, even if it's only The Grim Reaper we're trying to stop catching up with us!" He laughed freely and she joined in with him. He then quickly changed the subject,

"Do you know Harry well? The way he spoke of you made it seem as if you might."
"Well yes I suppose I know him quite well, we do work together in many ways, we're both of that *busybody type* you know? The kind of people who are on lots of committees and suchlike things, busy minding everyone else's business you could say! So we bump into each other at all sorts of social events and fundraisers too. I'd say we were more business acquaintances rather than actual friends though, why do you ask?"
"Oh, no particular reason, he's an interesting chap is Harry, I was surprised to hear that he bribed you into letting me stay here, that he funded my visit?"
"Oh…who told you that? Damn-it! I was under strict orders that you weren't to find that out! Sworn to secrecy I was! Oh well, we can't get the cat back in the bag now can we! Yes he did make a donation that perhaps coincidentally happened to coincide with your stay here, that much I will admit to!" She laughed, then went on,
"He's donated before over the years you know, or rather I think that he's steered funds our way from the deep pockets of his project's anonymous benefactor, the one who made the whole Folks Factory a reality."

"Right… erm… look, the main reason I came to see you was that I was wondering exactly when I'm to receive, well not to put a finer point on it… *the order of the boot* so to speak, you know…err… is my stay fourteen nights, or fourteen days? How's it been arranged?"
"When you must leave us? Oh, well… look, I suppose it's true, all good things do have to come to an end! Listen Bill, I don't have anyone going into your rooms until Friday, so if you can vacate the room on Thursday morning say? Would that be alright? I feel terrible having to… as you say, boot you out! But that is the reality of it I'm afraid!"
"But that's two more nights, well days… so three more nights! Bloody hell yes! That's absolutely fine and dandy with me!"

"Bill, isn't there any way you can be persuaded not to return to your old life… you know, going out there? Out in the cold, being homeless? Why on earth can't you accept the offer of a room at The Folks Factory? Look at you in just the two weeks that you've spent here, how much better you are for having been fed well, kept warm and safe and from enjoying the benefit of a roof over your head."

Bill shook his head, she could feel the warmth suddenly leaching out of their encounter, sense himself withdrawing from her, pulling back…
"Aye well, it's not all bad you know, being out there and close to nature, feeling that you actually are a part of it all and not remote from it… that you belong to it even. I always 'as t'Factry as a fall back an'all, if it gets too cold like…"

"Harry told me that you turn down his offer of a room everytime because you won't agree to the terms, you won't follow the procedure The Folks Factory have laid down before they can give you a room with a key to your own door, provide you with an address? That they have to have your full name and an NI number, is that why you don't feel able to accept it? You *are* running away from something aren't you, or at least you're hiding from someone? Are you in some kind of trouble Bill? Maybe Harry can help, even if it wasn't in a professional capacity, he is a very resourceful man."

He got up from his seat and stood with his hands on the back of the chair,
"Let it be love, please, just leave it alone. Thank you for all you've done for me here, it's been wonderful, you must be very proud of this place, leastways I hope that you are? You have every reason to be, it's remarkable! It's an oasis of love and care in that ever expanding desert of compassionlessness that's out there… Your work here is simply magnificent." With that he turned and headed for the door…

She called him back,
"Hey! Come on! Hang about a minute Bill! Look, if it is that, if that's all that concerns you Harry said, if I had to… as a last resort, that I could tell you that he'll make an exception for you, just for you and it would have to be totally on the hush-hush! That in your case he'll give you one of the rooms as long as you want it and with absolutely no strings attached, you can just be *William Williams* as I see you've been listed here by our Doctor… Oh, bloody hell it was him wasn't it? It was the doc who told you Harry was funding your stay? Hmm…

"Why not at least try it, keep on going down the road you're on now, the road to getting better? Why throw away all the good work we've done together in you short stay here?"
"He said all that? Harry did?"
"Yes Bill, he did! Come on man! There's being fiercely independent and then there's plain pig-headed stubbornness!"
"Aye well, I'll admit that giving him all those details were me chief objection to his offer and all of the rest of his bloody stepping stones *bull*… err… I mean, nonsense! I left that life behind me for a reason, so why would I want to be coaxed into treading back along a path designed to return me to it all?"

"Perhaps there could be a better way for you to live than you did previously, you know as part of society but in a different way to how you did before? Adopting a different mind-set maybe, finding a way of thinking about it all that would make it more acceptable for you, that you'd be able to cope with? But that's not even a step he's asking you to take right now, not a bridge you'd have to cross in order to have a place you can call your own and be off the streets. I know the *step-one* rooms are more

of a pod than a room, but Harry's talking about giving you a *step-two* appartment. You know what they are?"
Bill shook his head and shrugged.

"They are all on the third floor, they're accessed from a central corridor that runs right down the middle of the old mill building and they have lifts and stairs at the end that leads out directly onto Wentworth Street, so it's right at the opposite end to the Folks Factory refectory. They offer totally independent living for the people who live there. They're not that big, the one he's offering you only has one bedroom, but there's a bathroom, a separate kitchen and a living room. Why not at least take a look at the one he has in mind for you? What have you got to lose? You could try it out, do like you did here maybe? Give it a chance? You were more than pleasantly surprised with how you found things here weren't you? The one he's earmarked for you looks out over the canal, it's at the farthest end of the corridor so you'd be tucked away with no one coming and going past your front door all the time and being at that end it even has a window in the living room that looks out over the refectory!"
"How do you know all that?"
"I was involved back then in the planning of the upper floors, I used to have a job in… Oh look, it doesn't matter… I just do, the floors above have two and even three bedroom appartments, it's a wonderful concept and a marvellously creative use of all that space that the old mill had to offer."

By now Bill was stood in the doorway, having been unobtrusively edging himself ever nearer to it, he stood with one hand on the door handle as he said,
"Aye, well… Maybe I'll take a look at it, seein'as he's gone to so much trouble for me! Thanks again." With that he turned and left.

The rest of the day passed pleasantly enough for Bill, with him taking the long walk he'd planned through the woods before lunch and afterwards indulging in a pleasure that he had long ago forgone, that of reading! With his reading glassed perched upon the end of his nose he sat himself in a comfy armchair in the large resident's lounge, the wide bi-fold doors which led onto a large patio were wide open, the room was full of fresh, fragrant air and he could feel the warmth of the sun which was cascading into the room as it fell onto his legs.

Since he had received his two pairs of specs, he'd started using his reading glasses to take up again what long ago had been a favourite pastime of his, reading. He'd found a Sci-Fi novel by Ray Bradbury, read it and had then gone into the library to see if he could find any more of his books. One side of the shelving had been cleared of the old unread, leather bound volumes that were still in place along one of the other walls and had been refilled with contemporary used paperbacks!

Unable to find another Ray Bradbury novel, he came across a book entitled, A Kestrel for a Knave. The author was someone called Barry Hines's, the title rang a bell somewhere at the back of his mind. He read a little of the cover notes, it told of fifteen-year-old Billy Casper, who seems destined for a life in the coal mines of his home town, Barnsley. But Billy's discovery of a kestrel, and his dedication in training it, gave him optimism – however temporary that was it! He realised that this was the book Ken Loach's film Kes was based upon and why it had seemed familiar.

He remembered seeing the movie, Kes when he was still a teenager and how moved he had been after watching it, how it had influenced his own thinking about society and societal injustice, about how unfair life was in Britain. It had sown the seeds of him eventually embracing Socialism to be the only decent system to use to run a society. Sadly he had in later life come to accept that this was, at least within his own lifetime an unobtainable utopia!

He had devoured, more than read the book in less than two days!

Today though, he was reading The Gazette, the local rag. There was a piece on page six by that Jennifer Stainton, the girl who'd tried to interview him at The Factory, he smiled when he saw that she called herself their *'roving reporter!'* She was a really good writer he thought, as he read a very entertaining piece she'd written about the latest traffic flow alterations on the main routes in and out of town, hardly riveting stuff! But she made the issue of how the alterations to the roads, which were being carried out to allow for more bus and cycle lanes impacted on the people that actually used them, quite entertaining.

She pointed out that although these were highly commendable, very environmentally friendly and decidedly 'Green' projects... at least in theory... in practice and in the experience of the majority of the people who actually used the roads, who were drivers... they were hideously unpopular! In fact they deeply resented them, as all they appeared to achieve, from their point of view as car drivers, was to take out lanes they had been able to use previously and thus created massive tail-backs and bottle-necks, in other words unleashing mayhem and utter havoc, along with all of its associated frustration being inflicted upon the road users! All of this for the provision of bus lanes for an occasional half-empty bus and cycle lanes that virtually no one ever used at all ...

Most cyclists she said that she'd observed herself, or spoken to, in fact rode on the pavement as they felt unsafe on the roads! ...and who could blame them! The selfish and inconsiderate way that most people drive today! She added... *'I won't ride my bike on most of the main roads into town in rush-hour either!'* Yes there was the odd bus or two that sailed past the queues of frustrated drivers, but it seemed to them to be just rubbing salt into their already raw wounds!

She was balanced too though in her coverage and presented the other side of the argument, pointing out that the buses were actually available *for all* of us to use! That the pollution from all these cars was literally, albeit slowly, killing us! That it was causing breathing difficulties for our kids and creating a generation of asthma sufferers! So The Council had a duty to try and do something about it, to protect us from ourselves!

She asked pertinently, 'Have you noticed how many child-care & day nursery establishments are situated right next to these busy polluting roads?' Going on to add... 'Yeah... because they're handy places for *us* to drop the kids off as we *drive* into work! Handy for sure, but we're leaving them there breathing the filth from our roads all day long! We all know about the problems but we want it to be *others* who change their habits to make improvements and *not us! We need to grasp one simple*

concept... when we are sat in a jam... we are not IN a traffic jam... WE ARE the traffic jam!'
She was a bit of a radical too, which he especially liked as she suggested that making the buses really cheap might possibly be a good idea too? Subsidise the fares by putting it on people's Council Tax even? That way people would feel invested in the project... having effectively already paid part of the fare that would allow them to be one of the smug folks riding *on the bus*... and be one of those who were sailing past the queues of motorists! That they too could take advantage of all those lovely clear bus lanes to ride along into town!

Bill was chuckling to himself over what he was reading when he became aware that someone had walked over to stand alongside his chair, he looked up and was surprised to see Harry!

"Harry, what are you doing here?"
"Nice to see you too Bill!" He laughed as he dragged a smaller chair over and sat himself down next to Bill.
"I was up this way and thought I'd pop in and see how your stay has gone."
"Huh! What you mean is that *our Pat*, as in Patricia Melling MBE, rang you after her conversation with me earlier and suggested it might be a good time for you to do so, don't you? To strike whilst the iron is hot?"
"Well... erm... she might have done!"

Bill laughed as he folded the newspaper up and placed it down on the small table that was alongside him. As he took of his reading glasses and replaced them with his distance pair, he pondered on the thought of challenging Harry about him funding his stay at St. Jude's but decided not to, so instead he said,
"So I guess she's told you that she has me nibbling at your bait and suggested it might be a fortuitous time for you to come and try to hook me and reel me in?"
Harry scoffed, but he was still smiling as he said,
"You really are the most frustrating old bugger Bill, I can't understand why I bother with you! Pat says she's found you charming and quite endearing! I thought that somehow we must've sent the wrong person up, that the driver picked up someone else by mistake! That's really why I came up here, to check it was really you that was here!" The two men laughed

together until Bill got up from his chair and strolled over to the French windows, leading Harry outside.

He sat at one of the tables and proceeded to make up one of his rollies,
"They're not keen at all on anyone smoking here of course but, what can you do?" He licked the paper, tapped the end and lit up. Harry sat back and let the rays of the sun warm his face, he already had a ruddy complexion that could easily be mistaken for one of a spirit drinker's and it took little exposure to the sun to exacerbate the effect. He looked over at his obstreperous, old companion. Despite his unkempt appearance, with his wild long hair and thick, bushy beard he was still quite a striking looking fellow. Granted that was more so as he was today, with him being scrubbed up and having had a comb dragged through his hirsute splendour and the donning of some smart, clean casual clothes had improved things enormously too, but he'd always had a presence of his own, though it was usually tinged with a slightly darker and more brooding nature than today as he sat in the warm sunshine. If someone had said that he had once been a TV or film star, or maybe that he was an ageing member of a rock and roll band... you could have easily taken their word for it!

After a while Harry struck up the conversation again,
"I see all this reading has inspired some elegance into your speech! Looking at you now, it's almost as if the old curmudgeon we sent up here has been replaced with someone else!"
"Aye well, 'appen as 'ow if y'tends to folk a wee bit better, they responds similarly!"

The two men sat chatting together for a while longer, resulting in Bill agreeing to take a drive down into town with Harry and at least *take a look* at the flat he'd earmarked for him.

So it was that a little later on he was riding down the hill into town sat in the comfort of the passenger seat of Harry's Jag. Despite the many years that had passed since he had enjoyed such an experience... he was finding the familiarity of it all, although quite intoxicating, also somewhat troubling as it stirred memories that had lain dormant for so long. Memories of sitting on the leather seats in one of his own cars as he drove it himself...

Lost to his thoughts it seemed to take next to no time before he realised that they had pulled up into the smaller car park at the far end of The Factory. This end was far more gentrified than the business end, with which he was more acquainted, that frequented by the *clients*! The tall factory wall had been reduced to a fraction of its original height before it was topped off again with the original copings and one of the gate posts had been moved apart from the other to create a wider entrance. On either side of the tarmac the flagstones had been taken up and the area was now grassed over and had a row of small silver birch trees on either side. It had all the appearances of a factory conversion into luxury appartments, which in effect was exactly what it was.

Whisked up to the third floor in the lift, it was clear to Bill that Harry took great pride in what they had achieved with this project and he had to admit it was most impressive, the long corridor they found themselves on when they left the lift, ran the nearly the full length of the factory, seemingly narrowing into the distance as if it was in a movie, but despite its incredible length and only having the benefit of natural daylight at each end it didn't feel at all claustrophobic due to its width and height, aided by the light colours that had been used in the décor.

The flat he led Bill into through a door near the end of the corridor was superb and already fully furnished. After his cushy time at St. Jude's it looked to Bill to be an altogether far more inviting prospect than returning to his wild bivouac! He stood gazing out of the window looking over the canal and the few remaining streets there were before the moors to the north of town rose up as they did likewise on three sides of the town. How could he turn down an offer like this? He pondered to himself. Why would *anyone* want to turn it down?

His alter-ego chipped in a response...
Because it's a trap! That's why! It's nothing more than a tasty morsel dangling from their fishing line! Hung out there ever so temptingly before you, right in front of your hungry eyes...
Waiting for you to go for it...
Then comes the strike...

The bite of the hook…
Then they have you all over again…
Another voice asked him, look! What's there to fear? No forms to fill, no name to reveal, nothing…All of this can be yours… All you have to do is say that one word… Just say it, say *yes!*
Ah yes, that little word! But once you've said it, once you've agreed, said that one small word stepped inside… the moment that door shuts behind you… *you are trapped!*
You are *lost!*
They will have successfully made the first tiny cut of the thousands of cuts that will follow, cuts that will bleed the life's blood from your body, sap your life force until you are returned to being one of their mindless, unthinking zombies, living out your pathetic robotic existence lurching around, doing their bidding and jumping through their fucking hoops all over again…

Harry interrupted his reverie,
"Well what do you think Bill?" Then he added, as if he was a mind reader, "It's not a trap! You can walk out anytime, day or night, why not give it a try? If it's not for you, then there's nothing to stop you going back out there, out into the cold, if that's what you chose to do, decide that's best for you, there'll be nothing to stop you. What have you got to lose apart from being on your own out there in the cold, being constantly in danger and far away from any help should you need it… being utterly alone."
"Freedom Harry. Freedom and total unaccountability…" Was all he said in reply.

"Well at least have a proper look around will you, before you dismiss it and turn me down?" Harry took the grunt he got in response to be a positive one, as the recalcitrant old bugger then followed him around as he showed him the rest of the flat which consisted of the living room, a small corridor that linked it to the kitchen, the front door, the bathroom and the bedroom. In the corridor was a really large and very practical storage cupboard. The living room had a large window looking out over the moors in the distance, a TV, two chairs, a sideboard and a couch which Harry pointed out was also a bed-settee, there was also a small dining table tucked up against one wall.

"So what do you think Bill?" Silently turning his back on Harry, Bill just stood gazing out of the other window, his hands thrust deep into his pockets as he looked down into the refectory way below him. Becoming increasingly frustrated, Harry tried to distract him,
"There's a mobile phone there on the sideboard for you, it's got my number in it and a few others too that you may find useful as well." That at least piqued Bill's interest enough to get him to turn and go over to the sideboard, he picked up the small mobile phone which was plugged into a socket on the wall over the sideboard. He pulled the plug out of the phone and turned it over in his hand,
"You just flip it open, it's only a cheap little thing, I have a deal with a phone company..." Bill flipped the phone open, closed it again and placed it back down on the sideboard,
"Reminds me of the old Motorola V8..." He started to say but stopped short of elaborating further.

Harry just shrugged, what more could he do, you could lead a horse to water and all that…

Despite feeling a bit downhearted, Bill's cool response hadn't been that much of a surprise too him and after all he hadn't turned him down categorically either.

He dropped Bill back off up the hill at St. Jude's and headed back into town, he hadn't really had the time to spare for ferrying the old sod around, as he had a stack of paperwork sat waiting for him on his desk, the little jaunt had been a handy excuse to escape from doing it but it would still be there waiting for him when he got back…

CHAPTER FIFTEEN

Sat in his room with an open book on his lap that he was unable to concentrate upon, Bill was in a quandary over what to do the following morning when he had to leave St. Jude's. He acknowledged that it was a quite remarkable thing that Harry was offering him, he had removed all the obstacles of having to make the commitments that had always made the idea impossible for him to contemplate! How Harry was able to square it with his records wasn't his problem, but if he said he would do it, then that was good enough for Bill, he imagined there would be some *creative* accounting involved! Maybe he would be recorded as a live-in floor supervisor or something like that with the accommodation thrown in as part of the job? Or maybe he just had an empty apartment or two most of the time?

His main query though was, why? Why would the guy bother about him? Why had he bothered so much already? Why had he chauffeured him around personally like he just had? Bill knew how in all the time he'd known Harry, he'd mostly been rude to the man, at best he'd been begrudgingly civil with him! There simply wasn't anything in it for Harry other than the glaringly obvious conclusion that he actually cared about Bill. He guessed the guy spent his working life doing little else other than caring for all the other clients he hosted in one way or another, be it from simply feeding them or putting a roof over their heads for an odd night now and then, right through to housing them and getting them back off the streets altogether.

Now that he'd taken that first step by accepting the invitation to spend the time at St. Jude's and having benefitted so much from the experience, he felt more inclined to accept the offer than he would have been previously, the no-strings attached nature of it was reassuring too.
After all it wasn't a prison…
You could leave whenever you wanted to…

A line from an old Eagle's song ran through his mind, *'you can checkout anytime you want… but you can never leave…'* Hotel California was the name of the track he recalled.

He was up against a wall though here. A wall of his own construction, built out of hard bricks, bricks he had shaped and fashioned for himself out of the clay of his fears and from the damning conclusions he had come to about society. Then they had been fired in the furnace of his anger and cemented together with his pain. It was a strong, tall and defiant wall, built on deep foundations. The coiled barbed wire strands of suspicion of everyone and everything were tangled together along the top.

He knew that on the other side of the wall lay a land that he was familiar with, where he had lived all of his life until he could bear it no more, when he had left it behind...
A land for him that had at one time been one of comfort, of possessions, of family, friends, children, grandkids... All of which were most likely, still there.
But also on the other side there was an ex-wife, commitments, responsibilities, expectations and money... and all it could buy... Money... The gateway to alcohol, cocaine, gambling, sex...

It *was* a trap.

However sweet the tempting, dangling morsel may be... It was still bait.

It was still a trap.

Summer was on the way, so living outside would be okay, he had shelter if he needed it at The Factory if the weather was too wet, for too long. He could put off the decision till autumn at least, or until it started to get cold? Harry hadn't set any time limit on acceptance of his offer, had he? What if Harry left, or got fired? Where would he be then, whether he was in or out at that point?

So it was that Bill's last night spent at St. Jude's was a restless one of fitful sleep and he awakened feeling tired and unrefreshed.

Since he was awake anyway, he got up early and had a bath, he made a little pile on the bed of the neatly folded clothes he had borrowed and put his own back on. They had been laundered and ironed for him and he noticed that there had even been some repairs made with very neat stitching in a couple of places, both to his coat and his trousers! He kept the underwear and socks, wearing them and with the spare ones packed away in his rucksack, which he had taken back out from the bottom of the wardrobe where it had sat these last sixteen days, he placed it on the floor by the door, his coat draped over it, topped-off with his baseball cap. He went down to get his last breakfast in the dining room.

Once he was faced with the sight of food though, he couldn't summon up much of an appetite and instead settled for just a piece of toast and a cup of coffee. The worry of what to do next that had robbed him of sleep last night was now denying him his one last feed here! Once he'd finished his meagre breakfast he went to say goodbye and offer a final thankyou to Pat, the door to her office was wide open and as he went in, he was surprised to see his rucksack next to a chair that had his hat and coat over its back, there was also a bulging carrier bag placed on its seat.

Pat saw him come in and taking-in his puzzled look as he saw his stuff there, greeted him cheerily…
"Morning Bill! Thanks for having your room ready so early, the cleaners brought your stuff down so they could crack on getting it ready for the newcomer. Listen here, you really must take the clothes you picked out for yourself, they've put them in that carrier bag for you."
"Well it were… it was just that they aren't the sort of thing I'd normally wear… y'know… out there?"
"Oh no… Don't tell me you're going to turn Harry down? Awh no… He'll be devastated!"
"That's it though! Isn't it? Why? Why's he so bothered about me?"
"Oh Bill, you really are a clot! He may well have taken on the job as manager at The Factory simply *as a job… for the money!* In fact, he told me as much that that was how it was when he took it on, he may even pretend that's why he stays now! But he's totally devoted to it, it's become *his* cause now and *his* passion to help those in need. You're not the first person he's taken a special interest in, you do know that don't you? You're just the latest. He's quite the knight in shining armour is our Harry, you won't know this but I do, he offers this five star treatment package far more readily to any women that come through his doors than he does for the men! It's only a

reasonable thing to do though I suppose, a woman in that predicament is far more vulnerable than a man. He's more inclined to go the extra mile for young fellas too… He's a bloody good bloke is Harry, please don't let him down, take the helping hand he's offering you, it would mean so much to him and let's face it, it would be of enormous benefit to you… If only you could let your fear go…"

"Aye well… I'll take your bag of clothes and say thank you for them and for my stay here too, but regarding your advice… well I'll accept that it's all very well-meant and say thank you for it and we'd best leave it at that. Thank you Mrs Melling, I wish you well and goodbye!" She called after him,
"Do you want John to run you down into town?"
"No thanks I'll walk it. Bye…"
"Oh Bill! Hang-on a sec… The Doc told me to tell you that he wants to see you before you leave, can you pop in on him?" Bill grimaced, but in response grunted acquiescingly,
"Aye, 'appen as a'can! If a'must!"

He'd barely turned the corner in the corridor after leaving Pat's office when he ran into the doctor,
"A-ha! Mister William Williams, the very man I want to see! Please, walk with me back to my office."
"Aye, well I don't know why y'wanna see me, seems t'me 'as we said all as was needed at our last conflab!"
By now they had entered the doctor's room and behind Bill the doctor was closing the door,
"Please, take a seat Bill, I won't keep you long, I promise." The doctor went around his desk and settled himself into his chair,
"So, have you had time to reconsider your negative thoughts about meeting the specialist, y'know with a view to prolonging your life?"
"Nah! Course not doc! Thing is I'll die when I die, as intended if y'like? That Reaper fella's 'ad 'is eye on me for quite a while, sometimes feels as 'e's right there at me shoulder, ready t'tap 'is bony finger on it like!" He chuckled enthusiastically at this…
"But seriously doc, I do think… no I know f'certain, 'es bin following me for a very long time. I've 'ad more'n'me fair share of brushes wi'death, one way or another y'ave t'understand! 'E could've 'ad me on so many occasions I couldn't count-em…

in't'past like… reckless I were at one time, didn't care if I lived or died back then…

"So when 'e finally decides 'e's gonna 'ave me… well, that'll be it won't it? There's now't as I can do to change that! No? I'm right aren't I doc?"

"Well yes, if you want to put it like that I suppose so, but how is it that you think you're so different to everyone else, to *anyone* else? How different are you really to the tragic relics of humanity, as you refer to them as, that I come across here and in the hospital day-in, day-out? The one's with the gaunt faces, the mere remains of what was once a viable, vibrant person as they lie there on a gurney, often parked-up in a corridor, almost as if they've been abandoned, forsaken even, staring helplessly up at you with their pleading eyes, looking to you for something? For you to do something, to do *anything* for them, even if they haven't the faintest of clues as to what it could possibly be! They're looking for answers? For any answer, as to what the Hell all of this is about? How they've ended up there? How they got to be so helpless like this, to return to being as they came into this life as they were when they were babies? But with no Mummy this time, to save them… It's as if they're asking you, what happened? Where did my life go? How did it pass me by so quickly?"

"Aye well, what y'say's true enough. But they're where they put themselves aren't they? In 'ospital, that's the point I'm makin! See, I plan to die out there, *in* nature, as *part* of nature. To slip away in't'embrace o't'Reaper, restin' in th'arms o'is partner in crime… 'yperthermia!"

"Yes, that's fine and dandy… apart from some poor soul having to deal with discovering your rotting, fly-ridden and bloated corpse!" They both laughed!

"But here you are eh, Bill? Accepting the pills off me, even if you're not prepared to accept the treatment I recommend. So aren't *you* clinging-on too Bill? If only a little bit? Are you so certain that when, as you put it… you finally get that tap on your shoulder from your pal to say… 'It's NOW!' *Come in number 8! That you* too won't try and run, that you won't plead with him, *'oh no, not yet*! *Just a few more days… Please?'* That you won't try and cling on, clutching to anything, as a drowning man does? That instinct is so strong and is embedded so deep in our DNA! How can you be so certain?"

"Aye well mebbe y'right? Find out soon enough won't I, if what y's told me's right, eh? It's all a matter of degree though innit? Where y'draw y'own line in t'sand really, so yeah, okay! I'll tek me pills an'appen keep t'bugger at bay for a bit longer, but 'e'll still come when 'es good an'ready! God knows, like I ses, 'e's had enough chances already if 'e'd wanted to tek'em!
"I've 'ad me a good few days in't sun y'know doc, it weren't allays like it is now fer me! An I'm content enough to let what will be, come to be. If me ol'bodies clapped-out, then when it packs-up, then that's 'ow it's meant to be, we're not designed t'live forever doc! Y'should ask y'self that, yer 'ole profession should! Keepin' folks alive, just 'cos y'can in't enough, what y'needs t'ask y'selves is... *should* we be keeping them alive? Mebbe that's 'ow them folks got to be on them gurneys eh? Listenin t'likes o'thee an' running from t'reaper f'too long?
"So thanks, but no thanks doc!"

With a deep sigh, the doctor got up from his desk to see Bill out. He stopped at the door and shook hands with his intransigent patient and as he did so he placed a hand onto the old guy's shoulder saying,
"It's been a pleasure to meet you Sir! And also something of an education as well!"
"Aye well. Likewise for me!" Bill responded, a little taken aback.
As he went to finally leave, the doctor added,
"I'll just slip this into your pocket, in case you change your mind later!" As he spoke he slipped a folded piece of paper into the pocket of Bill's coat as it hung over his arm.
"It's the slip for your appointment with the specialist!"

As Bill walked away, smiling to himself at the last little antic of the doc, he was struck by how much the doctor reminded him of his father. Was it something about the earnestness with which he expressed himself, or the dogged determination he had perhaps? His Dad had been a staunch Socialist, a committed union member, a man who could never be swayed from the total belief that he was right (or more succinctly and less ambiguously 'correct') and that anyone who believed in any other system therefore, simply had to be mistaken. He'd even been a member of The Communist Party for some time! Yet at the same time also a deacon at the Methodist Chapel he attended, he saw no duality in that, even though to many it seemed an odd mix! He often told a tale about how his name had been on a list, a list compiled by *The Secret Service*! Who could know? Even back then things were pretty scary!

What he would've made of his youngest son becoming a 'boss' himself, becoming, one of *them*, him ending up being an employer? Of him hiring other working men to help him? Heaven alone knew! He'd never lived to see it, to be in a position to form an opinion about it, succumbing as he had to a work related illness leading to his premature death, fighting for his last breath a few weeks before his sixtieth birthday.

It was about three maybe four miles back into town, it was all downhill so it was nothing for Bill to walk it, besides he could take a more direct line than the main road did, as he walked down side streets and used the footbridges over the railway line and canal. It gave him time to think about what he would do…

By the time he walked through the stone pillars of The Factory's entrance he'd decided to *give it a go*! He'd tell Harry that he'd try the room out. But not tonight.

It would be Tomorrow.

He wanted to head out along the canal one last time, to spend one more night at his little bivouac home in the woods, to have one last memory of it, knowing that it was to be his last night there…
The time he'd left it previously, he'd always intended being back there that evening…
Maybe it was daft, but that was what he'd decided that he wanted to do.

Harry thought it was *bloody daft* too and said so! But he also said it was Bill's decision to make and he'd already said he could come and go as he pleased. He gave him the keys, there was a fob for the front door into the lobby and a key for his room, they were on a keyring, he noticed that the fob had a telephone number on it for recovery if they were ever lost and found.
"You know your way don't you? You don't need me to come up with you, do you?" With that he shook hands with Bill,

"Thanks for accepting this and I assure you, there aren't any strings attached, it's not a first stepping-stone or any of that stuff, I just want to know that you're safe and well. You really do need to look after yourself Bill… you're sorted with access to your medications now?" He nodded in reply.

Bill went up in the lift, it was odd walking down along the long corridor alone, reaching the end and looking down through the window into the canteen lying down there far below him. He went to his door, put the key in the lock, turned it, opened the door and stepped inside the flat… his own flat!

He dropped his rucksack by the door, placed the carrier bag on one of the chairs and went into the kitchen, he looked in the fridge, it was empty as were the cupboards. He'd need to get some stuff in! Now that was a thought… How was he going to fund his everyday needs now? His whisky and his baccy? He guessed that he would just have to carry on with his day job of begging? There'd be no Benefits coming in as he was retaining his anonymity.

Moving quietly as if he didn't really belong, he peeked into the bedroom, the bed was stripped but there was a large plastic bag full of bedding sat on top of it, with a smaller one alongside it that held some towels.

He looked around the door into the bathroom and then went out into the living room, took one more look and went back out to the front door. Leaving the carrier bag of clothes, he picked up his rucksack and went out into the corridor. He pulled the door shut behind him and put the keys in his pocket.

'Be back tomorrow morning'… he said to himself as he turned and headed off back down the corridor.

CHAPTER SIXTEEN

After taking the lift down and emerging at the *posh-end* of The Factory, Bill wandered back along the front of the long, tall building with a view to getting something to eat, his stomach was rumbling now that he'd settled on a course of action!

On the way he passed the area that was set out with the picnic tables, Nat the student was sat at one, she was writing away on a pad that was next to a pile of books on the table. She picked up a cup and whilst taking a drink from it, she noticed Bill walking down, she glowered at him and looked away. He shrugged and carried on, eager to see what culinary delights were left on offer in the refectory.

After a meal of baked beans on toast and a mug of tea Bill headed into town.

The day spun away as it ever did since he'd taken up this life, scraping together a few coins here and there, then spending them on a sandwich here, a cup of tea there… By late afternoon the weather was changing, the prolonged spell of sunny skies seemed to be drawing to an end, the wind was gusty and the sky was turning grey as Bill emerged from the corner shop with his quarter bottle of whisky and a packet of tobacco ready to head off along the canal for his final night out at his *country retreat!*

He enjoyed the walk and whereas it might have been taking things a little too far to say that he had a spring in his step … he found the walking much easier going than he'd been finding it prior to his *little holiday* at St, Jude's … as he mentally referred to it now.

Thinking in that way had sparked off memories of the many holidays he had actually taken, back in his old life, with his wife and kids… Nah… he stopped his mental windmill from turning at that point… He shook his head as he thought, nah we're not going there!

He eased himself through the rusting old gate, re-secured it and followed his unmarked path to his hideaway, thankfully finding that it was undisturbed! He breathed a sigh of relief, he was going to miss his little camp… But then what would be stopping him coming back any time that he wanted to?

He settled himself into his position, leaning back against the stone of the rockface, there was a small dip in the ground where he sat… he really did feel as if he belonged here, he thought as he unscrewed the cap of the whisky bottle, he took a little swig but wasn't inclined to take any more and screwed it back on, shoving it down into his pocket, he had no need of it tonight, tonight he wanted to savour the raw and unaffected experience of being there, of being here now, of just being…

Suddenly feeling tired and having restored something resembling a normal sleep pattern at St. Jude's, he soon fell asleep… but it was not to be peaceful night.

He found himself walking through a field of verdant green grass, it was quite tall, about eight inches or so high and it waved hypnotically, the heads of the grass making swirling patterns as their swaying stalks were gently caressed by the breeze …

Bracken shoots were appearing everywhere as they pushed up from out of the ground in search of daylight, the tightly curled up fronds seemingly reaching up from the soil, so that they could unfurl into the sunlight for another season's growth…
But now they were no longer bracken fronds… they were tightly clenched fingers on the ends of deathly grey arms! They were the hands of the dead reaching up, reaching out of the ground!
They were coming out of the ground everywhere around him!
They were reaching out for something!
They were reaching out to grab him!

He awoke, sweating! Stupid bloody dream! He scoffed but soon found himself sinking back…
Sinking into an inky black bottomless pit…

He was at The Haven…
In his room…
He'd been there a good while now, things were getting better, He was feeling like his mind was clearing, the therapy had been hard work but constructive…
He was with someone…

It was Zebedee!
No of course it wasn't his real name! He was there as a long term patient, he'd been in some sixties rock band and blown his mind on drugs to such an extent that he'd never be able to leave.
"Go on man! I'm telling you… it will free you! Trust me!"

Why had he taken the bloody papery thing and put it into his mouth? What possible advantage could it have for him? He was on the road to recovery now! Why risk everything?
He had though…

He could remember setting off from The Haven, he was on his way somewhere, it was somewhere special and he had to go there although he couldn't for the life of him remember where it was, or why he had to go there?

He walked down through the gardens to the stone wall that bordered onto the lane, he saw away over to his right, that the gates led onto the drive up to…

He vaulted the wall like a gazelle and picked himself up from being on the floor, why was he on the floor? He walked along the lane a little way, there was a gate in the wall on the opposite side, it was metal and had a curved metal fence in which it was set… it swung in an arc making a triangle-like shape, or more of a wedge, a wedge of cheese shape wasn't it? It was called a sheep-gate he knew that, all of a sudden! It was a gate for sheep? So how could he as a *human* get through it?

He stood looking at it in awe, as a man walked past with his dog. He got a funny look off him, so in response he stood-up straight to attention and then saluted him before returning to the problem of the gate for sheep…

Then he was walking on a hill, he was up *in the sky!* He was on that very hill that Julie Andrews had run across singing in The Sound of Music!
The hills were alive!
The grass was alive!
It was singing….
He was singing…

Way up high above him, ever so high up, he saw a buzzard slowly circling
He looked up watching the bird embracing the wind with its wings…
He was looking down…
He was flying…
He felt the wind beneath his wings holding him up in the air…
Circling…
Circling…
Circling…

"Over here!"
"I've got him!"
Hands on his shoulders and arms, sitting him up.
Hands on his shoulders again.
A coat wrapped around him.
No it's shiny foil?
"You getting me oven-ready?"
That's hysterical and he is laughing uncontrollably now.
"Take a sip of this…"
Water on his lips…

Sat on that couch again now.
"What on earth possessed you? You were due to leave us next week!"
"Will I still be able to? Leave? It was just a blip, honestly. I *am* ready!"
He is sat in that office, the stern faced man is talking to him…
He is the head man at The Haven.
"If it hadn't been for that chap who saw you at the gate, The Mountain Rescue wouldn't have had a clue where to start looking for you! They found you flat on your back like a starfish! What on earth were you doing? You weren't far off hyperthermia by the time they got to you! You'd been lying there for hours!"
"Oh… I was flying! It was wonderful!"

Bill was wide awake again now. The dream was still with him as he sat there in the darkness of the woods, listening to the wind whispering in the branches, rustling through the leaves.

His mind was going back to the time he'd spent at The Haven now. Damn-it! It was better left alone! But his train of thoughts

was a runaway now and he couldn't stop himself remembering more.
Once he'd been discharged from The Haven he'd felt a great deal better, at least for a while. He'd had high hopes that it had put him back-on-track, that he would be able to step back into his old life but aided by a new and less self-destructive perspective.

Why shouldn't he? He'd enjoyed a good life before he'd been grief stricken over the sudden death of his daughter and gone off the rails, but that was the nature of life wasn't it? Death and disaster? Other's had to face appalling grief too, they managed to move on from it, didn't they? Why shouldn't he? Here today, gone tomorrow that was how life was, there was no guarantee supplied with your kids, only the knowledge that whatever happened to them, good, bad or indifferent it would impact on you for the rest of your life, he now fully comprehended that this equally applied whether they were alive or dead!

Of course he'd always known this beforehand, but knowing about an *idea* and actually experiencing a *reality* cannot be compared! It was of course different losing someone who had been in your life for over three decades to losing them when they had only been with you for nine months, when they had never been in a position to look you in the eye... It was impossible and utterly irrational to try and quantify which was worse, it was totally irrelevant too, as his painful old memories had faded and the loss of his daughter still felt current and raw.

Other people dealt with far worst losses, he kept telling himself over and again, some had even survived the horrors of Auschwitz and yet they'd still carried on, but were they dead inside? Emotionally? He had done too, carried on and for a long time at some level at any rate. That was what he'd told himself he was doing anyway, the best he was able to do...

After the funeral, the minister at the church had told him that he had to *be grateful!* Grateful for all the years that she *had been* in his life, that was the blessing for him to acknowledge and that was what he should try to focus on, rather than fixating on the loss of the years he could have had with her had she lived, instead of seeing what had befallen him as a terrible curse!

Nothing could convince him though, they were years she *should* have had, not *could!*

Parsimonious twit that vicar was! He guessed he was only doing his job, but what sort of a job was it that he had to do? Why would anyone want to do it? I mean how do you try and convince anyone who isn't insane, that some, white-bearded, white-skinned old man who's up there somewhere, had planned it all out... that it was all part of His Plan? His plan had been for Abbie to be killed so randomly by a fucking lorry's wheel that had come loose, that had bounced down along the motorway, made it right over the top of the central barrier and was on a precise trajectory so that it put it right through the windscreen of her car... I mean, all that must have taken some fucking detailed and meticulous planning...

The Minister was keen to try and alleviate this obvious flaw in the benevolent nature of God's purpose by stressing that his grandkids, who were in the back of the car when it had happened, had both survived! They had been spared!

His response to the poor man had been brutal... he'd said that he found it difficult to be grateful to God and His immaculate planning! Firstly for ensuring that the wheel bounced precisely on the exact trajectory that it had, in order for it to hit Abbie's windscreen, rather than the front of her car or bouncing clear over it and secondly for letting his granddaughters survive and not killing them too, you know, why not make a proper job of it? Based on the fact that they were both so horrendously traumatised by the horror of seeing their mother turned into a mass of bloody pulp right there infront of their horrified young eyes... then screaming their lungs out in terror for what must have seemed like an age to them, as their car slewed across three lanes of the motorway, then spun around twice before ending up facing the wrong way in the outside lane... No it was hard to be thankful for all that, seeing that they would never be able to lead anything even remotely resembling a normal life thereafter!

The Minister had gone as white as a sheet... But he'd not finished with him yet as he went on, his voice getting louder and angrier as he ranted... '*You do know that I was following them on their way home? That I was in my own car right behind them don't you? That I saw everything that happened to them? That I nearly ran into them as their car went out of control?'* The Minister was shaking his head as he tried to back away, wringing his hands in front of himself, he was crying as he muttered over and over... I'm so sorry, I'm so very sorry...

Even as his two sons dragged him away from the poor sobbing clergyman, he'd yelled back at him 'why didn't your fucking lousy God take me instead, why wasn't Abbie following me? Why didn't the fucking wheel hit my car? Why didn't the fucking bastard take me?' The look on his eldest son's face was one of utter contempt as he snarled in fury at his father,

"Why can't you *ever* behave like a normal person? You always have to go off on one, don't you? You just have to go over the top! You're a fucking disgrace, that's what you are! You just have to give us all yet another one of your performances don't you? And here today, of all places... at our Abbie's funeral! You shame us all! *I'm* ashamed of you Dad! You're not the only one who lost Abbie! You selfish bastard! Me and Jake have lost our sister! Geoff's lost his wife for God's sake and little Fiona and Lucy have lost their mum! You're such a fucking selfish, self-absorbed twat Dad! Why can't you think of other people for once? Behave with at least a shred of dignity? You're a bloody mess, your whole life's a shambles! There's one thing you are right about though... there is no bloody justice, why couldn't it have been you instead!?"

Unnoticed by the three men, two women had approached the angry scene as they had been solemnly walking away from the funeral service at the church, they were arm in arm. Both were dressed in black, the taller of the two detached herself from the other to put a hand on the distraught vicar's arm, as he approached them walking away from the fracas. She placed her other arm around his shoulder to comfort him and spoke softly to him face to face. He rallied a little, even managing a small smile as she sent him on his way back to his church with a fond little pat on his back.

Her friend put her arm back through hers and they walked on, as she drew level with her sons and her ex, one of the women spoke out,

"Neil, my love…leave him be, don't waste your breath on the fool, he's simply not worth it. The pair of you just go! Go and find your wives and kids, they're with grandma, back by the door to the church thanking people for coming, doing what that idiot should've been doing!" She gave her ex-husband a withering look as she allowed herself to be steered away by her partner.

He'd tried to keep quiet, tried not to say anything more, but his mouth wouldn't obey him, it simply refused, it couldn't stay shut, he really had tried…
"Yeah you sneering cow, you waltz off with your fucking lezzy bitch! Waltz off from me *yet again*!" Neil grabbed at the sleeve of his father's jacket yanking at it, turning him away from facing towards his mother and Sue… his brother Jake grabbed Neil's arm to hold him back, pulling him off their distraught father who had slumped onto his knees and was now sitting back onto his heels…

"Oh, come on Neil, mum's right, just leave him be. There's no reasoning with him when he's like this!" Neil released his grip and let his father slump even lower onto the ground like a deflated balloon, all of the fight and anger suddenly dissipating, draining away from him as a wave of utter despair swept up over him. He sat there on the grass, helplessly crying with his head held in his hands as his sons walked away from him.

After a few strides Jake, his youngest son stopped as if he was making to turn back,
"Just leave him Jake! Come on!" His brother demanded grabbing his arm and pulling at him trying to get him to carry on back to the church, but Jake flicked his brother's hand off and turned back and walked back over to his Dad. He crouched down and put a hand on each of the sobbing man's shoulders. He looked up at his son, his face a tear stained picture of devastation… he looked deeply into his son's eyes,
"I'm sorry Jake… I don't think I can bear this… I know you've lost your sister… but she was my little girl… I lived for her…"
Jake let his Dad put his arms around his neck and let him sob onto his shoulder for a little while before gently taking him back up onto his feet with him as he stood-up.

Standing face to face, he pulled a fresh handkerchief from his pocket, unfolded it and gave it to his Dad to wipe his face with as he forced himself to smile kindly at the ragged grief stricken version of the face he had known all his life.
"Bit of role reversal eh kid? You sorting out *my* snotty face!" his Dad said, managing a weak smile.
"Come on Dad, I know you're devastated but you shouldn't carry on like this, let me get you back to your car, get you away from all this... please?" His father nodded and allowed himself to be led away from the church towards the carpark that was situated on the other side of the road. His elder brother who had been stood angrily watching them, his hands planted on his hips, just shrugged despairingly, his brother gave him a reproachful glance as he led their father away... utterly exasperated, Neil spun on his heel and marched off back towards the church.

Once he had him sat behind the wheel of his car, Jake asked him, through the open door,
"You'll be alright from here Dad? You're okay to drive aren't you? You're sure?" Then almost fearing the answer, he nevertheless felt he had to ask...
"Are you coming to the wake?" He'd wanted to say... *'you're not coming to the wake are you?'* It was so unfair not to want his own father to be there... at his own daughter's wake! But after the scene he'd just witnessed... then add in the effect that the copious amount of drink that the already distraught man would doubtless pour down his throat and... The thoughts of the inevitable consequences were just too terrible to imagine, the kids would be there too, to witness whatever kicked-off! Along with all the extended family and the friends of his sister, she'd been so very popular...

He envisaged Neil, who had a temper to match even their father's, ending up punching him out! Mum and Sue would be there too, if ever there was a red rag to his father that would be it! To his immense relief his father replied,
"Nah son... I couldn't bear it, all those jack-asses with their platitudes and simpering drivel! Nah... fuck-em all! Not you lad, you know I love you... love the kids..."
"Yeah Dad, I do! And I love you too even though you're a jack-ass, with all of your outrageous antics and outbursts! I mean... that poor vicar!" He couldn't help himself then and he burst out

laughing... His Dad joined him for a little while but soon the tears had started once more...

"The Vicar's face! Oh my God... you were brutal Dad, you'll have to apologise to him at some point!"

"Fuck that! He asked for it, they all do with their pious crap and all of their ceremonial bullshit. She's dead! Gone! Nothing can change that, she's not gone to heaven, she's not looking down on us now, she's not watching over her girls... she's just fucking gone!"

"Nevertheless he was only trying to do his job, as best he could and under the terrible circumstances he had been presented with, it was an impossible task at that!"

"Anyway, you're mother and that fucking cow she's with will do all the snivelling, grovelling and apologising that's needed to be done, you can rest assured of that! She'll fucking love it! She'll revel in it, be in her element apologising for me, then guzzling up all the sympathy for her having been married to me for all those terrible years of cruelty and abuse!!"

"Dad you know it was nothing like that! We all do, everyone does! Everyone knows you had a happy marriage... well a *happy-ish* one at least, not much different to anyone else's at any rate. But look at it from mum's point of view... We've had this discussion so many times already Dad!

"She did her duty, raised a family tried to fit into the uncomfortable boxes of a mother and wife that she never truly fitted into properly, we know now that she'd always been living a lie! Look at her today, if you could see past your anger, you'd see that she's radiantly happy! She's finally being true to herself, to the person she always was!"

"Yeah fine, but where does that leave me eh? My whole married life was a just lie, a sham? Oh leave it lad..."

"Okay Dad I will, but just think on this, no matter how much pain you're feeling right now, how much worse do you imagine Mum's pain must be? Abbie was a *part* of her, for fuck's sake, she carried her inside her own body for nine months!"

He'd just shrugged at that, then pulled shut the door and driven himself home, to the empty house and poured a whisky... his life had turned to shit, there was nothing for it, nothing anyone could say or do could help. Jake was a great lad but even he knew that Abbie was always his favourite... *had* always been... He had to accept things as they were... his wife was a lesbian, always had been... so what? His daughter was dead... so what? He drank himself into oblivion...

That was the theme *they* came back to every time... He had to let it go, that's what they had repeatedly told him. The psychiatrist, the psychoanalyst, the doctors and the nurses all kept saying it... over and over and over...They gave him therapy to help him get past the PTSD he suffered in relation to the actual accident, to *move-it-on* as they'd said. It had helped somewhat... its aim being to enable his tortured mind to move past being locked into and trapped in those tragic moments of unresolved horror on the motorway, so that he was continually reliving the experience and all of its terror, since it was impossible for his mind to file it away, unable to know where the experience could possibly fit into his memory banks. As a result it just played the whole experience over and over forever, on a loop in his mind... He remembered the floods of tears that had streamed from him as he sobbed from the fathomless depths of his despair after one of the more intense sessions of therapy...

He remembered that years before the tragedy he'd already taken up a new relationship himself! So it was natural enough that now that his wife had left him he'd felt in need of indulging another lady that was in his life! So he'd reinvested in his relationship with a very grand and dignified old lady! She was a 1955 Alvis TC21 saloon.

CHAPTER SEVENTEEN

The Alvis sat in his garage gleaming in black, grey and chrome, the colour scheme he believed all cars of that era should have, in his opinion she was quite frankly... *'magnificent!'*

The three litre in-line straight-six engine was concealed beneath a centre hinged, long-long bonnet, creating an aquiline nose for her, at the front of which was a sublime, chunky chrome radiator! Flaring-out on either side of her bonnet, were the most wonderfully shaped and elongated, curved mudguards that magically metamorphosed into creating her two big round eyes, in the form of giant chrome rimmed round headlights.

Just standing in the doorway of the garage whenever he'd opened up the door, looking at her as she sat there patiently waiting for him, so poised and elegant had always stirred his heart! Opening the front driver's door, always made him smile as they were hinged at the rear... *'suicide doors'* my arse! It was a far more logical arrangement and made it way easier to get in and out... Then sinking into the old and patinated leather seat as the unmistakable and sublimely blended aroma of leather, wood and oil delighted his nostrils... he was in heaven again.

This car for him was a solidified *piece of timelessness!* That seemingly nonsensical thought was what came to him whenever he looked at her! It was true though, for him at least, she was his very own Tardis! Once he was sat behind that fabulously large black steering wheel, with its three sets of four chromium plated spokes, behind which the expanse of the burr walnut dash lay, filled with many perfectly spaced, dials and switches... He felt transported to another world... the sad and confusing one he normally frequented would be left far behind him... Sat in this car he was transported back in time to a long gone era, a simpler time, a better time he considered in so many ways, a time when being English was something most people here were still proud to be, however mistaken a point of view that may in fact (at least from a historical perspective) have been.

He loved to hear the big old engine come to life and back in the day he would drive her sometimes for days on end, finding a hotel to stay at wherever he happened to end up... She was at her best on the open road, around town she was a tad heavy, he struggled sometimes with the synchromesh-free first gear too... despite Martin having gone over how to change down smoothly with him many, many times...

Martin... he was the guy who looked after his old lady, not that she gave him much trouble, but beyond the *tinkering with her type of maintenance*, that he could do himself, he knew his limitations. The great thing was that if there was a problem it was fixable, so unlike the unfathomable and unfixable problems that he'd faced with the other lady in his life! His wife!

He turned the key in the ignition and pressed the starter button...
There was a horrible grating noise...
No it was a roaring noise?
It was a lorry on the motorway bridge...
He must have drifted off to sleep again, lost in his memories.

It was still dark when he opened his eyes the next time.
An owl hooted somewhere off to his left... *'twit'*...
Another replied from his right... *'twoo'*...
It was cold.
Bill shivered and rummaged for the whisky...

It was first light when Bill properly woke up, it was drizzly and damp, the air was filled with the rich earthy aromas of the woodlands as they were refreshed and washed with life giving moisture. He shivered and rubbed at his legs, easing the stiffness out of them, the thought of his warm, dry flat waiting for him suddenly seeming more appealing than ever!

Those weeks at The Hospice had softened him up! He scalded himself, but he knew the rebuke was only half-hearted as he was painfully aware of how he'd been letting himself slip into a bad way, especially health-wise immediately prior to his little holiday! It had been a most timely intervention by Harry, he wondered how he would have fared without it?

He ate a few biscuits and drained his water bottle and then packed-up his campsite. He carefully, almost lovingly rolled-up the discarded piece of tarpaulin that had been his roof for so long and tied it up as he had every other morning, then crouching a little beneath his living vault of greenery he stood, bent over for the last time as he rested his gaze on his woodland *bedroom*...

Would he be able to adjust to living indoors again? He pondered, it had been so easy at St. Jude's with all the attendant facilities and care he'd been given, at his flat he would be alone, would he feel isolated? Is that how it would feel without the ever present buzz and activity of living nature or else the hubbub of the public surrounding him?

He was going to give it a go... That was his decision and there was no reason to change it. He'd just try it and see, that's what he'd decided he told himself, as he made his way back to the towpath.

He pulled the stiff-hinged gate back, for a moment he thought he would toss the old padlock aside, what the hell! But he reconsidered and placed it back exactly as he always had done.

The drizzle in the woods was more like rain in the openness of the towpath, it was still tranquil and beautiful nevertheless but in a misty, moist way today in the dull, early morning grey, overcast light. The hiss and swish of the traffic up on the motorway was ever present as people were rushing to work, or driving cargoes of goods to keep the wheels of society ever turning.

A gaggle of ducks stirred on the bank of the canal a little way ahead of him, pulling their beaks out of the feathers on their backs, where they had buried them to sleep, they struggled ungainly up onto their feet as they untucked them from under their bodies and waddled a few steps to launch themselves out onto the water of the canal, raucously complaining at him for disturbing them!

A little further along a lone magpie, disturbed by the ruckus from the ducks, flapped up and away from out of the rough grass at the side of the towpath, it too cawed annoyingly at Bill. *One for sorrow* he said to himself as he stopped dead in his tracks...

As he froze...
He blinked in disbelief...

He felt himself wobble on his legs which suddenly felt as if their task of supporting him was beyond them!

His left leg gave out beneath him and he went down onto his knee, only catching himself from falling further with his hand as it hit down heavily onto the gritty towpath, his other hand followed as he let himself kneel down, as he gasped for breath…

His head stopped swimming a little and he found the will to ease his arm up and let his rucksack slide off one shoulder and slip to the ground. He sat back onto his heels and let the other strap slip off and then he raised his head, lifted his gaze from staring at the gritty ground beneath him…

To look again at what had shocked him so…

It was real…

What he had seen was still there…

He felt himself gagging, but held it down as he pushed himself up onto one leg and then wobbled up onto his feet.

He took a faltering step on his unsteady legs towards the sight that had horrified him…

He looked down into the lifeless eye of Natalie Blunt as she lay on her back in the rough grass at the edge of the towpath. That bloody magpie had been at work on the other one!

He retched again but his near empty stomach had nothing to offer and again he managed to hold it down…

He stumbled to slump down onto the ground alongside her small body, he reached out and touched her neck to see if there was a pulse, all the while knowing that it was pointless, but it was what you did wasn't it? He could tell she was dead by the ghastly pale, bluish-grey tint of her skin, the glazed lifelessness of her dull staring eye…

He flinched away from her as he touched her, she was so very, very cold…

Her blouse was ripped and her skirt was pulled up exposing her navel and pubis, but there was nothing remotely attractive to this nakedness, the horrendous appearance of her exposed pale body, resembling far more the carcass of a dead animal at the butchers than that of a human being now.

He tried to tug at her skirt to cover her, but it was trapped underneath her. Unable to do anything more, he staggered up onto his feet, his tormented mind in a whirlwind of indecision! But it was obscene that she was so exposed! He desperately looked around for something he could use to cover her up with and caught sight of what he took to be her coat a few feet away, he stomped over to it, picking it up he returned to the prone body and carefully draped the long, plastic feeling material over her, covering her face and body down to her knees.

What to do now?
He felt his whole world was crumbling beneath his feet as a blind and desperate panic began to set in!
All his plans to move into the flat were being torn away from his grasp, the decision he'd agonised over was no longer of any irrelevance…
None of that was important now…
There was one thing that was crystal clear to him…
They would blame him!
They were bound to!
He'd found her, so he must have done it!
Also he knew the bloody girl, they'd met several times!
Why here?
Why was she on the route he took to and from his camp?
He had to leave!
He had to get away!
He grabbed at his rucksack and slung it up onto one shoulder.
Someone else would be along soon enough, a jogger or a dog walker, let them discover her and report it! It wasn't like it mattered to her any more did it?
He'd done what he could to give her a little bit of dignity back, preserve her modesty, hadn't he?

He set off staggering along the towpath in the direction of town, but after a few steps he remembered where he could duck through the loose bit of the fencing that he knew about, it would be a shortcut… He got stuck halfway through and flew into a blind panic, struggling and fighting against the grip of the fence. He stopped, panting breathlessly and tried to calm himself, he eased himself out of the backpack which was stuck fast and then was able to turn and release it and free himself.

Moments later, after he had pushed through the undergrowth he was back in the abandoned, derelict building where the gang of kids gathered, where he'd woken-up that day not so long ago. There was no sign of the yobbo gangs there of course at this time in the morning, they were nocturnal scum, druggies and wasters that so many of them were, although there was plenty of evidence of them scattered everywhere in the form of empty lager and cider cans, three litre plastic bottles, fast-food wrappers and loads of those little silver bulbs that had some gas or other in them that the idiots inhaled, they looked like soda-syphon bulbs to Bill.

He pushed through the broken gates directly out onto the street, there was a phone box somewhere along this road he was sure, wasn't there?

It was gone! A neat empty square on the pavement was all that remained! Apparently we don't need phone boxes anymore! Idiots! They were few and far between now… everyone has a Smartphone, don't they? *'Well I fucking don't!'* Bill growled to himself!

He remembered there were a couple of those covered phones things on the wall of the garage, it had a convenience store as well, it was just around the corner…

He walked across the forecourt having pulled his hat right down on his head, they'd have bloody cameras here for sure… He found the wall mounted phones, one had no handset, the metal cable hanging forlornly from the box, a web of small broken, coloured wires protruding from its end. The other one was still there though, he snatched at it and tremblingly put it his ear, he could hear the dialling tone… he punched 999 in on the keypad…
A voice crackled through the earpiece…
"Emergency Services, which service do you require?"
"Polis!" He barked out… Attempting to mimic a Glaswegian accent!

CHAPTER EIGHTEEN

Detective Sergeant Gideon Willis took one last drag on the... *ludicrous electronic piece of shite* (how he himself described his *e*-cig!)... that he was now using, weaning himself off his much preferred Silk Cut cigarettes... those perfectly formed little white tubes of tightly wrapped... death... the same ones which he had joyously consumed at a rate of forty-plus a day for the last twenty years or more.

It was true that the idiotic gadget fulfilled many of the behavioural roles of his smoking habit, the regular trips outside, the reaching out for it when he was getting stressed, plus the social aspect of having a shared addiction with others when out for a drink... But the ritual was slightly different, it was an imperfect substitute and as with any other form of such repetitive devotion, any deviation however slight, from the fixed mantra spoilt it... it lacked the flick of the ciggy pack lid, the click of a lighter or scrape of a match, the first drag on it to get it burning was missing too, the smell of that first waft of tobacco smoke, the soothing balm of the smoke as it filled your lungs... (*the cough!* ...okay, maybe not that?).

He still got his nicotine hit though, so it ticked that one vital box if nothing else... nevertheless it made you look like a prat, at least in his eyes and as far as it went for the flavoured shite you could get to use in some of the gadgets! A *fruit flavoured ciggy?* For fuck's sake? Those bloody menthol things back in the day had been bad enough! What had they called them? Consulate! Yeah, that had been it!

He was sick, but not quite to death *(...yet),* of being badgered every time he had to go and see Doc Strong for something or other, which as far as he was concerned at any rate, was totally unrelated to his smoking and drinking... or equally had nothing to do with his poor diet. He'd heard a whisper that the old bugger was ready for the off, sick and tired of all the bullshit that being a GP entailed today, that he was worn out by the endless problems that Covid19 had inflicted on his practice, his staff and himself.

He'd intimated one time, how frustrating he found the lack of any attempt at understanding by so many of their patients, of the pressures and stresses that they'd had piled today on them, on top of the already massive, existing pressure and stress the practice had been under for years, even at the best of times... *'it's all thanks to the miserable, bean-counting bastards who hold the purse-strings, that they hold tighter than a duck's arse'* was how he ever so eloquently had put it!

The old lad must be in his late sixties by now, so he'd have been able to have retired years ago if he'd wanted to... He thought fondly of the doctor, he was a grumpy old get, but he was straight talking and what he didn't know about doctoring... well as he'd put it, if he was ever non-plussed over something... 'I'll bloody well find out soon enough on this, as he pointed to his computer!'

He'd probably end up having some new doctor foisted on him when Doc Strong went, some fresh-faced child, straight out of Medical School, a kid who was full of themselves, all-knowing in theory but knowing fuck-all in reality! Cross that bridge as and when eh? For now he had to keep himself well enough to hang onto his job, he was on very thin ice and at fifty-eight he was the oldest Copper at the nick, well in C.I.D. at any rate.

All of his contemporaries had gone, many at the first possible moment they could too, jumping at the chance! Those who had done so mocked him now, on the rare occasions their paths crossed, for staying on, but he looked at them wasting their lives away, in the most part as least as he saw it, doing fuck all, swanning around, drinking or even joining the local Golf Club... playing golf!! Golf... ffs!?!

Being a detective *was* his life, he had no delusions that he was some sort of super sleuth like you'd come across in one of the endless number of TV dramas! He knew he was a plodder, he'd plodded his way through an anything but illustrious career from when he'd started as a uniformed wooden-top! Every step up the ladder had been well behind that of his contemporaries, often by more than just a few years too.

But despite all that he still loved his job! He'd had the odd unexpected success of course, with the cases he was handed...

but not for a while now... random chance would allow for that though, it didn't help that he only got the cases no-one else really wanted, they were never the exciting glamourous or newsworthy ones in the first place, anything like that went to whoever the rising star of the day was, went to one of the arse-kissing, sucking-up brigade whose more youthful, camera friendly face fitted better and would look good on the TV if they ever had to do a press conference. Putting his wrinkly, lined and ugly old mush infront of a TV camera was never going to happen was it?

He guessed that the love of his work, you could fairly call it his passion or even obsession, would fit nicely into one of those many moulds of a stereotypical TV detective, but without any of the shovels full of juicy and carefully selected clichés thrown in, from the seemingly inexhaustible list they had of them! Nah, he was happily married, had been for over thirty years, with two grown-up kids, now flown the coup. Neither he nor his wife had ever had an affair, been swingers or owt like that! He wasn't an alcoholic, he'd never used drugs, he took *all of his* annual leave...to go on holidays *with his wife*... he didn't drive a distinctive or classic car, he wasn't depressed, well no more than the average Copper was, or for that matter the average citizen... well anyone who was capable of actually thinking for themselves and was able to observe how rapidly our society was going to hell in a handcart! He was neither psychotic, nor paranoid nor any other such nonsense either! He was just a normal guy, yeah he was a smoker but he was doing something about that now, well wasn't he?

On his way back to his office as he walked along the corridor from his visit to the outside 'smoking area' a couple of the other lads, another DS and his bagman passed him by, heading out for their own fag break, the DS called out mockingly to him as they passed,
"What'cha got on at the mo' Brucey? Breaking up an Organised Crime Syndicate is it? Or tracking down a Mafia hitman eh? Or are you still trying to get a high enough pass mark, to get yoursel' through your course as a Lollypop man, ready for when they finally force you out to grass? Ha-ha-ha..." The other one who was also guffawing like the mindless dickhead he was chipped-in...

"That stupid old cunt couldn't find his own arse with both hands..." More mindless laughter...
Responding to their taunts, he called after them...
"Go fuck yourself Steadman! You wanker! Or why not get your boyfriend there to do it for you, he follows you around everywhere you go, with his nose up your arse already..."

At that very moment one of the bosses rounded the corner of the intersecting corridor's crossroads, she'd clearly heard what he'd said to Twat-Man & Bobbin... Chief Inspector Sally Pembrose was just as clearly... *not even remotely* amused!

"Gideon will you kindly restrict your disgustingly foul language to where it belongs... the locker room! The *men's* locker room at that! This is a Police Station! This isn't the first time you've been warned, make it *the last*!"

She scowled at him, before turning back to *the uniformed stiff* who was walking alongside her, he was wrapped-up in some posh, high ranking uniform... deputy commissioner? The clown even had his fucking cap on... Fuck! Don thought, bang goes any chance of ever getting a promotion now! He cursed himself for his outburst!

Meanwhile his boss had resumed her polite chit-chatting as they walked on! As he turned down the branch in the corridor she'd just come out from, he glanced back around the corner to get a sneaky peek at her from behind, *of* her behind... he had to give her that much, she *was* still in good shape! But then she was still only in her forties... and a fucking Chief Inspector too! There truly was no justice! The truth, in his experience though was that many of the women Coppers at this nick's language and their behaviour these days, could easily rival or exceed any kind of smut and foulness the lads could muster!

Still smarting from being addressed as *Gideon*, he mused that in that respect there actually was a similarity he shared with at least one of his fictional TV counterparts, the curmudgeonly Inspector Morse! In that drama he'd been saddled by his Quaker father with an even more God-awful first name ... Endeavour! Accordingly, he had opted to be known simply as 'Morse!' Gideon wasn't much better than Endeavour, but whereas

Morse's colleagues had the decency to go along with him and just address him as *Morse,* he had no such luck with people like Pembrose, I mean how hard should it be for her?

He'd asked her on several occasions to use either his surname, or just 'Don' to address him, Don was how his family and friends knew him... well how else are you going to shorten 'Gideon'? Gid? Or *Deon*! I don't bloody think so he smiled to himself!

Even the sneering nickname of *Bruce* was preferable to his given name and if it had been universally adopted he could have lived with that easily enough... it could even have been seen as a being a tiny bit cool? Except it was said only as a skit! I mean for sure in Don's mind, he and John McClane, the skeptical but good-natured New York City police detective portrayed by Bruce Willis in the movies, did have a lot in common! Well they were both so severely follically challenged that they shaved their heads... and Bruce did wear a goatee sometimes similar to the one that permanently adorned Don's chin... To hide his lost jawline... Suitably dyed to only leave a little of the ever more invasive grey...

Turning in through the door to the open plan office, he headed down between the desks towards his own cubbyhole at the far end, to call it an office would be ludicrous, he had to sidle around the desk and squeeze past his single filing cabinet to get behind it, a desk that was barely big enough to put his laptop and a single pile of files onto! Most DS's may not have an office but they'd usually have a reasonably sized workstation to operate from, so yeah no surprises about dead-end-Don's, pigeon hole!

He'd been surprised as he was approaching his glass partitioned hutch, to see that the door was open and his immediate boss, Detective Inspector Shazil Anwar was sat on the plastic moulded chair that was jammed in behind the outwards opening door, he'd left the door open... no doubt so he didn't die from the asphyxiating claustrophobia of the DS's hutch! He was reading a file through specs which he'd perched on the end of his nose, it looked like it could be one off the pile on his desk.

Shaz was an alright enough guy, he was in his late forties and he too had never fully adopted a lot of the *modern bullshit...* as Don referred to most, okay virtually *any*... new ideas, innovations or initiatives... methods and procedures that had been hatched by the latest Brainiac, who appeared at regular intervals, usually attached to a clipboard and with a big stack of handouts and a massive stock of arrogance, balanced out only by an equal and opposite mass of ignorance of any of the practical issues involved in whatever particular area of policing they were concentrating on bolloxing-up at that particular moment!

Shaz saw him approaching, closed the folder and placed it back on Don's desk, he smiled as he rose from the chair and moved aside to let Don squeeze past,
"Hi Don, how it's going?" Don smiled back a little uncertainly, it was not normal practice to be met like this by his boss, for his boss to come down, to be in his hutch... was this the day? Was this *the chat?* No, surely he'd have been summoned into Shaz's office, up on the next floor where suddenly it was found that people worked better in a larger, well-lit work space with lots of windows? Don had a theory that once you earned more by climbing the ranks, as you became more *important*, then a different formula kicked-in, one that once it was applied changed reality for you to suddenly make it completely understandable to you and seem quite logical at that point in time where you newly found yourself, that space, light and little luxuries are utterly essential to improve performance in managers! The strange by-product of this knowledge was being able to understand that all of these perks were totally superfluous for the underlings! In fact they worked better when placed in a pressurised environment...

"Okay Shaz... thanks. How come you're slumming-it down here in the bowels of hell?" He smiled a little awkwardly,
"I need to have a word Don..." *Shit! It was the chat!* Shaz was reaching down and taking out another file from his slim briefcase... Ah well, *I had a good run...*Don sighed...
Shaz looked up and caught a hint of the sad look of resignation and impending doom that was written across his subordinate's face, he held back from passing the folder to Don,
"You okay Don? You don't look too good, is everything alright with you?"
"Well... y'know? I do my best like... Try to get results out of the dregs of cases I get tossed, the one's no one else wants you know? *'Oh give it to dead-end Don!'*... By the way *Pally*-Sally

will no doubt be reporting to you that I was using bad language in the corridor just now, I was responding to some nasty taunts from Steadman and his pet DC... But hey, never mind, it won't matter much now will it?" (Pally-Sally because of her famed way of *chumming-up* to people, to get their guard down... to find precisely where to put the knife in!... all of her bonhomie was totally faked and to be resisted at all costs!)

DI Anwar, sat back a little in his chair, clearly taken aback somewhat ... He eventually responded,
"Erm... Don, look we're both of us old school, you and me... I know you've been in the game longer than me but nevertheless we did both come up the same way, the hard way and believe me *it was* the hard way for me as a young Asian guy back then! Yeah it's a different story for the youngsters coming in now, especially if they come in as graduates, your colour's a lot less relevant today, well at least in theory and a better thing that is too.
"That's part of the reason I'm here, I want you to lead an investigation with the new DS, he needs a steadying hand, someone with experience to lean on. It's a big enough case, and an important one too, it will get a lot of coverage so it needs to be handled carefully and with tact too, you must understand that."

"The new guy's the fast-track one who's just been seconded here?"
"DS Affan Ismail, yeah. You'll be an acting Inspector for the duration of the case." Yeah Don thought to himself, *acting* but with them not *paying*!
"You'll get an uplift in your salary to reflect the extra responsibility for the duration of the case of course." Huh! So what was this, a trap? He shrugged as if he wasn't that bothered...
"I've got the file here, Affan's been briefed that you'll be in charge, but please let him run his own team, steer him rather than outright manage him? I know your last murder went badly, so see this as a chance to redeem yourself perhaps?" With that his boss passed the folder to Don and rose from his chair,
"You know where he is? The office they've given him is a bit bigger than this erm... well, his DC shares his office normally so I've asked him to move him out and you can use his desk... I

didn't think it was necessary to get him to swap his stuff over so you could use his? You agree?" Yeah… like it would matter if he said he didn't!
"No, that's fine Sir, totally makes sense."
"Please, stick with Shaz will you?"

Then he was gone, leaving Don sat there in a daze, with the folder in his hands …for a fucking murder! A whirlwind of confusion in his mind followed, it was an increasingly spinning storm of conflicting emotions swirling around in there… *relief:* that he still had a job, *puzzlement:* as to why he had been given it, *worry:* about being put in over the head of a fellow DS, albeit a relative newcomer, but mostly *fear*… fear of being responsible for a *big case*! Fear of being placed under the spotlight, but most of all the abject terror that was tying knots in his stomach tight now… Of making another balls-up of it and then facing certain humiliation and the demanded retirement that would inevitably follow on from it.

Suddenly all the resentment he'd felt a few minutes earlier seemed like a snatched away comfort blanket that had suddenly and unceremoniously been taken away from him! His dull, routine but familiar existence was gone! The boring uneventful work he was given, he realised now was also familiar and safe, it was manageable, doable and with little or no prospect of anyone noticing any failure, nor getting any recognition over the almost equally unlikeliness of much success either!

He opened the file…

Fuck!! It was the murder that had just come in this morning!
He felt his head go hot, then cold and clammy with beads of sweat forming on his brow, the knots in his stomach decided to unravel themselves, making him feel like he may throw-up… He'd skim-read the first page, it was a report by the two DC's who'd attended at the scene with the uniforms, Amelia Robinson and Paul Cooper, he only knew them vaguely, as he turned the page he realised his hand was shaking…

CHAPTER NINETEEN

Bill had little memory as to how he came to be in the lift, he knew that he was back at The Folks Factory and heading up to the third floor, he'd been on some sort of autopilot since he made the 999 call, his mind had been so frantic, it had been unable to properly process the information being passed to his brain of the progress he'd made in getting across town. He was just walking, walking as quickly as he could, all he'd known was he had to get to the old mill… To his new bolthole… that had occupied all of his available focus, the singular purpose of his entire existence.

The lift sighed to a smooth stop and the doors swished open. He stood for a moment unable to move… placing a hand on the edge of one of the doors, where it disappeared into the recess, he leaned onto it, letting the shift in his weight give him the impetus to start moving out of the lift.

The corridor ahead seemed to stretch away to some far, far away point, it had the appearance of an endless, horror movie corridor, the side walls never meeting… Gripping with his left hand onto the handrail that ran along the left hand side, he made his way slowly along, Harry'd thought of everything… a stray thought fizzled through the turbulent storm clouds that numbed his desperate mind… even down to providing a fucking handrail!

Somehow he found that he'd made it to the far end, he was looking down into the refectory through the window that was at the end of the corridor, 'No… this isn't right?' His fuddled mind informed him…
He spun his head to look around, bemused and befuddled…
Searching for a clue that may tell him where he was…
There was a door…
The door to his flat?
Yes… it *was* the door to his flat!
He staggered over to it feeling as if he was really drunk and stood with both of his palms high up on the door, leaning his weight onto it as he breathed rapidly, his heart pounding heavily. He felt as if he was going to pass out…
'No… not yet, hold on…' He told himself,
'Keys. Keys… KEYS! Harry gave you some keys!'

He shifted his weight sufficiently to allow him to remove his right hand and he rummaged deeply down into his coat's right hand pocket, his trembling fingers desperately feeling around, searching the contents that were jumbling around in it, there was the small glass whisky flask… What was all the other rubbish? The conclusion he arrived at was that the keys weren't there…

'Fuck!' He cursed as he shuffled himself upright into a standing position, swaying gently as he removed his left hand from the stabilising solidity of the door.
This time he plunged his left hand into his pocket and came out with the keys gripped between his fingers, smiling at them like some kind of lunatic.
The keyhole was on the left hand side of the door… 'fuckin' stupid that is 'Arry!' He mumbled… there was no way he was getting the key in with his left hand!
He swapped them over into his right hand and tried to slip the key into the mortice lock, but the fucking hole wouldn't stay still!
What was that noise?
'Fuck'sake!' He grunted…
He leant forward, losing his balance, catching himself by banging his left palm onto the door just above the mischievous keyhole…
What IS that noise?
He managed to slip the key into the now stationary key hole and turned it. He felt it unlock, so he pushed at the door, it still refused to open.
Now… *less occupied with unlocking the door* his mindset shifted and he realised that the noise he'd been hearing was himself laughing hysterically. He stopped it, swivelling his head to look back down along the corridor to see if he'd attracted anyone's attention. The corridor was empty.
'Good!'
'Now… this fucking door!' He wobbled back to stand upright to survey his nemesis. For a fleeting moment he wondered if he could… *kick the bastard open*? Accepting that he could barely balance on both of his feet presently, he decided *'probably not, eh?'* A little voice somewhere echoed through his fracturing mind … *'I could've done it… once upon a time…'*
'What the fuck is wrong with me?' A flash of clearer thought demanded.

'Shock! You're in shock!' Came the response.
'Focus! Open this door! Now!' In response to the command he concentrated on his obstructing foe, now becoming aware of the shiny metal handle a few inches above the keyhole! 'Cunning eh? Who'da thought to use that?'
He wobbled forward and pushed down with his left hand onto the handle, the door having a good proportion of his weight now acting upon it, flew open and Bill fell in through the opening, landed on the floor in a heap. The door, now deciding to be *ever so cooperative,* slowly swung itself shut, clicking gently as it latched itself.

A minute or two… or maybe it was an hour or so later… he was incapable of discerning which it was, Bill found himself slumped into one of the armchairs that sat on either side of the French windows, both of which he must have flung open into the room at some point. He was gazing, unseeingly out through the grill of bars that were fixed across the opening to give the impression of a balcony that did not actually exist, outside of the doorway.
There was something wrong with him.
He had decided.
Oh yes, definitely…
'I'm in shock…' That was it… Yeah, already told you that!
'Hardly fucking surprising eh? Finding that dead girl lying there like that?' A furious voice yelled out at him from somewhere in his addled mind…
The image of her deathly pale legs, her private and most intimate parts exposed for all to see, her dishevelled clothing, her blank unseeing eye looking up at him… Then there was that hideous bloody socket where her other eye should have been…

He leant forward burying his head in his hands letting out an agonised cry as he tried to grind the images away from his eyes...

He reached down to his pocket… It wasn't there? No, it was in his coat's pocket. He looked up and saw that his coat was flung partly on top of his backpack, which he must have dropped onto the floor by the chair, it lay partly across the small table that sat between the two chairs. He leant forward and scrabbled desperately with the coat to find the pocket and his much needed whisky…

Once he had the small flask shaped bottle in his hands he slumped back into the chair, his hands weren't trembling quite as much now he noticed as he unscrewed the cap and took a swig... The neat spirit raced down his throat but rather than bringing him any comfort, it set him off into a coughing fit! He sat forward on the edge of the chair, coughing uncontrollably for what seemed like an eternity until it had subsided enough for him to lean back, exhausted.

He lifted the bottle up to his face to look at it, noting that it was still half-full, it was only then, that it dawned on him that his hand was uncovered, that he was without his usual fingerless mittens, he realised that it hadn't occurred to him until now that they had never been returned to him at that Hospice. He lifted his left hand up before his eyes as he tucked the bottle inbetween his leg and the side of the chair. He hadn't studied the back of his hand properly, in any detail... well, in years? He saw how thin it was, the bones and the thick, bulging blue veins both showing prominently through his thin pale skin.

He sighed as he let his hand rest down into his lap and let his head rest onto the high back of the armchair and closed his eyes. The face of a doctor from somewhere, swam into his mind telling him to lay-off the booze, at least the hard stuff! If he had to have a drink, just limit himself to a pint of beer, maybe two if he really had to! What was that all about? *'You have a fucking ulcer, you idiot*!' His inner nag angrily rebuked him. Aye but precisely what was in them tablets he'd handed him and made such a hoo-ha about insisting that he carried on taking? Eh?

He wanted to look at the labels on the bottles of pills right now, but he realised they were in his bag, on the floor... way, way too far away from him to be bothered with right now! He had a pretty good idea what the tablets would be anyway though, he muttered to himself, fuckin' anti-psychotics most likely, or some other chemically mind-numbing shite! That would be why he was feeling like this! Yeah... yeah... yeah... of course! And the fucking discovery of a murdered girl's body wasn't going to help him that much either was it? But he remained certain in his own mind that it was the fucking drugs that were the main culprit of this miasma he was immersed in, yeah, that much he was dead sure of.

He realised he'd sat upright again, had he been thinking to get the tablets from out of his rucksack? Before he'd decided it was too much trouble? Maybe, it didn't matter anyway, he thought as he slumped back, he'd just have to ride it out now, let the drugs clear his system he guessed, it wasn't as if he'd never had to do precisely that on many occasions previously, times when he'd over-indulged on one or more recreational drugs!

He rummaged around for the bottle that he'd put between his leg and the chair, the top had gone someplace but it had remained upright and un-spilt. He took another defiant swig and let his head rest back, closing his eyes as he let the spirit trickle down his throat…

Sometime later… once again an indeterminate amount of time, he felt a hand on his shoulder, gripping it, it was shaking him…
Now there was a voice too… calling out…
"Bill! Bill… can you hear me Bill?"
He opened his eyes to see Harry's face filling his vision, his worried face was huge as it loomed right there in front of his own…
"Whoa… back off a bit there Harry boy!" He managed to struggle out the words, before having to cough to clear his throat! That got the bugger to back-off, he chuckled to himself!
Harry who was now stood up looking down at him, was saying, "Are you alright Bill, you were proper out of it then, I had a devil of a job getting you to wake up."
"Aye well 'appen as y'should 'ave just let me be then, eh?" Bill growled as what had happened earlier on, hit him all over again, it was a veritable tsunami of horror! He felt the blood drain from his face and shook his head as if to attempt to retain some of it.
"Are you okay, you look like you've just seen a ghost, you've gone as white as a sheet?"
"No'Arry, me ol'chum, I most definitely am *not* alright! Yer damn near give me an 'eart attack, sneakin-in on an old man like that! Oow th'ell did y'get in any'ow? You have a key do ya? A key t'what's meant t' be me own flat? Tha's norr'on that in't!"
"Bill, you left the keys in the lock on the outside of your door! There is a spare key of course there is, but it's locked away in the supervisor's key chest! Why would I have access to it?"
"Aye well then… thing is I weren't doin' so good when I got t'door…"

"Right, well you hang in there then and I'll go and make you a cup of tea, have you eaten anything? I can make you a sandwich? There's everything you need here in the kitchen now you know?"
"Stop fussing like some ol'woman f'fuck'sake! But I *will* 'ave a mug o'tea though… *yes please*… three sugars an'all!"

A few minutes later they were sat opposite each other with their mugs of tea, Bill had recounted to Harry what had befallen him as he was returning to The Factry from his last night… *out in the wild*. "How I wish I'd just moved in 'ere straight away now, instead of insisting on doing that! Bloody ol'fool that I am." He'd bemoaned as he started to tell his ghastly story to Harry.

He hadn't got all that far though when Harry, whose own face had now drained of blood, held up his hand,
"Bill, you say this was very early on? When you found her?"
"Aye, be about five-thirty, I guess, mebbe a bit later why?"
"Bill it's gone twelve now! You have to tell all this to the Police!"
"No, no… NO! I'm not doing that! Fa-fucks'ake I've done now't wrong, t'weren't me 'as did-in't poor wee lass!"
"Of course you didn't, but…" Bill didn't allow him to finish…
"Are you fuckin'stupid or summat 'Arry? What d'ya think them pigs is gonna see? Eh? As they rubs their slimy 'ands together wi'glee? I'll tell ya what they'll see… They'll see some fucked-up, smelly ol'tramp, a wreck of a man and they'll assume that 'es most probably only livin'on't streets in't first place 'cos e's runnin' away from summat? Aye an'then, that it'll be most likely as be it's The Law 'es runnin' from, tryin' not to get caught! E'll be likely as not on't Sex Offenders Register an'all, they'll be thinkin next! Oh aye! 'E'll be a paedophile for sure! Well we'll easy stitch 'im up any'ow, whether or not 'e did it! Quick'n' easy does it! And another one off t'books!"

"Really Bill? You really believe all of that…"
"Come on after, all y've seen 'ere'? You know 'ow we get treated, how' t'pigs regards us. Y'onestly believe I'd get a fair'earin? Really?" Bill shook his head as he leant back and turned his gaze away, to peer out of the window up at the moors, far away off there in the distance, where he wished he was right now, still out there in the wilderness, that he'd never left it in the first place!

Harry muttered, "The poor girl… We have to do something!
"Listen Bill, I can't just sit around doing nothing now that you've told me about it."

"Why not? I've told ya I rung 999 and told 'em I'd found a body, and where it were."
"Yes but, you're a witness, surely?"
"Witness to what?"
"You said you touched her, that you covered her up, didn't you?"
"Yeah, worr'of it? I couldn't leave the poor lass like that, it weren't decent! It were bad enough as she'd been murdered in't first place like…" He trailed off…
Harry carried on, as if he was talking to himself…
"They'll see that as tampering with the crime scene then, I guess, will they?"
"Yeah!" Bill blurted out! "All the more fuckin' reason for me to stay outta it then, innit?"
"Oh Bill! This really is a fucking mess! They'll find your DNA on something you've touched, won't they? They'll know where the 999 call was made from, bound to? Did anyone see you there? See you make the call? Are there CCTV cameras around there… Covering the area by the phone?..."
"Whoa there 'Arry… easy lad! If they finds me, then so be it, they finds me. But I ain't volunteering meself that's f'sure. If you feel y'ave to turn me in, dob me up… again, so be it! Never 'ad ya down for a lousy snitch though!"

Harry flopped down into the chair opposite him, shaking his head slowly. This whole mess was seriously bad news… he couldn't help himself letting his mind run onto the ramifications for The Folks Factory, for him… For one thing, the girl had been around here for days leading up to this, plus she was only here in the first place because of the clients and now if Bill was correct, they'd be saying that it was one of those clients that had done for her! One of the *scum*, as the detractors like to put it, that it was he and his project that had encouraged them to be here in the first place! Oh my God, they'll have a field day! He thought of Jen, how she'd have to pick-up the story, it would be her job to do so! How much he'd given away to her about all sorts of stuff he'd most likely have been better keeping schtum about, at least now in hindsight, in the light of this tragedy… Then he thought about the poor girl, Nat… How could he concern himself with anything else other than doing all he could to help to see that whoever had been the perpetrator of this vile act was brought to justice... Andy! He remembered Andy! Oh that poor little sod... What would he do, his girlfriend so horribly murdered? They'd suspect him too surely? Didn't they always do that? Suspect the husband first or the partner in this case? His whirling mind was interrupted by Bill...

"Planet Earth t'Arry... come-in 'Arry? Now that you've 'ad 'alf-an hour as to get y'thoughts in order..." Bill exaggerated, "What are y'gonna do?"
"I, I... I dunno? No... Yes, yes I do know! Stay here Bill, don't move, don't leave! I'll go and get Alan, he's our legal beagle, he'll know what's best for us to do, I'm sure he will..."
"Wait, will y'give me your word, that y'll not just scurry off outta 'ere to go an ring't' Police?"
"What'll you do if I won't?"
"Fair point! Doubt as I'd be able to shove yer outta yon window..."

After Harry had left, Bill sat gazing unseeingly out of the window, there'd been precious little improvement in how he was feeling, but at least he wasn't quite as shaky as before. He guessed it would be the PTSD thing next, having to go through that shite all over again. Having... in the fullness of time, to eventually work his way past it all too... Well, if he lived long enough to do so that was! Yeah, that was what he had to look forward to now, that ever present, insidious terror that would slowly begin to creep in to replace that first shock of the initial horror of what he'd beheld, to lie dormant, lurking just beneath the surface of his consciousness, ever ready to pounce...

About a quarter of an hour passed before a knock came on his door,
"It's open! Come in!" He yelled unceremoniously.
He heard the door open and then click shut as a guy in his mid-fifties appeared around the corner into his living room.
The guy with the mass of combed back white hair...

"Hi, I'm Alan Jarvis, Harry's sent me up to talk to you. I understand you have quite a problem. He's sketched out what's happened to you, I know it sounds dreadful right now, but I'm

sure I can be of assistance to you in negotiating a route through these difficulties. You just have to keep your head and stay calm. May I sit down?"
Bill nodded and waved to the empty armchair opposite him.

"Aye, well we both know yer a great one fer *negotiatin' ya way* through difficulties aren't ya *Alan*!" The guy was startled and actually flinched backwards!
"Wha.. I..."
"Oh, just shut the fuck up Alan. I know you recognise me, that you know who I really am! It was all over your face at that gladhanding gathering when you saw me, there you were schmoozing and creeping around, doing what you're best at and then suddenly you saw me across the room! Your face! You looked like you'd seen a ghost! But you had, hadn't you? Eh? *Alan*?" He went on,
"Y'know I couldn't put my finger on it, when I saw you there, it was that you always reminded me of someone, I knew he'd been Eddie Shoestring in that old TV drama, but could I recall his name!"
"Trevor Eve? Yeah, I get that quite..."
"Oh yeah, I know... I know now! It came to me later. Pity you never had any of the attributes of the characters he played eh? Honesty, decency, integrity?" Alan sat forward, leaning towards Bill, and literally held his hands out, palms up in confession...
"Look Jos, I know I did wrong, I was in a mess... a terrible hole and I truly intended to repay the money... Honestly I did!"
"You must've thought it was your own private Christmas when I disappeared?"
"That's ridiculous! I was as worried as everyone else was, we all were, of course we were! It was a terrible time! Your family were desperate!"
"Yeah, I'll bet! If by *my family* you mean my youngest lad, Jake? Then yeah, okay, he probably was pretty upset..."
"*Pretty upset*! The fella was beside himself!"
"Yeah, like I said, Jake would've been! As far as the other one goes... well he'd have just been worried about how he'd manage to be able to take control of the company with me only *missing* and not having the decency to be on a slab in the morgue!" Alan nodded at that,

"Well, I can't deny that at any rate! That was precisely how I always perceived him to be in my dealings with him, a cold fish for sure, you're aware that earlier this year he had you declared dead! No, I don't suppose you will be, how could you be? The seven years required since you were last seen were up. He was in court on the seventh anniversary of your disappearance! Well the day after you were last seen! I only know this because I was informed in my official capacity here, due to your connections with The Folks Factory."

Bill/Jos chuckled to himself as he thought about what Jarvis had said about Neil! It was typical of him, he must have been counting the days down to when he could finally be in charge and rightfully take over what he already saw as his own company! It had always been as if he resented his father, couldn't wait for him to die, or at the very least retire and just fuck-off out of his way! It seemed that the fella had always felt he was entitled to take the reins, be *the boss*, be in charge! That he resented his father being there, the hostility between them at times was palpable.

It was bizarre, everything he had, had been handed to him on a plate! Yeah, for sure his father had made him start at the bottom working on one of the sites, he'd wanted him to know how the firm worked, be a hands-on boss, like he'd been. That was the way he'd done it himself, only he'd gone to work on other people's sites, he'd started off labouring, then picked up bricklaying and joinery, he was good with his hands but also sharp with his mind. He'd watched the bosses coming and going in their fancy 4x4's, saw the flash houses they lived in and that it was all child's play and he wanted it too.

After he'd saved enough money to buy a cheap bit of land, he'd built his first house, sold it and bought a bigger piece of land and as they say the rest was history.

Him and Neil were too much alike he guessed? Jake was so different, he'd always been more like his mother, back then he'd somehow been offended by any suggestion of that? Was that it? Because he was a mummy's boy, was that why a rift had opened-up between them? No, he considered, it was closer to the truth that they'd just never really developed much of a bond.

The seven years Neil had been forced to wait must have been purgatory for him to endure, all that time Bill mused, he'd have secretly been dreading that the old bugger might turn-up! It would almost have been worth it! To make a surprise appearance, get it on record that he was still alive! Part of him wished he'd done just that, maybe on the eve of the seventh anniversary of his disappearance!

The simple truth he supposed was that however he'd brought Neil into the business, he was always going to be seen as the *bosses son,* so he was never treated the same way Bill had been as he'd worked his way up, it wasn't possible for all he tried, to give him the same grounding he'd had himself, the little shit'd had a way too easy ride!

It had been a start so dissimilar to his own, him being the son of the boss, coming into a successful and medium sized building company, unlike himself who had literally built the whole thing up from the ground! His own father hadn't handed him anything, not in the material sense, all he'd given him was a strong work ethic and a will to better himself, instilled in him a belief that he was as good as anyone and that he could achieve whatever he set his mind to, if he was determined enough.

He thought once more about Jake, poor Jake, he knew how much the lad loved him. That was what hurt the most, accepting how unfair he'd been to him by disappearing.

It was sad too that Jake was the only one left who really cared. His mum was gone, she'd never really got past Abbie's death. She'd faded, turned in and escaped within herself. If it had been acceptable, they should have put *'from a broken heart'* as the cause of death on her Death Certificate.

Abbie had been like the daughter she'd never had herself, she'd been alone for ten, fifteen years by then, after his Dad had died, she had pretended earlier on that his wife Ruth fulfilled that roll but Bill saw through that little pretence! His mum had been one of three girls herself, her own Dad had desperately wanted a son so it was inevitable the way fate worked that she'd end up having three boys herself wasn't it? That was just another little example of how fate worked, how it toyed with us, cruelly and sadistically using us as its unwilling playthings?

Who else could there have been to mourn him? Both of his younger brothers had fucked-off as far away as they could! Had that been their way of dealing with their humble roots? One off to Canada & one to New Zealand. He'd not been in touch with either of them or even heard anything of them since his mum died. He looked back at the excuse of a man sat opposite him.

"So I'm dead now! It's official! It's no wonder I feel a bit wonky then is it?" The two men laughed, feebly together for a moment,
"So he'll have finally got what he wanted then! To be in charge! To be *the* boss! That kid resented me from the moment his balls dropped! He just saw me as someone he was destined to replace I guess? Even after I loosened the reigns, made him CEO he resented me still being there as Chairman!" Bill stopped abruptly…

"What the fuck! So when exactly did you get to know that I was the benefactor? I thought no one knew, not anyone who was still involved in the project at any rate! Who told you?" Jarvis smirked,
"I'm not as stupid as you obviously think Jimmy! Come on… *Jos?* Really? Don't you think you could have been a bit more creative? It's almost as if you wanted to leave a clue, to be so clever that you'd give it away to anyone as smart as you, smart enough to figure it out?… *Mister James Oscar Stanley*!
"Oh yeah your boy had a field day once he'd had you declared dead! He even changed the name of your company from Stanley Construction to Neil Stanley Enterprises! He gave your house to the younger lad too, oh yeah, after he'd sold off your precious car collection that is!"

"How do you know all this?" Bill demanded, Jarvis tapped his nose… he was enjoying this, he felt he'd seized the initiative,
"Oh y'know, wheels within wheels… I know their company accountant. We trained together at the same firm."
"What you know old Fred Kirkbride? He's at least twenty years older than you!"
"Who? Oh, I guess he'd be the guy Neil fired off soon after you went missing? No, it's Graham who I know, the current

accountant and I can tell you that guy is a crook. I'd have serious doubts about anyone who employed a character like him!"

"That's fucking rich coming from you!" Bill's face turned to thunder as he returned to the little matter of the theft of twenty thousand pounds!
"So I guess you'll have long since repaid that twenty k you stole, seeing as you've had over seven years to do so!" Jarvis blushed, his cheeks and his neck went bright red and he started waffling...
"I... I err... I do have the money... it's put away... *it's safe!* It's just that the books being all straight, you know after you found out what I'd done, I mean what you did? I couldn't believe it when you did it... repaid the twenty thousand from your own pocket into the company!"

Bill recalled the incident as he let the thieving shit squirm. Yeah he wouldn't have believed his luck when his accuser went missing! He had a little smile thinking that if he'd planned his *escape* a little more thoroughly, he could have left details of the embezzlement behind and made it look like Jarvis had done away with him!

The truth was though that he'd already been so close to breaking point... back then... on that day... He'd always had an eye for figures, he could smell-out a rat in a sheaf of accounts as easily as The Pied Piper! Jarvis had thought he was clever, but he wasn't, not to the trained eye, the fact that there was money missing had leapt out at him. He had to fight for every penny that they raised to keep the project afloat without using more of his own money, so they were all precious to him!

Jarvis had owned-up to his theft pretty quickly, turning from the bare faced denial he'd at first tried to tough it out with, to his sob story about his kid's tuition fees at private school, having a wife with extravagant tastes, all his debts... all the usual bullshit of the stuff people like him felt that they were entitled to have, to have without the justification of being truly smart enough or for their abilities to be worth enough to actually earn them! The man was pathetic! It hadn't been out of pity that he'd paid the money back in to keep the books straight himself, no he'd fully intended to deal with Jarvis when he felt more inclined to, more up to the task but at that moment he'd been teetering on the brink...

Examining the books, nit-picking over stuff, focussing on minutiae was the sort of distraction he'd sought out, anything rather than face the broiling torment of his own tortured mind.

Had this betrayal actually been the final straw, he wondered? It was a shitty thing for someone he trusted to do have done for sure, stab him in the back by stealing from his charity. Well the charity he *administered*... Was it the thing that had actually tipped him over the edge... to fall into the abyss... It was after all later on, in the evening of that very same day that he'd donned his walking boots, packed his rucksack and walked away from his life... never to return... until having to face it again today!

Returning to the conversation, breaking the silence that had hung in the air for a long moment, Bill/Jos/Jimmy feeling somewhat bemused questioned Jarvis,
"So you've kept that secret all this time? You've always known who I am?"
"No, I told you, I only found out when Graham landed the job at Stanley's..."
"So it wasn't until after I'd disappeared..."
"Are you okay Jos? You seem to be slow grasping what I'm telling you!"
"What? You devious bastard! If you don't think what you've been telling me would come as a shock, then..." Bill's face reddened in anger as he snarled out...
"So you thieving bastard, what you aren't saying with all of your drivel is the simple truth that you haven't repaid a single penny!" The manner in which Jarvis slumped back into the chair said it all, he was a defeated man... he was guilty as charged. It was 'Bill' who spoke next...

"Let me mek one thing clear to ya fella! S'far as yers concerned... ya knows nothin'! Yer's never seen me before up until today! T'you I'm jus' some ol'tramp that y'boss is tryin' to 'elp. Never forget as I know where y'skeleton's 'idden, an one word from ya 'bout me true identity to anyone, including 'Arry, an' y'll be off t'jail for embezzlement!"

CHAPTER TWENTY

Jarvis must have left at some point as when Bill started coughing and woke himself up, he was once more alone. Being isolated as he found himself now inside this room, cut-off from the world he normally lived in, he had no idea what time it was. He normally knew this from watching life as it busily passed him by, that was all he needed to tell the time…. back there, out in his world, living his life outside…

He'd been dreaming, going back again in time to the place where he'd been coming back from his amnesia, after awakening from the coma he'd been in following the attack…

His thoughts kept coming back to the presence of the woman in his hospital room, to Del, he was certain by now that it had been Del.

She was back to being the person he'd spent so many nights with, he was fully aware of her once more and of the part she'd played in his life back then. The haziness surrounding those months had cleared away as he'd recovered at The Haven, but he'd never set eyes on her again since that terrible night.

His worry that she'd been caught up in the attack and hurt or even killed had been mostly allayed, after he'd sought out again the cop who'd come to his bedside to take his statement regarding the assault. It had taken some time to track him down, enquiring at The Police Station initially, but then even longer to actually arrange a meet-up with him. The cop had been certain that there had been no woman involved or injured at any stage of the assault, at least not to his knowledge. No one he had interviewed about the incident, or the cops who'd attended initially had said anything about a woman being hurt. There had definitely only been one injured party and that was him!

He'd tried to find Del continuously for over a week, finding that he was hampered by the fact that for many months prior to the attack, he had been living in a blur of drunkenness, of being so high, or so drugged-up on cocaine or ecstasy or whatever else someone, anyone, would sell or give to him… He'd been living nocturnally at that time, falling into bed at his flat in town, or at

some random woman's flat, at some house, or in a hotel room... waking-up late on as the sun was already well and truly up but when the day was only just beginning for him.
It had only been in more recent times prior to the attack that he'd been solely seeing Del, as he was weaning himself of the drugs.

It had seemed to him that at that time the days had all been dismal, dark, cloudy, raining or windy or both... The sun had hardly ever seemed to show its face... It had probably been winter... He really couldn't recall...

He slowly began to come to terms with the fact that he knew precious little about Del, not even her surname! For sure... he knew every inch of her body... oh man did he know that! And getting to know that body had come as more than a little of a surprise to him too!

The truth was that he'd been living a truly hedonistic and utterly abandoned lifestyle at that time, in his quest for oblivion, to blot out the unbearable pain of being alive, of still being alive but having to endure living without his daughter Abbie and cope with his total disillusionment with life... it had driven him to seek refuge in this immersive and sustained bout of over-indulgent self-destruction.

Even at its most extreme, the escape was only temporary though... the relief was so fleeting... as it only pushed back for a time the moment when realities cruel, sweeping-in tide would crash back onto the rocky shore of his ragged and tormented mind, the harshness of the relentless waves beating on his aching brain was pure agony, accumulating as it did on top of the very real banging, physical pain of his endless, hangover headaches. Then the ebb of realities onslaught, sucking away all the vainly piled-up distractions he'd sought to use to keep out reality, the debris of his indulgences from the night before...
his ever more extreme...
and destructive...
mindless...
idiotic...
behaviour...

He'd met Del at one of the seedier clubs he regularly frequented back then, the one he was usually ending up at around then. It was one of the last ones to still be remaining open, at probably around sometime like three in the morning! She'd started talking to him as he was sat at the bar in a drunken, drugged-up haze, he'd been unaware that she'd sidled-up to him until she'd spoken to him!
By this time of the night that was normality for him, he'd be barely registering what was happening *around* him, or *to* him, where he was, who he was even! Only being vaguely aware of the presence of the maybe dozen and a half other punters who were still in there, the hard core of the other die-hard pissheads and druggies! The music would be quite low by now, most of it sounding increasingly incomprehensible… at least to him… it'd be jazz most likely playing… that jazz he considered to be the type where the musicians had lost their sheet music, were as drunk as their audience and were all playing randomly… In other words he had succeeded in feeling exactly as he'd set out that night to end-up feeling! Well and truly… Out of it!

"Hi there sweetie, I'm Del!" She'd purred, to which he'd slurred in reply, something along the lines of…
"'Course'y'are my lovely!" To his surprise she'd then reached over to him and ever so gently run her fingers through the flop of unruly hair that fallen across his forehead, lifting it back into place, she then let her fingertips run down his cheek onto his chin and gripping it ever-so-lightly, she used it to turn his head to face her.
"Lets' try that again shall we? Hi sweetie, I'm Del!"

Looking as he now was towards where the voice had come from, rather than replying as he'd previously done whilst carrying on staring into empty space! He became aware of the attractive face that was hovering about in space next to him, he squinted a little to get a better look… She looked quite attractive… attractive enough at any rate for this time of night! He'd not pulled that night, pickings had been slim and he'd been considerably less than amenable to the few women that he'd chatted with, or rather had tried to chat *him* up! They'd been so obviously prostitutes that he'd felt a bit insulted! Accordingly he'd not felt obliged to be particularly polite to them!

But this was a different prospect before him now! She was actually quite pretty, also she was clearly neither drunk, drugged-up nor intoxicated in any other way! She was quite sober!

He'd suddenly become aware of a new and very large presence arriving in his proximity, just behind him! He'd looked around over his shoulder … a little too sharply, nearly falling off his stool… Del had reached out a hand and caught his elbow to steady him…
"Steady-on there cowboy!" She'd chuckled as she nodded to the hulking presence of the bouncer saying sweetly to him,
"It's okay Donnie, he's harmless… aren't you honey?"
"So I'm harmless am I? Good judge of that are you Del?"
"Oh well done you! You remembered my name! I do like to make a lasting impression! In the state you're in sweetie I figure that was quite an accomplishment!"
"So, sweetie… is that Del for Della?"
"Why no sweet thing… How rude! It's Del for Del-icious!"

At some point later on he'd made the connection to realise that Del was one of the cabaret acts that were on in the less disreputable hours of the club's opening hours, between midnight and two.

He remembered waking-up the next day in a strange bed, in a room he'd never seen before… not that unusual in itself. He turned his head to see the back of a woman curled-up next to him… again not that unusual in itself either!

He'd tried to piece enough of the previous night together to try and determine who she may be… What her name might be? But it was a lady called *Sleep* who had reached up and hauled him back down into her dark, mysterious embrace…

When he eventually came around properly she was gone. There was a big mug of now cold coffee and a side plate with a couple of thick rounds of toast, thickly spread with marmalade. He grunted to himself and shuffled himself onto one elbow and shakily managed to grip the mug and slurp at the coffee. Despite being cold it was strong and sweet. He gulped thirstily at it once more before devouring the toast.

Laying himself back down for a moment he quickly realised that he needed to pee, so he struggled his legs out over the side of the bed and hauled himself up onto his feet, steadying himself against the bedside table as he wobbled about! In a similar manner he staggered out of the bedroom, glancing through a window as he went onto a small corridor to find the bathroom. He realised that he was in a flat somewhere, it seemed to be on the first floor, there was a busy street out there below it…

The next time he became aware, it was dark in the bedroom. He must have come back and climbed into bed he assumed.

A voice, right next to him woke him up, "did you find anything to eat?"
He shook his befuddled head and tried to say 'no' but only a croak came from his mouth… He coughed…
"Here, sit up and eat this!" A sandwich appeared on a plate infront of him. Dutifully he munched his way through it, the bread feeling like cloying cotton-wool in his mouth, virtually tasteless.
"Here drink this. It's tea. It's got sugar in it."
He drank the sweet tea and then lay back down…
He was briefly aware of her getting into bed alongside of him and rolling over so that her back was to him. He tried to turn his head to see her, it was dark though. He couldn't remember her turning out the light…
"Thanks…" He managed to mutter.
"Go back to sleep…" She responded.

There was an element of Groundhog Day to the next few days… they were virtually the same as each other, although he found he was gradually awake for a little longer each day.

Eventually he was sufficiently awake to pour away the drink that was left for him and rummage about in the kitchen to find coffee and some food. That wasn't the point at which he'd realised that she'd been putting something in the drinks, when it eventually had dawned on him, he'd found the idea an eminently sensible proposition and drank it regardless!

He'd tried to get a handle on how many days had repeated themselves, but beyond three or maybe four he was uncertain.

With a fresh mug of tea and a fistful of biscuits he switched the TV on to seek information.

He must have dozed off naturally this time, sat in the chair with the TV on, as it was about four in the morning when Del came in.
"Ah ha! Look who's back from the dead!" She commented as she flipped her shoes off and dropped her coat on a chair next to the small dining table.

She walked over to him, bent over him and gave him a kiss on the forehead. "How are you feeling?"
"It's Del isn't it? Pleased to meet you Del… meet you sober that is! I'm sorry if I've been rude to you? I'm aware… well vaguely, that I can be a total arse when I'm off my face!"
"No, you were a total gentleman, Jim."
"Jim? What, as in *Gentleman-Jim*?"
"Why, isn't Jim your real name then?"
"Err… nah… no, actually it's Jos. At least when I'm sober it is!"
"Okay *Jos*… you know, you were pretty sure it was *Jim* that night when we met!"
"Well I drink, get stoned, I do all of that to forget who I am, so it looks like I'm even more successful at it than I thought!"

He'd never asked her why she'd drugged him. Somehow she'd just known he had to come down, get out-of-it, if he was going to make it. He was just grateful for what she'd done for him. He knew he wasn't out of the woods by any means but he felt as if she'd put him on the right path, helped him take the first step towards something better.

After talking for a while longer they'd gone to bed. He was still wearing the men's pyjamas he'd first woken up in so he'd just climbed in next to her when she turned-in.
"Night!" Was all she said as she curled-up, with her back to him again.

"Did we…err?"
"No! Go to sleep!"

In time they *had* gone on to share an intimate relationship together, it became the most intense and also the closest relationship that he had ever shared with anybody. It seemed to him that he finally understood what it meant to give yourself to someone, completely and utterly with nothing held back… Was it love? He guessed it must be, how could anything else be so amazing?

It had been dark when they left the flat and he'd never returned to it again. He'd always met her at work, going to the club early enough to catch her act or she had come to his flat. Together they had carried on working towards weaning him off the drugs first and then gradually getting him away from the excessive drinking. It had been an exception that fateful night when he'd lapsed and got drunk again…

That was why he had no idea where she lived.

He must have drifted off to sleep once more, as a rough hand on his shoulder woke him, it was Harry,
"Look Bill I've spoken at length with Alan and we've decided that you have to go to the Police! I'm sorry, but if you don't go, I will. I've given it a lot of thought and I simply cannot see any other course of action that I can live with."

"Aye well… figured you'd come to that conclusion!"

CHAPTER TWENTY-ONE

Don was busily going through a stack of papers, one sheet at a time as he plucked them from the folder he had resting on his left forearm. After he'd made a quick appraisal of its contents he placed it down onto the relevant pile on top of the long desk in the incident room that was currently being set up.

He'd asked the *high-flyer* Affan, the new DS he'd had foisted upon him to help him do this, but already he'd been finding that the fella was good at not being around when there was any boring work to be done! Yeah, Don mused, that lad's destined to go a long way!

The Scene of Crime stuff was all in now, it consisted of an extensive list of all the evidence that had been bagged and tagged from the scene, a pile of photographs of the victim's clothing and a list of the items she'd either had with her, or had been found nearby. There was a small pile of witness statements along with those of the attending officers, a list of the girl's known contacts, from the analysis of her phone obtained from The Service Provider alone, as her handset had not been found and then there were all the photographs and so it went on…

He went through the pile of photographs, looking at each in turn as he took them from the folder, the first lot were of the crime scene. In the first one he saw that someone had covered the body with what they were assuming for now, to be her own coat. Considering the violence that had been inflicted on the poor kid, it seemed a strange thing for the perpetrator or perpetrators to have done. It chimed with the 999 call maybe though? He hadn't found the details of that yet…

It seemed probable that the call had been made by the same person who covered the body up, but why had they left the scene? Were they the perp? Had they felt the need to return to the scene to check for anything that may incriminate them, anything they may have missed in the dark? Had they felt a pang of remorse seeing her there in the cold light of day, when whatever insanity that had motivated them to behave in such a barbaric way had released them from its evil grip? Possible… More likely it was someone who simply didn't want to get

involved, maybe they didn't like the Police! That wouldn't eliminate too many people, he scoffed to himself, their popularity with the public after all was at a low ebb...
Could be someone who was *scared* of the Police? Had they something of their own to hide?

"Morning boss!" Affan called out cheerily as he breezed into the room,
"Well, yeah guess it still is... just about... *morning* that is!" Don attempted to be as gruff as he could, he failed as ever, it just wasn't in his nature and he found himself returning the guy's big boyish grin!
"Come on Gov! Let's get off on a good foot!" He joshed,
"Well if you want to do that, call me Don or if you have to be formal, yeah I guess 'boss' will do!"
"Okay Don, shall I start with the board?"
"Yeah okay, I'm still going through this..." He nodded down at the folder on his arm as he placed the photo that was still in his hand down onto the table. Arraf moved closer and looked down at it as Don peeled off the next one...
This one showed the girl lying on the ground without the coat over her...
Arraf groaned, "the poor kid, that's truly evil! How old was she, nineteen wasn't it?" Don nodded to the pile with the girls personal details,
"Start with them, centre of the board I want the photo of her when she was alive, so we know what this is all about!"

The phone that had been installed on the small desk at the other end of the room rang out. Arraf looked over to Don who nodded for him to take it and he went over and picked up...
"Murder Incident Room...."

Don shook his head as he mulled over his own mixed feelings about handling this case... yeah there was the kudos, the chance to shine, but also the downright nastiness of the whole thing to deal with too! He knew he was going to be haunted by that image of the girl lying dead, her clothes all pulled at and her nakedness... but Arraf seemed to be joyfully sucking it all up! He was so eager to get his teeth into his first big case, his first high profile case, his first murder! The lad would learn in time, wouldn't he? He tried unsuccessfully to convince himself? Nah, he suspected that he would leapfrog the ranks so quickly that he'd never have the time to actually connect to the awfulness of the crimes he worked on, seeing them as mere rungs on his supercharged career ladder...

Arraf called to him, "it was for you Don. I fielded it though for you, hope you don't mind? There's a solicitor downstairs with the guy who found the body and rang it in, shall I go?" Keen as mustard he was Don thought... So let's reel him in a wee bit eh?

"Nah, you can go through the rest of these and finish off setting up the board." He handed the folder to him on his way to the door, seeing his crestfallen face he added,
"Cheer-up lad! I'll be back to check over your work once I've seen what this is all about!"

Don nodded to the desk sergeant as he passed his counter on his way to the interview room. He paused for a moment to compose himself, then opened the door to the interview room and stepped inside, he paused again, as he shut the door and stood casually with his back to it as he took in the scene,

A smartly dressed middle aged woman rose from her seat and spoke up,
"Good morning! I'm Wendy Morrison, I'll be acting on behalf of Mr.Williams." She took a step towards him and offered her hand, He shook her hand and replied,
"Detective Sergeant Willis, shall we..." He motioned for the woman to retake her seat, nodding to the DC, Amelia Robinson who was also present, sitting opposite the solicitor, he noted she had been one of the attending officers at the scene.

"So my client Mr. Williams has prepared a statement for you." The solicitor slid a sheet of paper across the table towards where Don had sat down. He glanced down at it without reading it.

"Suppose instead that Mr. Williams tells me himself, in his own words what he saw, what he did and why he did it. Is that alright Mr. Williams?" Don studied the old guy who was sat across from him... He was clearly one of the homeless or making a damn good impersonation of being one of them! He was wearing a dirty baseball cap, from under which a mass of long grey and dark brown hair protruded, it was tangled for sure but looked surprisingly clean for a homeless person. Ditto his wild, long beard, it was darker and also greyer than his hair, but although unkempt it looked reasonably clean too.

He was wearing a large and heavy looking, dark coloured old coat. It was quite warm in the room... Odd? The man lifted his eyes and made eye contact for a moment, his eyes magnified through the lenses of the large black rimmed glasses. He glanced across at his solicitor and shook his head, an almost imperceptible movement.

"My client has provided you with the most comprehensive of statements, which you have before you. I suggest you read it thoroughly and if you have any further questions you may direct them through me. He does not wish to speak to you directly."
Don picked up the sheet of paper, it was several sheets in fact, stapled together. He sat back in his chair and carefully read through it, before handing it to his colleague.

It was precise and detailed in laying out an approximate timeline starting from when he had come across the girl's body, how shocked he had been and never having been in such a situation before he had been unsure what to do, however he had attempted to check to see if she had a pulse, although he had considered that she must be dead. This was confirmed by how cold her skin felt. He had tried unsuccessfully to pull her skirt down to cover over her private parts, but finding he was unable to so, he had found a coat with which he had covered her up. He then walked to a garage that was about a quarter of a mile from the canal and dialled 999. He felt as the poor girl was already dead and beyond help that this was sufficient action for him to have taken.

Don placed the paper down on the table.
"That's very thorough, thank you Mr. Williams. Let me be clear, I only want to *ask* you about this, you are *not* a suspect, you are only a *witness*. You should have nothing to fear, so why won't you talk to me?"
The old guy remained silent, blankly staring into space as Wendy replied for him, "Well, if there's nothing else? We'll leave it there I think detective, my client has done his duty insofar as he

reported finding a body and he has come here today with me, voluntarily and made a statement to you. I think you'll agree that this is all that he is obliged to do."

The DC Amelia glanced over at Don and then spoke up,
"But surely you can see that if he won't speak to us Mrs Morrison and he refuses to answer our questions that it's going to seem a bit suspicious to us, that all it is doing is making him look guilty of something,? Mr. Williams, don't you want us to catch whoever did this terrible thing to that poor girl. It might not have been the *correct thing* to do, when you covered-up her body as you did, but I fully appreciate that you did what you thought was the *right thing* to do. We don't for a moment hold that against you, honestly I for one don't. It was indecent, it was horrible for the poor girl to have no dignity like that! Do you have a daughter of you own Sir? Was that why you felt you had to do it?"

Wendy Morrison got onto her feet and she indicated to Bill that he should be doing likewise, accordingly he pushed himself upright from the table to stand unsteadily for a moment or two before nodding his agreement to her, the young detective spoke again,
"Thank you for coming in Sir, we appreciate all the help we can get and I can assure you that we will find whoever did this, but please reconsider speaking to us…" She held out a small business card towards him…
Wendy leant over and took it from her,
"Thank you detective, that will be all."
The old man glanced across at Amelia as he turned to follow Wendy towards the door, he gave her the tiniest of nods as their eyes met for a moment… the depth of sadness she felt in those eyes startled her, she had been about to say something else but it stopped her for a moment as she was rising from her chair.

When she looked up, Don was on his feet holding the door as the old man and his brief left. He let the door swing shut and sat down across from her in the seat Bill had been using.
"Well, what do you make of that Amelia?" She shrugged…
"What indeed?"
"So do you think he did it?"

"No way! Why… Surely you can't think he did? You don't, do you Sir?"
"Never say never love! Ooops!Sorry I mean *DC Robinson*, we have to be PC don't we DC, can't be calling you *love*?" She laughed along with him.
"Well I suppose at this stage we do have to keep an open mind… but I just don't see it Sir. The poor old bugger had a job getting up onto his feet never mind… well I mean, the poor lass *was* raped wasn't she?"
"Aye well, it looks that way, but we're waiting on the initial forensic reports to confirm it for sure, although the full autopsy is a day or two off, due to the shortage of a pathologist at the morgue!"
"That's all we need!"
"Don't rush to any sort of judgement Amelia, look at what's in front of you from all angles first and don't miss the most obvious thing about this case, this guy's homeless, he's a tramp if you like and yet he turns up with a brief and a written statement! Doesn't that set any alarm bells ringing for you? Then his statement explains away any of his DNA being found on the body, or at least offers a fig leaf of protection for him, enough to put a reasonable doubt into the mind of a juror perhaps?"

Back in the incident room, Affan had nearly finished setting-up the board, around the room a few more of the team had turned up, some of them were setting up tables and plugging in lamps, wiring-up computers and arranging chairs, others were leaning on the tables chatting.

Don let them get on with it and went over to the board, Affan was pinning a last item on,
"Will it do boss?" Don nodded, "good enough for now," He responded with a nod, as he cast his eyes over it. He then turned to the room and raising his voice spoke out loudly,
"Okay everybody, let's have a bit of hush!" The chatter and bustle died down as everyone turned their attention to Don.

CHAPTER TWENTY-TWO

Bill and his solicitor had been escorted from the Police Station by a young uniformed constable. As they stood next to the steps leading down to the car park, the solicitor turned to him and she made a half-hearted attempt at a reassuring smile,
"So Bill, I think that went as well as could be expected. I'm still not sure that it was the best tactic to adopt, but since you insisted..."
"Listen luv, give them buggers an inch an'y'll find yersel' banged up afore y'feet 'ave touched the ground!" Bill grumbled back in response.
"Well I suppose that you must have your reasons Mr. Williams..."
"It's *Bill*! Just Bill, I'm *not* Mr. Williams! I told yer that!" The woman visibly bristled!
"Well then *Bill*! I must repeat what I told you and Mr. Jarvis when you appointed me, if anything changes... if your status changes, I mean should you become a *suspect*... and I have to say again that the way you have instructed me to handle matters on your behalf so far... Well, I feel that you have definitely increased the possibility of that becoming a reality! If it does, then at that point I really must urge you to seek the counsel of a *criminal lawyer*, I am most certainly *not* used to dealing with criminal cases! It is a specialty I have never been involved with!"
"Nor 'as 'ad any inclination t'be involved wi'neither I'll bet!" Bill sneeringly interjected!

"I was given the impression by Mr. Jarvis when he spoke to me, that he has access to adequate funds for your defence should it become necessary. Engaging a Criminal Solicitor would be a far wiser use of them!"
"What makes yer think as I don't 'ave me own funds, eh luv?" The solicitor gave him an almost horrified glance before looking down without commenting, but she made to move away from him saying,
"So, you have my card... err... Bill. I must get going, err... can I... err, drop you somewhere?" The pained smile on her face almost made Bill burst out laughing, but he managed to just give her a little smile as he declined her offer and then watched how quickly, the greatly relieved woman scuttled off away from him down the steps!

As he sauntered back towards the town centre, Bill was replaying the brush he'd just had with The Law... Wendy was right, his tactic had only delayed the inevitable, the pigs would turn on him, sooner or later, if for no other reason than he was an easy target, who would care if he wrongly went to prison? If he was fitted-up? For the pigs it would just be a quick clear-up, good for their stats! Headlines reading that a dangerous criminal had been taken off the streets and there was one less of the homeless vermin that was infesting their town.

Although all things considered that detective hadn't seemed to be such a bad sort? Nah! He was still a pig though, he'd taken the queen's shilling, so he'd sold his soul!

One of the things that had stuck with Bill, from the avalanche (of what he termed *bullshit and nonsense*) that he'd found himself under at The Haven, had been... along with his introduction to the principles of Buddhism... had been the idea of synchronicity... *the simultaneous occurrence of events which appear to be significantly related but in fact have no discernible causal connection!* Accordingly 'synchronicity' had been added to his private lexicon of collected wisdom and quotations! The concept had chimed with him, it'd had a particular resonance for him. It was something that he had felt many times over in his own life, odd occurrences that almost seemed to have been *meant to happen*? After he had initially taken the path of discovering himself through following the guidance of The Buddha, he had found it had started occurring a lot more frequently, things just seemed to come his way on the path he was following, things that if he chose to see them, to acknowledge them, follow their cue, would be of help to him on the next step of his voyage of discovery.

It was with this mindset that he felt that it had to be more than random coincidence that he found himself standing on that particular corner, looking across the street at the Victorian building opposite him. It was a proudly built red brick and stone edifice that today was the home of The Gazette, the paper that reporter worked for!

Jenny Stainton was in the large open plan office she shared with the entire staff at The Gazette, apart from Gil Bamford The

Editor, who had an office at the far end, separated by a half glass screen so he could keep a watchful eye over his minions... all five of them! The office could easily have accommodated twenty staff but the times they had a changed eh? Being a local, one town paper meant that it was a miracle it still survived at all! She'd often tried to imagine the place in its heyday, packed and bustling...

Sat at her desk that morning however she was unconcerned about her surroundings, she was busy catching-up after being away visiting her brother and his family for the weekend. She was so engrossed she was muttering to herself without realising it!
"Whass-up Jen? Bad head after your dirty weekend?" Micky the office twerp chirruped-up right into her ear, as he bent his long, gangly body right over her to do so!
"It's this..." She waved an agitated hand about in the direction of her computer's screen... "This fucking story! This is *my* fucking contact! It's her! The murdered girl!"
"Shoulda kept your phone on like I've told y'before luv!"
"Don't *luv* me you stick insect!" Jenny was laughing as she reverted to the silly banter she had with her colleague,
Standing upright, the lad did a passable impersonation of Basil Fawlty...
"Well alright then Sybil! I'll just go and polish the silver then shall I?" She laughed despite herself but he stopped laughing with her as he saw she had tears running down her face,
"What is it Jen? Your family's okay, aren't they?"
She just pointed at the screen where she'd been scrolling through the updates and news stories on her computer and had just frozen on the shocking headline, 'Local student found dead on canal tow path! Police investigate... a headline from her own newspaper about the murder of Natalie Blunt!!

"I was working with Nat last week!"
"Oh shit, I'm sorry. Do you wanna coffee, I'm nipping out?" She nodded and wiped her eyes with a tissue as Micky strode away.

It was horrific that the poor kid was dead and that she had met her end in such a terrible manner, but what she was more than a little concerned about was that she found it equally horrifying that she'd been away! That she'd missed the story! It was the biggest story in her town since she'd started at the paper and the

story was about someone she knew, a girl she'd been working with... for fucks-sake! She was someone she'd been sat talking to only a couple of days before! Now she was dead! Her mind went into a whirl as she tapped at the keyboard desperately seeking more information...
'I always turn my phone off when I'm having personal time...
It's the only way to avoid becoming a 'sad old hack'...
You have to keep some separation!'
Her mentor Alistair had told her all that...
Yeah, that archetypal, personification of the term 'old hack' that he was!
She supposed that in his own way he was trying to warn her not to end up like him! Obsessed!
Oh hell yeah, I mean who'd want to be an award winning journo! Fat chance of that for her she sighed!
Her introspection turned away to think of the poor girl's boyfriend...

The poor little naive sod!
He'd be a suspect as far as The Police were concerned?
She nodded to herself...
But no!   Surely not?
He couldn't have done it!   Why not?
Anyone was capable of killing!   Wasn't that what they said?
What was his name? Andy...   What?
Robinson? Yeah *Robinson Crusoe*...   that had struck her!
One of her memory tricks...
He was a bit unshaven!   Red bum-fluff to match his hair...
Andy! Andy Robinson!   Yeah, that was it!
The poor little sod! He couldn't have done it, she decided, how indescribably fucking awful for the poor lad...
Her desk phone rang out!

"Hi Jen, it's Tracey here at reception. There's a... err... a *chap* down here for you. Says you know him? That you wanted to speak to him?... Hang on! No! He says that you *have* spoken to him and..." A loud voice shouted-out, sounding over the top of Tracey's
"*Just tell 'er it's Bill!*"
"I'm on my way down Trace... *do not* let him go!"

CHAPTER TWENTY-THREE

Jenny burst through the door into reception, startling Bill who'd had his back to it, he turned to face her,
"I tek it y've 'eard then!" He grumbled as she almost skidded to a stop next to him! She stood for a moment in front of the big old guy, in a state of confusion, she was so upset about Nat, she was still mad with herself at being away and out-of-touch and missing such an opportunity too and in that fleeting moment as their eyes met she saw a similar turmoil in Bill's eyes, but there was something else there in them, for him too… what was it? *It was fear!* The old guy was terrified! In that moment of connection with him, she felt it too… somehow she instinctively knew that Bill was going to get the blame! She stopped in her tracks, unsure what she should do. Put a hand on his shoulder, hug him?

Bill solved the dilemma for her, he just tipped his head towards the front door, "best tek this outside eh luv?"
"We can use my office?"
"Is it private?"
"Err… not really, but Gil's out… I think… Well I've not seen him today. We could use his office?"
He just shrugged and shook his head, so she responded,
"Okay, give me a minute I'll get my things then."
Heading for the door he called back to her,
"You do what y'must! I'll be in t'canteen at t'Factry. See y'there."

Ten minutes later Jenny was taking a seat opposite him, at a table in the window of the large refectory, well away from anyone.
"I got y'a tea. Never drink the coffee in 'ere!"
"So I… Oh my God Bill! What happened? I was here only a few days ago talking with Nat!"
"Aye well, I was one as found poor lass, ravaged and raped by some fuckin' bastards and dumped like a piece o'trash on't'towpath! It were terrible… horrible… it were an awful thing to see!"
"*Fuckin'Nora*! *YOU* found her? Oh my God Bill! I'm so sorry! I can't imagine… W-what the… what-the hell? What did you do?"

"I did all as'a I could to cover up poor lass's nakedness, t'weren't right, leavin' 'er there, all exposed like that… an' then I went and dialled 999."
"What happened when the Police arrived?"
"Dunno luv! I were long gone by then!"
"Oh… *what*? *Why?* Why didn't you stay with her?"
"Funnily enough phone weren't on a pole right next t'body! Oh yeah and me SmartPhone's battry were down! F-fuck s'ake girl!"
"Sorry Bill, I didn't think. But you could've gone back, surely? Waited with her?"
He just shook his head sadly. "She were past carin'…"
She recalled the look in his eyes earlier,
"You're scared of the Police? Was that it?"
"Anyone such as likes of me'd'ave to be a fucking nutter not to be… fuckin' pigs is bastards…"

Jenny was unsure what to do or say for once, the newshound was telling her to bite deep, sink her teeth in, lock her jaws onto her prey! It was urging her to scratch and pull relentlessly at the story, ruthlessly shake as much mileage out of it as possible! But she also felt some pity for the old guy too, she knew from her conversation with him that there was a depth to him that she had barely plumbed, there was so much left unknown to her about who he really was, what his circumstances had been before his fall into vagrancy, so why on earth would he consider the Police as allies? All they did was move-him-on or threaten to lock him up! Why should he have any faith in a society, or its rules and laws and systems when they had already failed him so badly, when it continued to shun him and offer him precious little help? If it weren't for Harry and his efforts here at his beloved Factry…

CHAPTER TWENTY-FOUR

The first full briefing was about to get under way for Don's team, he stood back from the board where he had just pinned-up the latest information and turned to face them. The babble of conversation died away,
"You are now all aware of our victim's identity, Natalie Blunt, nineteen, student at the college here." He tapped the central picture of her as he spoke,
"I know for a few of you, this will be your first murder investigation, so let me be very clear about this, there is absolutely no glamour to be had in any of this, this is something truly horrific and we owe it to this poor girl and her family to find out exactly what happened to her and nail the bastard or bastards that did this to her and left her like that!" He pointed to the crime scene picture of her body.
"Right, we have more information now and plenty to sift through from the phone lines"… he nodded and waved down the murmur of skeptical thoughts voiced on the value of information from the public… *'nutters, wannabe detectives, attention seekers…'*
"Yeah, yeah, yeah… despite all that some of them have included valuable information, including a sighting of Mr. Williams on Bentley Street which corroborates the CCTV footage from the garage where the 999 call was made from." He tapped the pictures on the wall…
"Why is all the CCTV we get always absolute crap?" Someone helpfully asked,
"As you will see, both show a large and scruffily dressed man with a backpack…"
"…and his cap pulled as far down as possible for the CCTV and his head kept down too! Is that the behaviour of an innocent man?"
Someone else added,
"Isn't it one of them Olympic Games hats?"
"Yeah that stupid logo looks like it is, 2012 wasn't it?" Don intervened,
"Okay, that's a good observation, but we now know that this is our very own Mr. Williams.
"We have a statement from the said Mr. Williams, you'll have a copy in the folder on your laptop. He admits to finding the body and to making the 999 phone call. This is the recording of the call…" He turned to Affran who tapped a key on his laptop…

"Is that the Police?
"Could I have your name please?"
"Never mind that! I've just come across the body of a young lassie, over on the canal towpath. By the look of her she's been murdered."
" Sir I need your name."
"No y'don't! Will y'shut ya gob and listen? She's no far west o' the ginnel as leads up from Bentley Street just up from the Petrol Station where I'm phoning you from. Have you got all that?" The line goes dead.

"Now there's something interesting about the call…" Amelia volunteered…
"I sat in when Mr. Williams was interviewed and although he refused to speak directly to us, from the little I did hear, as she spoke to his solicitor, he decidedly did not have a Scottish accent! He spoke with a local accent as you'd expect an itinerant of our area to do."
"Thanks Amelia,"
"So, he disguised his voice. Another question mark to hang over Mr. Bill Williams!" A voice came from the back,
"What do we know about him? This fella?"
"We have Terry and Jo looking into that now, but for now we know nothing, a big fat zero. No records on him."
"Me and Terry are going to The Folks Factory next thing, if he is a tramp, like he looks to be, he'll most likely frequent the place, someone will recognise him from the photo!"
"Good luck with that rabble! There'll be an epidemic of lockjaw as soon as they smell Police!" Someone *helpfully* interjected.
"Come on now! Be thorough there and speak to the staff first. We have an interview to do with Andrew Robinson, the girl's boyfriend. I'll take that with Affan."
"Crime Scene information now. We have various fingerprints and some DNA, although we're *still* waiting on the full autopsy, this is from the deputy at pathology, he has confirmed, *preliminarily*… he stressed that, as he told me… that the girl was raped… he's got DNA from semen… and he commented that she was quite badly injured during the rape…"
"Fucking bastard!" Someone muttered…
"We're having that stretch of the canal searched by divers to see if anything was dumped into it, at this stage the girls phone is missing, neither was any handbag found…"

"How was she I.D.'d Sir?"
"She had a student union card in her coat pocket."
"Anything on the prints?"
"We've run them, but no, nothing on file."
"We'll be getting yon ol'feck's prints to compare?"
"Of course, although in his statement Bill has covered himself to some extent…"
"Aye, by tampering with the crime scene!" A mutter went around the room…
"Be that as it may…"
"Is he a suspect Sir?"
"Of course, until we rule him out, and the boyfriend too although it's looking as if he's alibied, unchecked as yet, we'll be seeking DNA from him…"
"And our old tramp too?"
"Hmm… we could ask him to volunteer it? But even if he refused it wouldn't be conclusive…"
"Wouldn't look like the behaviour of an innocent man though!" Someone volunteered!
"Right… okay… I want a team to try and find out where this old tramp was coming from when he found the girl. From his statement it would seem as if he was heading on his way into town, so I want the area to the west searched. It was early morning, so he'd probably have been dossed-down somewhere along the canal, or just off it. If you need a dog unit I'll authorise it… no, make that *take* a dog unit, one guy with his dog will suffice. See what the dog can sniff out."

"Anyone got anything else? No? Okay, you know where I am if you pick up on anything and I mean anything! Let me be the one who decides whether it's significant or not, okay?"

"Boss? Pally Sally wants you! In her office… and now!"
"Ah fuck… that's all I need!"

Having stomped up the stairs to the Super's office, he was pausing for a moment outside the door to get his breath when the door flew open and the said Sally Pembrose almost cannoned into him! He stepped back to avoid her, but she froze when she saw him… She was red-faced and clearly very angry as she spat out…

"I was on my way down *to find you!* I sent word for you to come to see me *at once*! And that was at least half-an-hour ago!"
"I was conducting a briefing, I only got the message just now when I was wrapping it up, I guess the messenger thought it was more important to let me finish before they delivered it?"
"Guess all you like Gideon, when I say I want to see you now, I mean *now!*"
"Look, I came *as soon* as I got the message, so unless you think I'm psychic I don't see how you could possibly expect me to have got here any quicker!"
"Be that as it may, you'll adopt a more civil tone when you speak to me Detective Sergeant Willis! I am your superior!"

"Yes Ma-am, sorry Ma-am, three bags full Ma-am! Could you get to the point please and tell me why you've summoned me here, and why it's *so* very urgent? I'm trying to get a murder investigation under way here… you do know that? You do find out about little things like that as you're sat up here? You do get to know what the people who actually do the work around her are getting on with?"

The woman glowered at him, her contempt almost a shimmering and visible presence emanating off her, she was just about to speak… to say something in anger, but as he watched her face he saw it soften, as she reined in her emotions, as she composed herself to make a less heated but more targeted attack…

"I'm not sure if you recall *the incident* that recently took place in the corridor downstairs? When I was escorting The Deputy Commissioner out of the building and we passed you?"
"I have an excellent memory Ma-am, but I have no memory of an *incident* as you describe it! But I do recall that we passed in the corridor."
"Well I do recall *the incident!* I recall it very well indeed, as does the Deputy Commissioner and he was less than impressed with your behaviour, *significantly* less than impressed! His exact word in referencing it was in fact… *'appalling*!'
"As a direct result of that incident, I received a phone call this morning from him, you see your superiors who sit up here above you and elsewhere, are always aware of what the likes of you are doing and in particular, on this occasion specifically what *you*

are doing! Not only that and you may well be surprised to find this out, he was also already well aware of exactly who *you* are!

"His call was to inform me that you are not to be allowed to handle this murder investigation, that I am to take you off it at once and hand it to someone who presents a respectable face to represent the force, to be seen on camera and quoted in the Press and not... and I quote him verbatim now... 'not some foul mouthed old relic who should have been *put out to grass years ago!*' Oh how it pays to have friends in high place Gideon... or not as the case may be!"

Don who had remained on his feet throughout the entire exchange, stood there silently for a moment... there was no way on earth that the Deputy Commissioner had any opinion whatsoever about him, other than the one this vindictive bitch had provided for him! This latest dollop of career shite that was in the process of landing on his head had to be the last straw, he fumed impotently to himself even as it trickled down over him... his first big case in years slipping away along with it, before his very eyes...

But despite everything he'd had to endure, this had to be the biggest pile of shite that they'd ever dropped on him... and there'd been plenty. He felt the burning anger inside him begin to rise up, the pressure building up...
Until it just burst out...
"I know you've always had it in for me Sally, but this! This is beyond the fucking limit, you may have shot-up past me on the slimy ladder but you were never much of a copper, you never paid enough attention to detail, you were always too bloody lazy, always looking for quick and easy answers, you've never been anything close to the detective I am, even on my worst day!

"I don't know what I ever did to you to earn your contempt, but you have no right to be so unfair to me. I'm a decent guy, I've worked hard, I've kept my nose clean and this is my reward. Being picked-on by a vindictive cow who's been side-lining me for years, for fuck knows what reason... and who now does this to me!"

"Have you quite finished? I could have you thrown out on your ear *right now* for that insubordinate and insolent outburst Willis! Get out of my office, go and crawl back to wherever it is that you usually skulk and get back to dealing with the type of low level cases you are fit to deal with!
"I've already appointing DS Steadman as acting DI and you will hand over everything to him at once and you will co-operate fully with him. A single word from him to me that you are not doing so and you will have your pension plan sat infront of you on your desk within minutes of me hearing of it.
"Are we clear? Oh and just in case you have thoughts of going over my head, sneaking up to your old buddy upstairs… the chief super is presently on a week's leave! Not that it would make any difference of course as he too answers to Colin."

Don was stunned… As the impact of this latest disaster to fuck-up his career was sinking in, he was for once lost for words… He was also marvelling at what he had said to her in his little outburst! Part of him was attempting to hold him back, trying to be grateful for small mercies and to see to it that he still kept his job! It was almost as if he heard his own voice saying…

"What neither you, nor your dressed-up clown Colin, who you were with… and who you were shamelessly and I have to say sickeningly, smarming yourself all over… didn't hear, was the foul language that Steadman and his lackey had just thrown at me? What Steadman had said that evoked my response!
"And now you're giving the case to him! To Steadman! For fuck's sake! How can you hand a case like this to that idiot? The guy's a misogynistic moron! What about Affan? He was meant to be stepping-up to learn from me on the case, to co-handle it with me as part of his fast-track-overtaking-everyone-else career trajectory!"
"That will be all Detective Sergeant Willis.
"GET OUT!"

Resisting the temptation to pick up one of her pot plants… *fucking pot plants…* that were all around her office and hurl it through her window… or at her head… or to slam the door off its hinges… he just stormed out of her office and he did none of that, but he did leave the door open as a final… *yeah and pathetic…* act of defiance! It was only after he'd turned the corner and was stood at the top of the stairs that he paused for breath and to calm himself down. He slumped against the handrail and stared sightlessly down into the vertiginous gap inbetween the bannisters to the basement far below... It had been a long time since he'd had the thought about letting himself fall...

He let out a big sigh...

It had all been too good to be true... He should have realised! That bitch Pally Sally getting one over on him though... and it having to be this she used to do it! Such a big one! She'd been making life tough for him for years, she was a nasty vindictive bitch, but it seemed that she'd bided her time, waited patiently for the opportunity to bury her knife up the hilt in his back!

Of course he knew damn well why she hated him so much! The fucking spiteful bitch had to have a long memory though, as it had been many years ago, back when she was shagging her way up the greasy pole! She'd been addressing a briefing as a junior DC, on what had been quite a big case at the time, there'd been a lot of people there and she'd said something that was such a pile of shite that he'd had to speak up! Yeah he could've been more tactful in the way he'd pointed it out, but why should he have been? She was a jumped-up arrogant little bitch even back then. What he'd pointed out had already been transparently obvious to anyone with a grain of experience or brainpower alone, everyone else with more nouse than her, which included most of the people she was addressing! Perhaps it was because he'd enjoyed putting her down so much? Too much?

Was that what she'd always held against him? For sure, she'd been shown-up, humiliated even and in front of a room full of her colleagues and in the presence of her boss too! But so what, anyone else would've just sucked-it up, chalked it up to experience and been a damn sight more careful before they jumped to illogical and unsubstantiated conclusions in the future and definitely before opening their stupid mouth and voicing them!

It had made him popular with the other guys, they'd all have loved to take her down a notch themselves, or shag her, or do both, but that brief popularity he'd enjoyed was long forgotten now, unlike his sleight of her, at least in her mind apparently. Of course it had made little difference to the upwards trajectory of her career, perhaps the dent in her credibility slowed it down a little, but her boss although witness to her humiliation at the briefing had an upward trajectory of his own going on with her…

Don slouched his way back to the incident room, fucking Steadman and his pet mutt were already there,
"It's okay Don, I've been through all the paperwork on my desk…" He pointed with one finger to the room Don had been using…
"In what was formerly known as *your office*!" He dissolved into laughter before banging on the table,
"You can go Don… Now listen up everyone, from now I am acting Detective *Inspector* Steadman! I answer to most names, but Steve or Guv will do!"
'*Fucking thick-shit arsehole*' more like Don muttered to himself. The guy stood next to him had heard him, he smirked and gave a discreet thumbs-up that only Don saw.

"Right, we are now going to get down to doing some real business, some properly carried out police work! No more fucking pussy-footing around now that I'm on the job! You… Affan innit? Take Robinson there and go and arrest that old fucker Williams. I want his ugly mug shot up on here…" He tapped the board behind him…
"I want him finger-printed, I want to have his DNA sent off tout suite…"
"Won't we have to wait till we have him here… *guv*?"
Oblivious to the point the joker had made from somewhere at the back… *that what he'd said was French for 'right now!'* …he just carried on…
"Get it fast tracked! Once we have a proper mugshot I want it run through every data base you can find, I want to know who this old fucker is, chapter and verse, he had a life before he turned into a useless old piece of trash. This case is going to have the quickest and neatest clear-up on record. So, Affan… why are you still here? Fuck-off now, find the old bastard and arrest him!"

CHAPTER TWENTY-FIVE

Jenny turned in her seat in the refectory, responding to the noise of a commotion coming from somewhere behind her, "What's going on?"
She asked Bill, turning back to look at him she saw he was frozen in his seat, glaring in the direction of the noise. He took his glasses off and massaged the bridge of his nose...
"They've come for me... as'a said they would..."
Sure enough when she twisted around in her seat far enough she could see that the noise was from the rowdy jeering and heckling coming from the twenty or more other guys who had been sat having a brew... it was the presence of a uniformed constable in their territory! He was heading purposefully towards them, accompanied by two plain clothed officers, accompanied by shouts or 'pigs' and an assortment of grunting noises!

A tall Asian looking guy, approached Bill... He immediately recited the Police Miranda:
"William Williams I am arresting you on suspicion of murder, you do not have to say anything. But it may harm your defence if you do not mention when questioned something which you later rely on in court. Anything you do say may be given in evidence. Do you understand what I just told you?"
"Sorry lad, am a bit deaf, didn't quite catch it, *so no*, I didn't!"
"Please pay attention then and I will repeat it..."
The poor, slightly flustered chap repeated it over, word for word, as the other plain clothed officer, a petite woman in her late twenties smiled an uncertain and tentative smile at Jenny, who merely raised an eyebrow, but nevertheless found herself returning a tiny smile in response, after all she was just doing her job... it was funny as despite not really knowing Bill that well, she heard his imagined voice echo in her mind...
"Aye, lass is only *obeyin' orders!*"

As the cop was asking Bill to stand-up and accompany them to the police station, Harry came rushing over,
"What's going on? I think it would have been protocol to come and inform me of your intentions before marching in here!" The tall Asian cop turned to him,
"And you are, Sir?"
"Harry Protherow, director of The Folks Factory."

"Ah, I would love to have met you under better circumstances Sir, but I'm afraid I'm rather busy just now."
"What are you doing with Bill?" Harry demanded, Jenny chipped-in...
"They're only arresting him for murdering Nat! It'd be funny if it wasn't so bloody ridiculous!"
"Is that true officer?"
"We are arresting him yes. Other than that Sir, this is nothing to do with you, so please stand aside!" So saying he nodded to the uniformed cop who reached out an arm to herd Harry off to one side, she was very polite about it as she did so though,
"Please Sir, stand aside and let my colleagues do their job. If he's innocent then he'll be released." Harry went red in the face but reluctantly complied, he called to Bill,
"I'll have a solicitor there for you Bill, you say nothing till they get there! Say *absolutely* nothing!"

Bill who was on his feet now, nodded to Harry just as another jeer went up in response to a middle aged man in an ill-fitting suit having just stormed-in through the main doors and who was striding towards them, the two cops acknowledged him as he approached them,
"Is everything okay guv, we're still arresting him aren't we?" The Asian guy asked, whereas the woman just nodded with a little...
"Guv!"
Glancing firstly at Harry and then Jenny, the newcomer brusquely snapped...
"I am Detective Inspector Steadman, I don't know who you two are but I'd like you to step out of the way please." He turned to his detectives,
"Cuff him!" The tall Asian guy looked over to his diminutive colleague. She just shrugged in response... Jenny piped-up,
"Really? Is that necessary?" DI Steadman, reproached her,
"Madam I have asked you politely to remove yourself, now I'm telling you... get the fuck out of my way! Over there now" He pointed to where the cop was standing with a furious looking Harry.

Meanwhile the uniformed lad had produced a pair of handcuffs and stood holding them in front of himself...

"Sir?" He asked, his voice sounding uncertain and thin as he got the DI's attention.
"Very good! At least someone came prepared! Go on then lad cuff him!" The young copper fumbled the cuffs onto Bill's wrists as Harry protested,
"This is a bloody outrage! You haven't heard the last of this DI Steadman. Your behaviour is appalling!"
"Fuck-off back to your tramps, I know who you are… you do-gooder arsehole… just get out of my way! Right team, march the old cunt out, I have a reception committee out front waiting for him!"
"An outraged Harry blurted out, "You haven't heard the last of this! It's bloody outrageous!"

Jenny who was already on her feet nearly ran across the refectory to get to the main doors ahead of the cops, she could see that there was indeed a small throng of people gathering there, they were being held back by two more uniformed constables! Six cops to arrest one weak old man! This was ridiculous! Then she saw Sam the Gazette's photographer. That bastard Steadman had tipped the Press off that he was making an arrest! It was grandstanding, pure and simple!

She pushed her way past the cops at the door and through the little gaggle of other reporters to reach Sam,
"What the fuck Sam? What's all this?"
"A tip Jen, the cops tipped us off they're arresting the murderer!"
"He's not the bloody murderer Sam! Oh my God! He said this is what would happen!"
"So if he knew it would happen then?" Sam left it hanging…
"No, no! It isn't him Sam, I know it isn't and I'll bloody well prove it isn't if it's the last thing I do! Those bastards aren't going to lock up an innocent old man!"

The cop was now standing outside the doors, he was making some sort of announcement but Jenny wasn't listening, she had tears in her eyes as they met with Bill's. He was looking over at her, Steadman was standing next to him, shoulder to shoulder with one hand on Bill's shoulder and the other on his wrist making sure the handcuffs were clearly visible. As she watched he yanked on Bill's shoulder as Sam took his pictures… making sure that the photographers got full face pictures…

It was all a blur to her as Bill was bundled away into a waiting Police van and driven off. Sam came back over to her from the pack, "Alright Jen?" Seeing her distress, he softened his voice, "Oh my lovely, whatever's the matter? The old guy? Is it the old guy? What just went down for him?" She nodded, feeling utterly pathetic! Now she understood how people she was plugging for a story could seem dazed and somehow oblivious to what they had witnessed only seconds before! But she was a bloody reporter! It was her job to *not* do that! Bloody hell! *"Bloody hell!"*
She realised she had shouted it out as she repeated it in her mind! "Easy there…" Sam put his arm around her shoulder and she astonished herself by leaning into his shoulder and crying.
Sam let his camera swing from the strap around his neck and put his arm around her…
"Hey there Jen… It's okay, if he didn't do it you'll get him out, won't you?"

Coming to her senses, she shrugged Sam off… it was done in a kindly and playful way though…
"Gerroff me! You little perve, you've been waiting for a chance to get a grip on me for years!" He laughed, glad to get out of the awkwardness of the situation himself!
"Damn right! Oow…" He made a silly Les Dawson face, before becoming serious again,
"Seriously though, are you okay now Jen?"
"Bloody hell man, of course I'm okay! Bloody battle hardened newshound like me!"
"Ah… Bless…It's that time of the month isn't it love? Never mind, I understand!"
She thumped him hard on the arm!
"Sexist arsehole! That's it! I'm filing a complaint! Now, will you shift your arse and stop buggering about! We need to get back to the office. Come on! Now!" With that she started marching off…
"Err… My car's over here Jen!" He was laughing as he called out after her… She stopped in tracks and turned,
"Little shit!" She cussed him off, then went back to join him as they headed off in the other direction. Before they got to his car though Harry intercepted them,
"What the fuck Jen?"
"I know Harry. Un-fucking-believable! Oh Harry, this is Sam, The Gazette's very own Jimmy Olsen!"
Sam offered his hand which Harry shook as he said to Jenny,

"Look I have to get back to the paper, see that they don't fuck-up the photos I've sent over! Pleased to meet you Harry." He raised an eyebrow and mouthed… *'Jen'* eh? to Jenny, he smirked and then walked quickly away.

"Oh Harry, what are we going to do?"
"Don't worry, I'll have Alan find a criminal lawyer for him, look Jen I need to go and do it *right now*." He gave her a peck on the cheek, patted her elbow, "Don't worry love, I'll get the best one I can find, those bastards won't know what's hit them!" Then he spun on his heel and was gone.

She was still feeling dazed, and getting back to the office suddenly seemed less important to her, Sam had abandoned her, the little shit having picked-up that there was something going on between her and Harry and he'd shot off to leave them to it! To get back to the office and gossip about it too, no doubt! She was on foot now anyway so she wandered aimlessly across to the seats around the front. Nevertheless, part of her mind was screaming at her… *get back to the office, this is the story that can make you! What the hell are you doing?* Despite being aware of the insistent urgency of that voice, for now it was having no effect on her due to the magnitude of wrongfulness of the situation, it was all so unfair, so fucking ridiculous!

Another voice was telling her that she *would* write a piece about it, but it would an exposé about the shocking behaviour of The Police, it would exonerate Bill and at the same time point out to that idiot policeman who the real murderer was! You just need a moment to put it all together, somewhere you can think without being interrupted… Right on cue… just after she'd plonked herself down on one of the benches… *she was interrupted,* as she heard another voice, this time it was in her ear…
"You okay love? Y'look like yers just seen a ghost! I watched yers driftin over 'ere jus now, like yer was in a trance so I've brought yer a brew over!" She looked up and saw Jimmy's concerned face looking at her as he placed a proper pot mug down on the table, she placed her hand onto his forearm,
"Thanks Jimmy, you're a star…" Her voice trailed off into a sob,
"Oh eh there… Come on luv!" He said as he ran his arm around her shoulder and sat down alongside her,

"What the feck was all that about? You tell ol'Jimmy 'ere what's up…" As if to create a distraction for her, he pulled out his small Golden Virginia tin, flipped the lid open and took out one of his rollies. He tapped its end onto the tin lid…
"Can I have one Jimmy?"
"Sure y'can kiddo! Didn't know as y'smoked?" he said as he passed her the one he had in his hand,
"I don't." She said as she sucked at the flame of his lighter through the thin white tube of tobacco…

CHAPTER TWENTY-SIX

Sat in the back of the police van with the young copper as it drove to the Police Station, Bill felt something change inside himself, it was an odd feeling and yet one he recognised only too well. It was one of resignation, of surrender… It was a feeling of something draining away… his very life force draining away… Trickling downwards from his head, slipping down through his body, running into each of his legs to seep away, spilling out onto the floor to pool around his feet, to lay there evaporating away into nothingness, leaving behind an empty Bill shaped shell.

He'd been full of a raging and yet impotent fury as their cuffs had been locked around his wrists, then indignation at the humiliation of being paraded there before the rabble of The Press and nosey fucker-on-lookers!… Shown off as that dickhead of a detective's prize, to be used as a token… a thing for them to conveniently pour the blame onto for today's *unspeakable outrage,* a sap to be dumped upon, a mug to hold up as the *villain brought down* in today's headline before they moved on to the next bullshit distraction tomorrow…

All of that emotion had drained out of him now, he was totally empty, a mere husk of the man he had become when he'd shed his skin to step into that being his despairing mind had created out of its pain, shaped as a refuge for his embattled and increasingly deranged mind to inhabit! When he had put on the costume of 'Bill'! Bill, the empty husk of the man he'd formerly been, what was left after he'd walked away from his former incarnation as… *one of them.*

This was different insofar as it was not a new character being taken up to overlay the old one, this was effectively the deletion altogether of his existence as a thinking, functioning person. His mind seemed to be operating in super-slow motion, like one of those incredibly slowed-down movies they make…
…his thoughts were slowly dragging themselves…
…through a thick miasma of doubt & uncertainty
…of resignation…
…it was all over now…
…nothing matters anymore…

…it was inevitable…
…it had all been too good to be true…
…a fucking appartment of his own?… ha…. ha…..
…ha…
…ha!
Bill's retreating mind was unaware that the van had stopped, the doors were open and the cop was speaking to him, the sound of the words coalesced from being merely a noise into having a little meaning…
"…are you in their old fella? Come on, we're here! Time to get out." He gently placed a hand on Bill's shoulder steering him into moving towards exiting the van,
"That's it, easy now as you climb down…" He rested his hand on Bill's arm, he turned and looked at the lad as if he had no idea where he was,
"Thanks lad." He heard his own voice sound out from somewhere…
He weren't a bad young fella…
Something else had gone on after that. He'd been talked at, asked if he understood, moved about from here to there, each time he'd nodded uncomprehendingly or said 'aye' when so questioned.

He was made to undress, he saw his clothes being put into plastic bags and then he was put into a shower.
It was warm.
They gave him soap.
He was handed a towel.
He rubbed its roughness over his wet body.
He was given a grey tracksuit, top and bottom.
It felt smooth and soft on his skin.
His hair was still wet.
The water ran off it going down his neck.
His beard was wet when he ran his fingers through it.
The lights were so bright.
He was in a corridor leaving the showers behind…
Another person…
A voice…
A face…
That sneering bastard detective!
Steadman!
It was Steadman's face!
Coming towards him.

As he passes he deliberately lets their shoulders bump!
He is painfully jolted by it.
Supercilious, sneering, snidey, slimey, slippery, Steadman…
He spat onto the floor…
"Fucking cunt!" He heard his voice growl out…
A scuffle…
The bastard slamming him against the wall…
His face an inch away…
Shouting…
Spittle on his face…
A tussle…
The uniformed cop's shouted voice…
Mocking laughter…

Grey shiny walls…
A clanging bang.
A clicking noise.

Silence…

Stillness…

CHAPTER TWENTY-SEVEN

To his surprise Bill realised that he had slept solidly, there was a little light filtering into his room from the small window high up on the narrow wall opposite the door. He tossed the blanket that had been covering him aside, shuffled to his feet and had a pee in the stainless steel loo.

As his piss streamed into the water he noted absentmindedly that there was no seat to the toilet, nor was there a lid! His mind was wandering he noted, as he thought of how often he'd witnessed many of his fellow travellers, the other old guys that was, cussing as their pee only trickled, slowly and unwillingly from them as they'd lean against the wall of the washrooms at The Factry groaning... Guess I'm lucky then! Bill laughed to himself, in one thing at least!

That was one of the many lessons he been taught in therapy, or was it a Buddhist teaching? Gratitude? It smacked a bit of being a platitude, a way to keep folks down... '*be grateful for what you have*!' In other words don't look longingly at all that the rich possess, things you never will!

He was surprised that he had slept so well, so enclosed, the energy of the air so nullified, the place so quiet, sterile, still, dead. He was equally amazed that he hadn't lain awake all night on the hard bunk fretting and worrying either.

He'd given-up caring altogether it seemed...

He sat on the edge of the bunk and folded the blanket neatly and laid the pillow on top of it. The young cop had brought it in with a sandwich and mug of tea late on, before he'd been locked up for the night, the inference being that pillows weren't something you normally had. He was a decent enough young fella, shame he'd chosen the wrong career he mused.

He was thirsty so drank a few gulps of water from the tap at the small basin. Sitting back on the bunk his mind returned to his predicament and the concept of gratitude. He was warm and dry, he was well rested too and to top it all off... he was still breathing! I am here! I am in this moment. This is now.

His thoughts drifted to the beautiful young girl he'd met at St. Jude's, what was her name? She might have died by now, she was so fragile, she was like porcelain, that skin so pale and thin... Abigail! How could he forget her name? The name they had given to that tiny mite of humanity of their own, he saw her again as she lay in the arms of the vicar carrying out his ridiculous yet joyous ritual... bestowing the name that they had chosen upon her... '*I christen you Abigail*'... the memory normally excruciating for him, was just observed today with mild interest... he simply noted, quite calmly, that he had indeed *become detached*.

Detached... yes that was the word the psychiatrist had used wasn't it? It had all become so unbearable that the mind had simply said... *'that's it bud! I've had enough! I'm off, good luck with it all!'* And there you are, on yer tod! Gone are all the voices, so no nagging anymore, no suggestions, no do's and don'ts, no worries about saying the right or wrong things... just a calm empty space where the few thoughts you do have are just little vacuous clouds, drifting gently through the empty space of your mind, puffs of slow moving, insubstantial cotton wool, puffs of nothingness...

His languid mind drifted back to the van, the police van and his arrest... He recalled how he'd almost heard the sound as he was sat there, something going *<snap!>*, something had broken, a part of his mind had sheared away from the rest of it, like the wall of a glacier fracturing, detaching itself from the mass and slipping into the sea.... To drift away...

He was reminded of the feeling of running on *remote control* that he'd experienced, back on that night, as he was carefully packing the things he'd need into his big rucksack, putting on his boots and coat, ready to leave. To leave his home forever. There hadn't been a hat to put on! Well, there was a few, but none of them suited him? Suited him? What the fuck? He recalled how bizarre it had seemed to his resigned mind that suddenly a stupid, meaningless detail like that had mattered! He'd found himself upstairs in his youngest son's old room... the lad had left home years ago but there were a still a few of his things there. He remembered that he'd seen the hat hooked over the corner of the

mirror on the dressing table. It was navy blue, one from the Olympics, with the daft logo they'd used, his subconscious mind it seemed had decided that this hat was appropriate, the one he should wear as he walked away into his new existence! That it had directing him up there to seek it out! Accordingly he took it up, put it on his head and went downstairs.
For some reason he was drawn to go into his study, a room he had spent so many hours of his life in. It was a large room... it was a large house! No be honest he thought it was a sweepingly massive house! That was how he'd designed it, drawn the plans and then worked onsite with the builders creating it all. It was a curved structure that faced south, the whole of the exterior was glass, all the rooms on the front had windows or doors onto the area behind the glass! Beneath the structure was a garage, although it was more akin to a subterranean carpark by virtue of its size, being able to easily accommodate a dozen cars....

He'd shook his head as a dark realisation had come over him, what was the point of all of it? Of any of it? The house, all of the cars, the gardens and grounds? His eyes scanned around the room trying to find something worth taking with him...Was there anything at all? A single thing? His eyes fell onto the bookcase, and the writing desk that was alongside of it. Yes! There! There was the one thing that he considered to be worthwhile taking with him! It was a small leather bound book, a book yes, but the tooled leather covering had been made to be wrapped around it enabling it to be tied off, it was just as well too as there were many loose pages along with the bound ones inside of it. It was only about an A5 size, a compact little book, binder, whatever you'd call it... It was where he wrote his poetry, or stuffed in pages he'd written it on somewhere random.

It had been a gift from Abbie.

In the hall he slung his rucksack onto one shoulder, picked up his keys and went out through the front door! He'd locked the door, pushed the keys back through the letterbox, walked down the long drive, turned onto the street and never looked back once.

He looked around the small holding cell. Best get used to it, this will be the kind of place, he told himself where I shall be until I die now. His sluggish mind had already raced ahead and accepted that he would be tried, found guilty and locked away. It just didn't matter. He didn't care. What little fight that had remained within him had left him now.

Be grateful... He would be housed and fed three times a day, be warm and dry. In terms of the human suffering endured by countless millions of other people around the world who happened to have the misfortune of experiencing their own fleeting *Augenblick* in his shared timeframe ...during The End of Days? Having their own tiny blink of an eye at a time when our planet is spiralling towards ecological death... you could be forgiven for seeing it that way! No, for many being incarcerated in a prison would seem to be a luxury, however bad the conditions in England's prisons were currently being reported as! Besides it's where your mind is that truly matters and not the location of your physical body. One of his poems came to mind...

Dark mirror of water beneath brooding hill
Boulder strewn rocky, with heather so still
The valley holds her breath in expectant hush
Wispy mist lingers with no need to rush

The eastern sky lightens to darkest of blue
Night's dark cloak surrenders to subtler hue
Sounding from vantage points high in the trees
Birds cajole up the sun with enticing pleas

Lightening sky shimmers reddish glow appears
Avian chorus crescendos as diminish dark's fears
The valley glows red lit by early morning rays
The molten lake glitters where dancing light plays

Geese flock takes to wing with cacophony of calls
Through bars the sun touches my prison cell walls
Incarcerated in your gaol though my body may be
My wing brushes the lake as my spirit flies free.

It wouldn't be for that long anyway! Not if the doctors were right, he imagined the medical care in their cash-strapped prisons would be basic at best.

It was with this mindset that he ate the porridge provided by the same cop who'd given him the pillow the previous evening. He drank the hot tea as he munched the cold toast. He'd resigned himself to simply follow where he was led, endure whatever followed and say nothing to any of *them* from now on.

Later on he was sat back in the cell after being taken out and down along one of the strange smelling, windowless yet brightly lit corridors to a small interview room. A constable had stood by the door in the room with him as he was sat there. It was a long time before the detective came into the room. When he did come he'd done a lot of shouting and a lot of pacing up and down. The man was clearly unhinged. At one point he'd come up behind Bill, put his hand on the back of his head and banged his face down onto the table!

The young cop, who'd been standing by the door had dashed over and grabbed the detective's arms and pushed him back...
"Sir! Sir! You can't do that!" he'd shouted!
"Are you a'right?" He'd asked Bill.
"Get yer 'ands off me you cheeky feckin' woodentop!" The detective had fumed!

He could still visualise the lad's worried face, as it was, right up next to his as he'd asked him again...
"Are you alright?"
It was the same young lad.
He was a good kid.
He had a good heart.
You could tell.
Yeah he was a cop... but hey?
It was then he remembered, as he was thinking back, that he'd first noticed that the lad was black.
That's what they said nowadays, wasn't it?
He wasn't white... so he was *black*.
Like everything had to be black or white, or was it black *and* white?
Nah...He was *brown*.
He was like that girl, that reporter.
There was a hint of warmer climes in the occasional lilt that softened his voice too, like it was when he was concerned, like when he was asking '*are you a'right?*'...

Why would anyone want to bang someone else's head onto a table?
It was ridiculous.

"*Pick IT UP!*" The man had shouted. He'd been pointing at something on the table as he yelled. It was a small object, it was the same thing that he had hurled at him a few moments earlier, it had landed on the table top as he kept shouting at him… on and on and on he'd shouted!
Why? What was it?
Why did it matter so much to the madman?
So he'd picked it up, it was just a small cardboard box, why was it important?
He'd tossed it back onto the table disinterestedly.

CHAPTER TWENTY-EIGHT

Jenny was on her way on foot to The Folks Factory. After she'd briefly checked in at the office she'd wanted a breath of air to try and clear her head. She'd only slept fitfully last night after the drama of yesterday, but nevertheless, this morning she'd found a new determination to do all she could to aid Bill, to find a way to get him out of his present predicament.

She found Harry in his office, she'd knocked on the door, but felt they knew each other well enough for her to go in without waiting…
It was therefore something of a surprise for her to see someone was already sat infront of Harry's desk! A middle aged chap who smiled up at her, but before she could speculate further about him, Harry had jumped up, come around his desk and was introducing her…
"Detective Sergeant Willis, this is my friend Jenny, Jenny Stainton, she's a reporter with The Gazette." The cop stood up and shook her hand, he had a firm handshake and he looked her directly in the eye as they shook hands, he had an open face for all that it was a little worn and seemed to be carrying a weight of tiredness. His voice was soft and mellow,

"Pleased to meet you, I think I've seen you around, although we've never met properly. Maybe you'll be able to help us? I've come here this morning trying to find out more about the old fella Bill. I must say that I totally agree with Harry here, he should never have been arrested!"
"Thank God for *someone* in the police with some sense then!" Jenny said as they all sat down, she added,
"That Steadman's a real nasty piece of work!" DS Willis nodded in agreement,
"That's the least of it! He's also ruthless and unscrupulous, he's also as thick as… well let's just say that he's not much of a detective!"
"Unlike you?" She quizzed him, this cop growing on her by the minute!
"I like to think I'm at least capable, I do my best to be objective, thorough and fair. Mostly, all I want to do is uncover the truth, find out what's gone on, who has done what to whom and if

anyone is to blame under The Law. I don't want to bend the facts to fit a 'truth' that I've already decided upon." She smiled,
"Is that what Steadman's doing?" Willis nodded,
"It would seem so, unfortunately it is his style. I'm afraid I've been taken off the case, it *was* mine initially but... well that's another story! Anyway I'm still keeping an eye on things discreetly from the sidelines and apparently your old guy's just clammed up! He won't say a word now. Not a dicky-bird, he won't even *acknowledge* anything that's said to him. When he was brought up before the Custody Sergeant he was just muttering *'Aye!'* to everything that was asked of him, but now he's gone schtum! He won't even respond to being asked if he wants a solicitor!" Harry looked alarmed,

"But that's outrageous. I've arranged for one to go and meet with him. Surely she'll be allowed to speak to him." The detective shrugged,
"Not if he won't agree to seeing her and Steadman'll not be inclined to push him to."
Jenny interjected,
"But won't it look bad though, you know if it gets to court? That he hasn't been represented, that he's had no legal advice?"
"They'll just produce evidence that he was repeatedly asked and refused to answer."

Harry: "This is a fine mess! What happens when he's brought up before a judge, I mean if he's still refusing to speak? When they ask him if he's guilty or not guilty?"
Willis: It doesn't happen very often but I think under those circumstances, because the presumption of innocence must be maintained, a plea of not guilty would be recorded on his behalf. It will be a Magistrate in the first instance, not a judge, they'll pass it up to The Crown Court."
Jenny: "And he'll, be remanded in custody? Sent to prison?"
Willis: "I'm afraid so, since it'd be a murder charge, but don't forget he's not been charged with anything yet?"
Harry: "How will he go on at The Crown Court though, if he has no representation?"
Willis: "It can get tricky! He has the right to refuse to appear in court! Would he do that?" Harry and Jenny exchanged glances and shrugged, Harry vomunteering,

"Well the way he's behaving at the moment he could I suppose?" Don confirmed,
"Well if he did, he'd just be tried in his absence on a plea of not guilty."
Jenny: "We have to find a way of getting in to see him! To try and talk some sense into him?
Harry: "This is Bill we're talking about! How much sense have you been able to talk into him? The tragedy of all this is, I'd finally got through to him, after years of trying to! He was all set-up with his own flat too, if only…"
Jenny: "I know, I think I was starting to get through to him too, the last time I met up with him…"
Willis: "Look, I'll see if I can get a chance to speak to him on the QT before he's arraigned. Let's not lose hope just yet though, it's not Steadman's decision whether or not to charge him, maybe some common sense will come into play when it gets passed to The CPS."

CHAPTER TWENTY-NINE

"Result!" A jubilant Steadman exclaimed triumphantly at the morning briefing as he attempted to exhort his staff to bend to his will and give their all for him on this, his first major investigation and in his mind at least very soon to be his first major conviction!
He was brandishing a copy of The Gazette, held at arm's length, so that front page photo was clearly visible as matching the one on the board.
"Boy's and girl's...We have results!" A small murmur rippled around his less than enthused audience.
"Oh come on guys! You've done good, sifting the shit out of the phone calls and we have pulled-out two positive leads now. Number one is a bus driver who picked Bill up on the road into town, it's from awhile before the murder but useful anyway. We'll get the footage off the bus CCTV for confirmation of course but I want the team who went looking for the fucker's hideout to go back and start from the nearest point that you can get into the woods to the bus stop. This time take a whole pack of fucking dogs eh? Oh and don't let them come back until you've found it!" He was now pinning-up a small copy of a map with the bus stop marked on it.

"Next we have the You-Tube footage of this old get playing the piano like fucking Liberace! Right here in town too, in the Market Hall! It's a few years old, but it's definitely him." He taps a photo taken from the video, the *hhtp* listing printed out alongside it.
"Watch it, all of you! Note the way that our old fella scuttles away when he realises that he's being filmed! He's wanted for something, he's hiding from something..."
"Or someone?" A voice piped up,
"Could be a criminal, running from his bosses?" Another suggestion came...
"Okay, okay! Speculation is a waste of time unless it's followed up thoroughly. For now all I want is an ID, someone, somewhere knows who this old feck is. There's a mountain more of stuff to go through from the public, I know it's a ball ache, but in amongst all that shite could be another little pearl, so slog your way through it."
"Anything on his fingerprints and DNA guv?"

"Wouldn't I have said if there was! Come on, you're meant to be detectives! Can't you come to a simple conclusion?" Steadman roared back at the voice from the back...
"*Wouldn't be the first time you fucked-up...*" A mutter came back in response...
"*Has he even had them done yet?*" Came another...
Steadman, raised himself up and peered around trying to see who the smart-arse culprits were, all he could see was blank and *innocent looking* faces...
"Damn-it! Work with me people! Of course we've done the tests! The DNA will be back asap and there's nothing on the database for his prints."
"I see some of the nationals have picked the story up Guv, maybe that will get us something, I mean he's living here now, but who knows where's he's from? If you're on the run or hiding, going to another town's not a bad idea is it?"
"*Thank you*! For a bit of positivity! Yes we're getting good coverage, but it won't last, we all know how quickly the spotlight moves on. That's why we have to make the most of it. I'm doing an interview for the regional news to go out on the telly tonight!"
The hubbub that this raised in response was a muted conglomeration of sounds, noises and muffled voices, comments to each other, with a fair number of sniggers mixed-in too!

The following day after his TV debut, Steadman was almost beside himself, he was in the full flush of success, or so he imagined...
He pointed exuberantly to a second board that was now at the front of the room.
"CSI photos from where the old tramp was hiding out, it was quite a hide-out he'd made for himself, proper Bear Grylls as you can see, very well camouflaged, quite skilfully done. Not the work of a simple tramp? Anyway, well done team and credit to your little doggy friends! Pity you didn't do it properly the first time like but... hey-ho! Anyway, now thanks to the job being done properly, we know how he accessed the towpath, using a gate that wasn't properly checked the first time!" He tapped angrily at a picture of the gate in the rusty palisade fencing.
"So he had easy access to the towpath, it's on his patch so to speak and less than half a mile from where the body was found."

"Surely it's further than that?" A sensible voice queried, causing the acting DI to turn and look at the map as a flurry of wisecracks blossomed behind him…
"Maybe as the crow flies it might be, but that canal's bendier than a pole dancer!"
"Well you'd know all about pole dancers eh?"
"It's lap-dancers as he likes!"
"Maybe 'e really is a crow?"
"Well he does look a bit like one! Flap-flap of that big coat!"
"Yeah the crow… strikes again!"
"For fucks sake! Yer like a giggle of schoolgirls! Grow-up, will ya! Unless anyone has anything else sensible to add, that's all for now. No? Okay then, one last thing, the autopsy is finally being done this morning, I'm off there now."

With that Steadman strode purposefully from the room, the occupants of which breathed a collective sigh of relief! His departure triggered it to burst into chatter and laughter… In the hubbub one of the team took the opportunity to scrawl in thick black marker pen, alongside the mugshot of Bill, pinned right in the centre of one of Steadman's boards…

Adjacent as Bill's mugshot was to the photo of the one-eyed victim, it seemed sinisterly appropriate…

The Crow

CHAPTER THIRTY

Later that day, Don reported back to Harry that he'd managed to snatch a few minutes with Bill, but it had been unproductive,
"He's totally non-communicative, he just sits there staring into space, he can definitely hear though... I even banged on the table out of frustration at one point, when I couldn't get him to respond to me and he flinched, but he's either taken his right to remain silent too the *n'th* degree, or he's had some kind of breakdown. I asked the PC who was on duty if he's always like that and he confirmed it! Bill hasn't spoken a word since he was arrested!"
"If he's had a breakdown though, surely he can't be put on trial?" Harry suggested,
"Thing is he's been examined by a doctor and they say he's fully conscious and responsive to stimuli, that he's simply choosing not to speak."

"Shit!" Harry was at a loss...
"Yeah, that just about sums it up! For what it's worth, in my opinion that is, I think he's given up, thrown in the towel and accepted that he's going to prison! Maybe he sees it as a safer place than being out on the streets y'know, having a roof over his head and three meals for the rest of his days. I mean how many days has the poor old bastard got left in him anyway? Did you take a really good look at him?"
"Oh hell yes! I know all that, he was checked over in the weeks before all this shit kicked off, I even had him up at St. Jude's, of course you won't know any of this, but I'd even sorted out a small appartment here for him. He was going to be off the streets anyway! The bloody old fool insisted that he wanted to spend one last night out at his bivouac! He must have been on his way back from there when he found poor little Natalie."
"So you knew the victim?"
"Yeah, her boyfriend and her were writing up a piece about the homeless in our town and how the The Factry works, for a thesis or something, they're students, they spoke to Bill as well as a few other clients who would cooperate with them."
"Have you been interviewed by the police then?"
"Yeah, by that charmer Steadman and his attack dog!"
"What did you tell them?"
"Not much, I didn't know that much to tell really."

"They have a witness who claims that they saw a heated exchange between Bill and the victim, along the towpath."
"Shit! They're going to send the poor old sod to jail aren't they?"
"Unless he starts talking, it definitely looks that way. If he'd just agree to have a lawyer, someone to represent him, then we could do a lot. For one thing we could get our own psychiatrist in to do a proper evaluation of him."
"If only there was someone who could get through to him."

But they were unable to find such a person and Bill was taken to court, where he stood impassively as the charges were read out and when he was asked to speak in reply to them. When he did not, whether or not it was because he chose not to, or was unable to, a plea of not guilty was recorded. The report from the police doctor was read out, a brief summary of the case against Bill followed and that was that.

He was remanded in custody and taken in a prison van to a jail somewhere out of town.

It had all been a blur for Bill, he told himself that he wasn't really there, that none of what went on around him had anything to do with him. It wasn't real or happening to him, he was a bystander, a disinterested bystander. He was somewhere else. None of it mattered anyway. He was nothing to this system of theirs, he was outside of it all. He was an outcast who was solidly and deliberately ignored, shunned and left to fend for himself, alone on the fringes of *their* society, isolated and yet bizarrely amongst other outcasts suffering similarly. No helping hands, no money offered, nothing…

The only use men such as himself had to their society was to be used to pour blame onto… a girl is murdered, find someone to blame… he was ideal for the job. He'd been there, made his presence there know to the police, set himself up. He deserved to go to jail if nothing else for his abject stupidity alone!

In his current state of mind the ameliorating voices that would normally have challenged these stark pronouncements were muted, unheard to his shutdown mind. They would have reminded him of the generosity of the people who gave him money as he begged, or the ones who would buy him a sandwich, talk to him offering help at a hostel or suchlike, or the people at the Factry, people like Harry... who had offered him a flat of his own! Who drove him around from his stay at St. Jude's...

But no, these thoughts and the voices that may have vocalised them were shut away behind another steel door in Bill's mind now, locked away next door to the vault that held fast memories of all that had come in his old life before his fall.

It was better this way. He knew that much to be the case. He clung onto that as a certainty, something solid, a rock to cling onto. Even had he been reminded of the offered flat at The Factry, he would have dismissed it as having been some kind of a trap anyway. This was his due. He would be shut away as an example to others of how society dealt with problems such as he was.

He was scarcely aware of the journey in the van.
Just an experience of being shut in a small white moving cubicle.
The van going through gates...
Clanging and banging...
Being taken from the van...
Being led by his arm here and there.
Spoken at...
Shouted at sometimes...
Pushed and shoved a bit...
Sat down...
Stood up...
Corridors...
An office...
A doctor... *"Can you hear me?"*
A light in his eye...
Something in his ear...
Something on his arm...
His arm being squeezed...
"They've sent these over with you."
A plastic bag held up...
"Lisinopril and Aspirin. You saw a good old fashioned doc someplace then? No fancy stuff, I like it."
"Can you understand anything I say to you?"

"The report says you're in there, so I'll have to assume you can! You will carry on with these meds, from listening to your heart you certainly need them!"
Rustling of paperwork,
"Hmm... says here they want a full psychiatric rundown, so you'll be seen by our shrink. Right, that's me done!
"Good luck old fellow!"
A pat on his arm.
Another person,
"He's on D Wing, isn't he officer?"
"Yeah, with the other nut jobs!"

Another cell.
A window he can look out of...
Through the mesh...
A bunk...
Sleep...

A new routine then became established for Bill.
Get up when the bell goes.
Get dressed.
Go and eat breakfast.
Sit around.
Eat lunch.
Sit around.
Eat tea.
Sit around.
Go to bed.
Less frequently take a walk about outside.
Interspersed among this are the occasional visits he makes to see the psychiatrist. A man who talks at him... talks a lot.
Intermingled in his daily routine are faces, voices and the antics of other inmates...
The oddity and meaninglessness of the things they say and the illogical and pointless antics they performed in front of Bill and the rest of the inmates were of no interest to him.
He just drifted through the days in a hazy non-existence...
Similarly through the weeks...
Then months...

Beyond the incarcerating walls of the prison and Bill's tiny bubble of existence within them, out there in the big wide world, spurred on by a burning desire to reveal the truth behind all this, Jenny had become the very personification of the word *newshound!* Relentlessly seeking out every new lead she could, finding new scents and then beavering away at each and every one of them, desperate to sniff out and discover the reality of what had actually happened to Natalie Blunt in the minutes, hours and days before she was found murdered on that towpath. She worked hand in glove with Don, her police insider who was equally determined to clear Bill's name and in the process expose Steadman for the incompetent, corner-cutting, malicious idiot that he was and equally to highlight the poor judgement of that malicious and vindictive bitch Sally Pembrose in handing over to him Don's case, in the first place!

Don had become impressed with Jenny's skills of detection and her dogged determination and between them they began to create an alternative and more credible narrative to the unimaginative, limited and wholly convenient one that D.I. Steadman had promulgated.

By talking to as many residents as she could in the area immediately surrounding the crime scene, Jenny began to build up a picture of a culture of yobbery in the area, not particularly widespread, but occurring occasionally on some evenings and more particularly at the weekends, when quite large groups of adolescents, some of them as young as junior school age, would hang about outside on the streets. The anti-social activities of these *groups...* she wouldn't stoop to the level of gutter journalism, by using their exaggerating tactics in referring to them as *gangs...* centred on a large derelict site that had once been a factory or works of some kind.

Having been tipped-off in this way, she had gone along to investigate the site, she'd asked Sam to accompany her for security, although it was pushing credibility to consider Sam as a viable bodyguard... she doubted that he'd weigh ten stones wet through... but he'd been the only guy in the office at that moment in time, well... she doubted Gil would have wanted to get out of the car if she'd taken him!

They discovered once they'd squeezed in through the dilapidated gates that it consisted largely of piles of rubble, having been partly demolished and partly fallen-in of its own accord! Sam had made himself useful snapping pictures of everything as they went.

Viewed from outside on the road, he photographed the high stone wall that was still remaining, running along the pavement and joining up with the buildings on either side, but on the other side of the wall, inside the derelict site, it was ninety percent without any roof. He photographed the large gateway with the closed yet dilapidated gate blocking it and how it was loose and it was easy to squeeze around one end of it.

Inside they could see that along one side, still attached to the adjoining building, a short length of wall still supported a section of the roof, it remained hanging there in a most precarious fashion over one corner of the yard. Despite the rubble being piled-up everywhere else, there was a cleared area adjacent to the roofed-over bit, where it was evident that many a bonfire had been burnt, there was litter scattered all around.

Dozens of shiny little metal canisters lay around, all over the place, Jenny commented that they looked similar to the bulbs her mum had once used to charge her soda syphon. Sam made her aware that these were different and were used by the kids to inhale the pressurised gas that they contained, it was nitrous oxide gas he told her, laughing gas! Silly little sods she remarked! Later on back at the office, another one of her colleagues confirmed that it had become a fad for some time now and that the streets outside many bars and nightclubs were also littered with the things, what the users referred to as *whippets.*

The most revealing bit of evidence they discovered, at the expense of ripping her coat, as they scrabbled through a tangle of brambles that towered over their heads in places, was that there was a path through them, or there had been before the brambles… that she likened to a type of living and *bloody evil,* barbed-wire… had started to grow back over it, the well-trodden earth under their feet however still revealed the track of the path through the undergrowth. They fought their way along the path until it came to a stretch of tall and rusty, metal palisade fencing that held back the growth of brambles, it stretched out on either side of them, along the side of the canal's towpath.

Dragging clinging lengths of the green and barbed brambles off herself and treading them down, she was able to examine the fence more closely, finding that one of the vertical bars was not properly secured at the bottom, the rivet that was still fixed to the crossbar having rusted a hole all around itself in the vertical one, when she took hold of it she was able to pivot it on the remaining rivet that was still in place on the top rail, it was a squeeze but with Sam holding it up, she was able to get through and gain access to the towpath!

Stood alongside the canal she was painfully aware that this access point was only a few paces or so from was the spot where Natalie's body had been found, although she had no need of relying on her memory to inform her of this as a faded wreath was still tied onto the fencing to mark the spot. She helped Sam get through the fence and they walked over to see the remains of some bunches of flowers that were slowly rotting away around the base of the fence. There was a small figurine of an angel and a couple of soggy teddy bears too.

Jenny stooped down to pick up a small white picture frame holding a photo of Natalie, the eyes in her young and hopeful face gazed blankly back up at her, something else caught her eye as she placed the picture back down to lean against the fence, it looked like a small piece of cardboard with something printed on it. She picked it up and examined it, it was a bit worse for wear, looking like it had got wet and then dried out, it was an Underwood's Brewery beermat, advertising their 'UnterHund Craft-Bier'!

She smiled at someone's interesting use of a mix of languages to try to sell their product! She commented on it to Sam as she examined the beermat. It had a picture on it of a cartoon dog, it looked like the beer was aimed at the younger end of the market, had it been placed there by a fellow student maybe?
"Ever heard of it?" She asked Sam, showing it to him.
He said he hadn't, although obviously he knew of Underwoods Brewery.

She turned the card trying to read what had been written across it in biro, it was a scrawl and bits of the paper had begun to flake away, but after studying it for a moment or two, she was able to make out... '*so sorry*' she struggled to read the rest and with a little bit of guesswork she came to the conclusion that the rest of what had originally been written before that was... '*I'm...*' so it said... '*I'm so sorry*'. There was more but she was unable to make it out, so she took a tissue out from the packet she had in her pocket and carefully wrapped the beermat in it before tucking it away in her handbag. Maybe Don would be able to get someone to discover what the rest of the writing had said, it was probably nothing, nothing more than a drunken scribble from a fellow student, the beer looked likely to be something they would drink.

They walked back to where they'd come through the fence, standing back a little from it on the towpath it was easy to see how the opening through which they had just passed had been missed, looked at from this side the grass and weeds were growing high up all along the fencing, even looking more closely, the rivet at the bottom was still fixed to the bottom rail on the outside and looked the same as all the other ones, viewed from the towpath there was nothing to suggest that it no longer held the vertical bar in place.

Jenny was thrilled by their discovery, that there was direct access to the towpath from the derelict site, a place where gangs of kids obviously gathered, it meant that where the body had been found probably wasn't the crime scene at all. She telephoned Don at once and he joined them on the towpath a little later She demonstrated for him how the bar could be swivelled and they both fought their way back through the undergrowth into the derelict site, Sam deciding he was now superfluous to requirements had quickly volunteered to go back to the office!

Once at the area surrounding the site of the bonfires, Don packed as many empty bottles and silver bulbs as he could fit into a shopping bag Jenny had produced from her handbag! He commented that he wished they'd had a forensics team go over this place at the time. 'You never know though', he said, 'we might still be able to get something useful from here to use as evidence at some point...'

It was Don's idea to call in at the nearby garage and see if there was anything on their CCTV of the night before the body had been discovered. Thankfully their system retained months of data and sure enough there was footage of a group of lads passing-by on the street, heading in the direction of the derelict site, although the street was only visible in the top corner of the screen and the resolution was poor too, they could still see four or five lads and one girl walking past, the girl didn't appear to be under any duress, but although it was impossible to a hundred percent certain, she could very well have been Natalie.

Don agreed to write it up and take it to his superior. Later when he handed her the report he had an inkling about what she would do with it when she'd asked him if the file was the only copy of his report!

He said it was.

It wasn't.

As he predicted, she did nothing with it.

Sally Pembrose was only his direct superior due to Shaz being on extended leave. He did consider taking his evidence to someone else, to go over her head... However since his career was already hanging by a thread, he had to weigh at what point trying to save Bill and continuing to have a steady income would become incompatible? It was a vexing position to find himself in, but his old maxim of *'when in doubt do nowt'* held sway... at least for now. Maybe time would tell and something more conclusive would materialise.

Time passed swiftly by with an occasional tit-bit of new information coming in, or being gathered in response to the couple of articles Jenny wrote for her paper, in vain attempts to shed doubt and undermine the case against Bill. They had found that the beermats were in use at the student union bar, the rest of the scribbled message had been recovered on the quiet by one of the forensic people, as a favour to Don. The full message had read, *'I'm so sorry I didn't do more M...'* After the capital letter M the rest of the beermat had been too degraded to recover the rest of the word, they assumed it had most likely been the name of the author, and cursed the fact that they didn't have all of it. So all they knew from it was that someone was sorry, that they hadn't done something and that they were probably a fellow student whose name began with an M, it didn't narrow things down much!

Don had tried to be positive, "It's how cases often go, you get small breaks now and then with an investigation, you only take a baby step forward now and then, if any at all and for ages… but then it only takes one decent breakthrough for all of these little pieces to fit together, to give you what you need. The biggest obstacle we have is Bill himself! While he can't or won't talk, he's unable to appoint someone to represent him, it could be that after the psyche evaluation in prison the court will appoint someone to speak for him, if they consider he's mentally incapable to make the decision to decline counsel.

"Frankly it's all a bloody mess. I think we have to consider the possibility that somewhere in his mind he has accepted that he's not getting through this, that he's had enough and simply given up. He's resigned himself to the fact that he's staying in prison for the rest of his days! Let's face it, when you look at how the poor old bugger was living, it could well be the best thing for him! I mean, even if we could prove his innocence and get him released, get him back out… What would he be coming out to? A few more years living out there in the cold? How would that end?" Don had clearly not recalled Harry telling him of his offer of accommodation and Jenny let the conversation end there, what point was there in reminding him about the flat anyway?

Jenny felt that for all they tried, it was all just pissing into the wind! The mainstream press had decided that the guy… that they too had adopted the nickname of 'The Crow' for… was the murderer and the Police had their man. That was the end of it as far as they were concerned. She wondered why they were even going to bother having a trial, if and when they eventually got around to it!

The way the system made people wait for so long, holding them in such a terrible extended limbo, either on remand… which was locked-up without a trial… or as a prisoner in their own home on bail, accused but not yet having had the opportunity to defend themselves! It was cruel, unfair and totally unnecessary. It was just another symptom of the broken system, as she'd written in her article, the result of year after year of deliberately underfunding the Criminal Justice System, leading to the closing down of so many local courts and the savage cuts there'd been to Legal Aid... It made her blood boil, but so few of the public at large seemed to care, so few were even remotely interested in any of it, they didn't give a shit unless or until they had personal experience of the farrago themselves, till it was them or one of theirs who faced the creaking wheels of 'justice' or if they were amazingly lucky and the mainstream media decided to pluck their case from obscurity... make them one of the ever growing number of cases of a miscarriage of justice... that they brought to people's attention... for a day or two!

People were such mindless idiots she thought, they just allowed themselves to let the media lead them by the nose! Bloody sheep! She'd even been personally singled out by one of the nationals and given the label of being a '*bleeding heart liberal*,' an inexperienced reporter who was simply a misguided fool who had been *taken in* by The Crow! Somehow they had taken the information that she had disclosed in her articles, in her efforts to try and exonerate him... and categorised it as invalid tittle-tattle, because they said when she had interviewed Bill only days before the murder, she had *fallen under his spell*! Using that as evidence of her bias, rather than the truth of it, which was that she had through speaking with him been able to form a true opinion of his character! Her conclusion that he was a poor old sod who the system had broken and then spat out! Her editor had warned her off the story and told her that he wouldn't print anything else she put forward after that.

Stymied as they were feeling over their efforts to get Bill released, Jenny and Harry's romance had nevertheless continued to blossom. However rosy their own future may have been looking though, they were beginning to suspect that for all their efforts Bill's may be very much less so.

It was inevitable that with the passage of time, the lack of new information and with the everyday events that continually wrap us up in their needs and comforts... that as ever... life went on... Occasionally they would meet up with Don and swap notes, but all this did was confirm that they had nothing new or substantial enough to make a difference.

As the date of the trial loomed ever nearer, Don suggested that perhaps they should leak the information they'd gathered, expose the fact that Sally Pembrose had sat on the file he'd taken to her. Jenny pointed out that he would be putting his head on the block and from what he'd said about her, she would be more than happy to wield the axe!

Feeling suitably impotent, the day came and they could only watch from the public gallery as Bill went on trial, although calling it a trail was a travesty, it was more of a hideously grotesque pantomime! He just sat impassively in the dock, silently staring into space, totally disinterestedly. He never once glanced up to see them sat there, he appeared to be in some sort of a trance.

Incredibly the psychiatrist at the prison had given the all clear for him to be tried, citing in his evidence that he presented before them, that it was inconclusive that Bill was genuinely *locked-in,* as he was able to function in every other way that was necessary to sustain his day to day life, feeding and washing himself, etcetera... He also responded to external stimuli and was able to adequately comprehend the verbal instructions he was given. The fact that he was a zombie didn't seem to matter to them, their implication being that he was compos mentis and therefore him being the way that he was, was a matter of choice.

The *evidence* having been duly presented, the trial which had commenced on a Thursday was adjourned for the weekend and was set to resume the following Monday for the summing-up and for the jury to then retire to consider their verdict... as if they hadn't already decided upon one!

It was with heavy hearts that Jenny and Harry walked hand in hand away from the courthouse. They walked in silence to Harry's car, there was nothing left to say, they had failed and Bill was going to spend the rest of his days behind bars.

CHAPTER THIRTY-ONE

Just as she was packing up for the day, the phone on Jenny's desk rang out. '*Shit!*' She thought… shall I pick it up?… Her hand wavered for a moment but then she found herself saying into the receiver, albeit with a resigned tone in her voice…
"Hi!"
"Jen, there's a bloke down here asking for you, says he's an old friend of your pal The Crow!"
"For fucks' sake Tracey! I wish you'd all stop calling him that! His name is Bill! He's a fucking innocent man! He's just an unfortunate old guy who's been set-up and that's all there is to it!"
"Yeah, yeah… so *you* keep saying…Are you coming down to see him or not? I'm about to lock the door and fuck-off for home!"
"Of course I bloody am!"

Jenny shot down the stairs, unintentionally flinging the door open with a bang to hit against the wall, in her hurry and nearly falling through it into the reception area… Sue shook her head,
"Again? Can't you just open a door?"
"Well, that certainly is what I call an entrance!" A very elegant and nattily dressed guy exclaimed! He was leaning with one elbow on the top of the reception counter, one leg was crossed casually over the other at the ankle, his free arm akimbo. He'd turned his head towards Jenny as she'd burst in and now he beamed a smile at her showing a row of perfect, pearly white teeth… *Was he wearing lipstick? Was that a hint of eye-shadow? Was she actually looking at a guy at all?* …all this ran through her mind in flash!

Amidst her confusion she managed to bluster out…
"Jen… Jenny Stainton… you're an old friend of Bill's?"
"Well '*hello*' to you too gorgeous… so very pleased to meet *you*, Jen-Jenny! I'm Del and yes the wreckage of a man you refer to as Bill, is most certainly the same man I once knew."

"Can I buy you a coffee somewhere so we can talk properly, the Gazette's so run down these days there's not… well… and Sue, that foul-mouthed harridan over there wants to lock-up! We'd be more comfy across the road. Shall we?"

Del raised himself up from the leaning position Jen had found him in, brushed down the sleeve of his very chic, light grey jacket as it fell away from his lean body. He picked up a matching fedora from the counter top and placing it on his head, gestured with a flourish of his hand for Jen to lead on! He stood easily as tall as Jen, the word *metrosexual* sprang into Jen's mind as she led-on as she was bidden …

Tracey called after them, "*I'm* the one who's foul-mouthed? Really Jen?" to which Jenny flicked two fingers over her shoulder as she laughed…

Jen arrived with their coffees to the table where Del had sat, she noted that his jacket had been immaculately folded and laid on one of the empty chairs, the fedora having been positioned on top of it. She put the cups down and then took her seat, placing her phone on the table alongside her cup,

"May I?" She nodded to the phone,

"I'd rather you didn't Jen and no pictures either if you don't mind, you'll understand why when I've told you my tale!"

"Okay…" She made a point of demonstrably turning off her phone, "I have to say you're a damn natty dresser Del! I do love your style!"

"Well y'no shrinking violet yourself either my lovely, are you? And those your *work clothes*? Very understatedly chic!

"So, first things first… yes I wear a touch of make-up, but no I'm not any of the words you might attempt to use to pigeon-hole me with! I'm just *Del,* I'm *me* and I'm indescribable… *not* gay, *not bi, not anything* but simultaneously everything! Well everything that's *fabulous!*

"Right… so now we've got that out of the way…. I met Jos… that's who he said he was at that time… at one of the club's I worked at, the one I spent most time at actually, he was a regular there. We're talking about years ago now, maybe eight, even nine? Or it may be six or seven! I'm hopeless with time and dates! Anyway, we got to talking, he was always one of the last to leave… be around four… he wanted to stay drunk and stoned for as long as possible, back then it seemed like he had one hell of a lot of woes to drown… Look, can we sit outside, it's not that cold and I need a ciggy…"

Del drained his coffee in one gulp, stood up and put his jacket on, he stood whilst he positioned it perfectly on the shoulders of

his reflection in a handy mirror and did likewise with his hat, Jen had barely touched her own coffee...
"Bring it with you sweetie..."
"It's so hot how did you..."

Sat outside Del slipped a very thin and flat silver case from his jacket pocket, he clicked it open and took a thin black cigarette out from it, a matching lighter followed as he slipped the case back. He clicked the lighter to light-up, took in a deep drag...

Jenny was watching him carefully all the while as he did this, studying his every move, he had a style and grace about him to match his elegant appearance, he gave an occasional toss of the head as he'd just made as he exhaled the smoke from his cigarette, it intimated to Jenny that the blonde hair that was shaved at the sides and left a little longer on top, with a flop of a wave at his forehead had formerly been long enough to toss about! Or maybe he was accustomed to wearing a wig?
She realised that he'd taken in her studious gaze, as he smiled,

"Ah... that's better... You don't look like a smoker Jen, but I should have offered you one, sorry I was so rude!"
"No worries, so what were you doing at the club, sorry... I mean, not like, why were you there? But what was your job... err..."
Del laughed, tossing his head back again as he did... she could almost see his long hair as he did so... his laughter was so natural and infectious, it was almost musical, yet delicate and almost childlike too and Jen found herself laughing along with him,
"Oh, no, no, no, no-*no* darling! I'm not a hooker! Although... well, never mind that! No sweetie, I'm a singer... in drag of course, well I mean..." He swept his hands down the front of his body in an exaggerated flourish... "With this body... well! You should see me in a full length, sequined evening gown!

"But back to your *Bill*, now then, the clincher was that YouTube video clip of him where he's playing the piano... you see some nights after the band had gone, well it was usually just a pianist most nights, but anyway... very late on, Jos'd sometimes sit at the piano and play for me and any other drunk who was still left draped on or over the furniture around the place... He told me he could play pretty much anything if he had the music infront of him to read from, but the stuff he could play from memory was a bit limited…

"That was about it you see… what he played on the video was the same stuff, his little repertoire. I saw a tiny clip of it on the telly, that was what led me to it, it was a piece about the trial of someone the Press had named The Crow! Fucking vultures! No offence to present company! So I went online and got the full story, it eventually led me back to your paper, the *whatsama…*"
"The Gazette." Jen obliged.
"Yeah… I doubt the picture alone would have caught my attention, I had to really study it to see Jos in that old tramp's face… Nah, I'd've missed it for sure… it was only hearing the clip that made me look into it as closely as I did!"

"When I saw that he was due in court on Monday for the summing-up bit… Well, I packed a bag, borrowed my friend's car and shot back here!"
"How far have did you have to come?"
"I'd fled up to the north-east, near Stockton… I'd have flown from LA for Jos though if that's where I'd been!"

"So, what can I do to help? I can't believe for one minute that he did what they say he did to that poor girl, I got the impression from your article I found, that you don't believe he did either?"
"No of course I don't! We've been trying to help him for months, a friend of his and me, while he's been banged-up in jail… well he's a friend of sorts… the guy who runs the Factry, me and him and a cop too… not a bastard one, a good one, he's not the one who handled the case, well he was initially, but he got taken off it because…
"Whoa there! Easy does it… *slow down girl!…*" Del held his hands up theatrically.

"So, what's this *Factry*? Would that be The Folks Factory I read about in your article? You say your friend runs it?"
"Yeah, that's Harry! He's my boyfriend now as well!" She blushed… Del chuckled and pointed a finger at her,
"So you're not quite the goody two-shoes you try to come over as, eh? So, you do know that Jos would've been your guy Harry's boss back when I knew him?" Jen's jaw actually dropped…

"*What?*" She nearly yelled it out! Incredulously she said,
"*That was who Bill was?* Before he walked away from his life, became homeless... no! He was *that Jos*, before he *chose* to become homeless old Bill! That is totally and utterly fucking gobsmacking!"
"Brace yourself then love... He was only *pretending* to be Jos too! Bit of a theme he had going on there, eh? No he actually *was* the guy who put up the money for the whole shebang in the first place! The concept, the building work the whole thing! One Mr James Oscar Stanley... *almost MBE*... but which he turned down with a *'thank you very much for your offer your Majesty!'* He was the multi-millionaire owner of Stanley Construction, which you will be familiar with as it has to be one of the biggest companies to have its base in your town." Jen was aghast...
"Can I have one of your cigs Del..." Was all she could say.

Del clicked his lighter to the cigarette once it was in Jen's mouth, she took a drag on it, held it away from her face and studied it for a moment as she gently let the smoke drift out of her mouth and nostrils. It was black with a shiny gold band around the filter, an elegant looking thing, like Del, stylish and sophisticated... still a tube of *ready-death* though she scolded herself! She could see Del had a face that would be equally elegant as a woman and he had the build for it too, unlike a lot of the men who went into performing drag acts...

"Mmm... Sobranie... very nice...Didn't think you could still get them."
"Oh yes, you can if you know where to look, they use Black Russian tobacco you know darling!"
Del produced a cigarette holder from an inside pocket of his jacket, "would you like to go the whole nine yards my dear?" Jen laughed but shook her head,
"Part of your act Del?"
"Oh yes... it's not just Del actually, it's 'Del-*Icious*' darling..." he laughed and again Jen found she was laughing with him. She was beyond intrigued about him, finding him to be quite entrancing! All in all she was pretty mind-boggled by him! She took a drag on the cigarette and as she exhaled asked,

"So the poor old tramp, that ragged itinerant *Bill* who's sat rotting in jail, is in fact a multi-millionaire?"

"Well, who knows? What I mean is, whether or not he still is now? He certainly was back then! He never told me any of that of course at the time, to me he was just Jos, I only found out later. The thing is Jen, if his eldest son has had anything to do with it he *will* be penniless now... *shit!* If it's been long enough since he left, he'll have taken the lot, he'll have had him declared dead by now, won't he?"

"Well thing is if it's over seven years, he'll have been able to, but why, what was wrong with his son?"

"Jos rambled on one time about an ungrateful son, he just babbled about him *wanting it all*, without being specific about anything else or what *it all* was even! He told me how he'd made his son the CEO and stayed on himself as Chairman of their family business, but his son wanted him gone altogether, he didn't make much sense at the time and he never spoke about that again. He'd often do that you see, when he was drunk, talk and talk and fucking talk! It was as if he was trying to deal with so much torment in his troubled mind that he had to let some of it out? He often mentioned someone called Abigail, although I couldn't figure out who exactly she was to him though. It stuck in my mind though that he'd pretty much bragged one night that The Folks Factory was his, I couldn't get much sense out of him as to what he meant by that either though."

"I found out much later who his son really was... look this is getting to be a long story, are you okay sat here?" The evening was drawing-in and suddenly Jen remembered that on Monday morning Bill was going to be found guilty of murder! The man who built The Factry was going to be locked-up for the rest of his life! So she responded,

"Yes, I agree. Let me make a couple of phone calls Del, I need you to tell all of this to my friends, the ones who've been helping me try and clear Bill, we need to see if there's anything we can do, albeit at the eleventh hour to save Bill!"

When she rang Harry, he'd suggested to be discrete that they all met up in Bill's flat and an hour later they were sat around in his lounge digesting the new information that Del had provided.

Harry and Don had arrived at the same time as Jenny and Del, they'd both been aghast at the news of who Bill really was, Harry was outraged when Jenny told them that she'd suspected that Alan Jarvis had known all along who Bill was, she went on to recount how she'd seen the look on Jarvis's face when he'd caught sight of Bill, clearly he'd recognising him from somewhere and from right across the room at the fundraiser and how shocked he'd looked and then how he'd left almost immediately.

Harry burst out, "I can't believe that he knew all along who this Jos fella was and never let on to me! Even more to hear now that Jos was the money man behind the whole project! He shook his head…

Now that he was up to date, Don Willis the detective was equally amazed to hear what Del said as he continued his tale from where he'd left off with Jenny…

"Jos and me had a run-in with a couple of fellas one night at the club, they were hitting on me… not that anyone could blame them for that of course, poor saps… I was after all dressed as a woman, a gorgeous one at that, but I wasn't interested. They were clearly thugs, gangsters or criminal lowlife types of one sort or another. Well Jos stepped-in, he was very brave and very drunk as one of them was a big bastard, and both were mean looking fuckers, but he was so charming and drunk that he handled it beautifully…

"Nevertheless they weren't that impressed, but they did let it go, funny thing was although it didn't make much sense at the time, one of them said '*I'll let you off this one time Jimmy*' as they were leaving.
"It can't have been more than a week later when Jos had the shit kicked out of him!
"I'd been weaning him off the hard stuff for weeks by then and he was doing well, but that night we'd both had a few. Only alcohol though! I'd got a gig… oh that doesn't matter… we'd been celebrating. When we came out and we always left by the backdoor at that hour… the front had been locked for ages by then… we were jumped by the same two thugs. One of them pushed me over onto my arse and the other got Jos with a punch to the face, he stayed on his feet and give him his due, he tried to put up a fight, but he was drunk and the guy was a bruiser. The

other one told me to… '*fuck-off out of it and keep my mouth shut if I know what's good for me!*'

"So I took off my heels and legged-it! But I snuck back and hid behind the bins and watched. It was fucking awful, the other bastard had grabbed him from behind and held him while he was beaten senseless. When he was on the ground they started kicking him… Fucking animals they were! I was beside myself, I wanted to scream blue murder, I wanted to help him, poor Jos… but I couldn't do a thing.
"They left him lying there and walked off, I waited a minute then ran to him, he was semiconscious and rambling, I dialled 999 and put him in the recovery position, I kept telling him he was going to be alright, but to be honest I couldn't see how he could ever be alright again."

By now tears were streaming down Del's face as he recounted the horror he had witnessed. Jen, put her arm around him and he leant into her shoulder and sobbed. Harry asked if he'd like a whisky. He nodded and after everyone else indicated they would too, he got four glasses and a bottle out...

Suitably composed Del sniffled and went on, "the strangest thing was what the big ugly bastard said to the other one as they walked off, he said, '*'e's one mean son-of-a-bitch that Declan is! 'Avin us do that to 'is ol'man*!' The other one just laughed and said, '*aye y'd best believe it mon*!' It didn't make any sense to me until much later at the hospital."

He went on to tell them how the Police had questioned him at the hospital, he told them he only knew him as Jos, but he knew he had something to do with the Folks Factory. He guessed it was from that that they somehow got in touch with his son.

Harry was outraged, "So it had to be that bastard Jarvis who told them who his son was! It certainly wasn't me, maybe it was before my time even? Jos was in hospital so he must have been the only one here to deal the enquiry from The Police. Don't you see? This means that he must have known that Jos was really this James Stanley fella then too! Jenny and Don looked shocked, but Del just shrugged and went on,

"Much later on, while I was sat there at the hospital this guy turned up, he introduced himself as Jake Stanley, said he was Jim's son. He asked who I was and I said that I'd been leaving the club where I worked and came across his Dad on the ground. Thing is, I was struck by how much he looked like Declan, you see I'd seen him, Declan that is, with the same two thugs at another club I worked now and then, they'd been lording it up with the girls, like they were some kind of royalty, then it just fell into place... The remark about his ol'fella... So I just asked him, '*is your brother Declan then?*' 'Declan?' He says, '*oh you'll mean Neil?*' So I just nodded and he went on, '*yeah, the prat goes by Dec when he's trying to be a bigshot with some of the guys he hangs with!*'

Don interrupted at this point, "This is fucking unbelievable! It's dynamite! So what you're saying is that old Bill, is really James Stanley, a millionaire builder and his son Neil, aka Declan is a criminal who had two of his thugs beat the shit out of his own father!"
Jenny spoke up, "We've heard that name too from criminal sources at the paper, a bigshot called Declan or Dec..."
Don: "So have we! Believe me, but it has never been associated with Neil Stanley, owner and managing director of Stanley Enterprises, the biggest builder or probably biggest single organisation of any kind to be based here!" He went on,
"I *was* going to tell you that I'd just found out myself that Bill was Jos Armstrong, the one-time manager of The Folks Factory from a deep dive I had done on Facial Recognition, there was me thinking that I'd made a breakthrough! But now, to hear all this!"

Harry eventually broke the silence that had hung in the air for a long moment, "We have to do something now that we have this new information! Surely if the Judge is made aware of what we now know, of who Bill really is... well imagine if we let it come out! The Press would go bananas! It would make the trial so high profile that..."
Don: "Hang on! We need to think this through and think carefully too... First of all we have to get through to old Bill, or Jos, James, Jim, Jimmy... whatever you want to call him! Someone has got to go and see him and tell him that the game is up! That we know all about him and we will set about defending him properly with or without his help. Surely once he's aware we

know who he is it will bring him to his senses? But who's going to do it, he's steadfastly refused to see anyone of us since he was arrested?"

Jenny: "Regardless of that, don't you think that we simply must inform his son Jake? The poor lad hasn't seen his Dad since he wandered off years ago! Perhaps Bill would agree to see *him*?"
Don: "Well, so *we believe*... what I'm saying is, from what we know he's not seen him, but he *could* have been in contact with him, albeit on the quiet?"
Harry: "Either way, I agree with Jen, we have to include him, but we need to make absolutely sure that he doesn't let his brother know!"
Don: "Damn right! If he's as big a criminal as I think he might be, it could put Bill at risk, even where he is now in prison!"

Del who had been listening quietly spoke up now, "There's only one person Jos, or Bill as you know him, will agree to see and that's me."

Harry: "Don, can you set up a prison visit for Del for tomorrow? Can you do it without alerting that scumbag inspector who's in charge of his case?"
Don: "I can set it up, but he'll be able to find out if he asks the prison, I'm not sure whether or not they'd inform him as a matter of routine to be honest, but somehow I doubt it."
Harry: "In the meantime I'm going down to my office to call Jarvis and get him to come here as soon as he can."
Jenny: "Will he come, it's getting late, he'll have gone home by now surely?"
Harry: "Oh he'll come after I roast him for not telling me that he knew who Bill was!"
Don: "I asked my sidekick to look-up this Jake lad's address and she's just texted it back to me, so I'll get off and break the news to him. I'll bring him back if he's agreeable, I'm sure he'll want to meet the rest of you.

As Don was about to leave, as if on cue there was a knock on the door and Alan Jarvis walked in.

Harry quickly brought him up to speed and demanded the name of the best criminal defence barrister that he knew of in their area. He then instructed him to contact them at once, yes he knew it was Saturday tomorrow, he'd growled! Get him by whatever means you have to, even if you have to drive to his house, bang on his door and beg him! Tell him he'll have a blank cheque and this will be the biggest case he'll see this year when it all blows open...

Once Jarvis had agreed, he was summarily dismissed! Jenny queried, "You don't like that guy very much do you Harry? He certainly knows to jump when you say so too!"
"Yeah well... he's been a bloody rat for keeping quiet about Bill!"
It was an hour or two later when Don returned with Jake, he introduced him to Harry, Jenny and Del, as he shook Del's hand he smiled knowingly,
"I've met you before haven't I? I remember your name too and it wasn't Del! It was Rosie wasn't it? But... you were a woman last time we met! It was at the hospital wasn't it, you were the one who found Dad... but you told me you'd just happened upon him by chance? The fact that you're here now would indicate otherwise?"

"Okay, so I'm sorry that I lied to you Jake and yes I was presenting myself as a woman last time we met. So yes I did know your Dad, in fact we were the closest of friends. At the time I needed to keep a low profile, your Dad's attack wasn't random you see, it was deliberate and targeted! Targeted at him specifically! The bastards that beat him up knew me and they told me if I wanted to live I'd better say nothing. These people don't make idle threats either, so I packed my bags and left the next morning, this is the first time I've been back down here in years."

"My Dad was targeted?" An even more bewildered Jake asked. Don spoke up, "Jake, I'm afraid along with the good news about your Dad being alive, there are some things that are decidedly bad news that you need to know about. Firstly he's not in very good health, as I already told you he's in prison, so at least he's being looked after but... well there's no easy way to say this, it was your brother Neil who had your Dad done over, apparently he wanted him out of the company way more than your Dad intended to be!"

The five of them talked and drank whisky till the early hours, eventually Jake took advantage of Bill's bed and crashed out. Don let his wife know he was alright, somehow stitching together a plausible enough tale for her!

Harry and Jenny said goodnight to Don and they left Del to sleep on the bed settee, which he insisted he was more than happy to do, saying that one of them needed to be there when Jake woke up in the morning.

CHAPTER THIRTY-TWO

Bill was shuffling nonchalantly across the prison canteen, taking his tray back after eating his breakfast when he heard his name called out,
"Williams! Over here *now*." One of the warders, the one they called Jock, was stood by the doors to the canteen beckoning him over impatiently. He carried on to where the used trays were stacked, he placed his tray in the rack and then proceeded to amble over to the irritated looking man,
"Come-on, I've no got all day! You've a visitor so…"
Bill was already turning away from the guard as he dismissively waved away with his hand, the very idea of meeting a visitor! The guard took the remaining few strides over to him and clasped a hand on his shoulder, he gripped it hard.
"Nay so fast my lad! This isn'a visiting hours y'ken and this visit has been arranged by the Warden himself! Personally! Someone, somewhere has pulled some strings from very high places to arrange this!"
Bill shrugged so violently that the guard lost his grip, he spun round to lean his back up against the wall, standing up to his full height and holding both hands defensively, palm out at chest height in front of himself, all the while shaking his head from side to side.
Softening his attitude a little, the guard let go and stood back,
"Listen y'daft ol'fucker, I couldna care less if ya see this visitor or no, but I've been told to tell ya that ya visitor is one… *wha' tha' feck is tha'?…*"
The guard squinted at the strip of paper he had pulled out from his top pocket,
"A, an… *'M?'* wha'ever the fuck that means! M. Del *Lici-ou-schzenkha*! Wha' that fuck? Apparently, whoever arranged yon visit, knew as you'd been refusing te see anybody, they musta reckoned as y'would see them though, once you heard that name? Were they right then? Who the hell is this then?" He flicked the piece of paper, "some fuckin' Russian or summat?"
Bill slowly lowered his hands and nodded, the guard folding the paper up, smiled,
"Is that a wee smirk a see on y'miserable ol fizzog? Ha, ha-ha! Come on old lad and let's see why this *'M'* is so special to ya!"

Sat waiting at the far end of the large and otherwise empty visitor's room, Bill was intrigued by the news that Del, of all people was here to see him! For the first time in months he actually started taking an interest in his surroundings, he looked down the long, empty and clinical room where twenty tables were set out in five neat rows, two either side of a wide central aisle. It was a place to allow inmates a few minutes of contact with those who they had left behind out there in the world beyond the walls. Despite being brightly lit and having a row of windows along one wall, the heavy mesh covering them stopped anyone forgetting for a moment where they were. It was a cold, inhospitable place, smelling of bleach and fear. All the surfaces seemed hard to Bill, harsh and unforgiving, not even willing to absorb a tiny fraction of the soundwaves that hit their shiny surfaces, but bouncing them off to angrily echo around the stark miserable and depressing room.

Del… He thought about how he'd missed her when she vanished from his life after that dark night in the alleyway. He could still hear her voice… *'you'll be alright my love… hang-in there… help's on the way…'* as he lay there, unable to move on the cold tarmac, in and out of consciousness… For a long time he hadn't really known if it had just been in his imagination that she had been there with him at the hospital, when he eventually came round properly he'd asked Jake, but he said there had only been a woman who said her name was Rosie, who'd said she found him on her way home in the alleyway and called for an ambulance. It had broken his heart that he had never been able to find her after he was back on his feet again and he had resigned himself to the conclusion that the bastards who beat him must have done away with her, not wanting a potential witness to what they had done being left behind.

He was stirred from his thoughts by the door being noisily opened at the far end of the room, its clanging sound being echoed around the empty sterile room. A guard he'd never seen before came through, he held the door open and in she walked…

He stood up so abruptly his chair fell over behind him, the guard held up a hand to halt him from moving away from his table, then motioned for him to sit down as Del walked down the aisle towards him inbetween the rows of tables, or rather she *sashayed...* She was wearing a crisp, pale grey suit, very sharply cut over a matching waistcoat, a sparklingly white shirt, a deep purple Windsor-knotted tie, with a matching handkerchief artistically arranged in her breast pocket and a pair of very shiny black shoes... *men's shoes?*

He looked up at her face as she drew close to him, her silver grey hair was cut very short at the sides of her head but had been left longer on top and was swept back in an immaculate quiff, she was wearing a very pale colour lipstick (for her) and as their eyes met he saw she was wearing only the slightest hint of eye make-up... their eyes locked...
"Well take a look at you Jos! *What the fuck!* You look like shit!"
"Lovely to see you too Del!" Bill managed to grumble, but having been silent for so long, uttering the words set him off coughing, the use of his voice being unnatural and feeling strained. Del settled down in the chair opposite him, placing his hands on the table in front of him,
"I'm not allowed to touch you... although to be honest the prospect of doing so isn't really that appealing at the moment! Look at the state of you! What the fuck have you been up to Jos?"
His coughing having subsided a little, he croakily replied,
"More to the point, what have *you* been up to? Where the fuck did *you* vanish to? I thought those bastards had killed you! I fucking mourned you Del!" Tears were rolling down his face as he muttered out the words and he sobbed before rubbing the back of his hand across his face... Del went to reach out his hand to him but pulled it back, the guard's words still ringing in his ears, *'any infringement and your feet won't touch the ground till you're outta here, Warden arrange visit or not!'* Physical contact had been top of the No-List!

"Oh sweetie... I'm so sorry! I know I should have got in touch, I was fucking terrified though! But I *did try,* well eventually I did! I managed to get hold of your son's number and I rang him. He told me that you'd gone missing..."
"Jake told me that the woman visitor at the hospital told him her name was Rosie, was that you?..." She nodded,
"I had to protect myself, I was shit scared those bastards would track me down, when they asked me for a name it was..."

"I understand... look, I'm sorry... It's just that I was so worried about you! It's okay Del." She smiled at him,
"It was me who told the police who you were, I mean I didn't in fact know that for sure, not really for certain... But what I gave them was obviously enough to go on as they found your son from it."
"I thought it was me who told them to ring Jake?"
"No sweetie, your memory only clicked back in when Jake showed up, at least that's how I remember it. I had to stick with *Rosie* with the police too, if I'd given details of those men... I mean, I know they let me go on the terrible night, but that was only because they weren't thinking straight at that moment, they were too busy doing you over, but there was no way they would've left me alone, left a witness out there to what they did to you. Giving them up to the police would have sealed my fate, they can't protect you whatever bullshit they may tell folks! No once their boss, someone with a functioning brain... unlike the Neanderthals who beat you... was in possession of the facts, I mean once *he* found out..." She drew a finger across her throat... "I'd be a gonna!"
"You mean Neil? Or rather Declan?"
"Fuck! *You know?* You know it was him who had you done over?
"Not at the time, but I figured it out later, I think he might've meant them to kill me Del, I think the ungrateful bastard could've wanted me dead. But I didn't die and that's largely thanks to you, I'm guessing the sound of the sirens that stopped them from finishing me off were down to you?" Del nodded,
"As soon as I was out of sight, after they'd told me to 'fuck-off', I rang the police, told them where I was and showed them what was going on with the camera on my phone through the gap between the two big wheelie bins I was hiding behind. I'm sorry I couldn't do any more Jos, but look at me, I'm just a streak of piss compared to those bastards and the size of that big fucker!... I'd never wished more than on that night that I'd learnt Kung-Fu!" He made a couple of karate-like moves with his hands...
"I'd have diced the bastards!" He sighed before he went on,

"I felt so guilty, so bad for how little I was able to do for you... I didn't even tell the full story to your friends..."
"If you hadn't done what you did, they would have kept at it till I was well and truly dead, so you saved my life Del, leave it at

that." He laughed, "Although I do wish you had been a Kung-Fu expert! I mean it wasn't like you didn't have the time, you could easily have put the effort in to train, instead of lying stinking in bed all day like you used to... *lazy bitch*!"

They both laughed...

"That's better, I think I saw the old you for a moment then Jos! Underneath all that fucking horrible, and quite disgusting *mess!*" He pulled a revolted-looking face and brushed away with the fingertips of his raised hands, the mess he imagined to be there in the air between them, emanating from Jos's beard ...

"I'm so sorry Jos, I left town the morning after... the instinct for self-preservation kicked in! I've never been back here since, not until yesterday when I found out you were in trouble. I genuinely feared for my life, I've been living in Stockton... *aye, I'm up there in Geordie-Land now, manager of a bar, so I am bonny lad!"* He said in quite a passable Geordie accent.
"I think it was only the fact that you survived that they didn't hunt me down... But if the bastards had killed you and it had been a murder enquiry..." He shuddered.

Bill queried, "So what's with the get-up? You a man now, are you?"
"*How absolutely, horribly and fucking rude of you*! I thought you knew better than that Jos! I'd maybe expect shit like that from that horrible old twat *'Bill'* ...from the sort of tramp you adopted! But not from you Jos! Has being *him* so long turned you into someone I'm not going to like that much? I mean... *F-fucks sake* Jos... really? No one knows me better than you... well the Jossie bit of you does, if there's any of that lovely man I once knew left in there... no one knows better than he does *who and what I am!*"
He sat back looking cross and perplexed, letting the moment hang for a while, before carrying on again as if no cross words had been spoken,
"Listen, this is a special visit, sanctioned by the Governor himself! You've still got some friends in high places it seems, but I was told in no uncertain terms not to *take the piss* and make it last too long! Whatever the fuck, in *actual minutes* that means I don't know... But you have got to get your act together Jos,

your friends Harry and Jenny along with a cop called Don, have been working like mad to get you out of here, all the time you've been relaxing on holiday in here, swanning around like a zombie, they've been working frantically!

"Your son Jake knows you're alive too now, as of yesterday and that you are back in court on Monday, which *you do realise* is the last fucking day of your trial by the way! Before they lock you up and throw away the key! He is absolutely, fucking *desperate* to come and see you Jos and no, we haven't told that twat Neil about any of this! And yes, Jake has been sworn to secrecy, even to the extent that he has agreed, at least until after he's seen you not to tell anyone at all that you've been found and that you're alive! He is absolutely beside himself Jos, he wants to see you so badly. Will you agree to see him?"

"Aye well… *I will*, but not in here! After the court on Monday mebbe… Let me get back into my old skin eh? Before he sees me. I don't want him to see me like this, okay?"

"It's your decision Jos, I've done what I was asked to do and put it to you.

"Listen, I've brought clothes in with me, that head warden fella is it, one of the boss men, has them… Jake, *your son*, had kept all your clothes! *For fuck's sake*! What you did to that lad! He's kept them all that time Jos, for all those years… So by Monday morning, I want you to have shed this sorry looking shell, discarded this 'Bill' and returned to being Jos…
"No! You know what? Way more than that… *you bloody-well have to* become James Oscar Stanley *Esquire* again for us!
"We've even got a barber coming in, courtesy of the boss man, to unearth you from beneath that fucking jungle!"

A voice from the back of the room shouted out "Oi!" Del looked over his shoulder to see the guard tapping at his watch and then point repeatedly at the door. Del held up five fingers and gave him one of his most dazzling smiles…

"Five minutes Jos… So have you got all of this hun? Do it for Jake, do it for me, please Jos…" He looked at the almost unrecognisable face before him, unable to read any expression beneath the mass of unkempt whiskers, other than that held in his eyes, which she locked his own gaze onto… the eyes he beheld seemed dazed, empty, blank on the surface but beneath that he sensed an ocean of pain and misery… there was a long silence…

Finally Bill let out a long sigh leant back in his chair, took in a deep breath and shrugged,

"Okay then, why not?" Del unleashed his dazzling smile yet again, gave a little shake of his head and winked, pointing his index finger across the table at Bill …
"There he is! *That's* my man Jos!"

CHAPTER THIRTY-THREE

Harry was watching from where he was sitting overlooking the court from the visitor's gallery, sat alongside him were Jenny, Don, Jake and Del, as Sir Finnian Eustace Upton-Fredriksson got to work! Jarvis had turned up as well, but he'd had the sense to sit away from them, Harry had to hand it to Jarvis though, rat though he still considered him to be, he'd picked a winner in *'Freddie'*, as Sir Finnian was universally known in the legal profession. He was a larger than life character who it could easily have been imaged had escaped into the real world from out of the pages of one of John Mortimer's Rumpole of The Bailey books! His fearsome reputation combined with his initials and his penchant to set about reducing prosecutors to gibbering wrecks, as he mercilessly tore their cases to ribbons, had earned him the nickname… *'Fuck-Em-Up-Freddie!'*

Freddie had been as ever, ready to open the proceedings by grandly introducing himself, in his usual and highly theatrical manner, but he had been upstaged and forced to hold his act in check for a moment or two, keep it waiting in the wings so to speak, because as the Judge was making his way to his seat behind the bench, in all his bewigged glory, a look of consternation had crept across his ancient face, he seemed to be a little confused as he settled himself down, looking somewhat anxiously at the papers before him! Then glancing up again at the TV screen that had been placed facing him on the bench. Then as the court was about to be declared *'in session'* the bemused old guy, looked away from the screen to speak,
"Clerk to The Court, there appears to have been some sort of mistake, The Officer of The Court has brought the wrong defendant up before me here on my screen, or perhaps someone has plugged the wrong wire in somewhere!" He sniggered at his little witticism, then continued,
"This case before me *is* Crown versus Williams if I am not very much mistaken, *is it not?*" The Clerk set about rustling through his own papers as a clearly spoken and well educated voice rang out across the court from the speakers built into the TV screens,
"If it pleases Your Honour, may I speak?" The man on the screen was enquiring of him.

The voice was well-matched to the man who was visible there, the head and shoulders showed on the screens, was a rather thin but very well-dressed man wearing a well-cut, dark blue suit jacket with a bright red tie and a pure white shirt. He was clean shaven, with a full head of long, but well-groomed and mostly white hair which was swept back over his high forehead.
"You may if... well yes, if you have an explanation, then please do... go ahead."

Jos looked every bit as transformed to anyone who looked at him as he felt himself, a transformation however that was even more extreme had occurred out of sight, deep within his own psyche. As he was sat there before a camera and monitor screen in an anteroom on that Monday morning, he was once again fully aware of his surroundings, he was alert and ready... he bore precious little resemblance to his former incarnation as Bill.

As he'd been walked into the court earlier, escorted by the court policeman, on their way to the room that he would be using to appear on the video link, when he'd looked around properly, it felt like it was the first time he had been there, he had little recollection of his previous visit.

Through a window in a door he was passing, he stole a fleeting glance into the chamber, he slowed, then stopping to peer through it properly, as his escort kindly obliged him. His eyes scanned the visitor's gallery, his gaze ran along a row of people some of who he recognised, Alan Jarvis, a few people he didn't know or couldn't remember, then that cop, the one who had interviewed him initially, he recognised the face but had no name for him! This must be the cop Del said was helping them then?

Next to the cop was Del, sharply dressed as ever, she saw him and managing to catch his eye, she gave him a smile and a thumbs-up! Next to Del was that reporter from The Gazette, Jenny wasn't it? She was sat next to Harry from The Factry... he had his arm around her! Why, the sly old dog! He felt a small smile flicker across his lips... Then he felt a sharp knotting in his chest and he actually gasped, as his eyes met Jake's, his son had also spotted him! One of the lad's hands sprang up to his face, covering his mouth as he appeared to let out a stifled sob and

tears flowed from his eyes, Harry let go of Jenny and turned to Jake, putting an arm around his shoulders…
Jos had sniffed as he fought to hold back his own tears.

In the anteroom now, facing the monitor's camera infront of him, he took a deep breath, composed himself and replied to the judge who he could see on the screen in front of him,
"Your Honour I *am* the defendant, the man you know as William Williams."
"Well I never Sir! This is the most incredible thing that has…" Turning from the screen to the body of the court he stopped in mid-sentence!

The Clerk to The Court who had been stood in front of the bench all this time, now turned to the court to make an announcement,
"At the request of counsel for the defence, his honour has agreed to allow the defendant to appear here today via video link. The defendant in exchange has agreed to fully participate in the proceedings of this court with the proviso that his anonymity is preserved. The entire court will be able to hear what he says but his honour and the jury will be the only people who can see him on their TV screens." He pointed to the second screen that had been positioned on a stand infront of the jury.

The Judge thanked the clerk and then looked up and around the body of the court, he sat upright abruptly and pointed a finger at the counsel for the defence,

"You Sir! Yes you! Oh my dear Lord! I beg you to tell me that you have not taken up the defence of Mr. Willams?" Freddie smiled broadly and spread his arms out widely to either side of his tall and exceptionally broad shoulders, his palms open at waist height, greatly relieved to be allowed at last, to step out and take command of his stage…

"Your Honour it pleases me greatly to confirm that your eyes, aged though they may be… do not deceive you! Yes it is I, Sir Freddie Fredriksson QC at your service and honoured to be appearing in your court Sir and yes I am delighted to say that I am, *as ever*, acting on behalf of the defence!"

Freddie had informed the gang of four as they had been preparing for today, that he had known the judge for a great many years and that they had shared chambers before the old guy had been elevated to the dizzying heights of the bench. He'd told them how they had remained friends, if often highly combatant one's ever since.

"The Court will come to order."

Freddie who was still on his feet kicked-off proceedings...

"May it please Your Honour, having only had this Brief handed to me on Saturday, I feel... and I'm sure you will agree with me... that The Prosecution are presently at a distinct and totally unfair advantage, having had many, months to pursue their case and that my client, the man you know as Mr. Williams, having been unrepresented throughout that extended period of time... *granted it may have seemed to be that this was of his own choosing...* However, I am confident that having been provided with the mental health assessment that Your Honour had the wisdom to order be carried out and that it surely must confirm that the poor man was virtually catatonic, indeed that he had not spoken since the terrible shock he suffered upon being arrested so wrongly and on a charge of murder to boot!

"The fact is, the only crime of which he is actually guilty of was the one that *he* was subjected to, the crime of having to suffer the horrific experience of being the poor soul who happened upon this poor unfortunate girl's body! Although perhaps his real crime, or more precisely I should say, his real *mistake,* was made when he made that fateful decision... the decision to behave in the manner of any honest and dutiful citizen, in reporting to the authorities at once this terrible scene he had by chance happened upon, in the time honoured manner of dialling nine-nine-nine at his first opportunity.
"I have digressed a little..." The Judge looked to the heavens and said,
"As is your wont!"
"My apologies Your Honour... It is my opinion, an opinion I am certain you will by now share ...and indeed one that any right-minded person would have... considering the circumstances I have just elucidated, that it would only be fair for The Court to

grant a continuance of one month, in order to allow the defence to thoroughly investigate and research the validity, voracity and indeed the verisimilitude of the evidence that the prosecution has so gleefully presented against my client and most likely and probably even more pertinent to his defence to compile, the omitted evidence that they have hidden away and selectively not placed before the court!" The prosecutor leapt to his feet!

"I must object Your Honour! In the most strongest of terms! This grandstanding by Counsel is completely unacceptable! He is already making unwarranted and unfounded accusations against the police!
"This Counsel... who has been parachuted in at the eleventh hour, on the wings of his notoriety and at a time after which all the evidence has already been presented, when all we are left with is our procedural duty of summing-up... that alone is outrageous in itself! But to ask for a further delay of a month is preposterous! We have methodically presented a perfectly solid case against the defendant, to which they have refused to even enter a plea, in fact they have shown total contempt for Your Honour's Court and its proceedings with this ludicrous claim of being struck dumb! And now we have this high profile, infamous and most notorious of QC's coming here today, a man who has built up a scandalous reputation using his guile, his amateur dramatics, and his outlandish theatrics to regularly allow the guilty to walk free!" Freddie spoke up,

"Your Honour, please advise my learned friend to ameliorate his slanderous language! And perhaps to decide more concisely whether it was that I parachuted in here today or flew in on my big black wings of notoriety! " ...*'and to try and hide his fear and envy a little better!'* He said as an aside to his aide as he raised the black cape of his gown in a flapping motion...

"Thank you Mr. Fredriksson, that is quite enough of that! But quite so though! Mr. Parker, I can assure you that no-one will be allowed any grand-standing in my court! I will tolerate it from neither Mr. Fredriksson, nor yourself. You will apologise at once to counsel for the defence," Noting the nod that was given by Mr. Parker to Freddie the judge continued,

"And you Sir, will address this court with your remarks and this court alone! You will desist at once from your clever *attempting-to-be-witty* little asides, which you pitch at a precise volume to seem as asides and yet still remaining clearly audible to anyone with a keen ear! You will *not* influence the jury in *my* court in this manner Sir!

"However, whilst I do not appreciate unnecessary and verbose ramblings, I acknowledge that somewhere, albeit almost lost in the verbosity of your digressions, there was perhaps a grain of validity in your request. I accept that your client has indeed been indisposed and the timing of his recovery, however questionable it may appear to be to some, may well have been beyond his control, however inconvenient it may be for the defence and these proceedings and the prosecution, despite it at the same time appearing to be exceedingly convenient for him!

"I have read thoroughly the report on Mr. Williams's mental state and whilst it is inconclusive, as these matters often are, I feel however that I must tip the balance in his favour. After all a man accused is entitled to have the opportunity to defend himself and it would appear that up until today he has not been in a position to do so, or that he chose not to for whatever reason he may have had at that time. I hereby grant a continuance of one week."

Freddie leapt up at once,
"Your Honour, my sincere thanks for your understanding and indulgence, I am confident that even within this extremely contracted timescale we shall be able to demolish the case against my client, on the question of bail…"
"Mister Fredriksson, there is *no question* of bail!"
"Very well Your Honour, but may I ask you for one final indulgence? After your Honour's due consideration has allowed us a continuance of such an extremely short length of time, may it please you to allow my client to be held locally, to allow free access for myself and my defence team." …'*It would certainly please me!*'
"Very well. The defendant will be kept at the holding cells of the local Police Station for one week!" the judge leant forward and had a quiet word with the Clerk, looking across at the defendant on his screen, as he did so…

"This Court will adjourn for seven days."

The courtroom cleared as Bill sat in the anteroom, a knock on the door came and the officer who had been sat in with him opened it. Another of the court officers stuck his head around the door, he nodded to his colleague and then spoke to Bill,
"The judge would like a quiet word with you in his chambers! Most unorthodox if you ask me! Quite irregular in fact! You won't try and do a runner will you?"
A little confused Bill followed on as he was led back along a corridor and then through the now empty court room to a door at one side of the bench, they went around a corner to a large oak door.
The officer knocked, the sound of a loud and boisterous conversation could be heard through it, he knocked again and a voice boomed out 'enter!'
In the room Bill was surprised to see Freddie engrossed in conversation with the judge, both had glasses in their hands and a bottle of malt whisky was in evidence on the judge's desk!
"Come in, come in my dear chap!" The judge beckoned to Bill, as an aside to the officer he added, 'you can leave us, thank you!'
A little uncertainly the guy looked for a moment as if he might challenge this instruction, but clearly thought better of it, as he turned and left the room saying only, 'I'll be just outside the door then Your Honour!'

The judge smiled at Bill and beckoned to a chair,
"Please do come in, sit down. A whisky?"
"Just a small one, thank you Sir."
"Old *Freddie* here has been telling me all about you Bill, or should I call you Jim now?" Bill looked from the judge's face to Freddie's, he was somewhat confused as he had been unaware that making the judge aware of who he really was had been something that he had agreed to. Sensing this Freddie intervened,

"Listen Bill and we'll stick with Bill, at least for now, I've known our esteemed judge here forever, he is as trustworthy a fellow as you'll ever meet! He understands completely the necessity of keeping your identity under wraps from your son, the press and even the police. I knew your secret would be safe with him and it does not in any way undermine the integrity of The Court. However I felt that him having knowledge of who

you really are and the standing you once enjoyed in our community, before you went off the rails, would do you no harm, in fact that it would... well how can I say this... you would of course have received a scrupulously fair trial at the hands of my eminent colleague of course, but a nudge in the right direction doesn't do any harm either eh?"
Bill shrugged,
"Never been a big fan of nepotism myself!" At this the judge roared with laughter, commenting,
"So this is the same blighter who turned down an honour from Her Majesty isn't he? Well I say, *bravo Sir*! I do love a man who stands by his principles, however radical and mistaken they may in fact be! Listen to me Mr. Stanley, make sure you say nothing of this meeting to anyone, there's absolutely no harm in it of course, but nevertheless... *schtums the word!"*

CHAPTER THIRTY-FOUR

The following week passed by in the blink of an eye to the man formerly known as *'Bill'* as his long buried persona re-surfaced once more... He had asked to be known as *'Jim'* from now on, that was who he felt he had returned to being, it seemed to him that it was Jim's slightly bemused face that peered back at him from the mirror as he shaved each morning rather than Bill's. He hardly dare imagine what *Bill* would have had to say, what scorn he would have poured upon him for participating in such a meaningless ritual as shaving!

He felt as if he had awakened from the existence of blank numbness he had experienced since he had first been arrested, when he had retreated deep into the safety of the dark, murky depths of his mind. But he had awakened now in far more than the sense that he was simply *not sleeping* anymore, he was now fully conscious and alert, he was no longer simply existing as an object in a world from which he was disconnected, a world in which things simply happened to him and went on all around him, where he was moved around without knowing why and for reasons that seemed to be without any real relevance to him and equally of just as little interest....

He had found sanctuary in that place of isolation and resignation, accepting the fact that his second life, that of a free and unfettered homeless guy was forever over, that the rest of his days would be spent imprisoned within the confines of his own mind and the far more substantial and solid walls of the prison, built by a society that had shunned and disowned him.

The week he spent in the police station holding cell was a seemingly endless succession of visits, punctuated with meals and sleep, time moving quickly and everything seeming bright and focussed as his miasma further dissipated. He had spent a very intense hour on the afternoon of his court appearance in the presence of the esteemed Freddie Fredriksson, a man who's larger than life persona in court was greatly toned down to suit the confines of the interview room it had been agreed that he'd be allowed to use at the police station for consultations. His considerable physical bulk however was not similarly diminished!

Freddie was someone that Jim took to readily.
He had breezed into the interview room, seeming to be surrounded by a swirling cloud of invisible energy that flowed around and out from him, filling the room! He had held out a large and surprisingly rough hand to Jim, taking his hand and closing his other hand over them and with a very firm grip he'd shook it saying,
"You Sir, have had a *rum-old-time* of things these last few years! *By George* you have! Don't you think so Mr. Stanley? Stepping-out from your life so abruptly and completely and for such a long period of time too!
"*Welcome back Jim!* One day when this is all over and you're a free man once more, I would dearly love to sit down and spend an evening with you, along with a bottle of fine single malt to hear you recount your tale!"

Once the niceties were dispensed with, the brief had rapidly and methodically worked down the list he had in his folder, tackling each and every allegation made by the prosecution. He was one of those professionals that made you appreciate that there were in this world of ours, people who operated mentally, on a higher quantum level than most of us do, his elevated energy stimulating a responding increase in Jim's own awareness and alertness.

It only seemed that minutes had passed, before the brief was tying up the ribbon on the thick folder he had with him and was taking his leave, with the assurance that his team was already beavering away even as they had been speaking, unravelling each and every shred of *so-called* evidence that had been presented against him. When Jim, asked him as he was at the door leaving, 'What are my chances of beating this?' He'd laughed and suggested that he book a table for a meal at lunchtime next Monday to celebrate his freedom!

Since his arrival back in the holding cell at the local police station, Jim had been mostly looked after by the PC he'd met when he was first arrested. They were now on first name terms and he was being well looked after by Troy.
When he had first arrived back he'd been struck by how different the cell appeared to him this time, he could only recall that he

had been in a tiny, brightly lit space from his last stay there, the room now seemed to be significantly bigger somehow.

Troy had greeted him with a big smile as he'd brought his lunch in for him when they were first reacquainted,

"It's good to see you again Sir! I understand you've re-joined the rest of us 'ere in d'big wide world? Welcome back! I'm Troy, Police Constable Troy Prentice at your service Sir!"

"Yes indeed, it's a bit of a shock to an old guy's system to be fully functioning once more, but I'm most certainly back. I don't remember very much from my last stay here to be honest, but one thing I do remember, is how kind you were to me. Thank you Troy, if only all of your colleagues were as decent and conscientious as you are!" Jim had looked upwards as he referenced the Inspector who had charged him! He continued,

"I'm happy to be in your custody Troy and please, call me Jim."

Later on as Troy was bringing in Jim's evening meal, the detective who had first interviewed him had sidled in quietly around the door,

"Hi Jim, I'm Don, I don't know if your remember me? I was on your case when you were first questioned? I don't know if your friends have told you but I've been working with them to try and clear your name and get you released. You should never have been charged in my opinion and I can assure you that you never would have been if I'd been allowed to carry on handling your case!" He offered his hand to Jim, which he took and shook,

"Yes they've told me all about you Don, thank you so much for your help, it's greatly appreciated."

"Well apart from anything else, pursuing you means that the little scroats who did this awful thing are still running around loose out there!"

"It sounds like you have someone in mind then?"

"The journo on your team, Jenny, has been working on some leads, she's made real progress and if I'd had the resources that I would have had if this was an official investigation, I'm sure I would've nailed the bastards by now!"

"Why don't you? Have the resources?"

"Because the book is officially closed on the murder, why wouldn't it be? We have the guilty man! It looks like your man Fredriksson is ripping their case against you to shreds already! I'm working with them... on the QT you must appreciate, they're mostly a good bunch here, there's a lot of honest coppers you know, in fact most of us are!" He patted the shoulder of the constable stood next to him as he said,

"Guys like our lad Troy here." Troy chuckled,

"Thank you Sarge, just doing my job the way it's meant to be done!"

Don excused himself, explaining that he had to in-and-out as quick as possible since there was no way he could explain visiting Jim officially.

Once the detective had left, Troy told Jim that he had a visitor and was it alright if they came in while he ate his meal in his cell as his shift ended in less than an hour and his replacement was '*one of them*!' He explained that they would most likely adhere to all the rules they could and would probably deny him any visitors so late in the day.

Jim nodded as he tucked into his beans on toast! The menu although somehow seeming to be of better quality than during his last stay, still had a lot of baked beans involved in the menu!

Del breezed into the cell in his usual manner and plonked himself down on the bunk next to Jim, as he was finishing off his meal

"Oh my, looks like a truly gourmet diet for you sweetie! Bloody glad I'm not sharing this cell with you later! You promised to see Jake... well he's here now, are you ready?"

"Shit! Oh yeah, of course, yes! Do I look alright?"

"Stop fussing, you look fine!" he ran his fingers through Jim's hair taking it back up off his face, adding

"It's so good to have you back…"

Del went to the door, opened it and beckoned Jake to come in, slipping out as he entered. Jake was an inch or two shorter than his father and of a much smaller build, Jim had always seen that whilst Neil favoured himself in looks and build, Jake took after his mother... and more poignantly his beloved Abbie. There'd only been a little over two year's difference between them, and they'd often been mistaken for twins when they'd been little, Jake seeming to be determined to grow as fast as he could to catch-up with his big sister!

So it was primarily Abbie's face that he saw before him as the tearful man rushed into his cell, he was already on his feet to

greet him and his son strode straight over to him and threw his arms around his Dad, holding him tightly, as he sobbed into his shoulder, whilst Jim repeated over and over,
"I'm sorry son… I'm sorry… I'm so, so sorry…"

After what seemed like an age Jake pulled back and looked directly into his Dad's face,
"Fuckin' hell it's so good to see you Dad! God, how I've missed you. I still have to keep pinching myself, to make myself believe this is really happening! That you're really still alive!"

"I thought you might walk up to me and punch me in the face for what I did to you? Just walking out on you like that!"
"Dad, you were out of your mind with grief! I blamed myself for it for a long time, I felt that I should have been there for you more than I was. That I should have helped you more than I did! It's no excuse for me to say that I was grieving for Abbie myself, it's true of course it is, I was gutted, I was devastated… she was my Abbie too, my big sister, always there for me and however busy her life was she'd always made time for me… but she was your little girl, she was always your favourite, a true daddy's girl! I never resented that, I understood it even as a kid, she was just so lovely, such a lovely kid and then a wonderful woman too."

"She was, you're right, to me she was simply the most beautiful person in the whole world. Listen son, I don't blame your for one minute! You didn't abandon me, it was me who pushed you away… no, I *drove* you away. You *did* try and help me, you really tried. I saw it and I guess I even appreciated it at the time too, but I was beyond helping. Look at how I behaved at the funeral!"
"Dad, it wasn't your fault, you were destroyed with grief, you were just trying to cope, trying to deal with the pain that had engulfed you."
"I wasn't doing it in a very dignified manner though was I? That poor vicar's face! It's not even as if I was pissed out of my brains at the time, like I was a lot of the time around then, maybe it would've been a bit more excusable if I had been! I should probably go and see him and apologise perhaps?"
Jake laughed,

"I think maybe the ghost of someone whose funeral he held, turning up and apologising to him might finish him off! Sod him Dad, let's be honest, he was a bit of a sanctimonious old prick! Who'd want to do a job like that anyway eh?"

"It was him who did my funeral? Bet he enjoyed that!" They laughed together at the thought of it!

They were sat side by side on the bunk now as they chatted and in some way Jim was relieved, if there had been more space, if they'd been sat in one of the interview rooms, he could have been sat face-to-face with his son... it was much easier to be close to him and yet be able to avoid constant and direct eye contact with him as he tried to make amends for the way he had treated him.

"You know you and Abbie have so much in common, she was always a listener, a shoulder to cry on, someone who would let you talk as much and for as long as you wanted to, before she'd chip-in. I guess you both got it from your mum? I did love your mum you know, I mean, Abbie's death was definitely the last straw, but I'd been going downhill for years before that. Your mum and me had been happy for years, really happy too, there was nothing sham about it, it was only after you'd all flown the coup that we drifted apart, it's not uncommon, you must know that?"

"Yeah, I know that Dad, I saw it for myself, we all did and let's face it, her going all lesbo on you was something that most guys would struggle a wee bit with don't y'think?"

Jim laughed! He hadn't found it at all funny when she'd... *'gone all lesbo on him'*... as Jake had so typically put it! No, at the time he had been offended, highly affronted in fact! He was deeply hurt and had taken it all as a personal slur on him! Well, he'd made out that was how he felt! In truth he'd heard the angry words he spoke, and yet deep down he really didn't care, in fact in a way, he was glad that she left him.

'Stop making everything about you Jim!' Was what the therapist had repeatedly told him. You are for certain, at the centre of your *own* existence but you aren't at the centre of the entire universe! People exist outside and beyond you, each is their own centre, each with their own issues to deal with and their own lives to live as best as they can, in the way they see fit to.

Now looking back... older and wiser? Well, looking back from far enough away to see it more rationally at leaast, he could see that she had been like so many others of their generation, living in the little box that had been fashioned for her by 'society'? Her box had been the one that was stamped with, 'dutiful wife'. To be fair, she'd done all that the box she found herself in had asked of her, balanced her own career with that of being a wife, housewife and mother to their three surviving kids. It was little wonder that once the kids had gone and they were alone together, and by then living in an new and very different era, an age where individuality and the freedom to be yourself were becoming seen as a basic right, when self-sacrifice on the altar of some misbegotten thinking about how you were meant to live your life was being swept away...

It had been for the best, he could see that now. It wasn't that Ruth had simply been miserable, because she hadn't! Neither of them had been, he guessed she'd simply never had the time to think solely about herself, about her needs, her innermost desires and longings. He was happy for her, he realised now, as he thought about her for the first time in years. Susan was a lovely woman too, they'd both known her for years as friends, yeah she'd never married so she'd probably known who and what *she* was for years. Now he saw it as *bravo for her*! Back then he'd most likely have seen her as a predatory lesbian bitch who led his wife astray! He found himself asking his son,

"How's your mum doing? She still together with Susan?"
"Yeah, of course... oh you won't know that they're married now will you? Err... I don't know how to say this really..."
"That she was free to do so after your brother had me declared dead?" Jim laughed at his son's startled face,
"Look, I'm just glad it enabled her to get wed if that's what she wanted. I can see things so much clearer now. I'm just glad that she's happy. I never stopped loving her you know, I still do to this day. Love can change, it can morph into hatred even, but if it was ever genuine, one way or another it never truly leaves you completely."
"You've changed Dad. It's bloody marvellous just knowing you're still alive alone, seeing you, talking to you, they're all great too, but to know that you've moved on, got past that terrible pain you were carrying..." he put his arm around his

Dad's shoulder and drew him in as the tears welled up for him again...

"I bloody love you Dad..." They turned to face each other and hugged again as they sat there on the bunk.

"I love you too son."

After a few moments and a sniffle or two, plus a wee laugh at themselves, Jim spoke again,

"Please try and understand son that I didn't leave *you* when I walked out of my life... That was never what any of it was about, leaving anyone, leaving people behind. I'd been losing myself bit-by-bit, piece-by-piece for a long time, long before that. When I was beaten-up and nearly died it pushed me so much further down that road... I lost a friend too over that, Del? You've met her?" He looked sideways at his son's face...

"Yeah I've met Del, but *her*? Oh God... *Eh? What*? Oh I see... Bloody hell! Oh right, I'm sorry Dad, I'd no idea!" Jim laughed at his son's embarrassment,

"It's okay son, it's nothing like that! I've not gone gay or anything... *well?*... well, not in that sense, not like your mother has! *Oh whatever*! It's just that to me Del's always been a woman, that's how she was presenting herself when I first met her and to me she's simply feminine regardless of anything else, including whatever she says herself!"

Jake just sat with a little smile on his face, his only reply being, "Okay..."

"The thing was, something was already broken inside me on that night... the night I left I mean, it had been bent and strained so many times, in so many ways, it finally just gave out, snapped. When it did I actually felt liberated, for the first time in years I had a clear objective, I knew what I was doing and it all felt so right, so much as if it was meant to be. It was all so robotic as I packed my outdoor gear into my rucksack, putting socks in, undies, spare clothes all methodically done, as if I was going on a trek!

"It was as if I already had a clear plan drawn-up, I was simply activating it, following a map that it seemed my mind had drawn out ready for me to follow? I guess looking back now that's exactly what it was, it was part of my mind saying... that's it! That's enough! '*I*' have to take over here to ensure *my* survival. The idiotic clown who's been at the controls has completely lost it now to the extent that my very existence is actually at risk! So... *move over sucker...* I'm taking the wheel on our life from this point on!"

"And they did... I did... Part of me did at least. That's how life felt for me, that in that moment of clarity I had detached part of me from the rest of myself, I separated that part of my persona from the rest, the angst-ridden tortured part of my soul was shut off from me. I created a steel door in my mind and banged it shut on it all, bolted it and barricaded it away from what was left of me. Locked away all the pain behind it, left it there...

"Gradually I became a different person, I stepped into my role, I guess that's how you'd have to call it? It was hard at first but I felt isolated from it somehow, as if I was watching my life from outside of myself. The days turned into months and the months into years, I'd found a rhythm to my life. It was simple, basic and undemanding.

"I found peace in some of the things I'd learnt in therapy and on my retreats. I think I saw myself as a sort of roaming Buddhist monk? Living a life outside of society, a society that I no longer felt a part of, that I'd shunned and that I despised... I had a way of living that was like a perpetual meditation, a very mindless nihilistic type of empty meditation, one where the ego was lost and I simply existed, seeing what surrounded me, letting it engulf me in the way that a wild animal might... simple acceptance, pure experience, without judgement, without analysis, without opinion... I guess it could be referred to as a form of Nirvana? A perfect peace?"
Jake went '*pfft...*'
"... that's sure sounds different to how I imagine being homeless would be!"

"Oh don't get me wrong, it was really difficult at times! Fucking awful some of the time, sleeping in shop doorways isn't the best of fun believe me! Neither is trying to find refuge next to the bins at the back of shops, or risking going into empty or derelict buildings looking for somewhere to sleep, only to get into a fight with some other guy you find is already in there too! It seemed to me the ultimate of ironies came about for me when it got too

cold to be outside that I could take refuge in the very place I created…"
"You actually used the Folks Factory yourself?"
"I was off my trolley son, but not fucking mad! Why wouldn't I?"
They both laughed again.

In this way they chatted, laughing and crying as they gradually and lovingly created a new picture out of the jumbled pieces of the broken-up jigsaw of their previous relationship, until Jake had abruptly changed the subject,
"I can't believe what they told me about Neil Dad, that he tried to have you murdered!"
"I know! How are things between you two, you never really got on did you, chalk and cheese I always said."
"Nah, I never see him. Must be years now. We don't even do *family events* together anymore. When that detective told me what he'd done, I wanted to storm round there and punch the bastard's lights out! There's times when I'm so glad I don't live in America! If I'd owned a gun at that moment! But Don said that I had to keep *everything* under wraps, for fucks sake Dad, I haven't even told Liz!"

"Yeah well, that was partly at my insistence, but he has his own reasons too. We can't let Neil know I'm alive, or anyone else either. I know it's hard and I don't want you to have to keep secrets from your wife but… Well I'll be blunt Jake, those are my terms. I really want you back in my life but I cannot, I will not, try and simply step back into my old life. I left it behind for a reason and that's what saved me, saved me from destroying myself, I haven't really given it that much thought to be honest recently… I mean, about what I'll do if I'm freed…"
"*When* you're freed Dad! When! There's no question mark over that!"
"I know, Jake… okay *when*… But I do know that I won't be staying around here…"

"So you're just going to fuck-off someplace else all over again?"
"No, no, no… look we'll keep in touch, we'll see each other, I promise, but apart from you *and only you*, I want to be left to lie, to remain being dead and gone. Everyone who felt the need to, has grieved for me and then moved on, so it's nothing to them if

they never know the truth. Will you promise me that, please son?"

"Sounds like an ultimatum to me Dad! I can have you back in my life… as long as…"

"Let's not fall out over this Jake." He placed his hand on his son's shoulder, "I know it's a lot to take in but it truly is how I want it."

"Okay. Well, for now at any rate!" Jake had begrudgingly conceded.

"Anyway, what did you mean when you said that Don has his own reasons too?"

"He's put out feelers on the quiet to their serious crime people, also the drugs, vice and the fraud office and as soon as my case is out of the way he's going to unleash their dogs on our Neil! He won't know what's hit him, that's why he has to remain in ignorance of everything. That's why the judge is keeping me as Mister Williams, we don't want the Press to get a whiff of who I really am right now… or even afterwards for that matter!"

So what's this about your health not being so good, you don't look all that bad to me, well you know, considering everything?"

"Ah it's nothing son, you know what doctors are like, always out looking for work!" He laughed…

After they had parted, promising fervently never to let any form of gulf ever develop between them again… he felt that it had been a little soured by Jake's parting shot, in which he described his Dad's demands as his '*unreasonable terms!*'

Outside the police station Jake found Del was waiting, he was leaning on the railings smoking,

"Can I swipe one of those Del?"

"Course you can, that difficult was it?" Del inquired as he took a cigarette out and offered it. A click of the lighter later Jake thanked him, as he sucked at the black cigarette and coughed a little,

"Oh My God, these are strong! I rarely smoke to be honest, but yeah… that was pretty intense! I just don't get it, why he wants me to keep it a secret from everybody, that he's alive?"

"He's been to hell and back Jake, you know I think he actually lost his mind… and I mean that in the most literal sense, he buried away a big part of who he was in order to carry on living.

He'd never recovered from the death of your sister, you must already know that, it was all too much for him, but after the beating he took…" He went on,

"For sure, he's in a different place now and yeah, he appears to be *'back'* in many ways, but I can see that there's a shadow there, something dark hanging over him as well, he's fragile, he's not back to who he was before his life fell apart on him and I can't see that he ever will be, he's been through too much. I think we owe it to him to respect his wishes whether we can understand all of his motivations or not, don't you love?" Jake shrugged,

"I'm doing my best to see it from his point of view, really I am but… What about you two? I'm intrigued to know, well… What exactly is the relationship between the two of you?" Jake blushed a little as he asked adding,

"I never thought that my Dad was… well you know…"

"Queer?" Del offered, laughing at Jake's discomfort and putting an arm around his shoulders, he gave him a gentle hug before releasing him,

"It's okay love, don't worry, your Dad's not turned into some sort of raving homosexual, although why that should be a worry to you even if he had, I don't know…"

"Well my mum's married to another woman now, so why should I even be surprised if he was eh? There'd be a weird sort of symmetry in it wouldn't there?" They both laughed together now. Still clearly puzzling over it all, he asked,

"But did you… y'know, I mean were you…?"

"*Really* Jake? You want to know about your father's sex life from me? Hmm… I totally *do not* think so!" He shook his head and frowned, a little too theatrically and it turned into a smirk as he stubbed his cigarette out in the metal container fixed to the wall.

"You coming for a drink, it's probably what you need right now! There used to be a half decent pub around the corner, but it's years since I was here, nothing stays the same anymore, seems like people have to bugger about with everything, it's probably been totally gentrified and turned into some sort of fuckin' eatery by now! Mind you they'd've had to change the name, it was called The Dog Inn when I last went in!"

Sat in a corner of the pub, which fortunately hadn't been gentrified completely and still had half its space set aside for people who just wanted a drink, Del carried on with their conversation,
"The thing is Jake, if I'm to describe the relationship me and your Dad once had in any meaningful sort of way, you need to understand a bit more about me, about who I am first off, and yes… I do mean *had*! We won't be taking it up again, I've moved on with my life, made a new start elsewhere! Don't get me wrong though, I'll always love him, but it's been years and years since we were together and neither of us are the same people anyway, I ran for my life, I left the old Del behind, she was too dangerous, too easily recognised, she's only made a bit of a comeback this last year or so! No I became this guy you see today, up until I came back here, I've been *Derek*.

"Anyway, back to me… *my favourite topic*! The thing is I don't fit into any of the lovely little boxes that society lines-up to put us in and I never did, all those stupid pigeon holes we are meant to accept we belong in and then once we have acquiesced, we have to live by the rules we find posted-up on the wall inside of our very own, private little piece of hell!

"I always knew I wasn't the same as all the other boys I came across from my school days onwards! I never was. First off, I had the most amazing stroke of luck in the accident of my birth in that it led me to be brought up by a maiden aunt, my mother having been a child herself when she had me, she'd got pregnant at fifteen and consequently I was nothing more than an enormous embarrassment to her ever-so-lovely middle class family, right from the off, so they just farmed me out!

"Aunty Mabel was a wonderful old lady, she was my saviour! God knows what would have happened if I'd grown up in the bosom of that nest of vipers! Oh my God! The very thought of it, living with that man! My grandfather, I suppose you'd have to call him, I never saw any of them, well not properly, ever again! Aunty lived on the east coast, ninety miles away, far enough for me to be out of sight and all that! I often wondered if my mother ever thought about me? I never saw her again either, not that I can properly remember, anyway she never saw me more to the point, she never made any attempt to see how the child that she made inside herself turned out! Pah... she was nothing but a child herself though.

"No it was Aunty who was my real mum, she saw me for who I was straight off! She saw everyone for who they were. She had a wisdom and vision that's very rare. What she did for me was something most parents are utterly incapable of doing, she simply let me be *me*, no unnecessary corrections to my behaviour, unless it was because I was being rude or unkind, but other than that she let me express myself more or less however I wanted to and in any way that I wanted to.

"Of course she understood the narrow-mindedness that was out there back then, how judgemental, critical and just plain nasty people could be when confronted with anything or anybody that didn't conform to their own narrow vision of what was deemed to be *normal*, of what was right and was therefore acceptable! Being aware of all this prejudice she helped me to deal with it, to cope and to be able to blend in enough when I needed to, to learn that it wasn't always worth the effort of railing against the mindless bigotry and prejudice I would inevitably encounter, but to pick my fights, to discern which battles were worth the effort of fighting over and making damn sure that they were ones that I could win!"

"When I met your Dad I was singing in a night club, it was a pretty hard core club, one that catered for hard drinking, fast living types and it definitely deserved the description *'night'* if you know what I mean! Seeing it on the outside in daylight showed the place up for what it really was, a run-down dump! To have described it as seedy would have been a compliment! But by night, with the neon's blazing away, to the drunken eyes of the clientele they targeted it towards, it was sophisticated, dark and alluring!

"Your Dad was in a very dark place of his own when I first spoke to him, so you could say that he'd found his natural habitat I guess? As I got to know him it turned out that at that time, he was sleeping till the afternoons and then when he did eventually wake up, getting off his head as quickly as possible. Man he was hitting everything back then! He had money you see, a totally fucking lethal commodity to have at your disposal for someone

in the zone he was living in at that time! It facilitates whatever you want, it allows you to indulge in anything and everything however much you *really should not* in fact to be doing any of that to yourself.
"Basically he was, without even being conscious of the fact, committing suicide in agonisingly slow motion…"
Jake interjected,
"So you swooped in? Why? Why would you? Your clientele as you describe them must have had more than few such basket cases such as him? So why pick him?"
"Oh my word! You're a suspicious little shit aren't you? So what you're really saying is… what did I imagine was in it for me?" Punching Jake's arm, ostensibly playfully but considerably harder than he liked, Del's ire was up as he went on,
"Oh yeah! I saw him as a source of endless lines of coke, a ticket to a free ride with him on his super de-luxe roller-coaster of self-destruction and death! Whooopeee…"
"Okay, okay… I'm sorry Del, it's kinda hard to see my Dad as some pissant, lounge lizard, slouching around as you describe him…"

"But there we have it love, the fact is that you *weren't 'seeing'* him Jake! He was there, in your world too, there for you to see, but you just didn't go looking for him did you? You didn't see past the camouflage, the illusion, the shell of normality he had to protect him, to keep him safe when he needed to function out there in a world he no longer felt he wanted to live in." Jake looked upset, he sniffled back his tears,
"I… It was hard for all of us losing Abbie… you're right, Dad did put up a wall between himself and the rest of the family… It was… I guess…" Del patted his arm,
"It's okay luv, I'm not trying to beat you up over it, but please don't jump to the wrong conclusions about me either. I'm a good person, I wasn't just some leech waiting to attach myself to a likely mark! Although God knows I would've had plenty of chances to do so, if I'd wanted to! But it's not who I am, I've never done drugs, I hardly drink, okay yeah, so I smoke… so damn me for that, if you must … but *I am* a good person!

"I saw your Dad and I'd inherited or maybe learnt some of Auntie's way of seeing through the camouflage people use to hide behind. I can usually see something of the face behind the masks we put infront of ourselves, to play the different roles we think we have to play in this pantomime farce we call life! The obedient child, the friend, the lover, the clown, the husband, the wife, the father, the son, the employee, the boss... the masks are endless and what happens for most of us, is that we end up forgetting who *'we'* actually are!

"By that time of night and that far down his road of self-destruction, your Dad's choice of concealment, the drugs and booze was getting pretty damn shaky anyway, so the guy I saw, propping the bar up from his barstool, was a tragic man, a man teetering on the brink, a broken-hearted man. I just sat on the stool next to him and basically I just listened. That was all he wanted, someone to listen to him.

"I should add, well maybe I should have said much earlier on... To provide you with a bit more context! Okay... Rewind to this scene... we're in a bar, it's dimly lit, you look around and can see it's set in a fucking dismal, seedy night club! There's this guy sat on a stool, he's slouched over, with both elbows on the bar, a ciggies burning in the ashtray, the smoke rising up to coalesce with the cloud of despair that's already hanging over his head... and all around him...

"So the guy hears me start singing, he turns his head and looks across to the stage where in the beam of a brilliant spot-light, stands someone in a glimmering sequined outfit, shimmering in the darkness... *il voit une vision de la beauté!* You see the thing is luv, he sees on the stage, this heavenly vision of loveliness and beauty, he sees a gorgeous *woman*! So to your Dad, that vision he first saw of me back then, will be how he always sees me, as a woman."

Back in his cell, Jim lay back on his bunk. He was only a little tired physically but mentally he'd had an awful lot to take in that day and although his mind was back firing on all cylinders there had been a lot to process. That niggling pain he had in his chest sometimes was back too, maybe it actually was time to let the doctors do what they'd told him they wanted to do for him?

Lying back he realised that returning to being Jim Stanley, beneficial though it was in many ways, had necessitated unlocking that door, the barrier behind which he had held back all the pain and memories of his old life. Talking with Jake about

Abbie had pulled-up so many memories too, including ones he had especially, most deliberately and actively supressed…

He sighed as he lay looking up at the blank ceiling… it was something he was going to have to face, it was no good imagining himself to be rebuilt, repaired and restored after his eight year exile and imagining a genie such as this one would stay shoved quietly away in its bottle and if he never put himself to the test, he would never know when it may decide to manifest itself? It would be better to face it, deal with it now, get it over with perhaps?

He allowed his mind to delve, to go where it had been barred from going for so long… it went straight to his daughter…

Oh Abbie, my lovely girl… How I blamed myself for your death he thought. He knew it was ridiculous to think in that way, he'd gone over and over it in therapy but the heart is linked to the subconscious mind and logic and reason often hold little sway there.

It was a fact that she was only driving on the M56 in the first place, at that time of day and on that particular day, because he'd asked her if she fancied a day out to Llandudno with him and the kids, as he'd seen a very nice MGB GT V8 that was a private sale and it was over that way. It had been on the market quite a while, probably the asking price was too high, but that didn't bother Jim back then, if he wanted something he'd pay what it took, he had the money, after all he was rich!

That thought took him back to the previous year, on another day out that he'd had with Abbie and the kids, they had been on their way home, the kids were thirsty so they stopped at a service station to get supplies, he recalled the scene, Abbie was happy, she was all smiles, the kids were dancing about around her as they did, laughing and chattering as they walked from the car…
"Go and get a bottle of pop each and a bag of sweets… 'A' bag… that is *one* bag each! Look Pa, look at that!" She pointed to a big poster on the window advertising The Euro Millions lottery, "A hundred million quid! Wow! We're getting a ticket!" He remembered frowning at her,

"What the hell Abbs? Haven't you got enough money already? Your job pays well, Graham's got an amazing job too! I mean the dividends you get from your shares in the company alone could keep you all!" She laughed as she pushed her sunglasses back to hold her shoulder length blond hair back up and off her face,

"Oh I dunno, don't think it would quite do that! Don't get me wrong Dad, I'm not ungrateful, it's still very nice to have, but we do like to *spend*! Nah, thing is Dad...! She pointed at the poster, "*that* would be *money to burn*! To just splash-out and waste, to be given away, something to be totally stupid with! Can't you see that?"

"Hmm... not really, no I can't say that I do. It sounds frivolous and ridiculous! Nay, stupid!"
"Okay grumpy-grots, what would you do with it, if *zap-da-da-da-da-DA!* you had a cheque for one hundred million pounds in your hands!"
"Okay, so this cheque, is it made out to me?"
"Very funny! Stop avoiding my question! Come on!"
"Bloody nonsense this is! You do realise that the chances of winning the jackpot on these things is tens of millions to one against you don't you?"
"Avoidance! Someone wins it! I'm asking you what you'd do with it *if* it was you!"
"I dunno! I'm a millionaire several times over already so even buying a ticket would just seem plain wrong in the first place to me somehow, don't you think?"
"*Avoidance*! Dad will you just answer the bloody question!"

He knew she was only joshing with him but nevertheless he caught a whiff of that lightning flash of temper she shared with her mum, with his Ruth! He'd caught her mutter '*fucks-sake!*' under her breath!
"Right, well I guess I'd see it as something I didn't deserve to have in the first place so I think I'd most likely give it all away!"
Unbid, his mind had jumped back to the one pound Premium Bond he'd had as a child, recalling how for years he had waited patiently for it to win the big prize it inevitably would and for his life to be transformed by it! He'd still had it back then, but also along with the maximum holding of Premium Bonds that you

were allowed to have, something that he'd acquired much later in life after his accountant had suggested it! He couldn't recall if the £1 one had ever won anything, but he didn't think so…

"So! We make progress, slowly and painfully but nevertheless… Right then, to what and to whom would you give all this lovely money?"
"This is ridiculous Abbs, we're stood here in a shop debating this bullshit while the kids are going nuts over there!" He pointed towards the checkout. Abbie called out to them,
"Oi! Come here kids, take this and pay for your stuff, then go and sit in the car." She pulled a twenty pound note from her purse and gave it to Fiona the eldest of her girls, "Get a receipt and keep the change safe!" She'd shouted after them…
"So what are you spending it on?"
"Okay…" He knew of old with Abbie that once she had a bee in her bonnet there was little point in trying to brush it aside. It was his own fault really as he'd played many a game like this with her endlessly, from when she'd been a little kid. He'd wanted her to learn how to discuss ideas without getting involved to the extent that it became a quarrel, about the progression of an opinion, of the idea that each and every action led on to the next one, how each decision opened up a different set of new possibilities which in turn… They'd called them *mind-games*, or simply *possibilities*…
Knowing that he may as well indulge her, he side-stepped it for now,
"Okay missy, you asked for it… but on one condition though?"
"What?"
"It's back in the car on the way home!"
"Why?"
"Because it'll take us all the way home for me to explain it to you…"
"Right you're on!" She then marched to the checkout and purchased two 'Lucky Dips' for them along with an assortment of even more snacks and drinks!

On their way walking back to the car she started on him again,
"Look Pa, got us one each! Which one d'ya want? Come on…"
She waved the tickets before his face with her free hand as she carried the bag of tuck in the other, "Come on!"
"Oh for *f*… you keep them both!"

"No chance! Here!" And with that she shoved one deep down into the breast pocket of his sports jacket with her fingers! Wrestling playfully with him as he half-heartedly attempted to stop her!

Back in the car he hoped she'd forgotten, but fat chance, so in response to her demand of *'come-on then'* He'd launched off on a ramble...
"So the first thing I would do is find a disused, empty and dilapidated old factory building, one of those great big long buildings, somewhere on the edge of town, but not too far out. It's a crying shame that they aren't put into use again or even worse when they get pulled down! So I'd redesign it to be a place where anyone who found themselves homeless could have a roof over their head."
"That's a bloody great idea Dad! Then you'd tell me all about it and I'd get involved too!"
"I would? You would? So you'd do that as well as being the deputy head of a massive Comprehensive?"
"So you'd do it as well as being the CEO of a massive building company?"
"I'd let Neil take over?"
"As if!"

"Are you going to shut-up and let me carry on? We could provide pods and flats and things like that, all inside and under the one roof, so they could have an address and be eligible for benefits..."
"Yeah brill... and we'd get lots of the charities involved too, they could have rent free spaces for their shops and pass on stuff direct to the clients! We could have a doctor visiting too for them, a dentist could come even? Oh it'd be a great thing.."
"Who's story is this Abbs?"
"Nah... this idea's out the bag and she's a rollin' now daddy-o! We'll call it *The* Factory! Cool eh? *No!*... I've got it! Oh yes! This is way, way better... we'll call it The Folks Factory..."

He'd forgotten all about the ticket of course, although having a brief reminder of it, his premium bond fever had left him many decades previously! Abbs had asked him a couple of times if he'd checked it, he just said he had and that it hadn't won anything... he'd never actually bothered to look.

It was a month or so later that she'd called round,
"Dad, look me in the eye and tell me you actually did check that lottery ticket!"
"What? What lottery ticket? Oh you're not still going on about that are you?"
"Did you? Dad, did you *really* check it?"
Yeah… of course I did?"
"Honestly?"
"Yeah, said I did, didn't I?"
"Say honestly! Say honestly! You always promised me as a kid that if I needed to find out if the tall story or tale you were telling me was true, that I could ask you to say *'honestly'* didn't you? So?"
"Okay then, *honestly*!"
"Very funny! Say I checked the ticket, honestly I did!"
"Get lost Abbigail!"
"See! I bloody knew it! They're going nuts because nobody's claimed the prize Dad, a hundred and eighteen million quid!"
"I thought it was a hundred?"
"Oh you were listening then? It goes up sometimes if people get lottery fever! Where is it? You'd better not have thrown it out! I'll bloody kill you!"
"Really? I think I'll disinherit you, you ungrateful wretch!"
"Oh do shut up! Where is it?"
"*Greedy, ungrateful wretch* at that!"
"Where's your jacket? I bet it's still where I shoved it, isn't it?"
"What on earth are you two shouting at each other about?" Ruth asked as she rounded the corner coming into the hall from the lounge, to see what the commotion was all about?
"We've won the lottery mum, I'm sure we have! The old fool's not even checked his ticket yet, where's his sports jacket?"
"Which one?"
"The horrible old one!"
"Oh that one! In his wardrobe, in the dressing room I'd guess!" Abbie shouted back as she charged up the stairs,
"It's been on the news, the ticket was a Lucky Dip bought at a Service Station on the way into town! Here! Our town! I went into the garage where we bought the tickets and they have a sign up saying winning ticket bought here! It's got to be us!"
"What is she on about?" Ruth asked,
"Lottery fever, she'll calm down when she realises it's not the winning ticket!"

……. But it was!!…….

That came back full circle bringing him back to now, providing another reason why he felt guilty for her death. He gave each of his kids five million quid, he'd wanted to give them all a fifth of it, but was persuaded not to do so by Ruth and funnily enough Abbie had backed her up! The argument was how too much money could often ruin people's lives. Five million to blow was enough. He'd remarked *'so it's okay for it to ruin my life though?'*
"But it won't will it Jim, you already have millions so *you'll* make good use of it won't you!" Had been Ruth's less than helpful response.

He'd ended up with five million more than he'd reckoned too, as Neil had refused point blank to take any of it. 'Just hand over the running of the company completely to me and retire. That's all I want from you!' That was all he would say.

Abbie spent some of her money on the most expensive Range Rover money could buy. The car she died in. A big tall ugly brute of a car, one that sat high-up on the road. The lorry wheel would have cleared a smaller car…. That started the *'if onlies'* off…
…if he hadn't asked her to drive them all down to Llandudno
…if only they'd set off a minute earlier or later
…if only she'd followed him, it could have been him that died
…if only the fucking lorry had been properly maintained!

He knew it was stupid thinking like this…

They'd had a wonderful day out together, Abbie had dropped him off to look at the car and they'd arranged to meet at a café for lunch, one that they'd often visited on previous trips, one that was on the promenade, up near the pier. He would either drive up in his new car or get a taxi.

He was made up with car, it had a relatively low mileage on the clock, well for a 1978 car and it was still with the original owner, a very rare find. To the great delight of the old guy selling it, without bothering to haggle, he simply agreed to pay the asking price and within an hour, which he'd spent on his laptop, adding the car to the other six cars he already had on his classic car insurance policy and notifying the DVLA, he was driving along the promenade looking for somewhere to park. He saw the bulk of Abbie's black Range Rover and found a space a few cars back from it.

He really was *made-up* with the car, she was a real beauty, the big three and half litre V8 purred like a kitten, yet give a little blip of throttle and she had a wonderful growly roar!

Having reversed the car into the space, he clambered up from the comfy leather seat to get out of the car, bought a ticket put it on the dash and locked the car with the key, in the old fashioned way. As he walked away he turned to look back at her, to admire her shining beauty, the dark blue colour toned perfectly with the black rubber bumpers, she looked simply *magnificent*!

The details of the rest of the day had somehow become less clear to him, he had impressions of happy laughter, paddling in the sea, building sand castles, walking along the promenade... a bright yellow windmill on a wooden stick that Fiona held up to show him, spinning round and around with the sun glinting off it... Packing the buckets & spades into Abbie's car, along with the assortment of pebbles, shells and other bits and bobs they had either picked-up or bought for the kids... he clearly remembered all that and little Fiona being strapped into her car seat, then Lucy waving from her side on the back seat and of course Abbie... Sat in the car with the door open still chatting with him as she put on her seat belt, slid her sunglasses down off her forehead where she'd pushed them as she always did, whilst she'd loaded the car with him. She shook her hair loose and ran her fingers through it, flashed him a beaming smile as she said, "It's been a great day Dad, see you back at home."
"It has for sure, you drive safe. Oh listen, I'll follow you, I think the MG's burning a bit of oil, don't want you to be breathing that all the way home!" She pulled the door shut, the window was still down though as she started the engine up, "Is that you a few cars back?"
"Yes, give me a minute and I'll follow on."
"See you later alligator!" Abbie had sung to him, the kids waved to him as he walked away heading back to his car, a few minutes later he pulled out and tucked-in behind the Range Rover.

The image of her sunlit face as she sat smiling at him, one arm on the window cill of the car, the other resting on the steering wheel, her blond hair being gently rustled by the sea breeze was burnt into his mind…
The end of their perfect day out at the seaside.

The last time he saw her.

She had often come to him in his dreams, before he locked his agonised mind away, her smile was always there, sometimes it filled his mind in intricate detail, the precise shape and detail of her lips, even down to the few wrinkles she had at the corners of her mouth, her mouth moving as she spoke and the shapes of her white teeth as her lips drew back when she laughed…

He had rarely seen her angry in real life, but in his dreams she would sometimes be furious, her face red and distorted in rage, her mouth no longer soft and laughing but the vicious and venomous maw of a snarling beast as she hurled out shouted accusation after accusation at him… *"It's all your fault! All of it! I should still be with my Lucy and Fiona, you sent me away from them! You should have died not me! I hate you! I hate you! I hate you…."*

He'd always known it wasn't true and also that Abbie would never have said anything like that… but the broken heart knows no logic.

The drive home had started off going well, the MGB was peachy, she was barely ticking over as he cruised in overdrive along the motorway at around seventy. He was happy and contented, the day had gone swimmingly well and he was really pleased with his latest acquisition to add to the small collection of classic cars he was steadily accumulating.

Following on behind Abbie's Range Rover looking at the road ahead over the lovely shape of his new MG's shiny, dark blue bonnet, he thought to himself that he was a lucky man…
The MG had sat on the drive of his house for many months after The AA had delivered it back there following the accident, increasingly dirty and neglected, with black mould creeping-up

around the windows… everyone forbidden to as much as touch it.

Could he face going over the memories of that dreadful accident again, what was the point? What good would it achieve? Hadn't he gone over it enough in the past? It had played on a loop in his mind for weeks and weeks afterwards, then he had relived it in therapy too… with both therapists… hadn't The CBT guy got him past it?
Unbidden, another voice answered him!

> "Yeah! You got so far past it …
> that you went ape-shit and ran off?
> *Well?…*"

But how will it help raking it all up though?
I went *ape-shit* for a reason, to leave it all behind!

> "And how did that go for you then?"

I survived!

> "I suppose you '*could*' call it that!
> If you're going to open that door again…
> Unleash all those memories…
> Return to being '*normal*'…
> Don't you think you'd better face it all first?
> Deal with it now rather than let it
> bite you in the arse at a later date?"

Maybe…

It had all happened in an instant…
A split second…
A moment that separated… *then* …from… *now!*
The front of the Range Rover had bucked-down, as if the brakes had been jammed-on… but no brake lights?
Then it had slewed, at the same time pieces of something were spraying up from it and then…
The vison of the deep black rubber tread of a giant tyre on a wheel hurtling towards him, leaning at an angle as it hit the road right in front of his car before bouncing up and flying over the top of it and out of his view heading towards the hard shoulder…
Then brake lights?…

The back of the Range Rover seemingly hurtling at him…
His foot jammed to the floor on the brake pedal…
'1970's brakes!'
'Shit! I'm going to hit it!…'
Back wheels locked…
Sliding…   ….*'no A.B.S.! Ease off the pedal…'.*
Swerving…
Rounding the inside of the Range Rover…
Jammed-on brakes…
Car stopped…
Car lurching… *'it's stalled'*… *red light on dash*…
'Get out… get out!'
Trapped, fighting against something…   …*the seatbelt!*
Button!… *press the button*!…
Stood by the driver's side window of Abbie's car…
'Oh God! Her face is gone! …She has no face!!'

"Stop!"

How did you get to be stood by her car?"

'What? Why I ran back as fast as I could of course!'

"Okay, Now think, when you went to see Abbie at the mortuary, how did she look?

'What do you mean? She looked like Abbie!
Only she was *fucking dead*!'

"Did she have a face?"

'Of course she had a face!'

"How did she look?
Did she look peaceful?"

'She was fucking dead! Of course she looked peaceful!'

"So her face couldn't have been *'gone'* when you saw her through the window, could it?
They didn't put it back on for her did they?"

'What? Well no… but there was so much blood though…'

Screaming!!!
A girl screaming repeatedly… over and over…

Fiona!
The kids! Sat in the back!
His mind leapt to them!
Open the back door!...
"Fiona! Hush now… undo your seatbelt!
*"Shut-*up!
"Be a brave girl now, for grandpa!
"Help me get Lucy out of this seat!
"Do you know how to…"
"Like this grandpa…"
"Come on, get out of the car…"
Lucy clinging to my neck, Fiona's hand in mine…
…such a small hand…
Holding them both…
For a second…
Standing... *in the fast lane of the motorway!*
But there's no cars?
Lifting her over the barrier…
"Here sit here…"
"Let me help!"
A woman? Bending over them, comforting the kids…
The kid's faces in the bright lights on a bed in the back of an ambulance…

"Hang-on! How have you got there? In an ambulance?"

'What?'

"A moment ago you were stood behind the barrier of the central reservation!"

'I was… then I remembered Abbie! I had to get to Abbie!

"Why were there no cars in the fast lane?"

'What? Oh… Someone had pulled their car into it and stopped…
'Yes… there was another car in the middle lane too…
'They had their hazards on!
'There was a guy with a high-vis on, waving his arms like a madman too…
A man is already in the passenger seat of Abbies car!
Kneeling on the seat with his back to me…
"What are you doing? She's my daughter!"
"I'm a doctor…"
He's turning in the seat to look at me…

His face says it all…
He shakes his head…
"I'm so sorry, she's gone…"
The woman in green is stroking Lucy's head…
A torch in my eye…
A very black policeman's hat. It has a chessboard all around it. It's so big, so close to my face.
"Can you hear me Sir? Is the MG your car?
Do you know the driver of the Range Rover?"
"Abbie… My Abbie… My grandkids…"
"Can you give me your name Sir…"

"How did you get into the ambulance?

You were talking to a doctor a moment ago

alongside Abbie's car?

"This way Sir.
Come this way…"
He's leading me across the motorway…
Across the inside lane…
"What? *Look out! The traffic!*"
"The road's closed Sir, you're safe with me…"
A hand on my shoulder guiding me…
A glance back down the road…
Lights flashing everywhere…
When did it go dark?

Sat on the passenger seat of a car…
The man asking questions…

The hospital…
Bright lights…
So bright…
So noisy…
Hussle and bussle…
A quiet room…
Tea? A cup of tea in my hand…
The policeman, without his hat.
Asking something?
Graham's face right in mine…
Jake's face…
"Come on Dad, let's get you home."
"He blames me doesn't he?"

"No one blames you Dad, it was an accident, a terrible God-damned awful, fucking accident!"
"Graham does! I could see it written all over his face..."

Jim wiped a tear from his eye as he rolled onto his side, he felt the release of sleep slipping over him and surrendered willingly into its embrace...

He was woken by a hand on his shoulder, he turned his head on the pillow to see Abbie was sat on the edge of his bunk next to him,
"Hi sleepy." She said
"Hello love..." He replied, adding...
"It's been so long since you came to visit me!"
"You locked me away behind that door along with the rest of your old life Dad!"
"I know, I'm sorry Abbs... It all hurt too much."
"Well, you've opened the door again Dad and that's good. Maybe you needed to step out of your life for a while, but it's been long enough now. You need to get out of here, I'm glad that you're going to fight this idiotic case against you, glad that Jake's back in your life too. He missed you so much Dad..."
"I've missed him too Abbs and you... but I couldn't bear to let either of you in..." A tear rolled down his cheek,
"Never mind, you look so much better without all those whiskers! You must know in your heart that I don't blame you for the accident don't you? We'd had such a lovely day out at Llandudno hadn't we? You know if it had to be my last day on earth, then I don't think I could have spent it any better than being with my Dad and my kids at the seaside... It was such a lovely sunny day..."

She put her hand lovingly onto her Dad's cheek,
"You've finally moved on Dad. It's time for you to let me go now as well, can you do that for me? Let me move on too?
Jim nodded as the tears flowed again.
As she leans over and kisses him softly on the cheek, somehow he knows it will be the last time that he will ever see her,
"I love you Abbie,"
"I love you too Dad, back then, now and always..."

Jim woke in the middle of the night, to some sort of commotion going on outside his cell, he'd been in a deep sleep and felt sweaty as if he'd been a little feverish. He swung his legs over the edge of the bunk and sat with his head in his hands as a drunk was locked-up in one of the other cells, a kick of the door and a stream of obscenities later he must have passed-out or gone to sleep as silence descended once more on the corridor outside his cell.

He splashed cold water on his face from the sink, rubbing at the stubble on his chin as he dried it off, it was thick and grey… this shaving malarkey was a total pain!

The room was only dimly lit from the little window in the door with its heavy mesh built into the glass and from the streetlight that must have been outside, nearby to the high level window, but his eyes were acclimatised to the dark.

He looked across to where Abbie had been sitting earlier, it had been hard sometimes, before his fall into vagrancy to tell whether her visits had been real, or imagined, or if they were drunken or drug-induced hallucinations, or part of the dreams that haunted him. The dreams were the worst, the replaying of the accident…

Whether they were imagined or truly were visitations didn't matter to him, he'd always relished them anyway. He'd learnt to accept them and not raise questions about her being alive, or if he was dreaming and run the risk of it waking him up, but to relish them. She had never said goodbye to him before though, whether that was what had given him the feeling of finality as she left him this time or not he wasn't certain about, there was no uncertainty though in the feeling of finality.

He swilled down a couple of painkillers that Jake had brought in for him, Freddie having asked him as he'd departed if there was anything Jim needed and Jake had obliged him. He lay back down on the bunk onto his back, with a groan waiting for their effect to kick in.

His mind did feel clearer he thought, he'd been unsure whether recalling the accident all over again in his mind, would be a sensible proposition, but the compulsion to do so had been overwhelming. It had been traumatic unlocking the memories, but he hoped it would be cathartic this time? Hoping that the period of separation from his old life, the interval of eight years would provide some punctuation, would be enough of a pause for things to have settled somewhat.

It seemed so, he wasn't the trembling wreck he'd been on previous occasions when the memories had occasionally forced their way around the door, nor was he hung-over from trying to blot them out with drink or drugs either.

As the pain reduced with the warmth of the drugs floating around in his bloodstream, his mind began to wander once more, the pale face of the lass at St. Jude's swam into his mind, Abigail… he could hardly forget her name. He resolved to go and see her if he got out… *'when! He got out…'* He heard Jake's voice saying in his head. His stay there had been enormously helpful to him he recollected, all of it because Harry was such a good hearted man. He felt a moment of pride well-up inside him, then the ever so familiar of late, tears welling-up as he thought about Harry and The Factry and all he had put in place back then… It seemed so long ago when he had been enthused with the excitement of the whole barmy idea cooked-up by him and Abbie after she'd bought those bloody lottery tickets!

Oh to be able to go back and change things! He would rip the fucking ticket up and throw the pieces over her head, laughing like a maniac as he did so!

But then if he'd done that, then he'd never have put all that work into creating The Factry would he, he asked himself? Yeah, okay but *why* not? The lottery money had been the catalyst for it, for sure but it wasn't as if he hadn't had the resources to do it without the bloody lottery money anyway, was it?

It had something to do with Abbie's silly notion of *'money to burn, to waste, to do something good, or just stupid with…'* that had been the catalyst, that was the damning conclusion that he was drawn to. He had been too selfish and mean-spirited to do it with his own money. A wave of chagrin swept over him, he felt ashamed that it was only Abbie's idea of *'free money'* that had initiated the project in the first place! The more he thought about it the more he felt an undermining of what he had done... *don't be so fucking stupid...* part of him said in defence of his actions, the Folks Factory is real, it's there, it's working, it *is* helping the homeless in your town! Mission accomplished... you could have bought a luxury yacht with the money or a Bugatti to add to your collection! How many other millionaires & billionaires are there in England? How many Folks Factories are there?

It didn't matter either way he resolved, the place *had* been created, it was doing good and that was all that really mattered. Recriminations and condemnations of his motives were just him being '*self-indulgent and narcissistic!*' It was Del's voice in his head that made this assessment! It was precisely how she would have ticked him off if he'd shared negative thoughts such as these with her about The Factry!

It had been great fun working on the project though, whatever the motivation, or lack of it before the windfall, especially the involvement of Abbie early on, as they looked for premises that they could use. The starting point was vital, it was no good diving in with the first property they found only to discover half way into the project that it lacked features that it would need further on down the road.

Abbie had been great, she'd straight off said they would have to take into account local opposition to the plan, that the location was therefore vital, that the place they worked with needed to be absolutely *right* in that respect. It needed to be out of town enough, but near enough to walk to and in an area that wasn't too residential. The town had been an industrial and manufacturing powerhouse in its day, those days now long gone of course, but it had a legacy of a great many old buildings, old works and factories, many disused and falling into disrepair, the list they worked through was long but he still vividly recalled the morning that they'd pulled up across the canal from The Armstrong Mill...

They'd managed to get lost once again, as Abbie drove around the maze of streets in the old industrial area of town, Jim's *help* had been less than appreciated as he tried to steer her down what he thought were the right streets! *'Oh belt-up Dad! I know where*

I'm going' had been her response! Maybe it was fate that got her to make that last turn, to drive up and over the humped back of the narrow stone bridge, a glimpse of the canal afforded to them as they mounted its crest and there a little way further along the canal, looming huge and grey was the shape of a giant building! *'See! There it is, I told you!'* She'd burbled as she swung the car down the next turning on the left and pulled up on a patch of cleared wasteland where a building had once stood, no doubt one that would have been not altogether dissimilar to the massive mill building that still remained standing opposite them, on the other side of the canal.

It was a damp, grey and still day, patches of mist were lazily hanging around over the murky waters of the canal, reluctant to clear, resistant to the warmth of the weak sun. The mist seemed to be clinging to the stone and brickwork of the gigantic old monolithic structure, it's vast length creating an impression of endlessness as it vanished at either side into the gloom.

It looked simply *magnificent*! He had smiled to himself as he realised that he'd whispered the word out loud as he was standing next to the car alongside Abbie, she had hugged his arm and kissed him on his cheek,
"You love that word don't you Dad?" The sun had lost its battle with the mist for a moment or two and a little shiver ran through him, he pulled his jacket a little tighter around his body as Abbie added,
"You're right Dad, it *is* magnificent! This is it, isn't it Dad? This is the place where we're going to create our Folks Factory. It's bloody marvellous! How can something as magnificent as this be left lying idle?"

Built at a time when the only viable transportation system for anything to be moved in bulk had been the canals, it would have been obvious to the people embarking on the monumental task of constructing this colossal building, that the main façade on the front of the building would be built to face the canal and so it was that from their vantage point on the opposite bank they beheld the central section of the great building, flanked by two small towers rising out of columns in the brickwork, each topped-off with dome-like structures atop their intricate stonework. Built-in and formed out of raised bricks within the

brickwork, the name of the edifice was proudly proclaimed…
ARMSTRONG MILL.

Life had become a whirl from then on, the joint vision that the pair held, driving them on relentlessly. At Abbie's suggestion they told everyone as they became involved in the project that Jim Stanley was merely a go-between, he was acting on behalf of a billionaire investor who had decided to return and have a base back here in his home town, the town from where he had first started his business empire half a century previously and where he now wished to return and to do something, to put something back, in the same spirit of the Victorian philanthropists of bygone days. They told anyone who enquired further that the mystery benefactor had many homes in cities dotted all over the world, that he travelled between them for most of his year but felt he now needed a base back in his hometown, a place that would feel like a proper home. Somewhere that he would eventually end his days. It was in this way, she had insisted, that her Dad would be cushioned personally from any adverse repercussions the project might generate.

They decided that they would have to employ an architect in the first instance and set about finding someone who was not only qualified and capable but would also share their passion for the project. Abbie came up trumps with the name of a guy who had already designed several projects in the town, projects that had won awards for their concept, in that they created affordable housing for people, but at the same time offered the same appeal in their design and amenity as the majority of houses that were being constructed at that time, homes that were more lucrative (for the builders) being at the luxury end of the market and priced out of the reach of ordinary people.

The guy had proved to be exactly who they needed for the job, he had applauded their motives and inspiration from the moment he became aware of them and had given his all to take the first step in bringing their dream into reality by creating it all before them virtually on his computer screen and on great big sheets of paper.

With the designs and specifications complete and having been created by the hand of an award winning architect, they put their scheme before the relevant authorities, the purchase of the old building having been the simplest of tasks to complete once sufficient money had been wafted around under the noses of the present owners!

Jim had found the web of contacts and friendly faces he had come to know through his business connections and his membership of the town's Rotary Club, now paid dividends. His insider knowledge helped him get to the right people straight away and to then receive a sympathetic ear to their proposal. The location had been a key factor in minimising opposition and without significant delay the project was given the green light.

The next twelve months had been a maelstrom of activity, the costs on the project inevitably soared, but to Jim and Abbie it didn't matter, they had their billionaire backer behind them didn't they? They would laugh about it together as they knew that everything that they were achieving was at the expense of their *free money* as Abbie had put it.

Once the main structure had been fully inspected and any deficiencies that were discovered had been repaired and made safe, the plans could be made for the utilisation of the interior. The biggest single piece of work to get to this point had been the stripping and replacing of any defective elements in the roof, covered as it was by hundreds of thousands of large Welsh slates. The scaffolding which on its own had been a major and highly costly component of the project, was all down now and removed off-site, so the building was ready-to-go and the morning of Day No.1 had finally come! This was to be the exciting part of the project, bringing life back to the interior of The Armstrong Mill, reincarnating to become The Folks Factory.

So it was that Jim was there early-on that morning, before anyone else had arrived, he parked at the end where the car park would be created and walked over to the east end of the long building. He unlocked the double doors in the wall of steel and glass, this was to be the *business end* of the project, the end of the building that would open onto a large area of car park. This would be where anyone homeless… or not for that matter… where anyone could come and be able to receive a welcome of food and shelter. *A glorified soup kitchen*! Had been one the less than helpful remarks he'd had to deal with. But yeah, so what if it was? Those had only existed in history because of the pressing need there had also been for them back then! A need, that although it should be inconceivable today, was just as real again once more.

It would as time went on not only provide vital nourishment but would also provide extended help to anyone in dire straits, help them in many ways too as they had all sorts of plans from charity shops being based there to visiting doctors, dentists and even chiropodists. They were particularly keen to get an organisation such as Shelter involved to help in giving advice to people, but the main scheme behind it all was in the first instance to create pods, a small space for people to use, to call their own and to give them the all-important address that they needed to access benefits!

Once he was inside he turned, locked the doors behind him and looked around at the vast empty and echoey space where he was now stood. He craned his head upwards to take in the height of the glass roof so far above him. He was stood in the main area of the project, what would become known as The Refectory, an enormous volume of space created from where the massive and long gone steam engines had once stood, sold off as scrap metal no doubt many decades ago. It was now finally cleared, the floor had been repaired and it was ready to have the tables and chairs put out, they were stacked in piles near the entrance for now, awaiting being arranged and put into place. It was bizarre that their plans to have a ceiling put in over this area, creating an additional floor above it had been blocked, ignoring their arguments about heating costs and practicality, on the grounds that they were under an obligation to preserve the integrity and fundamental design of the building, which had strangely become of value after their proposal to utilise it and save it from its decline into dereliction and had resulted in it being awarded a Grade Two listing.

Stood in the still, almost cathedral-like emptiness of the refectory's vast space before the army of volunteers turned up, Jim allowed himself to feel a real sense of achievement, it had taken an enormous amount of work to arrive at this point, from finding the building onwards. He remained intensely modest about it all, about what he and Abbie were trying to do, it had started off almost as a bit of fun, but today stood there in this enormous space he couldn't help having a sense of history, a feeling relating to the same motivation, of purpose and yes of pride that Ephraim Armstrong himself must have felt when he had stood there himself, two hundred years previously on his own *day one* of his new buildings life, poised as it was to become part of that massive enterprise that had become known as The Industrial Revolution.

There was still a massive amount of work to be done yet before the 'Grand Opening Day' which was now only a few weeks away, but the structural work was done, the builders and all the various trades people associated with that side of the task had gone.

He was walking across the empty floor when his phone rang, he pulled it from his pocket,
"Hi Abbs, you're not due in till later on today are you?"
It was then that the bombshell had dropped. Through the tears and the sobbing at the other end of the phone he learnt that his granddaughter Lucy had been diagnosed with leukaemia.

He had tried to make his reply sound as confident and hopeful as he could …
"She'll be okay Abbs, they have amazing treatments now, especially for kids, keep your chin-up love, you'll have to be strong for her now…" As all the while he spoke he could feel a terrible coldness washing over him, sweeping down through his body, his head feeling light and numb, his lips cold, his heart heavy and sinking…

The call ended, he slipped the phone back into his pocket. Leaning against the wall to the kitchen area, he let himself slide down it and sat there. The shine had gone from the vast space now, in an instant it all began to seem pointless. He tried to tell himself that his words of encouragement to Abbie *were* valid, that there *was* hope, it was the earliest of days in their battle and it might not be too severe… But nothing he thought seemed to lighten the weight he felt in his chest.
Had that moment been the first time that he'd begun to feel that the whole project was cursed? He couldn't be sure, but it had

been what decided him to become Jos Armstrong. It seemed a way to distance himself from the bloody project, he imagined it might be too late, surely he'd be recognised? But a pair of black framed glasses had worked well enough for Clark Kent hadn't they? Plus he'd kept a pretty low profile up until then anyway... Later though, after the accident, that horrendous event when Abbie was taken from him, the idea that the money was cursed that had then taken root in his mind, began to grow, to poison everything for him, including his work at The Factory...

It had been a slow poison though and he'd hung in and remained dedicated to the project for many months, albeit as Jos, Abbie had tried to give as much time as she could, from the sidelines, to help in the setting up of the add-ons that were so vital to its success, but she was preoccupied now with the more pressing needs that her daughter's illness imposed upon her. Nevertheless they'd got through the grand opening and the show had got on the road.

He'd seen less and less of Abbie, she was exhausted mentally and physically with the stress of doing all she could for her own sick child and naturally enough helping hard-up strangers had seemed less important to her. She gave up her job, spending her time between endless trips to specialist hospitals and therapy centres and all the other plethora of things that accompany the dreadful curse of having a child with leukaemia, she had little spare time and when she did she was too exhausted anyway. It had been apparent that she too felt something of the helplessness and meaningless that the *free money* had brought to them, also the pointlessness of trying to make the world a better place when you were unable to do much to help your own child. She had however throughout it all urged her Dad to carry on, see the project through, he'd felt sometimes that she shoved it all onto him, but in truth the obligation he'd felt to her to do so had probably been the only remaining motivation that he felt.

So it was that by the time he lost Abbie in that terrible accident, Jos had put in place all he needed to take a back seat in the project. He had a business manager running the show, seeing to the catering staff, the accommodation, all the running issues such as maintenance and the other myriad things that went into keeping the show on the road. He had set aside a fund managed by trustees to carry on funding any gaps in the money his manager was also tasked in raising for the day to day expenses.

Having been busy on the project, he had effectively left his eldest son Neil to run the firm and he made that official now in resigning as CEO and appointing himself as Chairman of the company. Remembering that particular event with the addition of hindsight brought a sad smile to his face, that had gone *so well* hadn't it?

He had actually realised what was happening to him, as even at that time he'd felt himself beginning to slip away, becoming less in touch with what was going on around him. When his wife had announced she was leaving him, she told him that she was going to rediscover who she really was with her new lover... another woman... Apart from the odd descent into hurling childish abuse, he had in reality barely blinked, or really noticed her absence. Her comment that the money he had given her from the winnings had finally allowed her the freedom she needed, only added to the evidence that the money was cursed... Leaving him? Ruth was merely being true to herself? Getting a life, a life she'd been denied whilst she had the kids to bring up?

They were all very fair and reasonable assumptions to have now, but back then he didn't care less, he understood that now, despite his stupid protestations at the time. Just pour another whisky had been the answer... Find another nightclub to spend the endless nights in, to blur his reality with, to find yet another woman to take to bed to work out his frustrations with....
His mind always came back to that drive... returning home after that wonderful sunny day spent at the seaside, a day when Lucy was several months into her treatment and was feeling a lot better and brighter... When the dark clouds hanging over Abbie's head had seemed to have lifted a little. A perfect day spent with Abbie and her girls... the last day he ever had with his Abbie...

CHAPTER THIRTY-FIVE

It was the warm lilting voice of Troy, the young black PC that woke Jim the following morning as he sang out, deliberately reverting to his home accent,
"Room *serve-eece*, we got scrambled eggs for Sir this *lov-el-ey* morning," He laughed merrily adding, "would you like a morning paper Sir?"

Jim rolled over from facing the wall to look-up at the smiling face, unsure for a moment where he was...

"*Do you have a copy of today's FT my good man?* Ah, you're a good lad Troy! Tell me, I've been meaning to ask you, whatever decided you to become a copper?"
"Ah y'know, t'change de rotten system from within? They had a drive to recruit ethnic minorities you know."
"So how's that going for you?"
"Some days good, other days... hmm... well, not so good! Guess you *no so fond of de police?*"
"It's what they stand for really as an institution I don't like, rather than the individuals involved, I suppose there's good cops and bad cops, there must be some who want to do good, like yourself, but I think basically the problem is that the job also attracts a lot of the wrong types, ones who just want to have power over others and at the end of the day the police enforce the will of our rulers, enforce *their* laws, laws they make for us to follow, to keep us in line to suit their agenda whilst they live as they please and consider themselves largely above them."
"That... is a very cynical viewpoint... but not entirely inaccurate I'm sad to say!" He drew closer to Jim, tapped the side of his nose and whispered,
"I'll give you an example of a good cop... Don Willis, detective who on your case, 'fore de asshole take it on! Don been workin' wid whole lot o'decent cops, all very 'ush-ush, all on de QT to get to de truth 'bout you an'd'rotten case Steadman put up against you!" He laughed with Jim.

The rest of the week rolled by quickly and in what seemed like no time at all Monday morning had come around. After shaving and eating his breakfast, Jim was sat on the bed sipping his tea when Troy brought his suit in,

"Your suit Sir! Brought in just now by one of your defence team and a mighty fine suit it is too, tailor made I'd say! Mind you it'll no fit yer like it were made to no more. Man you gone skinny!" They both laughed,
"Suit like this cost a pretty penny, you musta had money once man?" Jim laughed as he took off the tracksuit and started buttoning up his shirt,
"What do you call a tramp in a suit?"
"Ha ha, 'ow about... The Accused?" They both laughed again.
Once he was dressed, Troy straightened Jim's tie,
"There... now you be all ship-shape and Bristol fashion! I wish you good luck today my friend." They shook hands and Jim was escorted to the waiting police van for the short trip to the courthouse. Jim was interested to observe that the van passed by the front of the building, where he could see that a small band of journalists had assembled, there was even an outside broadcast van parked nearby with its big satellite dish on the roof!

"Looks like you've attracted a decent turnout!" The cop driving the van commented as he swung down a side street to a rear entrance, adding "And friends in high places too! This is quite unusual... you being sneaked in round the back like this!"

So suitably 'snuck-in' Jim was now sat waiting in a small room with one of Freddie's staff, a pleasant enough woman in her forties who had introduced herself as Beryl and then gone on to outline the strategy that her boss would be using and explaining that he would be *in-camera* once again.

The court session was started only briefly before Freddie requested to have a conference in chambers with the judge, Beryl who was sat at his side smiled,
"With luck this will be when Freddie demolishes the case against you to such an extent that the next thing we see, will be the judge coming back into court on that screen and dismissing all charges against you!"

The judge was clearly in a most garrulous mood as he stomped out of the court to his chambers, followed by counsel, muttering "This had better not be one of his bloody tricks, I'll have the blighter for contempt if it is..." The two opposing counsels stood in the judge's chambers waiting for him to take his seat behind the large desk. The Clerk had followed them in and he closed the door and sat at a smaller desk to take notes.

Sat behind his desk the judge barked at Freddie,
"By the God's Fredriksson, this had better be good!" Freddie offered his most soothing of smiles as the counsel for the defence added,
"This is all highly irregular your honour, I feel you grant too much leeway for…"
"This is my court Sir and you will not make comments on how I run it!"
"My apologies Your Honour."

Freddie in the meantime had placed a file in front of the judge, a matching one on the desk in front of him and also one in front of the prosecutor, both counsel were still remaining standing. He opened the folder,
"If your Honour would turn to page one please, you will see that I have prepared a list of items, each item is a total repudiation of the so called evidence that has been presented against my client. I would in the normal course of events have taken their case to pieces in the courtroom, but I think you will agree, once we have gone through the list that it would do no service to justice to have the disgraceful behaviour of the police in this malicious and unfounded prosecution made public in open court!"
The judge harrumphed and motioned for Freddie to *get on with it!*

"Firstly Sir, there is the photographic evidence showing a condom packet under the ground sheet at the defendants bivouac. It was shown in the autopsy that sexual intercourse had taken place with the victim and that condoms had been used. This is labelled with the notation PRB/4, the forensic photographer's initials I believe and the number in the sequence of photographs that he took. It shows a flattened, cardboard condom packet on which my client's fingerprints were found. I now present my exhibit also labelled PRB/4 which shows the same shot but with no packet visible.
"This photograph was obtained directly from the forensic photographer by one of my team. When asked about the photograph labelled PRB/4 presented in evidence he stated that it was *not* his photograph adding that the quality of the picture

showed without any doubt whatsoever that it had not been taken with the same ultra-high quality resolution camera that he used.

"Item two your Honour, this is a still from the CCTV footage at the police station, it shows acting DI Steadman entering the interview room where my client was being held, you can see he has an evidence bag in his hand. The next picture shows him leaving with no evidence bag.

"Item three your Honour, this is a statement by PC Prentice corroborating the following statement made by my client regarding DI Steadman...
'While I was being interviewed the Inspector threw a small packet on the table in front of me demanding that I explain how it had been found at my campsite, he yelled repeatedly, for me to look at it, when I did not respond he pushed my face onto the table next to it and demanded that I *pick it up*! Which I then did. He then produced a DNA testing kit and swabbed the inside of my mouth.'

"This Sir is why my client's fingerprints were found on the empty condom box. You will find in evidence only one DNA test having been officially carried out on my client and that was recorded as taking place on a date three days after this incident. Somewhat surprisingly, we were unable to find any record of the interview in question having ever taken place.

"Item four your Honour, this is a still from the police station CCTV footage showing my client being taken to the showers by PC Prentice, please note the timestamp, then the timestamp on the second still showing them leaving, then the timestamp on the last two showing DI Steadman entering and then leaving the shower room.

"Item five your Honour is an independent forensic report my team have commissioned, it shows that pubic hair identified as belonging to my client found on the victim and entered as evidence, shows traces of soap identical to a sample of the soap in use at the police station. No traces of this soap were found on any other hairs presented in evidence.

"Item six, this Sir is page three of the forensic DNA report, showing the DNA recovered from the victim, you will see that there are three additional and unknown traces recorded. Please note Sir that only page one and two were presented in evidence, the fact that there was other DNA evidence present, as listed on page three, having been kept from your court.

"I put it to you Sir that the DNA found on the victim was planted there by DI Steadman, the pubic hair having been harvested from the drain screen in the shower at the police station. We have shown that he had the opportunity to do this and further we have copies, next in the folder Sir of the logs for the autopsy, showing DI Steadman's presence. A statement from the pathologist states clearly that DI Steadman was already in the room when he arrived.

"Item seven Sir, is a forensic analysis of the DNA presented as having been found on the victim and belonging to my client confirming that the sample was from saliva and not from either sweat or semen.

"Item eight your Honour, is a still from the same service station CCTV as used by the prosecution showing my client on his way from the crime scene, but this was taken on the previous evening showing the victim and four youths passing by on the pavement in the direction of the crime scene.

"Item nine, shows photographs of what we now believe to be the actual crime scene, you will see various empty bottles discarded about it, there is evidence of a fire and also many small silver canisters. These photographs were taken in a derelict site a hundred yards further up the street from the service station, the site is fenced off but the gate is not secured, furthermore the site backs onto the towpath of the canal with palisade fence running along the border. Viewed from the derelict site a path clearly runs towards the fence where a bar of the fence is unsecured at the bottom, allowing it to be moved aside and allowing access to the towpath. There is considerable undergrowth inside the derelict site at this point making it difficult to see it from the towpath.

"Item ten, shows fingerprints lifted from the bottles shown in the previous photographs, two of which are those of the victim, four others as yet unidentified fingerprints were also found. DNA samples of the victim were also found and likewise three other as yet unidentified samples.

"Item eleven is a copy of a report compiled by DS Gideon Willis detailing the additional evidence presented in item ten and his statement that he presented this report to one of his superiors, Chief Inspector Pembrose eight weeks ago. You will see that he was assured that she would *look into it*, you will also note that he states that she enquired if his report was *the only copy*? When he asked her several days later what action she was going to take, he alleges that she told him there was no point in wasting valuable resources, they had their man and that he should concern himself with his own case load. He claims that she also raised the issue of him taking early retirement!

"Item twelve is a comparison analysis of the sample of condom lubricant taken from the victim and that of the lubricant used in the brand of condoms claimed to have been found in the box allegedly found at my client's bivouac. You will see that they have a quite different signature on the spectroscopy graph shown.

"Item thirteen..." the judge held up his hand,
"Oh for goodness sake man, sit down will you and *stop*! No not you Sir!" the judge rounded angrily on the counsel for the prosecution!
"You Sir can stay on y'feet! What do you have to say for yourself?"
"I... err... well Sir, surely we must take time to consider the voracity of these accusations? I accept that perhaps there has been some, well perhaps, less than thorough investiga..."

"Less than thorough? This Sir is a catalogue of deceit!" The judge roared, banging his fist on the paperwork on his desk before him, "It is a deliberate and wicked attempt to perpetrate a flagrant miscarriage of justice." The counsel looked down,
"I apologise your Honour, I only work with the evidence that is presented to me by the police."

"This file will be presented to the CPS Sir and to The Chief Constable and your part in this deception will also be thoroughly investigated by them! Make your excuses to them!"

With that the judge ordered them back into the courtroom.

The court was brought to order and the judge spoke,
"Is Chief Inspector Penrose present in court?"
A buzz went around the chamber and looks of consternation were exchanged between the small contingent of police that were present, no doubt waiting for their victory in what they thought would be the guilty verdict. A flustered looking woman stood up and answered uncertainly,
"I am your honour."
"You will take the stand." Sally Pembrose regaining her composure strode purposefully to the stand, where she stood shrugging her shoulders to her colleagues,
"I remind Chief Inspector, that you are under oath. An allegation has been made against you that you wilfully ignored a detailed report presented to you by your subordinate colleague Detective Sergeant Willis, providing you with an alternative version of events to the one presented to this court. How say you?"
"DS Willis was not working on the case your Honour."
"But he was initially?"
"Well yes, but he was reassigned after the first day."
"I see, so you deny that he came to you with a file?"
"Why would he your Honour, it was not his case?"
"Answer the question!"
"No Sir, he did not."
"So you stand before me and blatantly deny that DS Willis handed you a copy of *this* folder, this report that I now hold in my hand, a report that details an alternative narrative to that which you presented to the CPS for their prosecution in regard to Crown versus Williams?"
"Ah... I do apologise Sir, I do recall that now! Yes... DS Willis did bring *a folder* to my attention your Honour, I have so many folders put before me you must understand... however I do remember now, at the time I dismissed it out of hand, that was how it managed to slip my mind! I considered it to be nothing more than sour grapes, you must understand that there is a rivalry between Willis and DI Steadman, because I took him off the case due to his level of incompetence."

"In all my years on the bench, never before have I been presented with such an appalling attempt to pervert the course of justice Madam! Officer of the Court you will arrest this woman on a charge of contempt and take her to the cells. I will personally have The Chief Constable before me this very day to see to it that he sets in motion a full investigation into this despicable debacle! Is Detective Inspector Steadman present in my court?"

A middle aged man stood up.

"I am DI Steadman Sir." The agitated judge pointed down...

"You Sir!" A uniformed PC sat at the back of the court leapt to his feet!

"Me Sir?" The tall Afro-Caribbean PC asked.

"Yes, you officer. You will come down here and arrest Detective Inspector Steadman on a charge of attempting to pervert the course of justice. Do you have a set of handcuffs with you?"

"Why yes Sir, that I do!"

"When you have cautioned him, place them on his wrists and escort him taken to the cells."

PC Troy Prentice struggled to keep a grin from his face as he walked down the court to make the arrest, as the judge pronounced,

"Mr. Williams, the case against you is dismissed! You are a free man, you leave my court today without a blemish on your record or a stain on your character. Members of the jury, I thank you for your service and you are discharged."

"All rise!"

A noisy hub-bub went around the court as people stood and began chattering with each other, in disbelief and greatly amused to see the shocked faces of the other police as they watched Detective Chief Inspector Pembrose being led from the witness box and some jostling taking place as Steadman was placed in cuffs, all this contrasting with the looks of jubilation on the faces of a group of people in the public gallery as they hugged and laughed together joyfully.

Jim was met a few minutes later in the anteroom by his barrister, he shook hands with Freddie, thanking him for ensuring his release. The larger than life guy had just chuckled, it was a deep

resonant sound from within the voluminous depths of his cavernous chest,
"Have no fear my friend, I am already in receipt of handsome remuneration and for a mere week's work! I hope you can find a way to manage with all the multitude of trials and tribulations our troubled world will present to you once you leave the confines of the four walls you have become so acquainted with of late."
"There is one more thing you could do for me Freddie, to justify your no doubt exorbitant fees! Money well spent I hasten to add! Would you sneak me out of the building please?"

"Have no fear, we have of course already arranged for you to leave by a private entrance at the back, but not the way you were brought in, your anonymity has been assured and you need have no worries regarding our esteemed judge, he has more weighty secrets to keep than the one regarding your identity! I've been informed that your friends have organised a meal to celebrate your release, somewhere very discreet and out of the view of the public, your son was telling me only…"

"I'm sorry to interrupt you Sir Freddie, but it's more precisely all of them that I want to avoid, even more so than the press and the public! I'm not ready for anything like that, I know they mean well and *they* do deserve a celebration for all their efforts in getting me out. Would you do me one last favour and go in my stead, I'm sure a chap such as yourself would relish a good meal, some fine wine and jolly company, no? Please thank them on my behalf would you? Tell them that I will thank them all personally and individually once my head has settled down."
"If you're sure that's what you want to do, certainly I will facilitate this for you. Please wait here."

Five minutes later, he returned,
"Okay, come with me." Jim was led back through the courtroom and then the side door and along to the judge's chambers,
"Here we are Alistair, one recently freed man for you to assist in making yet another escape!" The judge shook Jim's hand vigorously,
"Congratulations on your freedom Sir! I apologise for the appalling treatment that has been meted out on you! Bloody disgraceful abuse of power! I will personally make sure that

those responsible suffer for their deplorable actions! Seeking compensation for a wrongful and vexatious prosecution would seem to be a justifiable course of action to take next, what say you Freddie?" Before the barrister to reply though Jim blurted out,

"Oh no, I don't want anything like that! I just want to put it all behind me."

"Very well then Jim, I can appreciate that you're not quite ready for centre stage again yet! There will be time a plenty to reconsider. But now, regarding the immediate future though, I totally understand your reticence. Here, put this on," he handed a large, heavy and tan coloured mohair coat to Jim,

"And pop this on y'noggin as well old chap," having helped Jim get the coat on, he placed a large bowler hat on his head,

"There now, just keep your head down and when you get outside, go straight to the back door of the Silver Cloud that will be pulled-up just outside, it's not the way you were brought in, just get straight in and my driver will whisk you away to wherever you wish to go. Here, take these with you as well, just leave them in the back of the car when you get out."

He handed him a large rolled-up, black brolly and a battered old briefcase,

"That completes the illusion beautifully! Better still by George… you Freddie, get one of the chaps from the court to go out of the front doors with you, keeping his head down and seeming to be deep in conversation! People will assume it's Jim as he is there alongside your mighty, towering and intimidating presence! They will automatically assume you are escorting your client out to his newly acquired freedom!" Freddie roared with laughter,

"Splendid! A splendid suggestion! Your Honour it has as ever, been of the utmost of pleasures to work with you!"

Jim did as he was bid and went out through the door, finding himself in a wide passageway at the side of the building, he paused for a moment to take a first breath of the air of freedom once more. Looking to his right he could see thirty yards away a small group of people stood by the rear entrance he had used earlier. He was able to make out Harry and Jake amongst them, he felt a moment of shame for letting them down but walked across to the gleaming old Rolls nevertheless. With his hand on the door handle, he looked up along the side of the car to the other end of the passage, where it met the main street, a barrier was across it and a gaggle of reporters and onlookers were being held behind it by the police. He raised the brolly in a salute to them and dived into the back of the old limo.

Sat on the wonderful soft, old leather seats of the Rolls, he leant back as the old car effortlessly glided away. He kept his head down as it shot through the parted crowd and the opened barriers and swung away onto the main street,
"Where to Sir?" The driver asked… Without thinking, he heard himself saying… "St. Jude's, do you know it?"
The driver nodded.
"On our way Sir."

CHAPTER THIRTY-SIX

Jim watched the view sliding past, silently outside the window of the smoothly gliding Rolls, the old girl offered quite a ride he had to admit. He'd never ridden in a Silver Cloud before, his collection of cars although extravagant had never been at the more opulent end of the market! When the car swished up to the front entrance of St. Jude's, he hesitated for a moment, remaining in his seat with his hand on the door handle.
"We're here Sir!" The driver called to prompt him, Jim still remained seated, unsure now whether coming up here had been all that sensible of an idea,
"Would you like me to open the door for Sir? Make a grand entrance for you?" The driver asked him, having turned around in his seat to look into the back of the car, he noticed that silent tears were running down the old man's cheeks,
"Oh, I'm sorry, I had no idea. You take as long as you like Sir."
He turned off the engine and leant back in his seat, taking off his chauffeur's cap,
"It's a beautiful place this is and no mistaking. Do you have a connection with it?"
"I helped with the initial funding for it, although it was many years ago now."
"Did you really Sir, by gove? A fine gesture if I may say. And your visit today?"
"I don't know really, I just had to get away from all those people at the court. I didn't feel up to facing them. It was the first place I thought of."
"Quite understandable Sir, the press are like a pack of rabid dogs. I can take you somewhere else if you can think of somewhere else you'd prefer to go?"

Before he could think of anywhere else to go, his decision was pre-empted by the approach towards the car door of the director of St. Jude's! The driver, with his hat firmly back on his head, must have also seen her approaching as he was already around the back of the car and at Jim's door and was opening it before he had quite realised what was happening,
"We're here Sir!" he said respectfully adding,
"May I take your coat Sir, you'll not be needing it inside!" The woman addressed him,

"Good morning, well I should say *afternoon* now, shouldn't I? I'm the director here at St. Jude's, are we expecting you Sir?"
Jim had little choice left to him other than to exit the car, so he did so, letting the coat slip off his shoulders into the hands of the chauffeur, he smiled at the woman standing before him and he held out his hand,
"Jim Stanley at your service Mrs Melling, we have met although it was many years ago."
"Ah yes, of course! Please, call me Pat. It's lovely of you to call on us of course, but is there any particular reason why you are here today?"
"No, not especially, I was passing and thought it would be good to see the place before I leave town, I err… I shall be leaving for pastures new shortly you see." The chauffeur chipped-in,
"Will that be all Sir, would you like me to wait for you or will you make your own arrangements from here on?"
"Oh yes! No, thanks ever so much, you get off now. Thanks again."
"My pleasure Sir."

Jim turned back to Pat,
"That's not my car you understand! I was offered a ride in it to come up here by a friend I'd been… well chatting with earlier."
"Oh that's a shame, it's rather a beautiful old thing…" they both turned to watch as the car swung around and whooshed away from them.
"If it's at all inconvenient for me to visit…"
"Why no, of course it isn't! Please come, I'll have some coffee brought to my office for us, if you would like some." Jim nodded and she led on.

After exchanging pleasantries over a coffee as they sat in the director's office, Jim asked if he could be permitted to have a wander around on his own, with a suggestion,
"I'm sure you have better things to do than accompany me, I'll not be a bother to anyone…" he had added.

It felt strange as he walked around, visiting today as himself and not as the bedraggled old persona of Bill the tramp! He made his way to the lounge hoping to find Abigail but instead finding Eleanor sat in an armchair on her own, she was looking out through the French windows, her chariot as she referred to it, parked alongside her. As he approached her she didn't appear to see him, so he sat quietly down in a chair nearby, one not quite facing her and remained silent, waiting for her to notice him. However she remained impassive, continuing to gaze out through the window at the gardens.

He was beginning to wonder if she was still in there, when without averting her gaze from the window she spoke,
"So you return Captain? And considerably less hirsute than on the occasion when I last encountered you!" She finally turned her head to look at him now and narrowed her eyes a little,
"Ah yes, still troubled I see however and yet also I find you to be considerably reanimated today... to your former self would that be? Pray tell me who would that former self be that I find sat here in the place of the disheartened old pirate captain that I previously beheld? Grand old fellow that he was!"
"Jim Stanley m'lady, at your service!" He held out his hand and once again took gently in his, the feather light and tiny hand of the old lady.

"Pleased to meet you Sir. To what do I owe the pleasure of your company today? More pertinently, to what end do you return here and furthermore and far more fascinating to know... how is it that this metamorphism has occurred?"
"A long story and one I will gladly share with you, but before I do so please tell me, have you seen Abigail today? I would love to meet her again."
"Alas my dear Captain, well my erstwhile Captain, I have the saddest of news for you, dear sweet Abigail has passed onto the other side..." She sighed and turned her gaze back to the window, letting her head rest onto the back of the chair as her tiny frame visibly sagged.
Jim felt the same way as a wave of sadness washed over him, taking his breath away a little, certainly taking the wind out of his sails. He turned his gaze away from her to also stare out at the gardens beyond the windows. They sat in silence for a few minutes.

"Her poor mother." He eventually said.
"Indeed. Abigail has shed her own burden now, for her the ordeal has ended, but poor dear Samantha... Her daughter was

her life, how she will manage with the massive hole in her life that Abigail must have left I simply cannot imagine."
"Samantha, that's right yes I remember her, they were so alike. Losing a daughter is something you never get over..."
"Ah... the sadness and melancholy of your voice, speaks of experience. I feel your pain, your suffering my brother. There is neither rhyme nor reason to be found in this world Captain for all we may seek to find any! Look at me, a pathetic old relic, little more than skin and bone remaining of me, a withered and diminished shadow of the grand lady that I once was and only by the grace of God am I still compos mentis and not one of the dribbling mindless ones I have so many of surrounding me here! Although sometimes I do wonder occasionally, which of us is really the better off?" She giggled to herself,
"Oh to be blissfully unaware of one's predicament!"
"Ah no... They often seem frightened, the ones with dementia, retaining your intellect as you have, is a gift to be cherished Eleanor."

"Hmm... Maybe so... It seems we have little say in such matters though do we? Look at a wonderful, talented child such as Abigail, with her whole life ahead of her... for her to be taken... for her mother to lose her in such a way... Why? What possible purpose can there be in such a tragic waste? In allowing such cruelty, how can anyone reconcile such events with any form of belief in their being a loving God watching over us?"

"They'd tell you that their God's purpose is beyond our limited understanding?" Jim volunteered, albeit half-heartedly, "That's the usual line isn't it? We just have to have faith? A blind, trusting and unquestioning faith, or as I see it a totally illogical and irrational faith?
"I'm with you Eleanor, the *have faith* pitch was the point at which I parted company from them and it's why I've no time for organised religions now of any shade or variety! I see them as no more than systematic programming or worse still even as brainwashing. The only place I've ever found any comfort at all is in the teachings of The Buddha and I have to say that's largely because I don't consider Buddhism to be a religion anyway."
"Ah yes, a set of teachings, a way to live rather than the usual dogma of *thou shalt and shalt not,* do this and that. Along with all the other commandments but rather *to live with loving*

compassion for all living things. Yes my dear Captain, a conclusion I myself came to many decades ago."

She continued…
"I particularly love the Buddhist story that tells how Buddha told his followers… *"do not believe anything anyone tells you unless it passes the test of truth within your own hearts!"* Today of course that would have to include any information received from the myriad sources that continually assault the senses of the poor unfortunates who dwell in this dystopian reality… unless of course, they have learnt to refuse to allow their senses to be so bombarded! And I'm sure you will know, today the veracity of what is presented as truth is often a convenient lie in a flimsy concealing wrapper of partial truth…

"It's the second part of this story though that I like the most, it is so unlike what you describe as having to put one's trust in what we are told, Buddha went on to say, *"…even if it is myself who is telling you!"* In other words he taught that we should only believe what our heart accepts as the truth.
"But then Buddhism teaches us that we already have all the answers we will ever need within ourselves doesn't it? If only we have the wisdom to seek them out, to learn how to sufficiently still the incessant chattering of the monkey mind that would otherwise drown them out, to find the stillness needed so that all can be revealed to us."

Jim nodded, "And yet you still thank 'Him' for *his* grace? I mean, when you put it, as being thankful to God that you are still compos mentis?" She chuckled,
"Silly boy! We all are our *own God*, if we do but realise it! God lives within us…" She tapped her forehead,
"He… or I personally prefer to call her *She*, is what animates us, She is the vital spark, the scintilla of living stardust that transforms the animal body from the sack of meat and offal it otherwise is, hanging there on our framework of bones, animates it into the living and vital *person* that we are. We do but reside for a time within this shell, we are not of the shell but rather we are pure energy, we are spirit, we *are*… God."

"So do you think that we go on, I mean once we shed this shell of ours, leave our carcass behind?"

"That my boy is one question I have yet to discover an answer to... or not as the case may be!" She smiled at him, then went on, "So my friend what are your plans now you are reincarnated on this plane once more into your former self?"

"I'm still formulating them... they're somewhat vague just presently..."

"Ah... Well I'll do something that I rarely do, I'll give you a little piece of advice! I've lived a very long life and I'd like to think I've not done that bad a job at living it too! But for all that I've seen and done and sought out, the single most important answer I've found is this... Learn how to be at peace... both with the world outside of you, but more importantly with the world within yourself. So whatever you decide to do, I'd be sure to seek out a path that enables you to pursue that goal."

"Thank you Eleanor, I will do that." With that he rose and took her hand once more, she closed her other hand over his,

"Goodbye Captain!"

"Goodbye Eleanor."

He shared the very real sentiment he felt was there in her voice, that this would be their final parting.

Elsewhere down in the valley, far below them, in a private dining room of one of the swankiest hotels in town, there was great disappointment when Freddie walked into the room unaccompanied by Jim.

He made eloquent apologies on Jim's behalf and begged their forbearance, as he assured them that the man of the day had promised faithfully to thank them all personally as individuals, but on a one-to-one and more private basis when he felt more able to do so,

"We cannot for a moment begin to understand where the poor fellow's mind is at this moment, for us it is a great triumph, a time to rejoice and to congratulate ourselves on the fruit of our endeavours and to celebrate his release from incarceration, his restored freedom! But alas for him it is a reawakening to the realities of this often cruel world, with all its many slings and arrows! Returning to everything that his troubled mind ran away from all those years ago, no doubt the same fears and memories that were there when he left, still remain here waiting for him? And then for the last few months we must not forget he has been cocooned within the confines of his own mind, a prisoner in his own head, a man who was more or less catatonic... Please let us all sit and eat, drink and be merry! I for one am famished! Let us celebrate together for him, on his behalf!"

As Jim wandered back towards the director's office Eleanor's parting question to him had rekindled his wondering over what he was going to do now? As he was about to knock on her door, which was already slightly ajar, Pat fully opened it and was stood there infront of him before he even had chance to wonder how she knew he was at the door, she was already explaining,
"I saw you heading my way! On the CCTV!" She laughed,
"It's a vital tool for keeping track on some of our more, well... wandersome guests! Please come in and sit, did you see all you wanted to? I saw you talking to Eleanor, quite a tête-à-tête you were having, she's a remarkable person isn't she?"
Thinking how nice it was that she referred to Eleanor as *a person* and not simply as *an old lady*, he replied
"Yes she truly is. I was greatly saddened to hear from her of Abigail's death, such a tragic affair..."
"Oh, I wasn't aware you'd met the dear girl, how did you..."

"Before I tell you that, please tell me more about Eleanor, she's a fascinating person, so astute and despite her frailty her intellect is razor sharp! Would you mind telling me how old is she?"
"She's well into her nineties and yes she really is a remarkable lady, did you know that she was once a concert pianist, a child prodigy in fact. She was forced to take more of a backseat out of the limelight quite early in life though, due to the onset of chronic arthritis in her hands, she was only in her early forties I think, bizarre how life treats us sometimes isn't it? The cards that fate deals out to us? I mean a brilliant pianist is struck down with a disease of her hands of all places and then the arthritis that wrecked them goes into remission a year or so afterwards!"
"Indeed, it seems to me that fate is a little over fond of irony! Take Beethoven as an example, a brilliant if troubled genius of a composer, one of the greatest who ever lived..."
"...and he goes profoundly deaf!" She laughed,
"Yes fate can be a cantankerous and breathtakingly cruel bastard, like it was for Abigail..." He was a little shocked to hear such a word from her gentile lips but quickly steered her away from speaking again of Abigail,

"Please tell me more about Eleanor, after she was unable to play professionally, what on earth did she do?"

"Oh, well… She founded a school for gifted youngsters, an academy for teaching piano. She came from money you see, old money, her ancestor was some sort of Victorian tycoon, in cotton I think, she never married so she remains an Armstrong to this day…" Patricia carried on speaking but Jim's mind was reeling after he'd heard the name of Armstrong… He felt the blood drain from his face and suffered a strange vertiginous sensation as if he was spinning, falling into a bottomless chasm, it was as if the fates were weaving some sort of swirling net to trap him within…

His face must have given away his inner turmoil, as the seemingly disembodied voice stopped speaking and asked him,

"…Are you alright Jim, you've gone very pale!"

"No I don't think I am… I had a bit of a funny turn just then… I'm sorry to have interrupted you Patricia, but could you do me a great favour please? I sent the car away earlier thinking I could call when I was done here, but I seem to have left my phone on the back seat or in my coat pocket maybe. Could you ring for a taxi for me please?"

"Of course, but are you sure that you're okay? Your colour *is* coming back a bit now!"

"Yes, yes, please don't be concerned, I have health issues, but they're not life threatening!" How he hoped that was true!

"Well, there's no need for a taxi, I'm sure that Gordie'll be more than happy to drive you down, I'll get him to come up for you," She went to reach for the telephone on her desk,

"No need to drag the fellow up here, point me in the right direction and I'll go and find him. I'm fine now honestly"

"Okay, it's really no trouble to…"

"Really, please I've been enough of a nuisance to you already!"

"Oh alright, well you'll find him," she glanced at the clock on the wall, "Most likely at the back of the canteen, having his dinner, if not go out through the back and around to the garages, he has quarters tacked onto them."

"He lives in then? Lucky chap."

A bizarre thought occurred to Jim so he asked, "Pat, I don't suppose you know who had this place built do you, I mean who the original owner was?" Even before she spoke, he knew what she was about to say…

"Why yes I do, it was Josiah Armstrong! Funny isn't it how Eleanor came to end up living here, in the home of her ancestor?"
Jim was utterly flummoxed once more by the turn of events, all he could manage to say was,
"Thanks again Mrs Melling,"
"Pat, please just call me Pat and do come again won't you... you never said how you knew Abigail?"
"Another time Pat, thanks again..." and with that he made a rather hurried exit!

Despite having managed to retain the outwards impression of calmness, his mind was a wild flurry of questions... *Eleanor was an Armstrong!* She was back living in the house her ancestor built! The fucking bizarreness of it all! I mean, he asked himself, was it just blind coincidence? Was it fate? Or was it synchronicity at work? Was there any significance in it, did it mean anything at all? Once again he had that feeling of being watched over, toyed with, manipulated by some force or entity... by Fate?

When he got around to the back of the kitchen he found Gordie was finishing off his dinner, he was sat at a small table set to one side for the kitchen staff to use, Jim recognised him from when he'd driven him up to St. Jude's for his previous visit. He strode over to him,
"Hi, you must be Gordie? Pat says if I ask you nicely you'll run me back down into town, I stupidly left my phone on the back seat of my car when I sent it away."
"Was that your Silver Cloud I saw earlier? Beautiful motor! Wouldn't want to pay for the petrol she uses though! What'll she do... ten or twelve to the gallon?"
"I imagine so, but to be honest it wasn't my car! I was offered a lift up here in it by... err... by an old friend!"
"Lucky you and some friend you must have! Yes I've finished here, my pudding can wait!" He patted his rounded stomach as he rose from the chair,
"I'd probably benefit from missing it all together actually, these lasses feed me rather too well!" He laughed with a couple of the busy kitchen staff as he led the way out through the back door. As they walked across the back of the old house, he carried on chatting away,

"I've put the bus away for the night, so I'll run you down in the Humber."
"A Humber? Hmm... Now I *am* intrigued!"
"It's my own car of course, had her from new too, a 1966 Sceptre Mark two!"

Having come to the garage, Gordie pushed a button on a remote he'd fished from his pocket and a large triple width roller-door rattled up infront of them. Inside the large garage was the minibus that had brought Jim up on his last visit and alongside it and dwarfed by the bus was a tidy and very shiny old Humber, finished with a two tone crimson red and cream paint job.
Jim walked all around the car giving it admiring looks and firing questions all the while at Gordie, when he got back to the front he complimented him,
"She's a credit to you Gordie, she's a splendid old girl, how long is it since you had her resprayed?"

Eventually after more *car-chat*, they were sat in the car and ready to leave, the two men continued sharing their passion of... even more *chatting cars,* for quite some time.
Eventually when there was a lull in the conversation Gordie started the car up. Set side by side in the centre of the dash was a neat row of four small, chrome bezeled gauges, to accompany the quiet purr of the engine, three of the four needles on the dials jumped into life. Jim smiled and turned to face the proud driver of his very own classic car, nodding to himself,
"She's magnificent Gordie!" Was all he said but Gordie smiled to himself and nodded knowingly. Putting the car into gear, he slipped the handbrake off and they set off rolling across the yard.

"So where to?" Gordie asked, fortunately by now Jim had formulated the outline of a plan,
"You know the Folks Factory... erm, I'm guessing at least that you will?"
"Why of course, that's where I picked you up the last time we met!" He turned briefly, to face Jim in the passenger seat smiling,
"I wasn't sure where I knew you from when you first came into the kitchen, but the more you chatted, the more I was certain we'd met before, then sat here in the car chatting it came to me!

You certainly look a bit different today, but when you said *'magnificent'* and the way you said it… "

Shit! Jim thought to himself, as he realised that keeping his anonymity was going to be a lot harder than he'd initially imagined!
"You must be mistaking me for someone else Gordie!"
"Okay… really? Oh, no problem. My mistake." The guy smiled to himself as he clearly not only relished driving his car, but also recognising who his passenger really was.

Approaching the outskirts of town on their way down from the hills, Jim spoke up,
"Gordie can you pull up for a minute please?"
"Sure thing." Parked at the side of the road Jim asked,
"Would you mind making a phone call for me please? I've left my phone somewhere. See if you can get through to the Folks Factory and ask them to get hold of Harry… they'll know who you mean… ask them to get him to ring you back? I'd really appreciate it. I need to set something up for when we get there. Would you mind hanging on here then afterwards, waiting for a bit until he rings back?"
"No problem, but there's a nice little pub half a mile down the road, once I've rung him, we could get a pint while we wait, if you like?"
"Sure, sounds like a plan."
After fiddling with his phone for a bit, in order to find a phone number for The Folks Factory, Gordie did as Jim had asked and they headed off for that pint.

CHAPTER THIRTY-SEVEN

Harry met Jim in the lobby at the far end of The Factry. Despite feeling irritated by the old guy's behaviour, he sensed at once that things weren't well with him from his whole demeanour, his body language and the flatness of his voice when responding to him as he asked him if he was okay. He backed off from any reproach he might have felt like voicing for his behaviour earlier in leaving the court, simply saying,
"Everyone was sorry to miss you after the court, we went and had a little get-together, to celebrate that you're free, me and Jenny, Freddie, Don, Del and your lad Jake… we had a meal… Jake wants to meet up with you, when you feel up to it, will you see him?"
"Right now Harry I want to sleep, I *need* to sleep and nothing else, if you don't mind. Have you a key for that flat, I'm hoping it's still available for me to use? Maybe I'm assuming too much?"
"No, no of course it's still there for you…" He fumbled in his pocket for the little bunch of keys,
"Do you want me to come up with you?"
"Nah, just let me have the keys and you can get on with whatever you should be doing."
"You're sure? It'd be no trouble. You'll need some fresh milk and…"
"Stop fussing Harry! Thanks for everything, I really mean it, I'm eternally grateful to you for all your efforts on my behalf, but right now I *really* need to sleep… and for a long time! It's been a lot this last week and before that having been locked-up for all those months… I just need some time to readjust, time to myself, some peace and quiet, okay?"

Handing over the keys, Harry placed his hand on Jim's shoulder,
"Sure, I understand, really I do. Oh just one thing though, Del said to say… err well…"
"It's okay! Knowing Del as I do, it would've been something like, 'tell the miserable old twat *you're welcome* and *goodbye*!' Yeah?" Harry chuckled,
"Well, near enough!"
The old guy smirked a little before turning away to press the button for the lift. Harry made to leave,

"I'll get off then, leave you to it… Can I call around in the morning?"

"Make it after lunch!"

"Okay." Harry was about to leave when he called out,

"Oh Jim, hang on! I nearly forgot, I've got your hat and coat in the car that Freddie passed on to me!" He went to the car, retrieved them from the back seat and handed them to him.

Taking them, Jim turned and got into the waiting lift. He pushed one of the buttons, lifted a hand to Harry and as the doors slid shut he was gone.

Inside *his appartment*… the notion of that… seeming a little unreal after his accommodation at Her Majesty's pleasure! He stood looking out of the window for quite some time, trying to let his new situation settle in. He needed to decide what he was going to do next. Harry had told him before he was locked-up that the flat was his as long *as he wanted it*. He'd no reason to imagine that would have changed so he had a place to stay, but was that what he wanted to do? Stay here?

The thought of wandering off into the big outdoors wasn't very appealing somehow, he had lost his anonymity in this town now, 'Bill' was blown now as an alter-ego, as an effective alternative to being Jim Stanley. One way or another, he had to move on to something different, that much he did know, but equally he was certain that he had no desire whatsoever to try and slot himself back into the empty hole that the life of Jim Stanley had left empty… There was simply no way he would fit into that! Even if he could somehow circumnavigate the fact that he was dead, officially at least!

So what was he going to do? He yawned and decided that as he'd told Harry earlier, he needed to sleep, desperately.

He kicked off his shoes and lay on the bed dragging the covers over himself and sank almost at once into a deep sleep.

He gently became aware of his surroundings in the early hours, light was seeping in through the open curtains, he rolled over and dozed off again after he had assimilated where he was, but his sleep was patchy now and filled with dreams, troubled dreams in which he was being chased by a mob of people baying for his

blood for murdering the student girl! The twisted hate-filled faces of the ranting lynch mob vivid in his mind!
Then there was Abigail from St.Jude's, pale and thin, but radiant, somehow angelic now, saving him, ... smiling at him...
Eleanor calling out to him... 'Captain! Captain!'
Harry and Jenny dancing on the flags outside The Factry by the coffee truck... Waltzing...
Jake reaching a hand out to him...
The door to his cell clanging shut...
The hangman's solemn face...
Del...
Del running her fingers through his hair calming him, soothing him... *'It's okay Jos, it's okay, you're safe, you can get through this... I'm here, I'm not going to leave you...'*
He felt the bed give as Del got in and snuggled up to him, she put her arm around him and spooned with him,
"Sleep now Jos, you're safe... I'm here..."

A loud knocking at the door woke him.

He rolled over and peered around for a moment getting his bearings, he got off the bed and made his way on his stiff and shaky legs to the front door.
Harry was standing in the corridor with a carrier bag in his hand,
"You okay, you look a bit... dishevelled?" Jim dragged a hand through his tangled hair, pushing it off his face, his hand feeling the rough stubble on his cheek...
"Yeah, guess so, come in Harry..."
Harry went through to the kitchen and set about putting the kettle on and unpacking the bag he'd brought, Jim excused himself and went off to the bathroom.

When he reappeared he had changed into a tee-shirt he'd found and had a wash and run a comb through his hair,
"Coffee's there Jim." Harry pointed to the table next to where he was sat,
"How are you feeling, now that you're a free man again, it must be a lot to take in?"
Jim sat down, took up the coffee mug and held it in both of his hands as he looked out at the hills in the distance, he sipped at the coffee and remained silent for quite some time before replying,

"You're right Harry, it's not just about being free again, it's everything… I don't know who I am anymore! I feel as if Bill's gone forever now and to be honest I don't think I could live like that anymore anyway. His absence however has left me in a vacuum, I'm not Jim Stanley, that much I do know, I remember who he was… I know I used to be him once but…"

"You'll need time Jim, you just need to give yourself time, don't try and rush anything. But for now, well right now anyway, finish you're coffee and we'll get something to eat. You must be famished? When did you last eat?"

CHAPTER THIRTY-EIGHT

Hearing the backdoor bell, Jim had gone through to meet the postman, he was now sat back in the cottage's living room unwrapping the flat parcel that Steve had just dropped-off. It was symptomatic of where he was living now that you quickly got to be on first name terms with most of the people that you came into regular contact with, it was just that sort of place. There was Nessie, the woman who came to deliver the groceries from the village stores twice a week, Lesley who was the letting agent, who dealt with any problems he might have with the cottage and his nearest neighbours were Marion and Julien, although they were over half a mile away, down the little country lane at the top of the track that led down to the cottage and he purposely hadn't fostered any kind of a 'pop-in-anytime' relationship with them.

Inside the parcel was the draft copy of Jenny's book, for his perusal and then hopefully his approval, it was good of the girl he thought to be so considerate, she could have just written her book, had it published and be damned! He wouldn't have blamed her if she had either, particularly after the way he'd brushed her off, along with Del and the detective who'd helped Jenny trying to clear his name. The idea of sitting down surrounded by so many people immediately after the courtroom drama had been too much for him, his spur of the moment decision of doing *a flit* as Jake had described his behaviour, had at that time seemed the only logical course of action for him. He had been far more calculated in his decision, and equally convinced that it was the right one, at least as far as he was concerned, in making his second decision to move away the very next day after he'd been released!

Although Jake had struggled with his Dad's decision, thinking it to be extremely rude and more than a bit unfair, he'd accepted that if it was what Jim thought was best for him, then far be it for anyone to stand in his way, or to try and force him to face-up to making an attempt at re-establishing himself back in the land of the living and in some way to try and pick-up his old life? He realised there would have been just too much entailed in such a venture. If nothing else all the endless repeated explanations to everyone, every time he met someone again for the first time!

Basically he was just so grateful to be involved with his Dad again himself, that he had decided to respect his Dad's wishes and let everything else go. He'd lived through the last eight years thinking that he'd never see his Dad again, that in all probability he was dead, although there had always been a part of him that refused to completely accept that! He'd dismissed it at the time as mere wishfulness and childishly foolish thinking, now he wondered...

He still harboured a little resentfulness over Jim's continuing insistence that his return was to be kept from the rest of the family and also from the world at large, the last time the subject had come up however, he'd gone as far as adding a little rider, a condition of his own to his continuing complicity in the secrecy, he'd added.... 'Okay then... *for now* I will!'

Jim took the book which was in the form of an A4 bound-up-binder, it was printed only on the right hand pages, making it quite thick and heavy. He settled into a chair by the window, in the warmth of the spring sunshine that was cascading in through the window and laid the folder on his lap. It was titled:

'A Road from Riches to Rags (and everything in between).'

Jenny had explained that a simpler title, such as something like: 'Riches to Rags' had been used by many other authors over and over again!

The first page was a rough layout for the front cover of the paperback, it was a drawing of the old mill where it had the brick lettering 'Armstrong Mill' built into it, it was the view from the canal side. It was in the state of neglect it had been when Jim had first seen it and there in the foreground was a sketchy impression of Jim Stanley, from behind as he stood looking across at the old building. The next page was a layout for the back cover, it had a similar drawing of the Folks Factory again, from the same perspective but this time it was a shadowy sketch of the dishevelled figure of Bill who was stood in the foreground.

A tear came to Jim's eye as he looked at the proposed front cover, as he thought to himself of the terrible omission that there was...'Abbie should be stood alongside of me! An image of

Abbie simply has be put into this picture alongside of mine!' He saw that there was a pencil in a loop on the inside cover of the binder along with a handwritten note sellotaped next to it,

Jim/ Please use the blank pages to make any notes you may like to, I would dearly love to have your input and perspective. Please, please, please... do correct any errors I may have made!
Jen x.

Accordingly as instructed he took up the pencil and sketched a second figure stood next to his own form and also added a rough outline of the back of a Range Rover parked next to them. He added:

Jenny, My beloved daughter Abigail should be stood next to me on the front cover, along with her Range Rover. She was inspirational in the original idea.
Jim

He found the book a fascinating read, he scoffed at more than a few parts of it and had a good laugh at some other bits, there were many sections which he dismissed as being the product of the *'poetic licence'* Jenny had told him that she'd have to exercise at times when writing the story, having not been there to hear the actual conversations that people had between them and only being able to go on what he had imparted to her. He was greatly amused to discover that he'd been known as 'Gruffalo Bill' by some of the guys at The Factry! He could quite easily see how they'd arrived at it as an appropriate nickname for old '*Bill*'!

He thought back to the day that he'd departed from The Folks Factory, for that final time, now with the comforting gap provided by hindsight, it wasn't without a twinge of guilt that he recalled that it had been on the very next morning after his release! What was done was done though, it had seemed to be the only thing he could cope with at the time.

He cast his mind back to when he and Jake had both been sat in his flat eating the breakfast his son had brought over for them, when he'd told his son of his intentions, that he'd decided what he was going to do next.
"Listen Jake, I know you'll most likely kick-off when I ask you this but… Can you get away? Like, now you know, take some time off from work?"
"I've booked a fortnight off already Dad, I did it the day after I found out you were still alive! My bloody head was well and truly mashed you know finding that out! I couldn't think straight, or sleep properly, let alone do my job!"
"Great! Because I want you to run me down to Wales!"
"What? Wales? When?"
"Now, well as soon as we've finished eating!"
"But Dad! You promised to meet up with Jenny and Don!"
"Did I? When was that? It's news to me!"
"You did! And you know it and after all they did for you, don't you think you owe it to them?"

The old man had just huffed! He changed the subject rather than respond,
"Anyway, I hear that Del's already gone home?"
"Oh Del, yeah he left straight after the meal, the meal we all had together to celebrate *with you* after *you* were acquitted, the one that you so bloody rudely ducked out of coming to! He said you'd understand him just buggering off without saying goodbye… a goodbye he added that you'd had your chance to say, but chose to run off from instead! Do you? I mean understand him leaving like that?"
"Yeah… I guess so. He'd said as much to me, that those were his intentions, once he'd done what he came for. What we once had between us is long ago in the past, so he'd moved on, I feel the same too, you have to go forward, looking back's for losers!"
"So me driving you down to Wales…that's how you're planning on going forwards then is it?"
"Damn right son, precisely so!"
"Have you given any thought as to how you're going to live, when you get down there? Are you taking to the wilds again, will it be a case of new place, but same hobo lifestyle?"
"Don't be ridiculous lad. I left you with plenty of money are you going to refuse to fund what I want to do?"

"No Dad! Hey! Don't get your back up! You know I've got plenty of money, I've barely touched the five million you gave me, I'm not extravagant at all, what we've spent has been more than made up again by the interest!

"But Dad, that *is* something I do want to ask you about though, where's the rest of the money? I can't believe you spent all of it on your *little project* at The Factory, did you?"

"Nah, it took a damn big chunk out of it buying and restoring the place, but you're right, after I gave you, Abbie and your mum the five million each, you'll remember Neil wouldn't take it? I put thirty million of it into a trust to run the Factry in perpetuity. I gave away millions upon millions to charities too but there *is* a pot of money stashed away. The details are inside the frame of the picture of the mill, in the office I used when I was playing at being 'Jos'. The accounts in your name as well as mine and since I'm dead it's all yours now and you'll have full access to it. I don't want it, I just need some way to provide me with funding to live off, other than that do whatever you want with it, there was fifty-five million in it when I left, so it will be quite a bit more by now."

"Dad! What the hell am I going to do with it?"

"For fuck's sake lad, use your imagination, give it away for all I care! All I need from you is a bank card and funds in place to meet anything I use it for. It won't be for anything extravagant either, so it doesn't matter what kind it is, debit or credit and it doesn't matter that it's in your name either, give me the PIN, then I can use it to pay for whatever I need and to get cash out if I need to from any hole in the wall. You'll get the statement and you'll be able to see that I'm still alive!"

Jake was looking a little shell-shocked by now as he attempted to take all of this in!

His eventual response ended up being, "I suppose I'd better go and pack a bag then hadn't I?" But before leaving he took out his wallet and pulled out a couple of cards,

"Here take these then, I hardly use the credit card anyway and I can get a duplicate for the other one."

"Thanks son." Jim peered for a moment at one of the small thin, oblong shaped bits of plastic as he held it up inbetween his finger and thumb to look more closely at it. He marvelled at how as if by magic, this little thing could at a stroke, change everything in your life! He remembered how desperate he had once been to receive the odd coin or two as they were gifted into his outstretched hand, or dropped into his begging cup... *one of his Costa Coffee begging cups!* ...how vital those few coins had once been to him... Making the difference between having an empty belly or not.

The card had... MR. J. STANLEY ...proudly embossed in raised letters on it, Jim smiled to himself, thinking, *'yeah that'll do nicely!'* He said as much to Jake,

"It's even got my name on it!"

"Yeah I guess it would have, well near enough eh? No 'O' for Oscar though eh Dad! That's a blessing in itself!" They both laughed.

"Jake, one more thing before you go to get your bag, will you nip down and find Alan Jarvis, if he's not in his office he'll be about somewhere. Tell him I sent you to get the bank details out of the picture frame, it's the one of the Factry from across the canal... Oh you'll need to get a screwdriver from somewhere, I screwed the picture to the wall, to be safe like!"

"What's he going to think when I start unscrewing a picture off the wall in Harry's office?"

"Who gives as shit what he thinks?" They both laughed,

"Tell him I want to see him up here at once too."

"What about the bank details, shall I come up with them?"

"What the hell for, it's you who needs them not me! Just get them, tell him to come up and then go and get packed."

Before he left though Jake had insisted that Jim at the very least, phoned Jenny to thank her for all she'd done in helping secure his release!

"Where's that phone Harry said that he got for you? He told me he'd left you one here in the flat?" Having found it on the sideboard, he'd copied Jenny's number into its contacts,

"Promise me you'll ring her Dad. Do it now! Please! Do it while I'm getting my stuff!" Had been his son's parting shot, as he left the flat promising to be back shortly.

After fiddling for a while with the unfamiliar menu on the little 'Doro' flip-phone Jim managed to get it to find Jenny's number.

He determined to ring her as soon as Jarvis had been dealt with. He was going to skin the bugger alive!

Alan Jarvis when he arrived, was a much humbler man than he had been when Jim had last encountered him, even before Jim could speak he pulled a sheet of paper out from his pocket and placed it down on the table in front of Jim.

"This is the bank statement showing when I repaid the money I stole with all the interest added as well, you'll see it shows as an anonymous donation. After you tore a strip off me I did some really serious soul searching and I want to sincerely apologise to you for what I did, it was unforgiveable and if you feel you need to turn over the details to the police I will not only fully understand but I will also co-operate fully with them in every way I can. I let you down Jim, I let Jos down, I let the Folks Factory down, but most of all I let myself and my family down and I will carry that shame with me for the rest of my life. I let myself get carried away with it all, the bloody stupid lifestyle I felt we just *had to have*, that was somehow *owed to us*? The cars, the house, the holidays, the school fees... I felt I couldn't live without any of them. When I got so far in over my head I panicked!

"But then afterwards, after we talked, when I looked at all of it in the context of what I discovered you'd put yourself through, looked at it through the eyes of old Bill, that bedraggled old tramp who seemed to have absolutely nothing, but in reality who had millions stashed that he could have accessed at the drop of a hat, at any time... but denied to himself! I was utterly humbled by it Jim, by Bill, by you! You opened my eyes, it was like I'd been blind! I looked around me at the vision you had in creating all of this, right from the outset, all of it entirely for the benefit of others, others who were less fortunate and had fallen upon hard times, helping those in need and all the time you were doing it, you shied away from taking any credit for it, hid behind pretences... I well, I..."
Jim held up a hand to say... stop!

"Bloody hell Alan, that was quite a speech! I'm glad you've paid back the money, it wasn't that it mattered to me, a drop in the ocean really, it was that it was just *so* bloody wrong of you. Easy

for me to say? I guess, whatever... I did have every intention of handing you over until a few minutes ago, but if you promise me one thing now, I'm prepared to forget about everything." The relief on the guy's face was immense, a tear rolled down his cheek as he said...
"Anything, I'll do anything you ask! I swear to you that I will!"
"All I want from you Alan, is a commitment that you will devote yourself to keeping the place going and work your rocks off to make the housing projects a success."
"I will... Is that all you want from me? Really? Oh God, thank you Jim! Thank you, I give you my word that I will."
They shook hands and Alan Jarvis left with a feeling of lightness and a hope in his heart that he hadn't felt in a very long time.

Jim smiled to himself at the outcome of his meeting as he dialled Jenny's number. He was still on the phone talking to her an hour later when Jake had returned!

Jake had brought a spare suitcase with him and between them they packed into it all the spare clothes that had been provided for Jim and been left in the flat's bedroom drawers and wardrobe along with the toiletries they'd also provided. Jake had raised an eyebrow when they were ready to leave, as Jim had pulled his dirty old rucksack and old coat out of the closet, saying... "I'm not going anywhere without these!" Stopping and going back to take off the peg on the wall... and proudly holding in his hand... his filthy old baseball cap.
"Recognise this lad?" He laughed as he followed Jake out into the corridor!
"I never really understood until now, why I took the trouble to go and get this hat to take with me, but I realise now that it was because it was yours Jake! It was like I'd still have a tiny piece of you with me..."
Jake laughed, as his Dad held the cap in his hands, "You've made a fuckin' mess of it Dad! Look at the state of it!"
They both laughed as he placed the hat back onto his head.

It was with a twinge of regret and a fleeting dash of uncertainty that Jim pulled shut the door to *his flat* as he stood, ready to wheel his suitcase off down the corridor... He locked the door and handed the keys to Jake,
"Give these back to Harry for me, will you?"

He knew that he was also closing a door on an opportunity too, walking away from a possible future, a comfortable and known quantity of a future, one he could share with people he knew, or in the case of Harry even regarded as a friend. That was what life was though, wasn't it? It was a series of the decisions, of compromises, it was composed of all the choices we make, each one effectively creating a new crossroads, only they were crossroads each with a myriad of different directions to go in rather than simply four! Each choice of travel heading off towards somewhere different, the path chosen changing the future for the traveller, leading to somewhere new but equally so, leaving other places and possibilities behind.

Coming out of the doors once on the ground level, pulling his suitcase behind him onto the car park Jim's face had lit up when he saw his gleaming old Alvis parked up there waiting for them! His face was transformed into an expression quite unfamiliar for it, one that it hadn't had to pull itself into for quite some time! A wide smile that blossomed into a mighty grin! He walked over and laid a hand on the glorious black curve of the front wing.
"Oh well done son! Well done!"

Jim's days were spent pleasantly enough now living in the remote, rented cottage, it was situated a quarter of a mile or so up from the wild coastline of the Llŷn peninsular where he had chosen to settle, a couple of miles out of Aberdaron. He'd made the decision after a couple of days spent in Llandudno with Jake combing through the offerings of the estate and letting agents, and then scouring for more on his son's laptop. They had eventually come across the cottage and driven down the sixty-odd miles to view it.

Jim soon fell in love with the place after he had got over his first unfavourable impression as they pulled up at the bottom of the narrow lane that led off the country road they had turned off a quarter of a mile back up the hill. They had parked alongside the letting agent's car and were at the back of the house and a little above it, the rear elevation of the house being cut into the hillside. The key the agent had was for the front door so once they had walked around to what was clearly the front of the house, everything changed! The view over the bay was stunning and from this angle the cottage looked picturesque as it nestled into the hillside.

Inside it was cosy, with low ceilings but extremely well appointed, clearly it had been the subject of an extensive renovation which the agent happily babbled-on about. At one side of the building it was evident, at least on the inside that it had been extended, doubling its original size. Jake called through from the next room,
"Dad, come and see this, it's a clincher! I'd already spotted it on the pictures they had online, I knew you'd missed seeing it, so I left it to be a surprise!" Jim went through and as he entered the room, his son went…
"Da-da-d-da-da-da DA!" And flourished his hands towards the ancient upright piano that was nestling against one wall!
"Oh yes! "The agent had enthused, "When the owner was living here, he bought the piano after he had the extension added, it's very old apparently, early 1900's he told me. He had it completely re-strung too and he kept it regularly tuned as well, do you play?"

It was *the clincher* as Jake had put it, although the setting was just perfect anyway and exactly what he had been seeking! Duly satisfied that the cottage would meet his needs and after telephoning the agent and agreeing to lease it, Jim had bid farewell to Jake and booked himself in at a local B&B while he waited for the cottage to be made ready for him and for all the paperwork to be finalised. The B&B was located right on the seafront in Aberdaron.

Jim placed Jenny's manuscript down on the coffee table next to his chair, the spring sun was bright in the vast blue vault of sky that domed over the cottage, he looked out of the window as he went through to the kitchen to make himself a brew, taking in the vista of the brilliantly sunlit slope of shrub and greenery that ended with the vast sweep of an aquamarine sea beyond it. He'd spent the winter months snug and warm at the cottage inside its thick old walls. Despite his new home being a really old building, it was indeed very well maintained and the extensive modernisation was unobtrusive. The cottage even had an internet connection, not that it was something Jim had used, but it would be handy he guessed when Jake came down.

The peace and quiet, combined with the stunning location and his removal from all that had stressed him previously, was amazingly cathartic for him. He found that he had regained the same peace of mind he had once found when he had lived as the vagrant Bill, but with the comfort now of a lovely home to return to. The piano had been his greatest single salvation though. He spent hour after hour playing it. He'd discovered that the piano stool was jam packed with sheet music and many books of greatly varied music too. He worked his way through many of them, finding some really challenging and testing his skills to the limit. Over time he further honed his skill, bit by bit... He remembered hearing that a famous pianist had once said when he had been asked how he had become so amazingly talented... Practice... practice... practice, then when you've done all that... *you got it*... practice some more!

One thing that the cottage was entirely lacking for however was clocks! The few that there had been scattered about the place when he'd moved in, were now safely tucked away and out of sight in the back of a cupboard. Jim's only means of knowing what time it was being to open up his flip phone. That was it, it was all he needed! He quite simply had no need to know what time it was! He got up when the light crept in through his open curtains at dawn... well if he felt like it, more often of late he would roll over and sleep for a few more hours unless an ache or a pain from some part of his body decided he shouldn't!

When it went dark he'd be sat by the fire or in his bed asleep! What was the point of clocks anyway, other than to enslave us? He remembered a poem he'd written, he couldn't remember it all so he rummaged out his old backpack and plonked it down on the kitchen table. He took everything out of it item by item... there was the empty quarter whisky bottle from his last night at his bivouac... he shivered at the thought of the following mornings events... His water bottle! He shook it, there was a small sloshing noise from within! Without questioning the wisdom of doing so, he unscrewed the top and tipping his head back, poured the contents into his mouth and swallowed the water... Water that *Bill* had filled the bottle with! Discarding to one side the bulk of the rest of the contents, he found his ragged old leather bound handwritten poetry book.

He took out all of the loose pages, setting them aside on the table, as he was aware that the poem he was seeking had been written onto a page in the book. He smiled when he found it, yes this was the one, he'd called it 'Edelweiss'. As he read it he was taken aback by the prescient nature of the words he'd written, written so many years ago, before Jake or Abbie had been born. Even before his building business had started to take off. He felt the sentiment contained within the words so strongly, here he was now… having attained his very own rocky paradise! A place where the clocks no longer held him in their slavery!

Edelweiss

Siren memories come from afar
As twinkling jewel of distant star
The windswept rush on mountain top
With eagle's view o'er craggy drop
The hillside clad in purple heather
Changing colour with the weather
The silver cascade mountain stream
Then fade as waking does a dream
I prowl and pace as in my cage
I futilely strive not to rage

Wondering if this humdrum life
Is worth the trouble and the strife
Selling my soul to get the cash
To trade for all the worthless trash
That we are brainwashed into thinking
Will make us happy in this stinking
Cess-pit world we have created
That leaves us spiritually un-sated

Why do I in my prison stay?
Battering my wings day after day
When within the bar's an open door
Through which I could fly and soar

What is it keeps me in this hole
Squandering my life till I am old?
Is it habit guilt or fear
The needs of others I hold dear?
Or that I've simply not got the guts
To get myself out of the ruts
I've worn so deep into my fabric
Where joy can only show as manic
Bouts that alleviate the feeling
Of depression that has me reeling
Longing to pack and somewhere go
Where nobody will want to know
How I am or what's to do?
But leave me in my pain to stew
So that I can just exist
With no more pressure to persist
In vainly others trying to please
But be alone at peace at ease

Wandering some ancient highway
Where will neither watch nor clock say
When to get up eat and sleep
In its clockwork slavery keep
Rise with birds and morning sun
Let whatever maybe come
Feel the kiss of gentle rain
Wash away some of the pain

Travel far and with each stride
Still the turmoil deep inside
So that painful memories pass
With the whispers in the grass
Safe in my rocky paradise
New hope may grow like edelweiss.

He sighed, sat back in the chair and pondered once again about his poetry. Whenever he went back to read any of it, he often had the feeling that it couldn't be anything that he had written himself, so removed as they often were from the way he spoke or wrote things down normally. He found many of the ideas they contained to be way too profound to be anything that he could have come up with too! He was always grateful for them though, he imagined that they had maybe come from someone else, from another dimension, an alternative reality, where an alternative Jim resided perhaps? Or from a part of him, buried deep within his mind that was normally inaccessible to him maybe, but belonged to his shadow self? Or perhaps they just came from his shadow, from *The* Shadow?

All this pondering had let sleep creep up on him, he felt its embrace gently closing his eyes and surrendered willingly in the still and silent warmth of the cottage..

The entire cottage was heated throughout by a state-of-the-art ground source heat pump that somehow warmed the stone floors, in addition there was a large fireplace fitted with a modern log burner and just outside the backdoor there was an appropriately sized log store. All of this made his home a very comfortable place to live, he often thought of it as being not dissimilar to a Hobbit hole!

After he woke and was sat back by the window with a fresh mug of tea, Jim let the manuscript lie for a while as he remembered his trip down to Llandudno with Jake. It had been a natural enough choice of towns to head to in order to carry out his search for somewhere to rent, suitably located as it was, but there was also an element of attempting to seek some closure in his choice. He was aware that it would be painful, returning to the last place he'd been with Abbie, where he'd spent that last day she'd been here with him in the flesh… But it also felt somehow that it would be for the best for some intangible reason.

The day spent there with Jake had turned out to be unremarkable, the weather wasn't that good and although he had Jake for company it was as if it was a different place altogether.

As they strolled along the promenade he couldn't help thinking about how the kids had been running around on this very pavement the last time he was here, Abbie's two girls, Lucy and Fiona, it came as a shock to him as he remembered the Leukaemia that Lucy had been diagnosed with. Randomly as far as Jake was concerned, he'd blurted out,

"How's little Lucy, did she get past the Leukaemia, did she survive it? Is she still alive?"
"Yeah, she's fine now Dad, although she's not so little anymore! Are you sure you don't want to see them, see my kids too?"
"No son, I've thought this through very carefully and this is the path I want to travel now. I've been out of their lives for so long, I think it's best left that way."

Back when they'd been leaving The Factry, after they'd put the suitcases in the boot, Jake had offered the keys for the Alvis to him, but he'd declined.
"I think it's probably for the best if you drive lad, it's been a long time since I was behind the wheel, besides I haven't got a licence anymore, never mind insurance… seeing as I'm deceased!"

So it was with Jake driving that they set off for what Jim believed would be the last time ever that he departed from his home town. They journeyed in silence for the first dozen or so miles, Jake sensing from his Dad's silence that there was something going on with him, after all he was leaving everything he knew behind. It was eventually Jim who broke the silence,
"So Jake, how is it that you've got the Alvis?"
"She's yours whenever you want her back, you know that right?"
"Like I said, I don't even have a drivers licence! What would I do with her? You didn't answer my question."
"Oh right, yeah well the thing was, I got this text message from Martin, a proper odd message it was too… from your guy, the car man?!"
"I know who you mean,"
"So I rang him and he told me that Neil had asked him to sell your entire car collection! This was like only about three years after you'd gone AWOL. So I rang Neil right away and asked him if it was true and when he admitted that it was, I asked him what the hell he thought he was playing at! I told him that he'd no right to do that. He just told me in no uncertain terms to f-off! '*So sue me!*' I think he said. So I shot round there Dad! I was fuckin' fuming by the time I got over there… Oh I didn't say that Neil had moved into your house, or did I? He didn't stay long like but… Did you know? Anyway, he had. I was like screaming at him, '*Why? What's this about? Where's the need? The garage has room for another six cars, plus they're not even yours to sell, you've no bloody right to do anything with them!*' But you know

what he can be like! What a bastard he is when he wants to be! He just sneered at me and said, '*you can have half the money I get for them, if that's what's upsetting you!*' Martin was there and he tried to calm things down, but I was furious, beside myself! I really lost it, I'm not like that Dad, you know me, I'm placid to the point of being a wimp!"

"You're no wimp son and your brother's a fucking bully, he always was and you were correct too, he had no right whatsoever to sell my cars, well not until he'd had me declared dead at least. But if that's what happened, then how is it we're driving along in the Alvis right now?"
"Oh well, thing is. Like I said, I *totally lost it* Dad, I went raving ape shit! '*You're not selling his fucking Alvis!*' I screamed into his face, '*you can steal the others and sell them off like the common thief that you are and you can keep all of your ill-gotten gains, but I'm keeping the Alvis for when my Dad comes home. You're not fucking having that one, I'm having her!*'

Amazingly he just backed down! '*You can take the fucking old piece of junk if you want it, what do I care? But you're completely fucking delusional if you think the old cunt's ever coming back*!' That was all he said. So I got in her, drove her out of the garage... I couldn't change gear though and stopped on the road outside. Thankfully Martin came out and offered to drive me home in her!

"I've not driven her that much since really, but I've had Martin take her out for a good run now and then and he's kept her in top condition. He's very fond of the old girl himself."
"And you wonder why I don't want anyone other than you to know I'm not dead? Do you have any idea what prompted him to want to sell all the cars, it's not like he needed the money?"
"Fuck knows Dad, I think it was most likely just out of spite? The company's been in a bit of a mess since you left, he thinks he's so clever but he constantly rubs people up the wrong way, you've lost a lot of business because of him."
"I've lost now't! It's nothing to do with me lad, I'm a ghost! But I am so pleased that you held onto the old girl. It's funny really, you know if I'd had to pick just one single car out of them all, it would always have been this one. The others were great, I mean who wouldn't want an E-Type Jag, a Ferrari or a TR6? But in the

end they were just silly toys, indulgences, whereas this car is something else... That's the greatest thing for me though, that you feel that way too."
"Oh I do love her Dad! But she's a bloody handful!"
"Like any worthwhile female!" They both laughed at that.
"Yeah for sure! But 1950's technology is something of a shock when you normally drive a modern Hybrid! Seventy years of development and refinements aren't to be sniffed at! It took me best part of a year to be able to change into first and second gear without grinding the cogs, Martin nearly gave up on me! And around town... well! She's real *heavy man*! On a run like this though she's in her element isn't she?"
Jim had just nodded as the countryside continued to flash past outside their windows...

Jim woke up, he hadn't felt the sleepiness creeping up on him. He shivered a little as he yawned, the sun had gone behind a bank of cloud that was advancing up and over the sky from the west, a change on the way he thought, there was still a chill to the early spring air yet. The tiredness was something he'd become increasingly aware of as he ventured out and about outside into the countryside around the cottage. There were endless walks to be taken along the coastal paths but the one that took him down to the beach was his favourite. He could sit for hours on the shore listening to the incessant rolling in and out of the breakers, then the sloshing and sucking of the waves as they determinedly sought to tear away the land, hurling themselves at the rocks that kept the mighty sea at bay, he loved watching their unending and ever patient persistence in pursuing their task, as all the while overhead the gulls wheeled and cawed...

He also loved to sit with the wind beating directly into his face, his long grey and white hair streaming out behind his head from under his cap, his thick beard combed neatly back by the cool fingers of the breeze. He had regained a couple of stones in weight since his return from vagrancy, not that he ever weighed himself, but he could feel his bones had a bit more meat covering them these days, he remained lean however and was more stooped now as he battled against gravity to get back up the hill to his cottage, leaning ever more onto his stout walking stick. He'd wondered to himself on that morning on his way back up how many more times he would be able to make the climb...

He knew perfectly well that he should by now have registered with a local doctor, how that would go though in reality he was a little uncertain, him being *deceased* at least according to James Stanley's NHS records! Harry had been great though in arranging for his prescription drugs, or rather the ones prescribed for 'Bill', to be posted down to him every few months. He'd made his peace with Harry in a long phone call very early on in his self-imposed exile.

For all that he was now living comfortably enough, he was aware that all was not well, he still had the pains in his chest and some weakness in his limbs on his left side, although that had improved a little. Not smoking anymore and the abundance of fresh air from the sea had helped with his breathing too, plus he ate well now, Nessie saw to that when he rang his order through to her! He did however maintain his regulated consumption of whisky, the only difference now being that a rather nice single malt had replaced the gut-rot he'd previously metered out using the quarter bottles in his incarnation as Bill!

He lit the fire that he'd laid earlier on in the log burner, before his morning walk and settled down into the chair next to it, the wood crackled and burned as the flames licked eagerly over the kindling sticks and up over the logs. He picked up the binder and put his specs back on…

He'd had the book a week or two now and was on the last chapters, which he was finding fascinating as they were new to him as they were recounting events that had taken place after he had left for Wales with Jake in the Alvis.

He was particularly fascinated to read that the police had finally apprehended the actual perpetrators of the crime for which he had been wrongly imprisoned awaiting trial, the horrible rape and murder of poor little Natalie. The matter had finally come to a very abrupt end, even though newly promoted, Detective Inspector Don Willis was already closing in on them. One of the boys, unable to cope any longer with the guilt and remorse he felt for not preventing what had happened to the student, a lad called Matty… it had eventually emerged that his only part in the attack had been in restraining her, in holding her down… when he had tried to hang himself, only to make a botched job of it and to be saved by his horrified mother, to who he then confessed all! Despite having burns and abrasions to his neck she had marched him straight into the police station where he had made a full confession and given up all of the others who had been involved.

Despite not one of them admitting to their horrific deeds, the evidence that Don and Jenny had already gathered had tied them to the crime. They were duly handed down the harshest of sentences possible, however Matthew Drury the boy who had confessed, was spared prison and given a long community service sentence in acknowledgement of his confession and the remorse he clearly showed for his part in the crime. Tragically his drowned body was found in the canal a week after his sentencing, on the stretch where Natalie's body had been found. He left a suicide note in amongst the flowers and tributes to Natalie saying he was sorry, but he couldn't live with the shame of what he had done.

He read with no small amount of pleasure that the cop Steadman had also been sentenced to a spell at Her Majesty's pleasure for his crimes! And also that Chief Inspector Sally Pembrose had been investigated and subsequently dismissed from the force for gross misconduct.
There was a little justice in the world after all he mused!

It was with mixed feelings that he read about his eldest son Neil being jailed for fraud, tax evasion and money laundering. It was what he deserved, that much he didn't doubt for a moment and no doubt what they'd got him on had only been the tip of the iceberg of his real criminal enterprises. Regardless of what he had done though, this was the man who had once been the little lad who he'd bounced on his knee and taken on so many family holidays... He was his own flesh and blood, should he feel some pity for him? He found he had none, the only thought he did have was an unpalatable one, one he immediately felt ashamed for thinking...Why the hell was Neil still alive when Abbie wasn't? That was one piece of injustice that no one would ever be able to explain to him.

This man who was now in jail was nothing to him any longer, he was a complete stranger to him, he had been even before he'd gone AWOL, as Jake had put it! He'd always seemed to be so over-eager to replace his father, it must have been some sort of compulsion that drove him he guessed? As his father, was it his fault the fella had turned out this way? Was he somehow to blame, was his mother? Had they failed him in the manner in which they'd raised him? How could anyone know the answer to such a question? Jake had turned out just fine after all. He pondered for a moment what Ruth, his mother must think about her firstborn son today!

He walked down to Aberdaron to post the book back to Jenny in the envelope she'd sent with it, it was now full of notes that he'd made which he hoped she'd find helpful. A couple of days later she phoned him and thanked him, promising to send a proof copy to him of the final draft before she published.

Spring turned into summer as it invariably does and Jim was happy to be one of those who was here to witness the annual transformation that crept over the countryside all around him as he settled more and more into his new lifestyle, one of a retreat not dissimilar to the ones he had been on when he was grappling with hanging-in-there to his old life. Looking back now he realised that we all have a point at which we can take no more, an *elastic limit* he smiled as he recalled his Physics teacher explaining that concept in relation to any given material's physical strength. We were similarly tested by the slings and arrows that came our way during our lives, we bent we stretched, we tried to deal as best we could with whatever was flung at us but ultimately for all but a very tiny number of us, unless we were spared such brutal testing…
We broke…
We snapped…
Something gave way eventually!
He supposed some never exceeded their own *elastic limit*, they were the lucky ones.
But once we snapped, the only difference after that was whether it was total or partial, followed on by whether it was recoverable from or not and in what form of altered state of existence thereinafter our life would be lived.

The years that Jim had manifested in his existence as 'Bill' were becoming somewhat romanticised for him by his memory now, as the days of his new life rolled seamlessly by, the freedom he'd had, the state of oblivion that he had mostly enjoyed in the mindless, mindful state in which he had passed the days had great appeal to him once more. Yes, for sure he was at peace now with everything, with himself too, he felt that his life had turned full circle from the days of childhood, his first childhood as he now thought of it… turning into the days of what he felt were the days of his final childhood, a time when he had unburdened himself from all and everything that there was that had ever troubled him.

He was happy and content living the life of a hermit, well virtually a hermit that is, as he spoke to the people who called round for whatever reason they had to do so and those who he was acquainted with when he saw them in passing, but he visited no one and no one visited him, not in a regular sense at least. Jake came down twice during that summer and he spoke to Harry now and then on the phone.

Jake had brought down an old PC of his and in a wave of enthusiasm, not long after arriving he had gone about setting it up for his Dad, "I remembered that there was broadband already laid on here Dad, from when we first looked at the place, so I rummaged through the paperwork I had and I've sorted it out for you. It's back on and in a few minutes… Eh voila!" He had exclaimed as the monitor sprang into life, a few minutes later he had the thing up and running!

He went on to set up a new Gmail account for Jim and accessed the Facebook account that Abbie had set up for him, "You'll be able to log in and see what the family are up to, just don't comment or *like* anything you see eh? That really would put the cat amongst the pigeons eh?"

"Can't other people see that my account is active though?"
"Yeah well, let's hope no one notices then!"

Facebook hadn't turned out to be something he'd used that much after the initial curiosity had worn off, he'd used it to look at things his family posted, but he felt a bit like he was spying on them? He'd opened a new account though and used it to join other groups that interested him, ones about old cars, about nature, Buddhism and politics… although he quickly stopped looking at the latter!

It was around September that Jenny phoned and asked if she could bring the final proof of the book down for him to approve, it was a long drive for her, but she insisted that she wanted to come. In the end he agreed and gave her the details of the B&B he'd used when he first came down, he did have a spare room but wasn't inclined to offer it to her, he felt a little twinge of guilt for being selfish but it never occurred to him for a second, to change his mind about not inviting her to stay at the cottage!

When she texted him a few days later to say that she'd arrived in Aberdaron, he walked down to meet her. They met in one of the pubs there, having agreed to have lunch together.

When he walked in, she saw him and got up to greet him, she'd changed since he first met her, she had hair now! She was sporting a large and very attractive afro which was tamed by a colourful headband, she had the same wide, disarming smile though as she held her hand out to him,
"Hiya Jim! Oh my you're looking good! Quite a different person today, more of a rock star look about you than the scruffy old tramp vibe you had goin'for ya back when I first interviewed you!" He shook hands with her and then he gently lifted her left hand up and as he did she twiddled her fingers for him showing off the ring on her third finger…
"What's this I see then, little Jenny wren? That looks very new and sparkly! So who's the lucky man, not that old Harry surely?" She knew from his chuckling that he was only kidding with her,
"Yes indeed! I'm lucky too though, he's a lovely man!"
"Well there's no accounting for taste my dear and after all they do say that love is blind! Just as well for Harry eh? Nah… I'm only kidding, he's a great guy and I owe him a lot, I never really thanked him, well not in any adequate sort of way at least, will you pass that on to him for me please, tell him how much I appreciate everything he did for me. I don't think I'd be here at all today if it wasn't for him."
"Of course I will, oh and he sends his best wishes too, he insisted that I tell you that. We'd been hoping that he'd be able to make it down with me, turn the trip it into a little jolly together but he's up to his eyes at the moment, well… even more than usual! Oh

and don't let me forget, there's a parcel for you in my car, he said you'd know what it is? He said it'd just save him posting it this month?"
"Oh right thanks, it'll just be my meds, I've not registered here… it's all a bit complicated…"

Changing the subject he said, "I do like your hair, I mean you looked amazing with your head close-shaved like, I thought you were very brave too… It really suited you… I mean this does too like… Your hair grows quick doesn't it?" She was laughing as his intended compliment became so tangled-up that he tripped over it!
"Yeah man, amazing how quick it grows… as you pulls it outta the bag it come in! It's a wig Jim! One day I may tell you all about black girls and their hair… It's way too long a story though for today! You can ask Harry next time you see him, he's slowly beginning to get the drift!"

Jim got them a drink each from the bar and picked-up a couple of menus. While he savoured a pint of Double Dragon and Jenny sipped at her white wine and lemonade, they continued to chat until a young lad, who introduced himself as 'Ewan,' came over and took their order. While they waited for their food, Jenny showed him the proof copy of her book.

As he held the paperback in his hands he was a little taken aback by how expertly the artist had created the cover picture, it had perfectly captured the atmosphere of that day so very long ago. Central to the painting was the looming bulk of the old factory, the name, bold and clear picked out in the red brickwork, in the foreground was the bulk of the back of a black Range Rover, viewed from behind, with two shadowy figures stood arm in arm next to it, gazing across the canal at the old factory, the edges of the painting faded away to white as they had done into the mist on the day itself.
He turned the book over in his hands and looked at the rear cover which was equally well done, but was presented as a background for the writing and barcode that was always found on the back cover of paperbacks. It showed the building as it was today, on a bright sunny day but with a lone shadowy figure stood to one side, a forlorn and bedraggled old tramp.

"Do you like the design?" Jenny asked eagerly,
"I do, very much. That's a really beautiful piece of artwork Jenny, who did it for you?"
"Open the cover, they're credited in there. They teach art at the college where Natalie went."
Draining his pint, Jim got up to go to the bar,
"Would you like another?" he asked Jenny, although he could see that her glass wasn't even half way down, *'manners maketh man!'* He heard his mum's voice in his ear, reminding him as ever to be polite, to mind his manners! It was anything but unusual for him to hear her words, as he often did, despite the fact that she'd been dead for decades, equally so with his Dad and his ever offered little *pearls of wisdom*, as he'd referred to them, but somehow today his mum's voice seemed to be closer to him than usual, he could almost feel her presence…

He found the same lad who'd taken their order for food was now working behind the bar,
"Jack of all trades eh Ewan? Can I have another one of these please?"
"The Double Dragon wasn't it?"
"Yes, a very nice drop of beer it was too, a Welsh brewery I take it, what with the red dragons and all?"
"Yeah, it comes up from down south aways, the brewery's in a little town just outside of Llanelli called Felinfoel."
"Is it by George! What a co-incidence! My mum's Dad was born in Felinfoel! Tommy Williams he was! The son of Tommy Williams!"
"Well you don't get much Welsher than that!"
He recounted his conversation with Jenny about the beer and its origins, she smiled sweetly but was clearly neither anything like as interested nor impressed by the coincidence as he had been himself.

"There's something I have to ask you Jim, it's all a bit awkward really, the thing is since the book's largely factual, insofar as it's not a completely made up story, although I know I've had to pen the dialogue and create quite a few characters that never actually existed, nevertheless it's fundamentally about you and what you achieved in creating The Folks Factory…"
"I know, although I do like the way you ended it differently with Bill deciding to go off and live in Scotland!"

"Well yes, I needed to do that for your protection, but the legal people have said that they won't allow me to publish without your permission."
"I thought that I'd already given you that? Haven't I?" She rummaged in her briefcase and produced a legal form…
"It's your specific and documented permission they're after!"
"Ah… I see. Hand it over love, I'm happy to sign it for you."
"No, it's for when you've read the book, the final draft and approved it, you can sign it then and post it to me."
"I trust you Jenny, I'm sure it's the same as the draft you sent me, I will read it though, anyway I can always sue you…"
"But read the print that you're signing under today there's…"
She laughed as he totally ignored her,
"Hey Ewan!" Jim called over to the barman,
"Can you come over and witness me signing this please?"
With a puzzled look on his face, Ewan came over and watched as Jim Scrawled…
Where indicated:

x *William Williams*

After lunch she drove them back up to the cottage, he showed her around and then he took her for a stroll down to the beach,
"It's so beautiful Jim, I can see why you moved here. Are you happy now? You seem to be, this place may as well be a million miles away and years apart from when we were sat talking outside the Factry… as you too, also do… I mean, from the person you were then…"
"Aye luv! I were a proper mess for sure back then, weren't'a?"
Bill replied to her, causing her to laugh along with him.

CHAPTER THIRTY-NINE

Summer turned into autumn as it invariably does and Jim remained being happy to be amongst those of us who are still here to bear witness to it. He was yet again here to watch the annual transformations of nature he so lovingly observed as it crept silently across the face of the countryside all around him.

As the season progressed he watched the leaves began to turn on those few trees that were able to grow up in the shelter of the dip in which the cottage sat, where they could withstand the windswept coastal environment. Lower down in the shelter of the nearby inland valleys the woods and copses were putting on their magnificent and amazingly colourful, annual performance in the most multitudinous displays of every imaginable hue of brown, red and gold.

The magnificent and glorious colours of autumn.

The herald's last call out before the onset of the washed-out whites and greys of the winter to come.

Jim had increasingly found comfort in reverting at least in part, to dwelling within the persona of Bill. Bill, he found really liked where he found himself living nowadays and as his persona took over more and more, he had made it even closer to perfection by constructing a shelter very similar to the one where he'd spent so many of his nights in his former days deep in the woods, he used found and scattered bits as he had previously, but this time there was also the addition of salty bits of flotsam harvested from the shore.

As he lay on the ground in his new hideout, not deep in the woods, but in amongst the brambles where a section of stone walling had collapsed, he could hear in place of the sound that had previously provided him with nocturnal company, the motorway's roar, seemingly coming from high up in the treetops, here he had instead the incessant roar and bash of the sea as its waves beat against the land, forever ebbing and flowing, all of these distant sounds carried up to him on the salty sea breeze. He loved reliving the experience, it was greatly improved from the previous version as well, in knowing that he now had the amenity of the comfy, warm cottage a mere twenty paces away whenever he needed anything!

As the days went by he found more and more comfort in re-inhabiting Bill's formerly empty shell, imagining that the feeling was something akin to what a sea creature might have felt if it had been able to retreat once more into the familiar and ever so welcoming coil of their own, once abandoned shell.

Recently feeling the nights starting to turn colder, he had invested in a good quality, outdoor sleeping bag on one of his outings into Abersoch, a trip made on the number 17 bus that ran from outside the post office in Aberdaron. He made the trip quite often and he found a certain pleasure in mingling with the last of the season's tourists, of mixing in with other people and yet still being totally alone. He toyed with the idea of donning his old coat and cap which he normally reserved for his walk down to the beach and sitting down somewhere to beg for coins... but thought better of it.

As he lay that evening on the ground in his den, wrapped-up in the warmth of his newly acquired sleeping bag and under a woollen blanket too, for good measure, he gazed up at the stars above him in the heavens noticing how they had slowly spun around throughout the night on each of the many occasions that he awoke.

The weeks had gone quickly since Jenny's brief visit, the dark nights relentlessly drawing in as daylight became briefer with each passing week, all the more so when his little retreat was under the heavy, rain laden clouds as they so often rolled in off the Irish Sea, as though they were on a heavenly conveyor belt. The ceaseless south-westerly wind, more often than not a gale, bellowed its wrath as it howled around, outside the tiny cottage, born of the mighty ocean that had spawned it a mere eighty miles over open water of sea to the south, as it zealously battered everything before it.

Bill found that he was waking early most days, despite the black cloak of night still being draped over his cottage for so much of the time. The dreams he'd been experiencing on a regular basis were becoming dark, more and more sinister and yet somehow felt strangely familiar, they were exotic and fearful expansions of his memories stirred-up from his past, added to them was a feeling about the way in which he was spending his days of late, as if he was gradually fading from existence as an individual, as if he was becoming completely at one with the wild grandeur of his environment, that in being at peace he was gradually losing his own identity… all of this lulling him back more and more into the old and ever so familiar, stripped down wraith that had been Bill… Was that such a bad thing though he pondered? He decided that probably it wasn't.

It was quiet this morning after the seemingly endless gales of the last few weeks, he'd gone to sleep listening to the familiar sound of sheets of rain being battered against the glass of his bedroom window, driven on by the moaning, whistling howls of yet another furious gale… that had been his tempestuous lullaby last night! It had blown itself out now and in the still quiet of his bedroom he abandoned his attempts at sleeping any longer.

A little while later in the living room, he rattled through the embers in the log burner to expose the glowing red heart they had preserved that was now sucking eagerly at the air it was newly enabled to breathe. It hungrily used it to generate the flicker of a flame that licked hungrily around the fresh kindling he carefully placed onto it, bringing the fire back to life from its slumber.

He carried out his well-practised routine with the coffee machine and sat sipping his coffee next to the re-energised fire, burning merrily now in the log burner with its doors wide open.

True to his re-embodied character he donned his boots and then slipped his shoulders inside Bill's old great coat, he watched in the mirror hung on the wall in the hall by the front door as Bill pulled down on the peak of the 2012 Olympics hat as he put it on his head, over the top off his long and once more wild, silver and grey hair. Picking up his walking stick he headed out into the first light of the day.

It was a crisp morning, the wind having dropped completely, to leave behind in its wake a dead calm, even the waves were only gently lapping at the shore, it was as if the entire bay had

breathed a sigh of relief that the storm had passed... or was it merely holding its breath awaiting the next onslaught?
He strolled along the rocky, shingly beach right down alongside the waves as today they gently licked at the crumbled land, the sea passive as a lamb... for now...

By the time he was heading back up the hill the sun was well up over the headland, climbing its way up into a wonderfully bright blue sky. He paused feeling a little short of breath, his legs seeming heavy as he came to the point at which the track he followed to and from the shore crossed over the coastal path. Remembering that there was a wooden bench a little way further along it, he turned his head towards it, saw it wasn't far and strolled along the path to it. It was one of those that had been put in place as a sort of memorial to someone or other, a once dearly loved and now clearly departed husband in this case he recalled, having previously read the shiny plaque that was screwed to the back of it.

He sat on the bench gazing out to sea, he could easily understand how this spot could have been dear to the old fellow and had then retained a special place in the heart of his wife, now a widow left to sit here without him, to be one of the many people he saw sat alone, folks such as himself. He'd often seen a small bunch of flowers placed on the seat as he passed by on days when he'd felt able to venture further afield and walk along the coast to the headland. He imagined the husband's spectre sat next to him on the seat that was dedicated to him, as his own head rocked gently forward and he felt the sleepiness that had eluded him earlier on that morning before dawn, well-up now to wash up and over him.

Jim found he was stood up! He was standing looking down at his shoes, they were planted firmly onto a pavement, it was a pavement of stone flags that was bright and shiny, slick with moisture. He lifted his gaze to take in the sight of a strange, otherworldly and unfamiliar street! It was night time, everywhere was wet although it wasn't actually raining now, it clearly had been very recently...

A streetlight is shining from somewhere although he doesn't see where it is. It is throwing its sharp, blue-white light around all

over the place, transforming the straight line of the kerbstone into a silver ribbon of shining metal, the light shimmers off wet walls, off everything, the very air glimmers, making everything sparkle, glistening with tiny stars that glint with lines of white energy...
The walls are tall, wet brickwork, wet cobbles, a narrow place squeezed in between the walls...
An alleyway...
'Where am I?' The question in his mind is urgent, panicked...
'Where the fuck is this place?'
'How did I get here?'
'Why is it so dark!'
'Has the streetlight just dimmed?'
'This is a dream!'
'That's what's happening!'
'I'm dreaming!'
'I must be!'
'I have to wake-up!'
'Wake-up! WAKE-UP!!'''

'So it's not a dream then?'
'I'm really here aren't I?'
'If it was a dream I'd be able to wake-up?'
'Wouldn't I?'
'So I must be really standing here!'
'But if I *am* awake, why can't I move my feet?'
'It *has* to be a dream!'
'WAKE-UP!'

'But no, I'm still here!'
'What is this place? Why does it have a familiarity about it...'
'*Fuckin-hell! Oh my God!* I do *know* this place!'
'I know this alleyway!'
'But why am I here?'
'How the hell *can I be* here?'

A terrible feeling of dread comes over him, an awareness that he knows precisely what it is that he will see, if he can only turn his head around and look back at it, if he can somehow find the courage he needs to dare to look behind himself!
'This is the place I was attacked!'

He knows that if he looks behind, if he turns his head, what he will see is a body lying on the ground!
He knows what he will see will be…
His own body lying on the ground….

'This can't be…'
'This can't be happening…'
'I *am* dreaming! This *must* be a dream?'
'Fuck! Fuck! Fuck!' A terrible awareness dawns on him, springing out from the muddle of the fear, denial, confusion and panic that has welled up inside his fevered mind, to his horror what emerges is a singular thought, it is a crystal clear and totally terrifying thought…

'I'm fucking dead!'

'My body is behind me, lying there lifeless on the wet tarmac…'
'I'm a fucking ghost!'
'So this is it! This is what happens to you when you die, is it? Where's that reaper fella then? Where's that bright shining light you're meant to go towards? Where the fuck are all the angels… or even the demons?'
'Nothing?'
'This is it?'
'Nothing?'

'Shit! Is that it?'
'Maybe I have to turn around? Is that it? Do I have to look at my dead body to know that I have truly left it behind, before I can totally accept that I'm dead… Before I can move onto whatever the welcoming committee may turn out to be?'
'Is that the final act we have to make in this world?'

He realises that he is not alone any longer…
'Who's there? Who is it in the shadows? The Reaper?'

Someone places a hand onto his forearm, he feels them give it a gentle squeeze…
Now there is a voice in his ear from very close, he can sense a presence right next to him, a face is close-up next to his, someone is talking to him…

"I say, are you alright old chap?"
The voice seems to be completely out of place somehow? There is something wrong about it? For some reason it seems to him that it should be possessed of that ever so familiar warmth, that soft, warm lilt of Welsh-ness? How was it that had he'd become so accustomed to hearing that in the voices of those he came across? Where was he? What was happening to him?

This was a voice from Scotland, it was a Scottish accent! Was he in Scotland?

Bill mumbled something, a jumble of words, trying to respond to the voice as his senses slowly returned to him, tumbling over themselves as he gradually became aware once more of where he was... he was sat on a bench... as his subconscious mind frantically cleared away the set it had created, furiously packing away the props associated with his troubled dream, scuttling everything away backstage, bundling up the panoply of his fears back into its dark place, buried deep within his mind, behind the curtain, behind the veil...

Clarity once more...

"Yes, yes thanks, I'm fine, I must have fallen asleep... I was just tired. Not been sleeping so good lately, that's all. Nothing to worry about... But thank you!" He beholds a kindly face before him, an old face, with many a line and wrinkle upon it, old like his but clean-shaven unlike his own! There is a mass of wild and curly, pure white hair, bunched out from beneath a black sailor's style hat. The palest of blue and watery eyes peer into his own from beneath wild, white bushy eyebrows to match his hair and all of this atop of a ruddy complexion!
"May I sit down, share your bench with you? Maybe have a wee chat with you?"
"Well it's not my bench, so feel free!"
"No, quite so! If it belonged to anyone I suppose that would be Mrs Algea Morningstar, or her dearly departed husband Clement perhaps? Although of course it states that it was gifted to all of us to make use of! A fascinating surname *Morningstar* don't you think? Most likely a corruption from the German name of Morgenstern, or I suppose it could be said merely a literal translation of the German *morgen und stern*!"

"Eh...what?"

"The plaque..." The man who was now seated alongside of him, tapped a finger onto the gold coloured metal plate fixed to the back of the bench inbetween them.

"Ah right, I'ave noticed that, but I've never bothered to read it, don't tend to bring me reading glasses out wi'me!" *'Why he wondered had he lied so unnecessarily about that?'*

"I've noticed you around, on my travels, when you were too, so to speak... on *your* travels! A-ha, a-ha, a-ha-ha-ha!" The guy had a laugh that could quickly warrant him getting a punch in the gob Bill mused!

"You live in the cottage up the hill there?" In response to Bill's nod he went on,

"Bwthyn yn y Bryn! I knew the old fellow who lived there, Gwilym Williams, a grand old chap he was, he was well into his nineties when he died. His kin sold the house, they live down south somewhere, in Swansea I think it is, they had no use for it. Sad really, all in all, after so many generations of the same family had lived there, right back to the time when it was built. Built by them, the Williams family it was, back then, it would be the last century, well before... Erm...

"It was bought by an American, an author I hear tell he was! He spent a fortune on it, having it all renovated ye ken? He had plans for a garage too, and extra rooms, they were all to be carved-out into the hillside and to be buried back underneath it all so as you'd never have known any of it was there, all of it out of sight, so no one would have even noticed them, not that anyone would have cared anyway! Ah, but then there was the planners... ah well, never mind. He became disheartened by it all I think, the author chappie, he lives in New York, this was meant to be somewhere else for him to come and write... I'm sorry I get carried away so easily! It goes with the job I suppose?

"I think he fancied that he had his ancestral roots here in Wales? So many of them do don't they? Colonials that is..."

Bill turned his head and looked into the face of this unwelcome interloper who had come along and burst in on his peace and quiet... Not that the bloody dream he'd been having had been anything remotely peaceful! The expression the vicar beheld on the face of his erstwhile companion was a mixture of something inbetween a sneer and a frown, wrapped in an aggressive look of horrified disbelief?

"Y'don't say?" He scoffed dismissively, as he noticed the dog collar... '*A fucking vicar!*' He thought! '*Fabulous!*'
"So, what do I call ya? Reverend, rev, minister, vicar, father, yer 'oliness? Eh?" A slight look of surprise danced over the man's face as he laughed...
"A-ha, a-ha, a-ha-ha-ha!" adding,
"Ah... I see we have a sceptic, a man who isnae a fan of The Church or mebbe it's only its clergy y'have nae got a liking for? Well now, in answer to your question though, most people just call me Al!" Bill chuckled to himself, the fucker had more or less said '*you can call me Al*', his ever-so-fucking-witty little party piece no doubt... and, he'd used it to leave his question unanswered, Bill noted.

To Bill's still slightly fuddled mind the clown who he had sat next to him was a *vicar* and that was that! Vicar was an adequate enough title for him, all he needed was a big red nose and an equally big and stupid painted smile, add to that his already frizzy white hair... maybe change the hat?... Eh voila! The very Reverend Bozo Bongo!

The guy was still talking... bla, bla, bla...' some rich guy who'd bought the house'... bla, bla, bla...
Not listening or joining the conversation Bill went off onto a different tack, butting in on the diatribe...

"So would that be Al for Alan, Al for alphonso, or Alec, Albert, Alvin, Alfred or maybe Ali? Would it be Ali Bongo mebbe?" The vicar stopped in mid flow, merely laughed,
"A-ha, a-ha, a-ha-ha-ha...No... no, it's no' that..."
"Howsabout The Vicar of Bray then? Y'laugh's like a feckin' donkey's after all!"
"A-ha, a-ha, a-oh my... Very clever! You're surely a fellow who speaks his mind are y'no'! An'yer no concerned particularly as to whether or no a body takes any offence either! Very clever linking the donkey to a Vicar by its braying! A regular wit it is that I meet this fine day! But I do have to insist that I hav'na any contortion in ma principles nor in ma beliefs unlike the vicar to whom you refer!"

Bill laughed, the strain of this nowadays, prolonged and unfamiliar vocal process setting him off coughing again... as it ever would on such rare occasions! *'Right, so he thinks he's a proper clever old cunt does he?'* He thought and to try and outdo the vicar he made an attempt at being an *even-cleverer-old-cunt!* He said,

"He looks around, around,
He sees angels in the architecture,
Spinning in infinity,
He says, *Amen and Hallelujah!*"

"A-ha, a-ha, a-ha-ha-ha… well now, if you're no in need of a bodyguard, I could try to be a stand-in for a long lost pal y'might have? *I can call you Betty too…* well if you'd like me to, but I'd much rather be knowing y'real name! A-ha, a-ha, a-ha-ha-ha…"

"So, firstly allow me to introduce myself to you in a proper manner, The Reverend Aloysius Fothergill at your service Sir!"
He reached out his hand which Bill took to shake, anticipating something akin to a limp, dead fish to be placed into his hand, but pleasantly surprised when the old guy had a firm grip… well for a clown! …and he appreciated that he'd held back from using his palm-held-shocker or squirting him in the face from a buttonhole too!

He replied thinking as he did so… *This'll set the old bugger off… matching my surname to the guy who previously lived in the cottage!*
"Bill Williams, I guess I'm meant to say, pleased to meet you?"
The vicar responded as predicted! Bill zoned out…

Eventually the verbose vicar had excused himself, maybe the lack of even a grunted response finally registering on him?
"So you're sure that you're alright? You do look a wee bit better than when I found ya, that's for sure, but ya still dinna look particularly well. Have y'seen a doctor here, I mean since y'moved to these parts? If no, I think that y'should."
"Well thanks for your opinion, but yer't wrong type of doctor eh? Thing is I'm past me expiry date, we're not meant to go on and on forever are we? What's it say in ya book Rev? Three score year and ten? Well I'm out of date then Vicar!"

"Well aye, but then there was Methuselah too in the bible? There's a sayin' God helps them as helps themselves, that springs to my mind too!"
"Thing is I've outlived me usefulness, back in Victorian times, I'd been dead twenty year gone! Aye an'there's another sayin' springs to my mind... God 'elps them as minds their own business!"

The Vicar who was now standing, looking down on his grumpy companion, just smiled at the intransigence of the old fellow, "Aye well I'll point m'nosey-ol'beak thataway and wend off in a southerly direction! I'll bid y'good day ma friend."

Turning on his heel he headed off along the coastal path, in the direction of the headland. Some of his waffle had been quite interesting, well the bits when Bill had actually been listening enough to remember any of it! He was a little unsure if the old guy had been simply telling him *about* an old church, the one that he was already familiar with, it being right on the coast bordering the beach in Aberdaron, or if he was saying he was actually the vicar there. From what he could recall from his trips into Aberdaron, the church was really ancient, it certainly looked very old from the outside at least, hearing the name Saint Hywn's was what had caught his attention for a moment or two! He determined to give the place a proper visit on his next trip, his interest having been piqued.

As he resumed his battle with gravity heading uphill along the path to the cottage, images from the disturbing dream he'd had when he fell asleep on the bench kept washing back into his mind... The embarrassing thought... 'I unintentionally *fell asleep* on a bench!' Came to him, the very thought of that was disturbing enough in itself! The dream though had seemed so lifelike, no it was far worse than *seeming* like anything, it had *felt* totally real, he still felt a giddying sense of disorientation even now and it must have been at least an hour ago since he'd fallen asleep...

What did it mean? Why should thoughts about that incident spring so aggressively up from his subconscious mind, it was an event that had happened so long ago too, so why now? He'd never had a dream about it before, well not one as vivid and all-encompassing as this had been, he'd truly believed that he was standing in that alleyway, that he was back there at that moment!

Dreams were just that, he told himself, bloody nonsense running on the empty screen of the sleeping mind, when there's no input from outside coming in, all of it down to one of the unoccupied filing clerks in the library of his mind who was probably lost somewhere, someplace where they were rummaging through rooms full of incorrectly filed stuff, obscure thoughts and experiences just shoved-in and the door shut on them, so it was most likely random? He should just let it go, he told himself even as he knew damn well that he would be incapable of any such thing.

Having made it to the cottage, he closed the front door behind him and let his heavy old coat slip off his shoulders, shoved it carelessly onto a peg and flipped his cap over the hump where it was bunched-up. His walk had not given him any sort of a boost today, normally he'd come back feeling invigorated after his brush with the wild expanse of nature, but today it felt more like he'd had a brush with death!

He threw some more logs into the fire and went to make a brew. Returning with his tin mug of tea, he shut the doors on the log burner and sank wearily into his chair. He was still unsettled by the dream…*'let it go* he told himself, *'it doesn't mean anything*!' But it was like a scab he couldn't resist scratching at…

Draining the last of his tea, he set the mug down, the warmth of the fire now filling the room combined with the weariness he still felt and he soon fell asleep again.

He awoke with a shiver, a chill had descended on the room, the fire had burnt itself right down to nothing, it was dark. He closed his eyes and drifted off again…

When he woke the next time it was with a start! The room was in total darkness, he could see nothing but blackness. His heart froze as a voice sounded out, it was a deep, soft voice and yet also disturbingly unpleasant and resonant…

"Are you ready yet?" It asked. He looked around desperately trying to find something, someone that he could see, anything he could focus his blinking eyes upon…

"It's been a very, very long time now, are you ready yet, are you finally ready to turnaround? Are you ready to face what you will see there?"

"Who are you?"
"Where am I?"
"What the fuck do you want with me?"

"Really? All that palaver, all of that blather all over again? It gets so tiresome, bla-bla--bla—-bla—-bla… You have no fucking idea how tiresome it becomes!"

This time he awoke with a sudden start! He gasped and sat upright as he took in the flickering glow of the fire, which was in fact still burning merrily, the familiar outlines of the furniture in the room still showing clearly enough in the dim light of dusk leaking in through the window.

The sound of *that voice* was still ringing in his ears…
'I must be losing it! I'm finally losing my mind…' he speculated, what other explanation could there be?

That he had died in that alley way all those years ago?

That everything that had happened to him since that moment in time, from that one recalled frame of a captured memory that he had retained of it… his sideways view of perpendicular wet tarmac, his cold cheek laying on it, the light bouncing off it…

Could everything he had experienced since that singular moment have existed only in his mind? Was it possible that it had all been nothing more than an illusion?

Was the cottage an illusion?
Was he merely imagining sitting here?

Ridiculous! He thought as he slumped back into the chair…

Why?

Why is it ridiculous?

What is perception anyway, what is reality?
Is anything *real*?
Aren't we told that *'we'* what we perceive to be *'ourselves'*, exist only as a loop of neurons chasing themselves around and around within a neural network that is constructed inside the biological computer that we have decided to call 'our brain'... that we are merely a ghost in the matrix, yes? The expansion and evolution of the same brains that we find in animals, with whom we share so many physiological characteristics, they merely lack this single loop of self-awareness in their brains that we have named *consciousness*.

After all the entire outside world is only something we can ever *perceive to exist* through interpreting the input from our external sensory organs, they pass on this limited and incomplete data that they have acquired along nerves into our... what shall we call it? Our *mind*? Yes that fits the bill. So we can only ever *'imagine'* what is out there. Build-up a picture from the somewhat suspect data we gather, from our far from perfect sensory organs.

Now, consider that a little further, our eyes see only a limited range from the total spectrum of energy that we call light, our ears can 'hear' only a limited range from all the frequencies available, so all that we actually have arriving at the interface with our brain is a series of electrical impulses, transmitted along our nerves, so it's very much akin to the signal a radio receives and in a similar manner to what the radio set does with that signal, our brain decodes the signal from the nerves electrical impulses, to create for us a perception of reality! Or more precisely *our* perception of reality, our very own and quite unique understanding of what is actually out there. But do we decipher that input accurately though? How can we know?

The internal counter to his mental debate asks... okay, so I get all that but everyone else is busy doing the same thing aren't they? Doing all of that too, perceiving everything in a similar

enough way to the way in which we do, so we can know from that, what reality is, can't we?
Does anyone else exist though?
Consider this, if you were a disembodied brain, or if you had no brain at all and were only a disembodied intelligence… could you also be imagining your own body? Your own world?

F-Fucks-sake!!.....

Was Bill's reaction to the dialogue in his extended internal debate!

He got up from the chair, turned on the standard lamp, threw some more logs onto the fire and went over to the Sony hi-fi that was stacked in the alcove formed by the chimney breast. It was an old system, dating back to the Yank who'd lived there no doubt, but it was real quality nevertheless, no doubt being state of the art and costing a small fortune once upon a time, back in the day! It was big and chunky with a separate shiny metal box for each and every different component, tuner, amp, CD player, even a compact cassette player and all of it topped off by a very swish looking turntable.

He pulled out the carrier bag, he'd leant up against the glass door to the empty record cupboard, still sat there since he'd dumped it down on his return from his last trip down to Abersoch. He'd spent an hour or two trawling around the charity shops there for LPs. It seemed they were something most people no longer cherished, evidently preferring the hiss-free, impersonal, and illusory *'perfection'* of digital sound! A bulging plastic bag full of paperback fiction, similarly gleaned, sat on the floor alongside the bag full of LPs.

He flipped through the LP's in the bag and found the one he was looking for, he quickly picked out the distinctive bright yellow jacket of on an old Deutsche Grammophon LP, it was one of his favourites of old, a quality recording of Beethoven's Fifth, played by The Berlin Philharmonic, conducted by Herbert von Karajan.

He turned the volume up as the needle clicked into the groove on the black vinyl and sank back into his chair, closing his eyes as the iconic first four notes rang out . . . .

He let the music carry him away…

Outside and unseen by him cocooned as he was, in his cosy bubble of warmth and music, the skies had darkened, the high clouds that had spread in from the sea, had been followed by a vast slab of descending darkness that gradually blotted out the fleeting glimpses there had been of the waxing moon. The first gusting fingers of wind were beginning to probe at the land, stirring up the piles of dried leaves, conjuring them to perform wild dervish dances as they fell under its commanding spell, forcing them to whirl up into higher and ever growing, higher spirals up around the walls outside the cottage. As the final crescendo of Beethoven's Fifth rang out, bringing to a close Bill's private concert, outside the cottage the gale was just tuning up, making ready for its own tumultuous performance, raindrops had started to splatter hard against the glass of the windows and once more the night began to howl…

CHAPTER FORTY

The storm was still battering the window of his bedroom when Bill awoke the next morning, he had slept heavy and long, his tot of whisky, intended to be purely for medicinal reasons, had turned into quite a few! It was nearly half-eight, he noticed on the clock in his bathroom, he'd long since dispensed with having one alongside his bed, he had no need to know when he went to sleep or awoke anymore, but he had eventually rummaged one out of the cupboard for his bathroom. It was perverse considering he had harvested them all and shut them away in the first place... but that was his nature now, he smiled to himself... *perverse* summed it up nicely! So he wanted to know what time it was when he got up now? So what?

Having done what he needed in the bathroom he pulled his thick woollen dressing gown on and went down to make a coffee. He set the insanely extravagant La Spaziale expresso machine up and went through to get the fire going. Once the flames were licking around the logs he went back to dispense his coffee and to foam-up a small jug of milk to top it off. That bloody Yank had way too much money he mused, as he frothed the milk using a machine that belonged more in a coffee shop than a tiny cottage in Wales! The thing must have cost the guy thousands! It made a bloody marvellous cup of coffee though, he had to hand that to him! But then shit like that was all relative, let's face it if you lived in New York and decided to have a summer home in Wales to come for the purpose of writing... spending a few grand on a coffee machine wouldn't seem remotely odd to you, would it?

Wiping the milk off the nozzle and tossing the dishcloth across the kitchen into the sink, he pondered on that, the fact was that he could have done all of that himself once upon a time, well in reverse, had a summer home on Long Island or even Santa Monica, he'd had the money to do it for sure, so why hadn't he? Sat by the fire sipping his coffee he wondered if he hadn't deserved to be rich at all in the first place, by virtue of his inability to shamelessly lavish luxuries upon himself? That was what the rich did, wasn't it? Was it some sort of carried over working class guilt that he'd inherited from his parents, or more precisely from his Dad? Was that why at some level in his mind, he'd decided to punish himself by living the life of a vagrant for all those years, to compensate in some way for his own years of excess, relatively minor though they'd been, for having too much? Possessing an unfair share of the material wealth that the world had to offer, well that life in The UK had on offer? When so many had so little? Had some deep seated vestigial streak of puritanism surfaced from the depths of his ancestral psyche?

He smiled at the idea, convoluted though it was, as he drained his coffee, immediately rising from the chair to make a second one! It was definitely a *two coffee* morning he felt as the heavy rain continued to lash against the windows and in the log burner, the hungry flames were spurred on by the roar of the wind in the chimney and the supercharged updraft as it rapidly consumed the logs.

His second coffee enabled time for a counter argument to emerge, hadn't he used his wealth to set up The Folks Factory? Hadn't he tried to do something for those who had nothing? Didn't that count for anything? He chuckled to himself at the resounding *'no!'* that the voice of one of his more implacable ancestor's boomed out into his mind! 'It was only after you won that *free money* that you did that any of that wasn't it though?'

By Ten o'clock nothing had changed outside, whilst there was a certain appeal in battling against the elements to go down to the shore, as he had done many times before, the reward being to witness a hint of the true raw power of nature, feel the phenomenal wrath that She was capable of as the sea was goaded and tormented into insanely hurling itself at the land as though it was possessed by a mightily furious Neptune himself. But all in all, it was bloody hard work, battling into the teeth of the elements on the way down and then the struggle of climbing back up the hill, hindered rather than aided by the battering of the wind at his back, as it made his footing, on legs that had seen better days, considerably less certain. He decided that it would require way more effort and energy, than he felt he had available that morning, so instead he opted to take a leisurely ride on the bus into Abersoch, he'd not been for a while and there was that old church to check out in Aberdaron on the way back home later on.

It was only about half an hour's walk down onto Aberdaron, so he'd get wet for sure but that didn't really bother him and it would be dry on the bus for the hour and a half ride into Abersoch.

He spent the day there as he liked to refer to it by... *swanning around*! Having no purpose other than to watch life go by, he wandered aimlessly around the small town until he was hungry when he had a pint and a pie at one of the pubs. After his lunch the weather had improved a little and he'd more or less dried out too. The wind had dropped substantially, the rain had eased and the windswept sky was clearing in places so he ventured around to the bridge, crossing the river to go and walk along the beach.

The tide was on the way out as he strolled along the sand, memories of happy days flooding back to him, of trips to the seaside with Ruth and the kids when they were little, memories of the family he once had... Had he truly appreciated what he'd had at the time he wondered? Or had he taken it all for granted back then, when time seemed such a different commodity to the way he perceived it now? Back then it seemed to him that time stretched out before him, way off to a distant horizon, akin to the great stretch of sandy beach that lay before him... that the future at that horizon was far too distant to discern, so far off that there was little point in straining the eye or the imagination to see what was there... waiting there, patiently for the day when he would arrive...

Now he was there!...

Time... The lines of that poem came back to him again... '*Wandering some ancient highway, where will neither watch nor clock say, when to get up when to sleep, in its clockwork slavery keep*'...
It was a strange commodity for sure, time was. But then it wasn't a commodity at all, was it? Wasn't it merely a concept? Something that man had conceived of, noticed it as an observation, thought about it some and then given it a name! Isn't that what the ever-so-clever little monkeys that we are do? Look, see, judge, quantify, categorise, pigeon-hole and then fix a *name* onto everything? Our ape-like predecessors had no concept of time such as we have, they spent their days simply being

monkeys, doing what monkeys do without any need to know what time it was, ergo what *time itself was*! It was either light or it was dark, hot or cold, dry or wet and that was enough. They were either hungry or replete, they were neither young nor old, fit and strong, or damaged and weak, they were simply alive! Yet they still had family groups and lived within an established hierarchy, they knew fear, contentment and love for their young...

Now time was a looking glass for him, through which he could peer backwards, seeing through it to behold all of his memories laid out across the span of time he had lived through, yet for all of his years of storing memories, it was a miniscule fraction of the width of a hair on a scale measuring the time the Earth has existed, but for him it amounted to the entirety of his experience, and his lifespan...Well almost, he wasn't quite at his own horizon yet, although it was looming-up fast now...

He strolled along the beach for about half an hour, the sea here just washing gently at the sand, then after a little detour made it up onto the path that ran around the headland. He eventually came to a sculpture of a larger than life man, it was made up from bands of rusting metal riveted together here and there and intertwined with thinner bars to form the shape of a bulky body, topped by a head. The entire thing was created to be a type of open weaving of metal through which you could see the sky behind it... It was unusual to say the least. There was a fine view from here of the next bay that lay a little further along the coast around the headland he'd just walked around.

From there he took a different path that headed up to the summit of the headland, from there he had a panoramic view of the sea and the beach stretching back to Abersoch, the wind had dropped even more and now it just buffeted him playfully as he headed back down towards the town and the bus that would take him home.

Back in Aberdaron he decided that he would go and take a look at the old church down by the beach, as he'd earlier planned to do. He read on the large board outside that it was called Eglwys Hywyn Sant or St Hywyn's Church and that it was nine hundred years old. It had more of the appearance of a stone barn from the side and the front, but once inside it was far more impressive, with a large window at the nave. He strolled around soaking up the atmosphere, it had a tangible presence, he could almost feel the weight of the centuries that were contained within its walls, feel its strength in having been able to endure all the fury of the weather that it must have withstood, rooted as it was so close to the wrath of its ever so close and terrifyingly mighty neighbour, the sea.

As he was about to make his way out a clergyman, who was perhaps a little concerned by the somewhat dubious apparition he beheld before him, wandering about in his church! An apparition of a tall if somewhat stooped old man, wearing a dark coloured, long greatcoat and an old baseball cap from under which flowed a wild head of grey and white hair that was matched he saw as the man turned to look at him by the wildest of beards!

When this wild looking fellow spoke however, it was with a gentle and educated voice... Bill having just realised that he'd put on neither his respectable coat nor hat that morning and truly was the manifestation of his old persona, exaggerated some extra culture into his voice...
"Good afternoon, it's a lovely old church you have here isn't it? You can almost feel the history contained within it, it's almost palpable..." Suitably reassured the vicar replied,
"Ah, yes indeed. Century upon century of history of the people of its flock coming and going. Are you a visitor... here in Aberdaron? Are you just passing through?"
The old man chuckled, "Am I a tramp looking for shelter, is that what you're trying to ask Vicar? Sorry, I have no idea if that's what your title is." The man blushed and was about to concoct a reply when Bill went on,
"Don't mind me, I'm only teasing you, it's in our nature to judge what we see before us, it's only natural... It's what keeps us safe! I may look like a tramp today, I put on my old coat without thinking this morning! I actually live just a little way up from here, you'll tell from my accent that I'm not from around here of course, but then that makes me a resident here by choice rather than by accident of birth doesn't it? And a fine and lovely place it is to live too, if a little wild at times!" At this point he held out his hand to the somewhat bemused man,

"Bill Williams, pleased to meet you, I live in the old William's cottage up on the tops, but no I'm not any relation!"
"David Morgan, pleased to meet you too Bill. I know the cottage you speak of, the last Williams to live there was Elis, quite the character he was too! The house was bought by some American it was, so I recall, although he was less than a year here I think, but no, he came and went back and forth to America… can you imagine, living like that? I mean why would you? He fell out with The Council and that was that, the For Sale sign went up!"
"So I believe, but he did me a favour as the place was modernised and is very cosy now. I only rent it by the way."

As they had been talking Bill had been making his way to the door, he was stood in the doorway as he asked,
 "Tell me David, do you know anything of a reverend Fothergill? I bumped into him on the headland the other day."
"No I'm sorry the name doesn't ring a bell with me, oh see… Here's Glenys, what she doesn't know about things hereabout isn't worth knowing!" Bill looked out through the door as he fully opened it, to see an elderly woman with a large bunch of flowers in her arms on her way to enter the church, she spoke up crossly,
"Wnewch chi symud eich dwylo o'r drws a gad i mi basio!"
The vicar replied, "Ie, wrth gwrs, gad i mi gymryd y blodau, ydych chi'n nabod y Parchedig Fothergill?" He added, turning to Bill, I've asked her about Reverend Fothergill for you."
However the old woman merely shrugged dismissively and ignoring his question, pushed her way inbetween the two men to get into the church, muttering to herself as she went!
"My apologies for Glenys, she does the flowers and is single mindedly tyrannical about them!"

Bill wished him good day, turned and went to head off, but had barely gone two paces when he felt the lightest of touches on his forearm, it was so gentle he barely noticed it. Looking around he saw a tiny and slightly built, old woman stood beside him, she was barely four and a half feet in height and was dressed predominantly in black, even her pure white hair was drawn back and held down by a black headscarf, he assumed that she must have come from around the side of the church,
"I heard you asking about a Fothergill is it?" She asked cocking her head on one side, to look up at Bill like a bird, with her one

good eye, the other being so misted over her iris was barely visible.
She crooked a finger at Bill and beckoning him with it said,
"Best come with me then old man…" He followed her as she headed around the side of the church, the side that faced the sea, for a little old lady she got a good stride on!
Once they had got to the rear of the church with the large stained glass window at its end behind them, she went diagonally up inbetween the stones, it was slightly uphill as there was higher ground to both the side and to the rear of the church giving the old stone building the appearance of being snuggled into the slope, or as if it might have been shoved into it by the persistent wrath of the battering gales coming in off the water!

As she made her way between the stones, he noticed that they were mostly very old, he'd already spent some time wandering around the graveyard on one of his previous visits to Aberdaron, the inscriptions on old gravestones having been something that had fascinated him for years. She stopped in front of one that was of a medium height, it was a slab of quite thin, greyish brown stone that was shaped around the top into a curve with little angles worked into it. It was very old and heavily weathered, the lettering worn down and indistinct in places but there was enough of it still legible to make out the word that the old ladies knobbly old and tiny arthritic finger was pointing at… Fothergill! It was no longer possible to make out the initials preceding the surname but they could easily have been imagined into the shape of Rev. A.

He looked down at his diminutive companion, she gave him a knowing looked and tapped her nose, before beckoning over her shoulder, "You can be buying me a tot of rum at The Ship for my trouble. There's something you'll want to be telling me about this I'm thinking?" Jim stood for a moment staring at the gravestone… This was bloody ridiculous! So what did this mean, that he'd seen a ghost? Was the old vicar who'd sat and chatted with him the spirit of the man whose mortal remains lay long dead here under six feet of dirt? He laughed out loud and looked around to see if the old lady had heard him, but all he saw was her back as she headed around to the front of the church, he stood for a moment longer, holding his chin and running his fingers through his beard…

His rational mind came up with a solution as he left the grave to follow after the old woman, he must have read the inscription on the gravestone on one of his previous visits, his subconscious mind had recorded the name, perhaps guessing the faint letters to be 'Rev' and 'A' then when he had fallen asleep on the bench, he hadn't woken up at all! He had dreamt the whole encounter! He laughed again as he rounded the front of the church to see the old lady was already out of the gate and heading towards the pub. As he was going through the gate, he trod on one of his shoelaces, he rested his foot on a rock and retied it, when he looked up again she was going into the pub through a side door.

Sat in the pub Bill was surprised to find it was quite modern inside, he'd half expected it to be very oldie-worldly. The old woman was very chatty and in no time at all he knew the entire history of the Williams's who had lived at Bwthyn yn y Bryn where he had made his own home now.

"So what was it that made you to be asking the vicar after the Fothergills? The Williams would have known him well enough a generation or two back that would be now, so how is it you knew of him?"
"I think the name must have stuck in my mind from when I visited the graveyard a while ago, it's an unusual name, I have a passing interest in genealogy you see, I looked the name up to see what its origins were, Scottish I think it was?" He failed to mention that he had only done this after his personal encounter with his ghost!
"Well now, there's a thing. The Fothergill that was a vicar was a Scot..."

It was a couple of days later that he heard a knock on the backdoor, it was the little old woman from the churchyard! She told him that she was called Gwenllian, somehow her name never came up last time they met. He made her a cup of tea and she chatted about how much the cottage had changed since the days when the last of the Williams had lived there... *'Much bigger it is that I find it today!'* She didn't stay long and the real purpose of her visit became clear as when she was leaving, this time by the front door. She took a small pouch out of her pocket, it appeared to be made of some type of fine hessian sacking and

was tied with a piece of rough looking string at the top. It looked like some sort of potpourri. Although she hadn't mentioned anything about the Fothergill's or of their graveyard encounter and subsequent chat in the pub whilst they had chatted today, as she placed the tiny bag down on the window ledge in his porch, she said,
"This will keep old Fothergill from bothering you again, he'll not be so keen on entering the house with this sitting here!" With that she carried on out of the porch, as she was leaving she turned and said,
"Don't open the bag! Or touch it either!"

He eyed the bag a little suspiciously as he went back in through the front door, but left it in the porch untouched.

He switched on his desktop and looked up *'Wales and witchcraft!'* After a few minutes he came up with the term 'spell bag' the write-up was associated with Celtic witches:
The magic of Cornwall often came in the form of small spell bags filled with either powders, folded written charms, or other magical ingredient. These bags did a number of things, from love conjuring, curse breaking, and spirit banishing to healing, luck magic, and finding lost possessions.

Well now! That fitted the bill well enough he thought, smiling to himself, of course the ghost of the old vicar hadn't made any attempt to come into the cottage! Well, not yet! What am I thinking about he chided himself? I dreamt the whole bloody thing anyway!

He was just heading through to put the kettle back on when the phone rang, it was Jake:

"Hi Dad, how's it going?" Settling back into his chair he responded,
"Same as usual really… still living the dream!"
"Really? Or are you just being sarcastic?"
"No, honestly things are fine. I've dropped back into the same type of existence as I'ad when I were Bill! Well sorta similar at least, kinda just being present in the moment, letting life flow by and being a *part* of it all, part of nature like, belonging to it and not feeling removed from it? Rather than looking at everything

and then feeling the need to set about naming, cataloguing and then categorising everything I've seen, that I hear too. Take sounds! You know they're wonderful when you actually take the time to listen properly to them... I used to take so much for granted, I missed so much, I just let so much pass me by unnoticed! Take the sound of the sea... Now that's something else y'know, it's incessant and ever changing, never the same again ever. And the wind too, when it gets up! Wow! It comes in here so strong, nothing to stop it is there? Howling and wailing all around the cottage."

"That's good, I guess it's very Buddhist and all that, living in the moment?"

"How about you Jake, what's new in your life?"
"Nothing much, Liz is away for the weekend with the kids to see her mum and Dad, so I've got the place to myself. You know, it really is the most spectacular house you built, At first I used to feel guilty living here after we'd not long moved in, I don't know why really? It was when Neil said he was going to sell the place...

"You know he moved in, a year after you vanished... or did you? Did I say? Then within a few months he's selling it! I imagined you were perhaps haunting the place and that was why he wanted to sell it! You'd driven him out! But he did say he'd only sell it if I didn't want it... well I was like... *what sell Dad's house?* No fucking way! It was given as a sort of ultimatum to me though, so I had little choice I suppose?"

"Well I'm medd-up that y'livin there, making use of it, so don't worry any over it on my account! I'm glad t'other bugger isn't lording it up there though!"

"No I won't then! It was easy though really, once we'd moved in like... well I mean, talk about having wow-factor! It's like a dream living here, I totally love it!"

"What about Liz, is she happy living there, what about the kids... are you *all* happy living there?"

"Happy? They all bloody love it Dad! You should see the kids when they bring their friends around! Liz too! They're so proud and so full of themselves!"

"Yeah, well... Oh, I dunno, do you, like... well, do you do what you can so that they don't get too feel too smug, entitled or boastful, I mean let's face it, they're pretty over-privileged living there!"

"Oh come on Dad. Let it be will you? You should come up for a visit… would you? I mean come up, if I drove down to get you? Damn-it! I should have asked you about it for this weekend while they're all away! I've still not told Liz… about you I mean! Like I promised you I wouldn't. I've wanted to tell her so many times, thing is she's been saying things like…

'Oh Jake, what's happened to make you so happy these days? Have you won the lottery and you're keeping it to yourself? It's not another woman is it? Are you having an affair?' Then we had a good laugh! She was only kidding me on! Don't worry, she doesn't really think any of that! If I let you know next time she goes away then… will you come?"

"Nah… I don't think so. It's in the past for me now and best left there.. Yeah I know I put a lot into it when I had it built, back in the day, but it's so… I dunno, grandiose, extravagant, totally over-the-top somehow? Don't you think?"

"Not a bit, yeah for sure it's big! I mean huge! The glazed-in front section alone is like the size of three normal houses on its own, but it works so well, it's like having your own Centre Parcs, you can go outside from so many of the rooms in the house, whatever the weather and you're still in the dry!"

"Oh I dunno, I just can't help seeing it as too much now, back then I just wanted it all, I was never satisfied with anything, look at all those stupid cars I had! But now I think, why should anyone have so much when so many others have so little. It seems a bit immoral to me now somehow… I'm sorry… look if you're happy living there, it's not for me to try and discourage you. Nor do I want to try and get you to see things the way that I do now, it's for you to find your own way through life, come to your own conclusions about everything and discover what's really important to you and what isn't, after all it's your life! You're happy, Liz is happy the kids are so… good enough!"

"Yeah of course they are, who wouldn't be? I mean apart from you and your sack cloth and ashes mentality? Oh, I'm sorry Dad, I didn't mean anything…"

"No it's okay son, if you've not been through what I have then I can't expect you to have even the remotest inkling of where I'm coming from today. Maybe it's one of those things that you finally discover when you're getting near to the end, when

you're looking back on it all, on what's happened to you, where your life went! You're looking at everything from a very different perspective? It's like they say, you can't pass on the wisdom you've gained from your own experiences, it's having the experiences yourself that gives you the wisdom and not hearing about them from others."
"Are you sure you're okay? It sounds like you think you're going to die or something?"

He laughs, "Hell Jake, I know I'm going to die! We all are, it's just that for some of us it will be a damn sight sooner than for others! I'm past my sell-by-date too so I'm into extra-time! I guess it focuses the mind somewhat more than previously!"

"Well I'm sorry you won't come up. I'll try and get down to see you, it's awkward though for me getting away and having to lie about where I'm going!"
"I know, don't feel like you have to, it really doesn't matter, I can talk to you like this and that's enough. How are things at The Factry, no problems there?"
"No, I keep in touch with Harry and he says everything is ticking along nicely there. Him and Jenny are getting married in March, I don't suppose you'll be there?"
"Not been invited lad!"
"No, well neither have I yet, as in I haven't had an invitation, but Harry rang me to let me know and he asked me to invite you! So will you come? I'll come down for you and run you back."
"Nah! Wish them well from me though will you? I'm right pleased for Harry, he's a lucky man and Jenny's one in a million. There is something that you can do for me though Jake, will you check in with Pat at St. Jude's? Make sure their finances are doing okay and make a donation if they need it? Hell just make a donation anyway!"
"How much do you want me to give them?"
"Oh I dunno, give them whatever the interest is?"
"Since you left? That's like four or five million!"
"Oh right, well give them half a million then, that should keep them going for a bit eh? It's such a wonderful place…"

"Do you hear anything of your brother, now that he's locked up?" He laughs…"Shouldn't laugh I know, but… Well it's nice

that he's got his come-uppance at last. Maybe I should come up, what are the visiting times, I could pay him a visit?"
More laughter... Jake continued,
"Yeah, it's not before time either, but I do feel sorry for his wife, well not so much for her, I never took to her that much really, but for the kids, can't be much fun for them can it? Having their Dad in prison! By the way, been meaning to ask you, do you hear from Del at all? Has he ...err I mean *she* got your number?"

"No I've no way of contacting her, you could ask Jenny if she left any contact details with her or if she's been in touch with her, if you'd do that for me, I'd appreciate it. Maybe she'll invite her to the wedding? But either way, it would be good to have a chat on the phone with her. She had to be cagey before, out of fear of your brother and his shady associates, but now he's locked-up? Well who knows?"
"Okay Dad, you take care."
"You too, bye."
"Bye."

The remainder of the winter passed in a Groundhog Day type of fashion, with each week being pretty much a repeat of the one before it... stack the logs, keep the fire going, take in the groceries, chat with Nessie and the postman if he happened to catch him at the door, walk down to the beach now and then, go down to Aberdaron...
He saw no more of Gwenllian or the vicar, either when he was awake or asleep, at home or on his walks although he always eyed the little spell bag warily, as he passed through the porch!

A printed invitation to Jenny and Harry's wedding had arrived in due course and although he initially replied to say he wasn't able to make the trip, he later decided he would travel up and watch the wedding, but do it from the sidelines. Seeing them get married was only part of the reason he'd decided to make the trip, he also felt a little homesick too, not for his old opulent life of excess, but for his simple life on the streets and the nights spent in his bivouac in the woods! He knew it was a case of looking back through rose tinted glasses, acknowledging that there had been many times that had been a lot less than enjoyable!

Using his computer, which he had picked-up again quite proficiently, he was able to book a ticket to make the journey by rail. He was a little taken aback to discover that it would take him around six and a half hours to make the journey, at least three hours longer than the time Jake said it took him to drive down. What did it matter though, he had nothing else to do did he? He'd just spend the day before the wedding travelling, it could be a little adventure for him!

It seemed like no time at all before the day came and on the morning before Jenny and Harry's big day, he was up early, he paused at the door as he was leaving and about to put his coat on, then perversely he decided to root out his old coat, normally reserved these days for his walks to the beach or along the coastal path! Then to finish off the outfit he pulled on his old Olympics souvenir cap too! Well, he thought, if I'm going back to my old stomping ground...

He caught the first bus out of Aberdaron arriving at Pwllheli in plenty of time to catch his train. While he waited he had a brew at the appropriately named Buffers Café. He'd looked at the map the night before on his computer and it appeared that Pwllheli station and the buffers at the end of the railway had always been there, it was a true terminus station and had never been anything else, unlike so many other towns whose railways were often truncated having run on for miles into the far flung reaches of rural Wales back in the glory days of the railway. It seemed that back in those halcyon days a train could be taken from Criccieth to Caernarvon, a far more direct route than the one he was having to take now! However the fact that it still had a railway link at all, was something to be grateful for these days!

As the train ran out of Pwllheli station he had a brief view of the harbour and then shortly afterwards the track ran along the coast, giving him a view of a sandy beach. The single track line ran right next to the beach in places and after a while turned south to carry on hugging the coast all the way down to an estuary just before Machynlleth, where it turned to follow the river inland.

He had to change trains there to catch one for Shrewsbury and this was how his journey went... change at Chester, change again at Warrington, change at Preston! By the time he'd arrived *home(?)* …okay, back where he used to live, he was beginning to wonder if moving away to the back of beyond had been such a great idea after all! But then again, he'd never intended to come back had he? He determined that he certainly wouldn't be making a habit of it, at least not by this method!

Walking from the station into town, he noticed that very little had changed in his absence. He stopped off at charity shop and bought a cheap and anonymous looking cap, then tucked away his tattered old Olympics 2012 hat out of sight in his pocket, thinking now, after purposefully bringing it, that it would have been too much of a giveaway to anyone who might remember him from before as *Gruffalo Bill* or even worse as *The Crow!* now that he had let himself return to looking like both of them with his wild hair and big bushy beard!

As he idly wandered around the shopping area of town, all the while heading in the general direction of The Folks Factory, he spotted one or two homeless guys along his way sat begging outside some of the shops and in other places that he'd once have regarded as *his specs*! Each time he passed one of them, he tossed a few coins into their hat, or into their outstretched hand or… and he had to smile to himself at this… as he tossed coins into a Costa Coffee cup! He made a point of saying something to each of them, either *'yer alright mate?'* Or *'there y'go buddy,'* or something similar as he'd always felt better himself when people acknowledged that he was there and at the very least a living being, another person albeit one who'd fallen on hard times and not just an object, *a thing*… something akin to those dreadful plastic effigies of kids that they'd used to collect donated coins in back in the sixties, they were rudely referred to as *'plastic spastics'* he recalled.

They were an effigy that stood as tall as you, you being a kid at the time, looking all sad, pathetic and pleading, he was dressed in a pale blue shirt, that exact same colour as they used for the… (cruelly named by us kids back then)… *Spaz-Chariots,* the tiny vehicles that they gave to people they branded as *invalids*… (In-valid- s!! *ffs!*) … and this shiny plastic kid would stand there, eye to eye with you in his short pants, a crutch under his arm and his leg in a brace, trying to make you feel sorry for him?… You'd find them lurking around by shop doorways, waiting for you as you were on the way out after your mum had been spending money on whatever, some of which they wanted you to get out of your mum now… they were just child shaped collection boxes after all, they were for The Spastic Society he recalled, the plastic kid had a fucking *slot in their head* for you to put coins into them! Some things had improved he guessed?

He decided that he'd like to go and take one last look at where he'd made his bivouac in the woods and not feeling like walking all the way along the towpath to get there, he got on a bus at the nearby bus station.

He got off at the stop nearest to where the path led away from the road up into the woods and eventually to the canal. He made his way uphill through the woods until he came to his spot… It was virtually unrecognisable now, he only found where it had been because of the presence of many loose and dangling, tattered and washed-out strands of POLICE - DO NOT CROSS tape, bits of which were still tied here and there to trees and bushes all around the area where his hideaway had been once been located. Most of the undergrowth had been cut back, although it was already beginning to grow back now, there were still areas where it had been trampled underfoot and the ground was still a muddy mess all around the area.

Saddened not to be able to revisit his *little outdoor bedroom*, he made his way up through the woods, with a view to walking back into town along the canal's towpath. He eventually made it up the hill to where the palisade fencing stretched across the woods and he could now see the canal beyond it. He worked his way along it until he reached the small gateway, where he stood chuckling to himself… *'got yer eye-wiped, 'aven't ya?* …as he referred to his assumption that he'd be able to slip through the gate as he had done previously, by twisting the faulty padlock that was holding the bolt… In its place now was a very shiny and obviously new, high security padlock! The bolt was held very securely in place!

Being forced to abandon his plan of returning to town along the towpath, he resigned himself to having to walk all the way back down through the woods to the road and then taking another bus ride back into town, so he wearily set off down the hill!

Arriving at The Folks Factory, he kept his head down on his way in and then got a brew and something to eat. Nobody paid him much attention and later on he got a bed for the night under the name of Al Fothergill!

Kicked out of bed at 7.30am as everyone always was, he lost himself in the crowd who went through to queue-up for some breakfast. Once he'd eaten he went for a walk to kill some time, passing a florist he bought a small wreath which he took in a plastic carrier bag that the girl in the shop kindly provided him with… to the canal. He walked along the towpath to the spot where he'd discovered Natalie's body and placed the wreath there, leaning it up against the palisade fence. He stood for a moment in silence with his head bowed before setting back off in the direction of town. He paused where the loose upright had been, the broken rivet at the bottom had been drilled out and a shiny new bolt was now fixed in its place, he pointlessly tested the upright with his hand, no one would be getting through there again in a hurry!

Intrigued by this, he walked the half mile back along the towpath to the nearest access point and then worked his way around to the main road where the garage that he'd phoned his 999 call from was. Passing it by, he came to where the derelict site should have been. The old gates were gone now and new metal gates had been securely fixed in their place. Looking through the gates he could see that the entire site had been cleared, all that was left was the strip of undergrowth that ran along in front of the fencing, hiding it from view, everything else had been scraped away, back down to bare clay, there were stacks of concrete drain sections just inside the gates and a large builders board had been fixed to the stone wall.

Checking the little mobile phone which he'd brought with him, for the time, he made his way back into the town centre and the cathedral where the wedding would soon be taking place. Once there he found a spot where he could watch everything from a distance without being seen himself. As the time got closer, quite a crowd had gathered around the doors of the church and by keeping to the rear of the little throng he was able to move in closer yet still remain hidden.

He didn't have to wait long before Harry arrived, he was pleasantly surprised to see that Don was with him, they looked to be great friends now, laughing and joking with each other, that made Bill smile. Ten minutes later a lovely old car... *his* lovely old Alvis arrived with the bride, the car had been dressed-up with white bunting and looked a treat! Jenny looked a treat too, he thought and his smile broadened when he saw Jake... suitably attired and even wearing a chauffeurs cap, jump out and open the door for Jenny! The bride to be...

She looked beautiful, her dress was a vivid purple with white trimmings, the skirt ended just above the knee, it was all very fancy and nothing like the usual type of wedding dress you saw! She looked stunning, what she'd done to her hair Bill couldn't even begin to fathom, but regardless of that it looked amazing. There alongside her in a slightly toned down version of Jenny's dress was Del! She looked gorgeous too! He couldn't take his eyes off her and perhaps that was what caused her to turn her head and look over in his direction... Despite being lost at the back of the small crowd, their eyes locked, she smiled and then winked at him!

Once everyone had gone into the church, Bill snuck in and sat right at the very back, declining the invitations of several of the ushers to move down nearer to the front. He watched the ceremony from there and then just as the happy couple were making ready to leave he slipped out quickly, as the doors were being opened for them to leave.

He took up a position some distance away so that he could watch them emerge and then hang around as they posed for all the photographs to be taken. It was a glorious spring day and they took their time, but eventually Jenny and Harry headed to the Alvis to make their exit, as they did so Bill moved in closer, he wanted to try and catch Del if he could and speak to her... She'd obviously had the same idea as she held back too, remaining by the doors to the cathedral as the rest of the folks drifted away. As the last of the guests had come out, he called over to her, she looked around and smiled at him as she walked over,
"Why are you hiding? You should've come in!" Bill reached a hand out uncertainly towards her, she brushed it aside before wrapping her arms around his neck and kissing him on the lips,

she leant back with her arms still around his neck and looked into his eyes,
"You've gone and let yourself go to seed again Jimmy boy! Oh dearie me, but haven't you? Look at the feckin state of you!"
"Well, you look bloody ravishing Del! Where's your fella?"
"Oh I sent him along with everyone else to the reception, he knows all about you so don't worry. Come on we'll go and have a drink at The Dog." With that she took his hand in hers and led him off!

Sat in a corner of the pub they caught up over a drink, she remonstrated with him for not letting Jenny know he was going to come,
"What's the matter with you? You should be there at the reception too! Well, if you'd cleaned yourself up a bit, like I had you present yourself when you went to court, looking like a normal human being again and not some wild thing! Then no one would have recognised you as the infamous Crow if that was what was bothering you?"
"Nah, wasn't that, but I'd have been recognised as the ghost of the deceased James Stanley perhaps? All those photos being taken! Don't forget that I'm dead and gone to my family and what few friends I may have had left when I died! There's only Jake who knows I'm alive."
"Yeah, yeah, of course… oh yeah, and Harry and Jenny and Don the detective, and that Alan fella, oh yeah… *and me!*"
"Yeah well okay… anyhow I'd rather be some *wild thing* anytime and look that way, than being anything remotely close to *normal*, thank you very much! Trying to be normal, trying to live that lie my life had become, was what got me into trouble in the first place. I love where I live now, it's so peaceful, I'm at peace now, with myself and the world… well the little bit of it that I have any interaction with and I can just be me as nature intended me to be, without all that awful scraping at my face… You should come down for a visit."
"Surely to God you could trim the damn whiskers back a bit once in a while though?"
"Anyway, I *did* see the wedding, from the back of the church."

They chatted for a while longer until Del made to leave,
"Well *I have* a wedding breakfast to get to, so if you're not going to come with me, I'll have to say au revoir." She picked up a

beermat off the table, rummaged in her handbag to produce a pen, wrote her telephone number on it and then handed it to him saying,
"We'll keep in touch, okay love?" Looking a little forlorn he took the beermat from her but said sulkily,
"Okay... I suppose I shouldn't keep you from the party, you always loved a party! Take care of yourself Del... I loved you, you do know that? I still do..." She smiled, took his hand and leant in to kiss him, it wasn't a snog but it was way more than a peck!
She turned to leave but then hesitated,
"Hang on here Jimmy, for just a sec..." She went to the bar and said something to the guy behind it, they laughed together and then he rummaged underneath the counter for a moment before handing something to her and continuing to chat as she held whatever it was in her hand. All became clear as when she was returning, she pointed to an upright piano she'd spotted over on the other side of the bar near one of the exits,
"Come on Jimmy, one last time eh?" With that she took his hand and led him to the piano, it must have been the key to the lid that she had obtained from the barman, he noticed it had a large wooden fob on it as she used it to unlock and then lift the lid. She pulled out the stool and beckoned him to sit,
"Oh I don't know Del, I mean... I was always kaylied at the club, back in the day!"
"Yeah, yeah, yeah... like you were on that You Tube video?"
"Yeah but that was different..."
"Jimmy, just PLAY!"

Begrudgingly he took off his big old coat and dropped it on a nearby chair, he sat on the stool for a moment at the keyboard, staring into space...
"Okay, so what do you want me to play?"
"Jimmy, will you just *shurrup* and play something for me... for fuck's sake!"

He played a few notes randomly, then launched into a really slowed-down and very soulful version of Neil Sedaka's bouncy old hit from way back in 1962... *Breaking-up is Hard to Do*...☦
It was so different it was barely recognisable...

After playing around with the intro a couple of times, ad-libbing and improvising, he shocked Del by starting to sing! This was something he had never, ever done... not even once in all the times she'd sung with him as he played at the club...
"Oh man..." She exclaimed..." That is so... *mm...mmm*..." She purred as she squeezed in next to him on the stool and took up the harmony...

By the time they were coming to the end of the song, the handful of people that were in the pub were crowded in around them listening, as he got to the last strand, he broke down into a sob... but Del ever the pro, seamlessly took it up and finished to a little round of applause.

Still sat at his side Del turned to him and wiping away his tears with her fingers, she took his face in both of her hands and kissed him, long and slow... A small cheer went up from the people who'd been watching before they drifted away again.

"Oh Jimmy, Jimmy, Jimmy... that was delicious, exquisite... Thank you. But now I really must go."

With that she got up and made ready to leave, as she handed him his coat, he asked her,
"Will you sing for your supper then?" She laughed,
"Are you kidding buster? Think I'd come all this way and not get myself into the limelight? Me and Mike are the entertainment for tonight, I'm off for a slap-up-meal right now in some fancy hotel, but the main 'do' is tonight, you know you really should stay... Mike's in a band, they play R&B mostly, but they can manage good stuff too when I boss them into it!"
"Mike's your fella then?"
"Oh Jimmy... you'll always be my fella... but hey, you left, I moved on! That's how it goes eh? Mike's Dad was an RAF pilot

☦ See back page

in the war, or perhaps I should use his proper name of Michał, his Dad's Polish you see, he came over here from Poland to fight Hitler in 1939. He was a pilot in the Polish Airforce when Poland was overrun by The Nazis, Flight Lieutenant Stanisław Rosiak...

He's a real life hero and Mike's so proud of him, he'll be a hundred next year.
"So if you're not going to come with me, I'll have to bid you farewell!"
"Okay, take care of yourself Del... Like I said, I really did love you, you do know that don't you? I still do... always will..." She smiled, took his hand and leant in to kiss him, this time it was just a peck. She then turned and went over to the bar, handed back the key to the piano and exchanged a few words with the barman. She held up her phone to him, pointed at it and mouthed *'You Tube'* to him! She'd only recorded their little performance hadn't she!
She turned on her heel then, with a broad grin on her face, blew Bill a kiss and called out as she left...
"I love you too Jimmy. Au revoir Cherie!"

With that she was gone, leaving only a lingering whiff of her perfume...
A silent tear ran down Bills cheek, as he somehow understood that her parting words of '*au revoir*' should more accurately have been '*adieu*'...

It was with an ache in his heart that he slung his old backpack onto his shoulders, headed out of the pub and went straight to the railway station. So, okay maybe not going to the reception was understandable, but part of him was yelling at him, telling him that it was *un-fucking-reasonable* not to visit Jake while he was in town! The thought however well-intentioned got short shrift from the more dominate voice in his head, that was telling him to fuck-off back to Aberdaron, to get away from it all again, to leave everything behind him, where it belonged...

His voice of reason had one last try...
'But Jake could run you back, you know he would...'
'He's at a party... best to just leave him be!'
'He'll find out you were here! How do you think he'll feel then?'
'Nah, Del won't say anything. Anyhow I've got a return ticket!'
'Oh... For fucks sake!!'
On the train he watched the countryside as it slipped smoothly by outside his window. The grumpiest part of him was cussing him for making the journey up north in the first place!

'Fucking stupid! All this fucking way to go to get home again now! Six and a half fucking hours!'

It took him a damn sight longer than six and a half hours to get home however, with the trains running at less and less regular intervals into the evening, until at one station he found that they had stopped running altogether for the night! As a result he spent hours sat around waiting at various stations on his journey home.

'This is what you get, rushing away without thinking it through, running away all over again, when you could have had a good night's sleep and set off in the morning!'

As he finally boarded the train for Pwllheli to make the last leg of his rail journey home it was ten in the morning, it was only then that he allowed himself to have a laugh about it and at all of his other *antics* as he referred to them… He hadn't been a happy old fella at all up until then!

CHAPTER FORTY-ONE

The moment he'd walked into the cottage on his return, he'd decided that something *felt-off!* Ostensibly it was still the cosy little cottage that he had left behind a couple of days earlier but… as he closed the front door behind him, he felt certain that something had changed. For one thing it felt decidedly chilly as he bundled his way in through the front door and dumped his backpack on the floor in the hall. The welcoming warmth of the little cottage would normally have been wrapping itself around him… He flicked the light switch and the lights came on, so the electricity was still on, but when he knelt down to feel the stone floor it was really cold. It was something less tangible than merely the lack of heat though that he sensed was wrong, it was more of a feeling, it was an emotional reaction rather than a physical defect in the building that was the source of his disquiet, the problem he was up against was that for some unknown reason it didn't *feel like home…*

He shrugged to himself, *it's the only bloody home you've got lad, so best get yersel' used to it again!* With that thought in mind, he went through to the kitchen and put the kettle on, while it was boiling he recalled the small room that was off the kitchen, he'd only looked into it briefly the once, that had been back when they'd been viewing the house and having no reason to, he'd never been back in there. It was part of the newer part of the cottage and it housed the mass of gubbins that ran the ground source heat pump that supplied the hot water to heat the floors. Bill assumed that the angry red light that was glowing on and off on the control panel wasn't there for decoration!

The kettle boiled behind him and he shut the door to what he newly regarded as the utilities room! With his mug of tea in hand he went through into the normally cosy lounge, it was of course chilly today and he set about getting the fire going once more. First things first eh? He mused to himself, the call to the agent to have the heating fixed could wait till he was warm!

Ten minutes later and finally out of his hat and coat he was settled into his armchair with a newly topped-up brew and a piece of toast, made with bread out of the freezer.

He banked up the now blazing fire with as many logs as he could fit into the log burner and shut its air intake down to get it to burn more slowly, the room having warmed up nicely by then. It came as no surprise to him at all that after his most tiresome journey back, that he was feeling quite worn out now and he readily accepted the warm embrace of sleep. He was to have little rest though...

Almost at once, he found himself back standing in *that fucking alleyway* again... as his befuddled, sleeping mind had decided that it deserved to be so named! He'd already been dragged back there several times since the first dream he'd had and everytime it had the same deeply disturbing feeling to it, that he wasn't dreaming at all! That he was being transported to this bloody place somehow, where he was being forced to relive what happened there over and over again.

He was amazed how rational he was able to be... he was fucking dreaming after all! But was he? He decided to look all around this time, to take in the details of his surroundings, as he observed everything more carefully, he was continually having to force down the panic that had always welled-up on his previous *visits.* If that is what they'd been? He could actually see the streetlamp this time, it was one of those old fashioned ones, with a big flat glassed lantern that had a sort of lid to it? He was bloody sure that there hadn't been any fancy lamps like that in the alleyway where he'd been nearly kicked to death!

There was more that wasn't right too, other things that simply felt as if they were wrong... The shining wet kerb was still there, the stone paving flags were too, but the road itself was cobbled, there was no tarmac! So how could this be where he was mugged then?

With that thought in his mind, he felt a little more confident and managed this time to turn around to see what it was that had scared him too much to dare facing previously and in not doing so had always awakened him from the dream... *If a dream it was...* A feeling of dread, that he had made a terrible mistake swept over him though, as to his horror he saw exactly what he had imagined to be there, had been dreading he would see... in his worst fears...

There lying on the shining, wet cobbles lay a curled-up body...

Cobbles? But there were no cobbles! They shouldn't be there! He raved once again! He could vividly recall the intricate, irregular shapes of the small, individual stones that were held captive in the tarmacadam road, when it was so close up to his face from when he'd been lying on the road, as he was clinging precariously to life...

Girding himself and clinging insanely onto this single straw of comfort, he crouched down alongside the prone figure to take a closer look...

What he found both shocked him but also at first relieved him... It wasn't him! The body wasn't his! *So what the-fuck?* He sprang back up onto his feet, his head spinning and feeling a little dizzy as he tried to cling onto the dream... *or was it to try and stay in the place he'd been transported to, to remain a little longer this time*? He bent lower this time, leaning over the prone body...
It looked too small to be his body now anyway, had it shrunk since he'd first looked at it? Was it the body of a child? What... No! That wasn't how big it had been just a moment before! It definitely appeared to be shrinking before his very eyes!

He quickly knelt down onto the cobbles... his trousers soaking up the moisture off them, he could feel the dampness spreading around the knees of his trousers...

He scooped up the body in his arms and knelt there, holding it in the silvery shining light, utterly bewildered, trying to look at the face that was somehow covered, wrapped in layers of clothing, wasn't visible to him...

Then to his horror the bundled child he thought that he was holding in his arms began to shrink again, even as he tried to cling-on more tightly to it ...

In a moment or two the bundle was so small he held it only inbetween his hands, he was now able to see that it was a baby he was holding... the baby looked up at him, their eyes meeting but only for a moment, before the already tiny bundle continued to shrink... smaller and smaller... he tried to close his hands around it, to cling onto it… but it was now so small that it slipped inbetween his fingers and fell down onto the cobbles…

It seemed now to his reeling senses that what was falling from his hands was a tiny, shining, opalescent little pearl! As it hit the cobbles it bounced up an inch, then rolled slowly across the slightly domed shape of the top of one of the cobblestones…

He dived down onto the floor to try and grab it…

But as he attempted to close his fingertips around it… it rolled into a crack between the cobbles and was gone…

He lay in a bedraggled heap on the cobbles and wept…

He was still crying when he woke up, the fire was roaring away and when he picked up his mug of tea, it was still warm… he had been gone only minutes and yet the time he spent in the alleyway seemed to have been an eternity… Discarding the tea mug, onto the arm of the chair he reached out his hands to rest them on his knees, half expecting them to be damp… But they were dry and warm from the heat radiating off the fire, burning away merrily in the log burner… Did that prove anything though? Why would his physical body have needed to be transported to the alleyway…

Pulling a handkerchief from his pocket he dried his eyes and blew his nose, he was still stunned by what had happened in the dream! Hopefully now that he had faced-up to whatever it had been that his subconscious mind had insisted upon him seeing, that maybe the dream would cease to reoccur? That would be a relief if it turned out to be the case, the more burning question however to his mind was, what the hell had it been about?

His immediate thoughts leapt to it being about Abbie, that was the most obvious conclusion, he thought that it was his subconscious mind, trying somehow finally to make sense of her loss, but working within the logic-lacking mechanisms of its inhibited mindscape. Then he thought further back to the two stillbirths of his other daughters, those two tiny bundles of promise that had both been denied that vital spark at the moment that it counted the most…

Why now though? That was the biggest question that sprang into his mind, why now after all these years? Over a year had passed since he had lifted the iron shutter and released the memories of his old life, unlocked that part of his mind once more, why would it wait till now to hit him? He'd already answered the question with his earlier thoughts he came back to, the subconscious mind lacked any concept of logic.

Wrestling with thoughts such as these, he was unaware that he had fallen asleep once more… *or had he been transported back to that alleyway?*

He found that he was once again there, still kneeling on the shiny wet cobbles, he noticed detachedly in a still part of his otherwise spinning mind that they were neat granite sets, the beautiful crystalline structure of the granite having the distinctive darker flecks intermingled with crystalline ones, all of this appearing so clearly to him shining there in their wet surface, making them seem to be polished…

The other part of his mind had already got his fingers working into the gap where the tiny iridescent pearl had vanished, trying to grip onto the four inch square cube of granite and wrench it free, in a desperate attempt to find that tiny pearl…
His fingers hurt and his nails split but he refused to give up, now clenching the cobble with both hands…

Suddenly it came free and he rocked back onto his heels with the lump of granite still in his hands, he let it fall away and lunged forwards to see into the gap where he had plucked it from…

The shock of what he beheld took his breath away… He was peering down through the four inch square into the opening where the cobble had been… straight through the road into open space beneath it!

What he could see through the small square opening was a vertiginous drop, as if looking down over the edge of a cliff to the broiling waters of an angry sea hundreds of feet below!
He felt an instinctive urge to get away from the hole, to distance himself from this inexplicable and terrifying phenomena, so he tried to shuffle backwards on his hands and knees but as he did

so, the entire row of cobbles either side of the gap left where he had removed one, fell away... The small lumps of granite toppling downwards away from him! Then in a sudden rush they were joined by the entire street that lay on the far side of the hole away from him...

Driven into a blind panic and in desperation, he now tried to shuffle backwards faster, but as fast as he went the cobbles, row by row fell away into the void... He tried to turn, in order to get up and get away more quickly, to run from the widening abyss, but as he scrambled up onto his feet he felt the cobbles beneath his back leg give way beneath him, he fell forwards landing heavily onto his right knee, glancing over his shoulder he saw the cobbles still falling away, row by row, nearer and nearer to his knee...

Then he felt a hand grab his left hand, which he had thrown up to balance himself as he'd fallen forwards, it gave a mighty tug and as it did he pushed with all of his might up as his flailing leg found some purchase, to land on his side on the stone flags of the pavement, even as the wave of falling cobbles swept past him at the edge of the stone curbing which miraculously had remained in place!

He leant back against the wall of the building that the pavement ran alongside, turning his head to try and see who had assisted him, but all he could see was the solitary street light, still firmly planted on the same pavement a little further along. Beyond the kerb at the edge of the pavement there was nothingness now, just a sheer drop, to the sea far, far below.

Surely this is time for me to wake up now?

But no... he closed his eyes willing himself to be sat safely back in his chair, warm and cosy by his fire. He risked one eye... nope still here in fucking Fucked-up-Land! It felt very precarious sitting where he was, the pavement now feeling that it was merely a ledge on the side of very high cliff... Who was to say that it wouldn't crumble and fall at any minute, just as the road had? So it was decidedly not the best place to be! He pushed himself up onto his feet, all the time with his back firmly up against the wall and then shuffled sideways in the direction of the lamppost, he kept the palms of both hands pressed flat against the brickwork. The pavement was easily wide enough for him to have strolled along down the middle… but he felt the urge to keep that precipitous drop as far away from himself as possible…

He kept his eyes fixed on the kerb all the while as he edged along trying not to focus upon the impossible drop that appeared immediately after it. He shuffled sideways until suddenly his fingertips felt something smooth in place of the rough brickwork, a touch further and he realised it was a frame, he looked down over his shoulder to see behind him, it was a doorway, he reached out with his left hand to grasp onto the handle, pushed down on it, felt the door open and shoved himself backwards against it to fall into a dimly lit room…

He rolled onto his hands and knees as he got his bearings, he could hear someone singing in the distance, the echoing voice sounded familiar… He got to his feet and realising that he was in a long narrow corridor, what else was there to do other than set off along it? Presently the floor beneath his feet turned into a staircase, as he went down the steps they got wider and wider… now there was a thick piled carpet beneath his feet…
The singer started a new song…

Now you say you're lonely
You cried the long night through
Well, you can cry me a river, cry me a river
I cried a river over you

He realised that it was Del singing, well didn't it just have to be? part of his mind reasoned, he could see her now as he continued on down the steps…

Now you say you're sorry
For being so untrue
Well, you can cry me a river, cry me a river
I cried, cried, cried a river over you

She was standing at a large old fashioned microphone, in the centre of a wide stage, the staircase he was descending ended at its rear …

You drove me, nearly drove me, out of my head
While you never shed a tear
Remember, I remember, all that you said
You told me love was too plebeian
Told me you were through with me and
Now you say, you say you love me
Well, just to prove you do
Come on and cry me a river, cry me a river
Cause I ………

She saw him and stopped abruptly…
The unseen orchestra ending on the same note as her!
She had a look of mild surprise on her face…
The stage beneath his feet suddenly vanished…
Disappeared into an inky void…
And he fell…
…and fell…
Or was he?
Was he actually falling at all?
He could feel no air rushing past him?

It was black everywhere for sure, but…
He blinked his eyes but could see nothing…
He could feel nothing either…
So was he floating?..
…*in a mosta mysterious way?*…
He laughed at that line of Bowie's…
He reached out again and heard a clanging noise…
He opened his eyes to see his tin mug roll to a stop on the flags of the floor in the cottage…
On the floor by the log burner…
In his lounge…

CHAPTER FORTY-TWO

When he finally ventured upstairs, he had to find some extra blankets to pile on his bed, half sozzled after trying to chase away the torments of his dreams by polishing off what was left in the bottle of malt that Nessie had delivered before his trip up north. The bedroom like the rest of the house had been chilly, he'd cussed himself for not getting around to ringing about the faulty heat pump, but he'd slept like a baby and the sun was up when he woke.

Pleasantly surprised by how well he'd slept, he ventured downstairs and put the kettle on, stoked up the fire and put some frozen bread in the toaster… He was on remote control, a robot running on its pre-programmed, regular morning routine, all to the accompaniment of the rhythmic hammering in his head…

He found the number for the agent and made the arrangements for the maintenance man to come out, he was impressed by the service… The woman said that they would be there around lunchtime! Millionaire Americans did like prompt service he guessed and would pay whatever it cost to be provided with it?

He'd come downstairs in his thick dressing gown, not bothering to get dressed, so after he'd eaten he went back up to have a bath, only to find that there was no hot water! Now feeling utterly miserable, he crawled back into bed!

He'd not been out of bed for the second time that long and fortunately had got dressed this time, when the backdoor bell rang… *'Hi, I'm Daisy here to fix your heating & before you wonder, I have a first class honours degree in Mechanical Engineering!'* …had been the opening shot of the very attractive lady plumber? Engineer? Heat Pump repairer…

Once the lass had fixed everything and it was all running properly once more, he had cause to question what he'd thought of as a 'millionaire level of service' the company provided. She told him, as they were sat having a brew that there was meant to be a regular three monthly maintenance inspection carried out on the Heat Pump and water filter units! She pulled up the schedule on her tablet to show him,

"What I can't understand is that there's no notes or anything a all indicating the suspending of the visits, they just haven't been getting onto the schedule." Bill offered his, *expert technical* opinion,
"A glitch in the system perhaps?"
"Yeah..." She laughed, realising that he wasn't being serious, "I'm new on this circuit, it was the run I wanted most when I started with the company, I love it round here."
"So that you'd be working on your home patch was it? You're local aren't you, I'm used to the accent by now,"
"Oh well done! Most err... sut i'w roi... err, *folks* who come from outside, just hear a Welsh accent and that's it! You must have a good ear."

It was very pleasant chatting with the lass, she was a proper Celtic beauty, with flame red hair and piercing blue eyes, he bit his tongue to avoid asking the obvious and utterly puerile questions that came to mind about her career choice! What business was it of anyone's? She was doing what she wanted to do, using her intellect to fix things, working with her hands as well as with her clearly very sharp mind? If Ruth or a myriad of girls of her generation had adopted the same, eminently more sensible approach... Well, things would probably be a lot better in the world today?

Despite finding it very pleasant chatting... Which he realised was something quite rare for him these days! He let her wrap up the conversation and get on her way, he found her parting shot of,
"See you in three months." Something to look forward to though.

Ten minutes after Daisy had left, there was a knock at the front door! No one had ever come to the front door in all of his time at the cottage, you were presented with the backdoor when you came to the cottage from down the lane, to get around to the front from there meant going all the way around the side of the building. The only way you'd arrive directly at the front door was if you came up from the coastal path, even Gwenllian had arrived at the backdoor! He wondered why she only placed her spell-bag in the front porch...

A cold dread washed over him, he had the insane notion that it was old Fothergill making a house call… The phantom vicar himself! His mind leapt to the spell-bag in the porch, maybe the magic drained away from them… did they have a *spell-by-date?* He couldn't help smiling to himself at his *little joke*… What was wrong with him? He was behaving like an fucking old woman!

He strode defiantly the last few paces to the front door and pulled it open rather abruptly! He was faced by a surprised and elderly lady, who was holding a small dog in her arms,
 "Bore da, dw i ddim yn gwybod i bwy mae'r ci hwn yn perthyn?"
"Eh? Come again luv?"
"Oh I'm sorry I mistook you for a local with err… well… so, what I was asking was if you knew who this little fellow belongs to?"

He got rid of the woman… and the dog as quickly as he could, without being overly rude to her! As he turned to go back inside, he eyed the spell bag warily, reaching out to touch it but pulling his hand back at the last moment! 'Bloody crazy old fool' he muttered as went in and closed the door behind him.

Remaining unsettled he went to pour out a whisky, only to find the empty bottle. Damn-it! He cussed, that meant a trip down into Aberdaron, Nessie wasn't due until tomorrow… She'd be ringing around teatime for his order…

He slumped into the chair by the fire, his headache had diminished now, but he still remained feeling decidedly ill at ease. The deep, dreamless sleep had done him some good though and had reinforced his hope that the reoccurring nightmare was at last, finally done with him. He'd remained unsettled by it though and in addition to the fact that the equilibrium of his daily routine seemed unable to re-establish itself since his trip up north. He wished he'd never gone now! Although he'd been really glad to see Del again, to chat with her and even to sing with her as he played! Although what she had done with the damn video clip she'd recorded of them, he didn't want to think about! The thought of being on You-Tube all over again…

He mused over how pleasant it had been chatting with that lass earlier, but why not? She was lovely and she'd fixed the heating for him too! Already the place was warming up, he could have that bath in a bit? The thought of getting undressed and wet… he couldn't be bothered… Later maybe…

Something had changed now. He came to the conclusion that any change there had been had to be within himself. The cottage was timeless, his routine was there waiting for him to step back into, it was him who felt unable to do so. His thoughts eventually coalesced into the opinion that it had all begun with his encounter, real, imaginary or dreamt, with old Fothergill, followed on by the old woman at the church, the gravestone, the spell-bag, the dreams… The notion that Fothergill was possibly a ghost, an apparition or spirit bothered him, all that stuff was bloody nonsense, wasn't it? Or was there something mystical seeping into him, living on this hillside in this ancient cottage, steeped in… what? Welsh-ness? He laughed at the notion of that!

He came to the conclusion that his thoughts were just chasing each other around in his increasingly confused mind and what he needed was someone he could talk it all out with. His thoughts spun back to all the endless therapy sessions he'd endured at his stays at The Haven. All of that psycho-analysis! Was that even something you could practically do, analyse your own mind? He suspected that realistically, such a task would be impossible.

Who could he talk to though? Really talk to? There was no way he could burden Jake with his woes, the lad had enough to cope with already, he'd caused him more than enough grief for one lifetime! Harry? What about Harry? They were only *sort of friends* though… He knew already that there was only one person in the world he could talk to, so why was he dancing all around her and not naming her? But did he have the right to ask anything more of her though? Didn't she deserve to be left to get on with her life without him, she was doing a pretty good job of it by all accounts, wasn't she?

There *had been* something in that kiss though, hadn't there? The one when she was sat right next to him on the piano stool. When he could feel the heat from her body, as it was right up against his own. They had really reconnected in that moment. And who had it been who had appeared there at the end of his surreal and insane dreamscape?

Somehow though, deep in his heart he felt it was wrong of him to cling to her, he was an old wreck of a man on borrowed time, what did he have to offer her? A life with him, in a burrow on a Welsh hillside overlooking the sea? Living like some kind of fucking, hermit Hobbits? Nah! She was a vivid and scintillating night bird! He smiled to himself as he visualised her... That idiotic joke-line, of being the *only gay in the village*, ran through his mind! She'd beat him up over that, categorising her as *gay*! Or categorising her in any way! She *so* hated labels!

He could go and live with her then? He laughed at that idea until it set him off coughing! Yeah, she'd look real swell with some wild old hill-billy type on her arm! He could clean himself up some... Yeah, sure...

But she *had* given him her number hadn't she? He'd put the beermat into the inside pocket of his old coat, he remembered doing it, to keep it safe... He went and retrieved it and sat by the fire looking at it for a long time, undecided whether to toss it into the fire, let it burn up and forget about her, let her be, let her go... Run away? Again?

He felt the damnable weariness in his body returning, it seemed to be coming on earlier day by day, his chest was aching again and he could feel himself getting sleepy... He fought against the feeling and aggressively roused himself from the chair, tossing the beermat onto the side table, he fiddled agitatedly with the fire to keep it going and then went through to make a strong coffee. Realising that he hadn't eaten all day, apart from some toast, he put a frying pan on the stove and made a cheese omelette. He zapped some baked beans in the microwave and wrapped the omelette around them before sitting and eating it.

Feeling a little more awake he tossed the dishes into the sink, filled the frying pan with water and went back into the lounge. His eyes were drawn to the beermat, what the fuck eh? He picked up the handset of the phone and dialled the number, it was late afternoon, what would she be doing? The number was ringing out...Was she living late again like she had when they'd

been together? Up all night and sleeping half the day? She probably wouldn't answer anyway, part of him hoped she wouldn't…
"The ringing stopped as his call was picked-up, he was about to speak when he realised that it was only an answerphone message… Del's voice rang out,
"Well it's looking like you've missed me! Oh poor you! Send me a text and I'll get back to you, but don't leave me a message! I repeat *do not* leave me a bloody message… I *never* listen to them! *Byeee…*"
That was bloody typical of her, he smiled to himself, it had been good to simply hear her voice though, he almost left a message but if Del said she wouldn't listen to it, then that *meant* she wouldn't!

It was a fucking nuisance nevertheless he grumbled as he unplugged the charger from his mobile, yeah Jake had already told him off for leaving it permanently plugged in, it was the only way he'd found to be sure it was always charged when he wanted it, routine… come in, hang keys up and if he'd had his mobile with him… put it on charge!

He'd have to go out to get a signal to send her a text message, there was no trace of one in the cottage and if there was one within a mile it was only stray and random!

'*Bloody woman*' he cussed her off, as he dragged his boots and then his coat on! But simply thinking of her, put a small smile on his face anyway!

CHAPTER FORTY-THREE

Bill was glad to arrive at the top of the track that led down to the cottage, it had been uphill all the way from Aberdaron and as the handles of the plastic carrier bag holding his whisky, a pint of milk and a loaf of bread repeatedly worked themselves into a strand of evilly possessed razor wire, on a mission to sever his fingers... he had repeatedly cussed himself for not taking his backpack with him... *'that's what you get for rushing out!'*

He'd sent a text to Del asking her to ring him and *thanking her ever so much* for not using her answerphone and pointing out the inadequacies of her preferred option for a caller who was using a landline! He could almost hear her saying... *'who the fuck uses a landline today?.* He supposed she had a point... *'old people!'* Would've been his reply! Jake had told him a while back that one day landlines would be phased-out completely! Progress? That was what they described all of their bullshit as! It wasn't how Bill saw it!

Halfway down the lane as he rounded the last corner before he would see the cottage, he froze... striding up the lane towards him was the lithe figure of The Reverend Fothergill! Had he been to the cottage? Bill's panicking mind queried... But there was a stile and a footpath leading off the track, a little before his backyard, he could have come from there perhaps? Unsure what to do and feeling foolish standing there dumbstruck, he pulled his phone out of his pocket and pretended to look at it as the old man strode closer to him, he caught his eye when he was a few feet away and muttered *'morning'* to him as he passed, receiving in reply a little a nod and a brief response of *'Aye!'*

He turned to watch as the old man strode purposefully away, around the corner and out of sight...

Nothing weird about that then? He tried unsuccessfully to convince himself as he continued down the track to the cottage. Perhaps he'd seen the same old man on his travels previously and used the memory of him to cast him into the role of the man he dreamt about? After all there was nothing to show that the old man he'd just seen was a vicar, was there? Nor had he stopped to pass the time of day with Bill, as the damnable vicar from his dream most assuredly would have done! He realised that he was giving attributes of character now to imaginary people from his dreams... Maybe a psychotherapist was what he needed rather than a chat on the phone with Del? There'd been a wee hint of a Scottish accent contained in the one word he spoken, in his *'aye'* though, hadn't there?

The rest of the day slipped away in much the same fashion as they usually did, other than Bill constantly looking at the phone! As afternoon slid into evening he was beginning to think she'd decided to let sleeping tramps lie, lie in the bed they'd made for themselves, to let it be... He decide to play 'Let it be' on the piano and went through to the new lounge, if it had been meant to work as a spell it did... for he had barely played the intro when the phone rang! He shot back through to the old lounge...

"Del?"
"Jimmy? You sent me a rather rude text?"
"I did, I did... Oh thanks ever so much for ringing me, there's no signal at my cottage, bloody nuisance it is, for the mobile I mean, so I couldn't leave you a message and you can't do a text from a landline... and I wanted to talk to... well anyway... *Fucks-sake*... how the hell are you?"
"So you wanted to talk did you? Was that to me specifically or to anyone daft enough to listen?" She laughed, then went on,
"Are you okay, you sound flatter than a pancake and yer gabbling away like some demented old turkey, that black dog sniffed you out again? Found y'hiding place has he? Or have you got a new one now, have you been adopted by a Welsh one? Famous for being on the miserable end of the spectrum them Welsh are!"
"Yeah, well the thing is, I wanted to chat with someone who would talk sense to me, so thanks for ringing... bye!"
"Very funny! No really, I gave you my number so you *could* ring me... I'm glad you did, what's up love? Is something bothering you?"
"I think I'm losing it Del..." The tears started to flow, he sniffed-up,
"I'm sorry, I didn't know who else to talk to..."
"Oh dear... Big telephone hug coming down the line... *Mmm... mm... mmmm!* Okay! So what's troubling you love?"
"It's everything... I guess I'm having another existential crisis?"

"Oh right, so nowt important then eh? Another one? Bloody hell, Jim, how many have you had?"
"They're on-going I guess... I had my first when my Grandpa died."
"How old were you then?"
"Eight... It was handled so badly, I never even got to go to his funeral."
"Ah, luv... That must have been really shitty for you, folks were so thick about dealing with death back then, mind you it's not much better now for many." There was a pause in the conversation, before Bill asked,

"How about you luv? How's things going for you? Tell me everything's fucking wonderful, that'll cheer me up no end, really... I do mean that, honestly I'm not being funny... Knowing that your life's good for you now would be a real comfort for me."
"What? You, trying to be funny? That'll be the day, there's a show coming on called The Tragedians, you should apply for an audition!"
"Very funny, but really how are things with you? And how's things going with your new fella?"
"Oh, I'm fine... Always am! Y'have to be doncha! Mike... oh, *that* fella... oh my, he's like a dozen guys in the past now!"
"What?"
"Idiot! I'm kidding, we're great! He's finally come around to the realisation that *I am the star*! Him and his *going-nowhere* little band are now *my* band! We're Del Delaney and the Delinquents!"
"Has a certain ring to it! I thought you were Del Diamond, like that was your stage name?"
"Yeah well, I kinda liked the hint at the Irish in *Delaney* you know? And then there's the Del theme in it and in delinquents... My idea of course!"
"Naturally!"

They blathered on in this manner until Jim/Bill was sat there in the dark. Inbetween silly trivia, nonsense and gossip he managed to pour out his troubles, telling her about the dark dreams, how vivid they were and unlike anything he'd ever experienced before, about the Rev. Fothergill... ghost, hallucination, dream?... whatever he was or wasn't! The gravestone and the old woman/witch and her spell-bag, the feeling he so often had that he wasn't alone, that there was someone with him... It all sounded so stupid he kept saying to her... But she listened patiently, making the odd comment now and then to try and help understand her friend, but it was the conclusion she came to that had made the most sense to him and even as she was speaking about it, he knew that he'd already come to a very similar conclusion himself, without even realising that he had...

"...the thing is Jimmy and I'm not really sure how best to say this, or whether I even should... I can't see how it's going to be of any help to you really and I don't want to scare you either..."
"Just say it Del, please, just tell me what you're thinking."
"Well, thing is, when Aunty was, err... when she was *really* old..."
"What you're trying to say is when she was dying, aren't you?"
"Are you going to belt-up and listen to me or what?"
"Sorry..."
"Okay then, something that you have to realise is that Aunty was way older than a parent would normally have been, she was pushing fifty when she took me on *as a baby*! Not like she nursed me or anything of that kind of thing! Hell no, nothing like that! She was well-heeled, she'd come from a very rich family, so she just hired-in a nanny for me until I was old enough for her to be able to cope with me on her own. Anyhow, when she was getting close to the end of her life... and she'd've been clocking on ninety by then... in those last weeks leading up to when she died and she was very frail by then... although she was mobile and still had all of her marbles too, well most of them! Anyway, how she described it was like this, she said that *the veil was getting thinner,* she'd always been into spiritualism, I should have mentioned that, so it could've just been wishful thinking like, but she said that she'd been chatting with people who'd *passed*, as she put it, or to you and me that would be *died*! Talking to dead people! Oh my Lord! That they'd been coming to her all her life in her dreams, but now they came to her while she was awake..."

Once he'd let her go, their conversation had definitely decided him upon the need for a glass of malt! He went through to the kitchen and opened the new bottle, it was a different brand to the one that Nellie usually brought for him, so he poured a little into a glass and took a sip, it was nice enough, smooth, mellow and not too peaty, it'll do he thought and poured a little more…

Sat back in his chair he thought about the implications of what Del had told him, about the experience of her ageing aunty, it wasn't particularly encouraging was it? The trouble was that it chimed with everything he already felt and rather than coming as a blow, in a bizarre way it was a comfort somehow, serving as confirmation of what he already felt… validating the conclusion he'd come to by himself… that his notion that he wasn't long for this world, was accurate! *The skids were under…* that had been another one of his Dad's *little sayings* too!

He took another swig of the whisky… did he regret not listening to the doctor at St. Jude's now, did he wish that he'd kept the appointment that he'd made for him with the cardiologist? Nah… The way he saw it then, his opinion about continually trying to fix things hadn't changed, all you would do was just add a few years on at the end of your life, at a time when you wouldn't be in a fit state to enjoy them, when you'd be better off being dead anyway! Better to go out when you were still pretty much operational, surely?

So death was another step closer to him? So he'd closed-up the gap between them had he? So what? He'd been dogging his heels all his life hadn't he? Wasn't that what the bugger did? Wasn't he always there with his big long sickle, or was it a scythe? What was the difference? Anyhow, he was always there with it poised, ready to strike you down at a moment's notice, ready in case you made a slip-up, took a wrong step, missed your footing on the tightrope known as *life…*

No, he thought that wasn't entirely true, that the shadow had dogged him *all* of his life, he'd first noticed it was there when he was eight years old, when his beloved Grandpa had died. That was when he'd discovered his presence, that was when the shadow had been given a name… He was called Death!

Being introduced to… what for him as an eight year old kid was this most unusual concept of *death…* had presented him with what he found to be the most peculiarly strange and perplexing of ideas for him to get his young head around! It clashed

violently with the illusion he had always felt of permanence, his mind had operated with a sense of continuity, the feeling based on his experiences up until then, that one day led to the next one and he'd not had any reason to assume that this wasn't how things would go on forever… Now he was being told that this was most definitely *not* the case! *'Everyone dies love'*… Mum had said, she'd said it all so normally, like she hadn't just pulled the pin out of the hand grenade that she had just placed in his innocent hand! That she hadn't just let a bomb off, right in her young son's face!
'Am I going to die?' He'd asked, the words spoken from a white and horrified, stricken young face!
'Yes of course, but it will be a very, very, very long time from now!
'Why? *I don't want to die!*' Tears now streaming…

James Stanley's existential crisis No.1! Unbeknownst to his eight year old self, to be followed by a great many more!

The worry over where his Grandpa was now, was what came next for him and he hadn't been remotely placated when his questions had been answered by being informed, that Grandpa had *gone to heaven!* Even at eight years of age, James's enquiring mind found this a highly suspect answer! He liked to pick over what he was told, pull it apart and see if was likely to be correct! This was the reason he had a need to seek out more information than was often at first forthcoming, why he needed more facts to substantiate an initial claim, it was the reason he continually asked '*why*?'

After due consideration he found the whole notion of 'Heaven' to be beyond suspect, in fact it was rather ridiculous! To his logical young mind, it was even more so in regards to the other place that you were meant to go to if you'd lived a bad life! I mean, where were these places located? The implication was that heaven was up in the sky and hell was down under the ground, this smacked of utter nonsense to his active, enquiring young mind. The core of the Earth, he had learnt at school, was made of molten metal after all.

Also he considered that being burnt in the *fires of Hell* and for *eternity* too, seemed pretty darn disproportionate, apart from the obvious fact that when things burned they were reduced to ashes... witness the coal fire... his innate sense of fair play and justice was also greatly offended, I mean if you'd lived to be seventy-six like Grandpa, but say unlike him you'd been a real bugger and you were told to sod-off when you got to Heaven's gates... *You'd burn in Hell for eternity?* How was that fair? Seventy-six years of Hellfire would be more than adequate as a punishment surely? Assuming you'd been bad from the moment you were born, but that had to be wrong surely, because babies didn't know how to be bad, did they? They only learnt that from watching and listening to the grown-ups, didn't they? Then there was the idea that you could just kneel down, put your hands together and say 'sorry' and that'd get you off anyway?

All that he'd been told was that his Grandpa had *gone away* now, that he wouldn't see him ever again and yes that he was in Heaven now! 'Funerals are no place for children' was what he and his brothers had been told... Looking back on that he still felt angry at his parents, more for their ignorance now, rather than for their stupidity in denying him the opportunity to share in the grief of his extended family at the ceremony. He understood that they'd only done what they thought to be *for the best*, as far as their idiotic and limiting Middle Class mindset had allowed them to do, it was an out-of-date idea even by the standards of the sixties he thought with hindsight, but they were very *old school* over many things, talking about death, emotional openness and any suchlike, *new ideas* had been scoffed-at by them.

So that was when he had come to know about his shadow, to understand that it was always there... Waiting patiently. He recalled how for weeks after his death he'd had nightmares about his Grandpa, he'd find himself sat talking to him one minute and then when he turned to look at him again, he wasn't there anymore, there was just a bleached white skull and some bones where the old man he loved had been sitting chatting with him only a moment ago!

He would lie in his bed at night, listening to his heart beating, feeling it beat as it lay there inside his little chest...
listening to the gap there was inbetween each beat and wondering if it might forget to make the next one...

when it did beat again he remembered…
to his newly discovered horror, that…
a day would come…
when it *would* stop…
that he would feel…
his very last heart beat?

He was eight years old.

CHAPTER FORTY-FOUR

Bill had a restless night, his sleep was fitful and full of disjointed and unrelated fragments of dreams, most of which evaporated away as he carried out his morning ablutions… what he called his first morning visit to the bathroom. The face that peered back at him from the mirror as he brushed his teeth, was that of a bleary eyed old man, he frowned at his reflection as he took in how his eyes were just narrow slits, with large puffy bags of pasty skin beneath them, he had a decidedly unhealthy pallor to his wrinkled skin, well, what was visible above the dense tangled jungle of grey, white and black whiskers.

He tossed his toothbrush back into the cup on the windowsill, dried his face and picked up his hairbrush, this was one thing he'd rarely done, when incarnated as the character Bill… brush his unruly mop of hair and beard! He dragged a comb through his whiskers before sticking it into the bristles of his brush and shuffling through to his bedroom to get dressed.

Downstairs he set up the coffee machine and rummaged for some bread, there was only a solitary crust left in the bag, so he put it in the toaster wondering once more what had happened to Nellie yesterday, she'd never turned up with his groceries, so unlike her, she'd never let him down in all the time he'd been living in the cottage. He determined to ring her after his breakfast.

While he was making his coffee the toast popped up, he switched the coffee machine over to heat up the steamer and went to get some marmalade out of the cupboard, only to remember that he'd finished the jar… it was on his order! There was half a jar of organic peanut butter that Jake had picked up at the shop last time he'd been down, it would have to do!

Peanut butter wasn't something he found that appealing but beggars, choosing and all that eh? He filled a desert spoon from the jar and placed it on the top of the toaster slot, pushing the lever down to set it going again, his toasted crust now sat on a plate next to the toaster. Having finished off making his coffee, he took the now warm peanut butter and spread it onto the toast… it was the only way to make the stuff remotely edible he'd found!

He took in the glory of a wonderful morning as he opened the front door and stood with his coffee in his hand, filling his lungs with the cool sweet air, it was fresh, fragrant and tasted like the finest of wines. There were little wisps of mist clinging here and there to the hedgerows and lying in any shallow dips in the grass. The sky was radiant blue, its arching blue vault soaring away over his head to meet the flat sea way off at the horizon. The sun had been up awhile and he could feel it's warmth on his face. Definitely a day to go down to the sea...

He plonked his empty cup down on the shelf in the hall, pulled on his boots, put his coat and cap on and headed off down the path to towards the sea. Crossing the coastal path he paused to look both ways along it as it wound its way along the edge of the land, half expecting to see the Reverend Fothergill or the old witch, but there was no one in sight, so he carried on down the hill towards the sea. He could smell the saltiness now in the air and hear the gentle wash of the small waves on the shore...

He sat on a rock just above the beach and let the sun warm him, he closed his eyes and lifted his face, a gentle breeze caressed his cheeks now and then as he let himself slip into a meditative state...

A small cloud passing in front of the sun as it floated lazily in off the sea creating a sensation of coolness on his face and the light visible through his closed eyelids darkened. He opened his eyes as the sun emerged once more bathing the land in its warmth, he closed his eyes a moment longer to savour the warmth and then took a deep breath, as he let his breath out slowly he stirred himself, he had no idea how long he'd been sitting there, that was a success then he smiled to himself, that was what meditation was all about...

He decided not to bother making the last scrabble down to be right alongside the water and started to make his way back up the hill, as he went he found that his legs felt heavy though, he paused for a moment, thinking to catch his breath but was shocked to find that when he made to carry on his legs felt completely leaden, a little stunned he lowered himself down to sit on the grass for a while and gather himself.

Instinctively he reached into his pocket, seeking his whisky… silly old fool! He chided himself, it'd had been a long time since he carried a quarter flask in his pocket!

After about ten minutes he struggled up onto his feet, where was Fothergill or the witch when you need the buggers? He grumbled! He further cussed himself for not bringing his stout stick with him… he *always* took it to go down to the beach! Well clearly not always! But why not today for fuck's sakes!

He stood-up, remaining motionless for a while on what were now, his rather wobbly legs before trying to push himself to walk on… He made it as far as the coastal path…
Not too far now…
Five minutes more…
More like ten though, shuffling like this!
What the fuck is going on?

He opened his eyes.
What?
Where was he?
For a moment he had no idea…
Gradually awareness began to slowly trickle down back into his consciousness…
He'd been on his way back up from the beach…
So what had happened then?
He pushed down with his elbow and lifted his head up a little off the ground…
He was lying on a grassy slope?
Away out to the west he could see the giant red disc of the sun as it was slowly sliding down into the sea.
He'd been lying here all day?
He remembered that he he'd forgotten to ring Nellie before he set out!
What?
His mobile!
He needed help!
He needs to sit up to find his phone…
He tries to push himself up, but his left arm is too weak, he rolls back down onto his back…
Shit! This is bad! This is really bad!

He tries to get up again, using his right arm but as he does his head spins…
 He opens his eyes, he is still lying flat on his back, the clear sky above him is dimming from dark blue to black…
Shit!
It's getting dark, I've been led here all day!
This is it then…
I'm dying?
Well, didn't you say that this was how you wanted it?
How you wanted to go out?
It's fucking perfect! A wonderful day, now slipping into night…
Just as you're doing…
Slipping into the darkness…
A moment of panic…
He laughs at himself…
If you'd rung Nellie she'd have been at the backdoor wondering where you were?
But I didn't ring her, did I!

He falls into a dreamless sleep, awakening to wonder if he had dipped into the darkness…
Tested the water?
It's quite dark now.
Stars are twinkling into life.
He blinks and the moon has sailed up high into the sky now.
It should've been a full moon… he thinks.
Would've been more fitting…

Next blink it has moved right across the sky.

The stars are spinning slowly in time lapse… in the moments he flickers into wakefulness

The air is cold on his cheeks…

He can see The Milky Way now, curving its spangled banner across the sky like a fountain of stars, it's so bright tonight!
The brightest I've ever seen it, he thinks…
The last time I will see it…
My last day has come…
Will I see tomorrow?
A moment of panic…

It's okay…
Everything's okay…

He opens his eyes.
The sky is no longer an inky blackness up above his head.
He tries to turn his head, but can only move it a little.
There is a light dusting of frost on the grass.
A sheep looks down at him disinterestedly as it chews away, before turning and wandering off.
A blanket of mist is lapping up the hill coming in off the sea…
He tries to lift his left arm, it is immobile… another stroke then he concludes.
He reaches up with his right arm and dusts frost off his coat, it requires an enormous effort and his leaden arm slumps back down to his side…
He's covered in frost…
But doesn't feel cold?
He feels warm…
The warmth when you die?
Hypothermia…

He opens his eyes.
Not long has passed though…
The sky is lightening away off to the east over the headland now.
He can hear gulls calling out…
He can see them wheeling overhead…

He tries to get up as an overwhelming panic sweeps over him, one last effort, one big push…
You can do it…
Actually he can't…

The realisation of his situation washes over him again, but as the last of his panic subsides it is in the manner of a warm wave washing onto a sunny beach…

After the guttering flame of panic has had its last flicker, it dies down into a deep and all enveloping calmness…
It is realisation.
It is resignation.
Acceptance.
Relief.

He smiles, thinking back to his eight year old self, lying in bed waiting for his last heartbeat!

Not long now kid…

It's been a long journey, a long life and yet…
It all still seems to be so close, in his mind…

He feels so close to that boy even now…

He opens his eyes…
He tries to turn his head, but is unable to…
He looks as far to his left as he can… there… He sees Jake!
Jake is sat in a chair by his bed…
He's in a hospital bed… How's that?
He tries to speak but all that happens is he has a weak cough…
"Dad!" Jake grabs his left hand, he tries to grip it…
He can only move his fingers a little…
"Dad, can you hear me?"
He blinks twice…
"You had a stroke in your flat! I found you there… hang in there…"
A terrible realisation washes over him,
'So this is my fate eh?'
Ending up a fucking vegetable…
'Why did I let them persuade me to stay here?'

He blinks his eyes open,
Watches as his breath curls away up into the sky…
'Huh… If that's what *being saved* would've looked like!'
'Ha-ha-ha…'

"Grandpa! Grandpa! Come and see…"
He looks down at the joyous face of a happy little girl…
She has her hand in his and is tugging him to run with her across a verdant field, wild flowers are growing everywhere…
He runs to the top of the hill with her, turns and looks back across the sweeping landscape…
His breath comes easily…
Jake beams at him saying,
"Bet you're glad you had the surgery now Dad?"
His hand goes instinctively to his chest…

He turns to looks around,
There is a tree ahead, on a small rise,
Beyond the tree the land falls away to a distant valley,
A broad river meanders lazily across it,
to a distant coast, the sea stretches endlessly away from it…
A mountain range rises as a misty grey smudge on the horizon…
Overhead a solitary eagle hangs effortlessly, gliding on the wind currents, as they rise up from over the sea…
He notices someone sitting on the grass, leaning-up against the trunk of the tree…
She has one leg raised-up at the knee…
Her hands are clasped onto it…
As he walks nearer to her, she turns to look at him…
She smiles and pushes her blonde hair back behind her ear…
He calls out… *'Abbie…'*
She beckons to him with her hand, inviting him to come over and join her…

A warm tear wanders down his cheek,
He blinks his eyes open…
He smiles as he thinks of Abbie, is she really waiting for him?

'This is the time of my death.'

His smile breaks into laughter, he tries to speak, but has to cough weakly for a while before he can say anything out loud,
Finding his voice he cries out…

"Come on then ya'bugger!
"I'm ready for ya!
"I held ya off though for all them years though, didn't I?"

'Maybe I should be shouting for help instead of yelling defiance into the face of the shadow…'
He ponders idly!
The darkest midnight hue of the sky slips away shade by shade, surrendering to the ever so gradual lightening… a deep burnt umber glow ignites along the horizon to the east, mellowing softly down to a tint of orange as the sky above it transforms into the palest of pale blues…

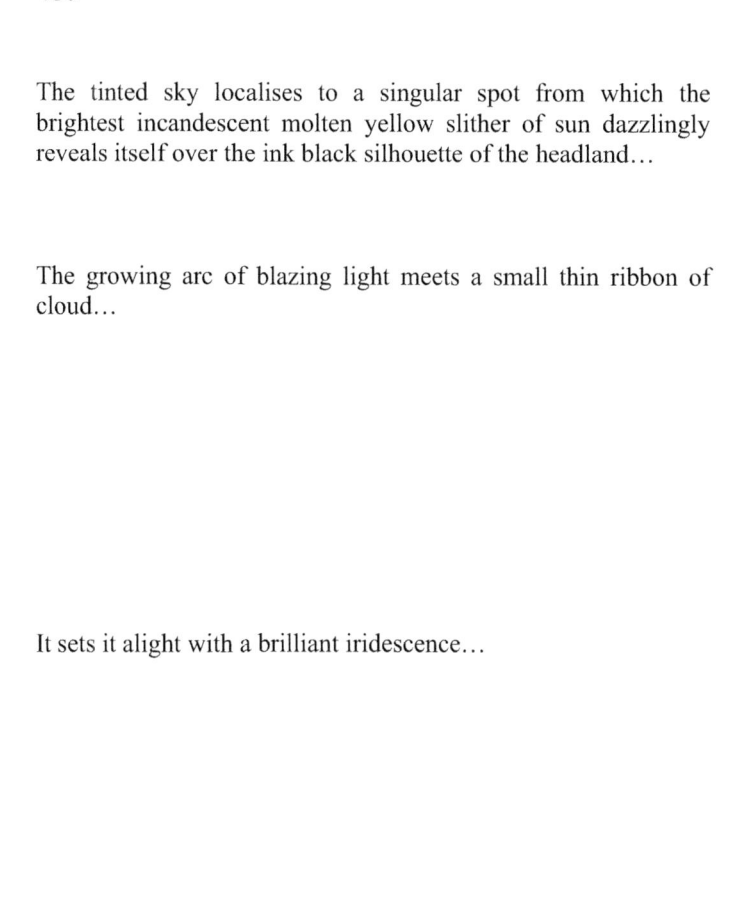

The tinted sky localises to a singular spot from which the brightest incandescent molten yellow slither of sun dazzlingly reveals itself over the ink black silhouette of the headland…

The growing arc of blazing light meets a small thin ribbon of cloud…

It sets it alight with a brilliant iridescence…

All the colours of the rainbow glow before him…

God's promise?…

Or just the refraction of the light?

It seems as if will melt before the sun…

A small shadow slithers up across the valley

Passes over him…

It is a new day…

"So, this is the last sunrise I will ever see…"

He became aware of the sound of his breathing as he exhales…

"Hhhhhaaaaaaahhhhhh…."

…as air warmed by being inside his body leaves him,
Streaming out of his nose and mouth.
He watches the mist of his breath as it floats away…
Mingling in with the sea's breath…
Blown up from the restless coast,

"Hhhhaaaaaaahhhh…."

In his ears the damp breath of the sea whispers to him…

"Hhhaaaaaaahh…."

On his lips he tastes its salt…

"Hhhaaaahh…."

Now a soft voice is there within the whisper………………………
. . . .
. . . .
. . . .
. . . .
. . . .

"Hhhaaah..."

           "Have no fear Jim..."

"Haaah..."

        "All is well..."

"Hhha..."

        "Everything is exactly as it should be...

"Hha..."

     "As it is meant to be...

"Hh........."

"I am here..."

"You?.....

  "Yes..."

"Hhhhhhhhhhhhh*hhhhhhhhh*ₕₕₕₕₕₕₕₕₕ
....
....
....
....

EPILOGUE

I do hope you enjoyed my story? These pages are left blank for you to take up your own pen…. For you to write you own ending, I mean… did Bill actually die? If he did… what happened next?

Skip Evans

The sun was high in the sky when the walker was alerted by the barking of his dog, the dog had found something

It's dark because you are trying too hard.

Lightly child, lightly. Learn to do everything lightly.

Yes, feel lightly even though you're feeling deeply.

Just lightly let things happen and lightly cope with them.

I was so preposterously serious in those days, such a humourless little prig.

Lightly, lightly – it's the best advice ever given me.

When it comes to dying even. Nothing ponderous, or portentous, or emphatic.

No rhetoric, no tremolos,

no self-conscious persona putting on its celebrated imitation of Christ or Little Nell.

And of course, no theology, no metaphysics.

Just the fact of dying and the fact of the clear light.

So throw away your baggage and go forward.

There are quicksands all about you, sucking at your feet,

trying to suck you down into fear and self-pity and despair.

That's why you must walk so lightly.

Lightly my darling,

on tiptoes and no luggage,

not even a sponge bag,

completely unencumbered.

Aldous Huxley

The Shadow

When as a child I used to play
I noticed a shadow appear one day
But every time I turned to see
I was alone there was only me

As out I ventured along life's road
I'd often feel I was not alone
But whenever to look, I'd turn my head
The shadows stayed still as if the dead

And when the dark at night I'd fear
I would feel my companion drawing near
So close that I could feel his presence
He seemed a cold and empty essence

So through life's fleeting joy and despair
My silent shadow was always there
Sometimes I'd miss him one or two mile
And blissfully share a happy smile…

Now life's long journey has tired me slow
Laden by sorrows that weigh my heart low
I journey at sunset lit by the last rays
My long shadow reaching out pointing the way

Now as the darkening skies draw near
A cold wild night I'd say to fear
The wind whips cruelly at my cloak
Scattering homeward tardy folk

The path winds narrow lost in gloom
The sky is dark laden with doom
My heart is heavy my legs are weak
When first my friend decides to speak

His voice is low but very near
He whispers softly in my ear
"We've travelled long and far have we
Let me walk now close aside of ye
And as this bitter night rides out
My presence here will calm your doubt"

'Look yonder there I see a light
A flicker of home through this dark night'
"Your footsteps falter my friend dear
Here take my arm and have no fear"

'My friend your arm is strong and true
And I lean more and more on you
The cold night shrieks its awful sound
But warm am I your cloak around'

"Dear friend let me carry you for this the last mile
Rest ye now in my arms for a while
Your journey is ending but not at your home
It ends where it started with me all alone"

"For though you have travelled awhile in the light
Your home is with me, back here in the night
To death's soft still darkness we now return
Your life's brief weak candle no longer will burn"

As I lie cradled in my friends warm embrace
At last my eyes lifted can see his kind face
Eternity beckons not cold as the tomb
I feel I am travelling once more to the womb

Skip Evans 25th September 1997

Other books by Skip Evans

The Alternate Reality Series:

The story of how a fifty-something man's personal crisis and Internet dating quest for sex leads him on a rollercoaster ride that will forever change his life! A romp through the curmudgeonly yet often humorous mind of a man right off the end of his tether and off his rocker! The story is told in sometimes graphic and sexually explicit language and is ONLY SUITABLE for broad-minded, adult readers.

The story of an ordinary, everyday and very average guy, who is already struggling with his grip on reality and life in general, when he acts completely out of character and sets in motion a chain of events that will take him on a journey that will inexorably change his life... and maybe the world!

Joe McKinlay as he is about to embark upon his final chapter, travelling to a world beyond his wildest dreams or imaginings, across time and space to another galaxy. Set in a not too distant future, in a world not all that dissimilar to our own.

Joe Mckinlay has now settled into a peaceful monastic way of life. However, disturbing events are transpiring in realms he has barely dared to explore. Now he finds that his mistaken decision not to destroy an AI could bring about the end of all of existence as we know it as something sinister is happening in other versions of our world!

Stand Alone books:

Set in 1958 nothing is impossible in Stuart's imagination and yet the events that unfold are beyond even his wildest dreams! This is an often humorous adventure, that a young lad undertakes with his teddy bear Joey. Told with a whiff of nostalgia and with more than a dash of pure magic.

I am Timbe... I am of The Land... The Land is a wondrous place where man lives in harmony with his Mother, The Earth. Many people here are sad. I say brothers and sisters I am Her voice speaking to you, listen to Her.... before it is too late...

Page 451 ☦

Go to:
https://www.youtube.com/watch?v=ngcrQ3DDjBM

Renee Olstead & Peter Cincotti - Breaking Up Is Hard To Do

Vocals – Peter Cincotti & Renee Olstead
Written-By – Howard Greenfield, Neil Sedaka
Renee Olstead - Topic
1.04K subscribers
Subscribe
51
Share
Clip

Find me on **facebook** *:* **Skip Evans Lancashire Author**

Printed in Great Britain
by Amazon